A

JASON ELAM
AND *STEVE YOHN*

NOVEL

PRESENTED BY

TYNDALE HOUSE PUBLISHERS, INC.
CAROL STREAM, ILLINOIS

A

*RILEY
COVINGTON*

THRILLER

MONDAY NIGHT

Visit Tyndale's exciting Web site at www.tyndale.com

TYNDALE and Tyndale's quill logo are registered trademarks of Tyndale House Publishers, Inc.

Monday Night Jihad

Designed by Dean H. Renninger

Published in association with the literary agency of Yates & Yates, LLP, Attorneys and Counselors, Orange, California.

Library of Congress Cataloging-in-Publication Data

Elam, Jason.
  Monday night jihad / Jason Elam and Steve Yohn.
    p. cm.
  ISBN-13: 978-1-4143-1730-4 (hc)
  ISBN-10: 1-4143-1730-1 (hc)
  ISBN-13: 978-1-4143-1731-1 (sc)
  ISBN-10: 1-4143-1731-X (sc)
  1. Terrorism—United States—Fiction. I. Yohn, Steve. II. Title.
  PS3605.L26M66 2007
  813'.6—dc22   2007038595

Printed in the United States of America

14 13 12 11 10 09 08
 7   6   5   4   3   2   1

DEDICATION

LORD, WE START WITH YOU. This has been, and will always be, Your project.

Jason thanks Tamy, the kids, and his mother, Evelyn, for their love and encouragement.

Steve thanks Nancy and his daughter for sacrificing so many evenings to this project.

Both Jason and Steve owe a debt of gratitude to Pastor Rick Yohn for his constant support and for being the biggest fan of this book from day one. Thanks go to Linda Yohn, also, for her excellent tough-love proofing skills.

Matt Yates, this bird never would have flown without you. Thanks to you for your practical wisdom and guidance (and, most importantly, for the "research" trip to Del Frisco's), and also to Jeana and the rest of the Yates & Yates gang.

We had so many go-to experts assisting us in making this a realistic book with a plausible scenario. Special appreciation goes to LTC Mark Elam for teaching us how to hurt people in really nasty ways. Also, huge thanks are owed to Troy Bisgard of the Denver Police Homicide Division, Kurt Peterson of the Denver Police Bomb Squad, and our friends at the Air Force Special Operations Command and the U.S. Secret Service.

Thanks go to Karen Watson and the rest of our new family at Tyndale House Publishers. We owe a huge debt to Jeremy Taylor for dealing with an editor's worst nightmare—two first-time authors. Also, we greatly appreciate Beverly Rykerd of Beverly Rykerd Public Relations for getting the word out so effectively.

Finally, how can we thank our small group enough for all of your inspiration and prayer through this process? You are the wind beneath . . . well, you know the rest. Our gratitude goes out to the folks at Lemstone Christian Store in Parker for the couch and the coffee and to Fellowship Community Church.

Lastly, we have been blessed by so many others who have encouraged us and prayed for us along the way. Thank you, one and all.

PROLOGUE

1991
ADHAMIYA
BAGHDAD, IRAQ

Hakeem Qasim picked up the small, sharp rock from the dirt. Tossing it up and down a couple of times, he felt its weight as he gauged his target. He glanced at Ziad, his cousin and closest friend. They both knew the significance of what he was about to do. Wiping the sweat off his forehead and then onto his frayed cotton pants, he cocked his arm back, took aim, and let fly. The rock sailed from his hand, across fifteen meters of open space, in through the driver's-side window of the burned-out Toyota, and out the other side—no metal, no glass, nothing but air.

"Yes!" the two ten-year-old boys shouted in unison as they clumsily danced together in triumph.

They had spent the better part of six days clearing this dirt patch, as attested by their cracked, blistered fingers and by the jagged gray piles in and around the old Corona. Hakeem took pride in the knowledge that his rocks were mostly of the "in" category, while Ziad's were mostly of the "around." But to have the final rock of the hundreds, if not thousands, that they had cleared from their newly created soccer field pass all the way through the car could mean only one thing—good luck.

Hakeem was the older of the two by seventeen days. Although he was small for his age, his wiry frame attested to his strength and speed. His uncle Shakir had told him, "You are like the cheetah, the pursuer." He wasn't exactly sure what his uncle meant by that, but he loved the picture it put in his mind. Often, when he closed his eyes at night, he dreamed of stalking prey out on the open plains. Hakeem the Cheetah—*watch out, or I'll run you down*. His complexion was dark, and his black hair was thick and wild. His eyes were a deep brown and had a feline intensity to them that he knew could be unsettling, even to his mother. "Hakeem, you have the eyes of the Prophet," she would say, sometimes with a shudder.

Ziad was the opposite of his cousin in build. Tall, square shoulders, large head—his father used to call him *Asad Babil*, the "Lion of Babylon," named after the Iraqi version of the Soviet T-72 tank. Ziad wasn't the brightest star in the sky, but he was a guy you wanted on your side in a fight.

As the boys scanned the dusty lot, Hakeem felt a tremendous sense of accomplishment, remembering what the field had looked like just a week ago. He glanced to his left, where he had tripped over a rock and badly cut his elbow—the impetus for their renovation. He unconsciously picked the edges of the scab; that rock had been the first to go.

A waft of lamb with garlic and cumin caught Hakeem's attention, awakening another of his senses. Well, his hunger would be taken care of soon enough. It was Friday, and every Friday (except for the day after the bombs had begun to fall last week) Uncle Ali came over for dinner. It was always a special event, because Ali Qasim was an important man. All the neighbors would bow their heads in respect as he drove by. Father would bow too, in spite of the fact that Ali was the youngest of the three brothers and Hakeem's father was the eldest.

Even now, Hakeem could see Uncle Ali's black Land Rover parked next to his house across the field. Beside it was the matching Land Rover that carried the men Ali called his "friends," although he never talked to them and all they ever seemed to do was stand outside the house looking around. There was a lot of mystery surrounding Uncle Ali.

Last month, in a day that Hakeem would not soon forget, Uncle Ali had invited the boy to take a ride with him. "Let's see how good my friends are," Ali cried as he hit the gas, burying the other Land Rover in a cloud of dust. They bounced down the dirt roads, laughing and yelling for people to get out of the way.

When they made it out to the main road, Ali had suddenly gotten serious. He reached into his *dishdasha* and handed Hakeem a small handkerchief that had been folded into a square. The boy's excitement grew as he opened one corner after another, discovering inside a bullet with a hole drilled just under the case's base. A thin chain had been threaded through the hole.

"Hakeem, this is a 7.62 mm round that I pulled out of an unexpended AK-47 clip that Saddam Hussein himself was firing outside of his palace."

Hakeem was still too afraid to ask what—or whom—President Hussein had been firing at.

"Feel the weight of it, Nephew. Imagine what this could do to a person's body. For centuries, the West and the Jews have tried to keep our people from worshiping Allah, the true God. You've learned about the Crusades in school, haven't you?"

Hakeem quickly nodded as he slipped the chain over his head. The cartridge was still warm from being kept against his uncle's chest.

"You know I'm not a very religious man, Hakeem, but I can read the times. Soon, because of their hatred of Allah, the Great Satan will come to try to destroy our country. But we don't fear, because Saddam will defend us. The mighty Republican Guard will defend us. Allah will defend us. And someday, our great leader may call on you to pick up a gun for him and fight against the West and defend his honor. Could you do it? Will you be ready, little Hakeem?"

Even now, as he fingered the long, narrow brass bullet hanging around his neck, thinking about how Uncle Ali's prophecy about the Great Satan coming to their land had been fulfilled only two weeks later, his own answer repeated itself in his mind. *I will be ready, Uncle Ali. I will fight for our leader. I will fight for our honor. I will fight the Great Satan!* Allahu akbar!

Suddenly, an ancient, peeling soccer ball bounced off the side of his head. "Nice reflexes, Cheetah," Ziad laughed. "What are you daydreaming about?"

"I was just thinking about Uncle Ali."

"I don't like to think about him. He scares me. People say he's friends with Uday. Could that be?"

"I don't know, Ziad. I think it's best not to ask too many questions."

"Yeah . . . I hope he leaves my mom alone tonight. I don't like the things he says to her or the way he looks at her."

Ziad was the son of Uncle Shakir, the second of the three brothers. When Shakir was killed three years ago while fighting in Iran, Hakeem's father had brought his brother's family—Aunt Shatha, Ziad, and Ziad's four-year-old sister, Zenab—into his own house.

The voice of Ziad's mother rang out from across the dirt field, interrupting their thoughts. It was almost time for *Maghrib*, the sunset prayer time.

"You realize that this will be the site of your great humiliation," Ziad taunted in the pompous language they used when teasing each other.

"Tomorrow, Ziad, your pride will be shown to be as empty as your mother's purse!"

That struck a little too close to home for Ziad, and he pounced upon Hakeem, quickly taking him to the ground. The boys laughed and wrestled, until the voice of Aunt Shatha came a second time—this time with a little more force and the addition of the word *Now!*

"We better get going. The field will still be here tomorrow," Ziad said. "I'll race you. Last one home's a goat kisser!"

"You got it! Ready . . . set . . ."

Ziad's forearm swung up, catching Hakeem right under the chin.

I fall for that every time, Hakeem thought as he dropped to the ground.

"Go!" Ziad yelled, bolting off to take full advantage of the lead he had just given himself.

Hakeem sat in the dirt for a few seconds, counting his teeth with his tongue. He was in no rush. He knew that no matter how large a lead Ziad created for himself, his cousin had no chance of winning. Hakeem would run him down, and then tomorrow he would make him pay on the soccer field for the cheap shot.

As he got up, he spotted his nemesis. Ziad was about halfway home, puffing with all his might. Beyond his cousin, Hakeem could see his mother and Aunt Shatha laughing and cheering Ziad on. Reclining on the roof were his father and Uncle Ali, shaking their heads and grinning. *Here's my chance to show Uncle Ali what his "little" Hakeem is made of.* Hakeem jumped up and began running at full speed.

Suddenly, the world became a ball of fire. The concussive wave knocked Hakeem off his feet. He lay flat on his back. Flames singed his entire body.

The first thing that entered his mind as he glanced around was *Look at all these rocks we'll have to clear off the field tomorrow.* The high-pitched ringing in his head was making it hard to think. As he slowly got up, a pungent smell hit his nose—a mixture of smoke, dust, and . . . what was that last smell? . . . Burnt hair?

What happened? Where is everybody? Ziad was running home . . . Mother and Aunt Shatha were at the door . . . and Father and Uncle Ali were on the roof. Hakeem looked around, trying to make sense of things and attempting to get a bearing on which way was home, but the dirt and grit in his eyes were making them water. Everything was a blur.

When he finally figured out which direction was home, he saw no roof, no door, no house, no Father, no Mother, no Uncle Ali, no Aunt Shatha, no Ziad. He saw smoke and dirt, fire and rubble. Hakeem stumbled toward where his home had been. He could only think of one thing: *Mama!* Now he began to feel the burns on his face, starting with a tingling and quickly growing to a fire.

Panic began to well up inside of him. *Mama, where are you?* Hakeem tried to call out for her, but all the heat, dust, and smoke had reduced his voice to a congested croak.

The ringing in his head began to subside, only to be replaced by a more terrifying sound—screams. Screams coming from all around him. Screams coming from within him.

People were running on his left and on his right—some carrying buckets, some covering wounds. Hakeem stumbled past a smoldering heap of rags that deep inside he knew was his cousin, but he couldn't stop—couldn't deal with that now. He had to find his mother. *Mama, I'm almost there!*

As he crossed his father's property line, he fell into a deep, wide hole. An exposed piece of rebar cut a long gash into his leg. Blood poured out, soaking his torn pants, but still he forced himself up.

Mama, I'll find you! Oh, Allah, help me! Allahu akbar, *you are great! Show me where she is! Don't worry, Mama, I'll save you!*

He grasped for handholds to pull himself out of the hole and felt something solid. He grabbed it and began climbing up the side of the crater. As he reached the top, he finally saw what he was holding on to. It was an arm—visible to halfway up the bicep before it disappeared underneath a massive block of cement and metal.

Hakeem instantly let go, falling back to the bottom. He twisted and landed on his hands and knees and began to vomit. As he hovered over the newly formed puddle, he could hear the screams all around him. He dropped to his side and rolled onto his back, closing his eyes tightly, trying to will himself not to look at the arm. As long as he didn't look up, didn't see the very familiar ring around the third finger of the hand, then maybe it wouldn't be true. Maybe he could just stay down here, and eventually his mother would find him. She would help him out of the pit, put ointment on his face, bandage his leg, hold him tight, and tell him everything was going to be okay.

But Hakeem knew that would never happen. He knew Mama would never hold him again. The distinctive ring he had glimpsed was one he had examined often as he listened to stories while lying in bed. It was a ring he had spun around his mother's finger as he sat with the women and children in the mosque, listening to the mullah condemn America and the Jews.

This has to be a dream, he thought. *Please, Allah, let me wake up!* Tears began and quickly turned into torrents. *I don't like this anymore; please let me wake up!* His heart felt like it would explode. He didn't know what to do. *Somebody help me! Anybody help me!!* He didn't want to look back up at the hand. He didn't know how to get out of the hole. He didn't know how he would stop the bleeding on his leg. He didn't know if he would ever stop crying. *Oh, Allah, please help me!*

Now his screams began again, and they continued on and on until finally Hakeem's world faded into an unsettled blackness.

2003
OPERATION ENDURING FREEDOM
BAGRAM VALLEY
HELMAND PROVINCE, AFGHANISTAN

His count was off. Second Lieutenant Riley Covington of the United States Air Force Special Operations Command was on watch at a perimeter security post. He had been lying at the top of a low rise, watching his sector, for four hours, and each time he had counted the boulders on the hill across the small valley, he had come up with thirty-six. This time, however, the count reached thirty-seven. *Keep it together, buddy*, Riley thought as he rubbed his eyes. He shifted slightly to try to allow the point of a rock that had been boring into his left leg to begin a new hole. *I have no doubt these guys scattered these rocks out here 'cause they knew we were coming.*

"You seeing anything, Taps?" Riley whispered into his comm. At the other security post, located on the opposite side of the harbor site, Airman First Class Armando Tapia was stretched out behind a small, hastily constructed rock wall.

"Everything's good to go," came the reply.

On this sixth night of their mission, Riley had chosen a less-than-ideal position to set up their camp. He didn't feel too bad, however; there were probably fewer than a half dozen ideal sites in this whole desolate valley. He was positioned on a low hill to the east of his Operational Detachment Alpha, and Tapia was planted to the north of the team. Rising on the south and west of the ODA camp were steep cliffs. If anyone wanted to approach their bivouac, they would have to come through one of the two security posts.

Typically, AFSOC missions were carried out singly or in pairs. The special-ops personnel were dropped in from high altitude to take meteorologic and geographic measurements, then silently evacuated. Very clean, very quiet. But Riley's team had lost three members in this area during the last two weeks. So it was on to plan B—take in a group and protect everyone's backside.

JASON ELAM AND STEVE YOHN // 7

The moon exposed the barren landscape, eliminating the need for vision enhancement. Riley shifted again and flexed his fingers to keep the cool night air from cramping them. A scorpion skittered up to check out the rustle. Riley's number-two man, Staff Sergeant Scott Ross, said these creatures were called *orthochirus afghanus Kovarik*; Riley preferred to call them the "nasty little black ones." A well-placed flick sent the arachnid careering down the front side of the hill. *Time to start counting boulders again.*

Riley Covington knew that if he could survive this tour in Afghanistan, chances were good that by this time next year, the scenery around him would look a whole lot better. He was two years out of the Air Force Academy, where he had been a three-time WAC/MWC Defensive Player of the Year and, as a senior, had won the Butkus Award as the nation's top linebacker. He was six-two, rock hard, and lightning fast. His nickname at the Academy had been Apache—later shortened to "Pach"—after the AH-64 attack helicopter. *Hit 'em low, hit 'em hard, hit 'em fast!* Riley had sent more opposing players staggering to the sidelines than he could count. Once, a writer for the *Rocky Mountain News* had compared his hitting ability to Mike Singletary's, the infamous linebacker who had broken sixteen helmets during his college days at Baylor. He still felt proud when he thought about that comparison.

Two years earlier, Riley had been selected by the Colorado Mustangs in the third round of the Pro Football League draft, and commentators believed Riley had the possibility of a promising PFL career ahead of him. However, his post-Academy commitment meant putting that opportunity off for a couple of years. In the meantime, he had spent his last two thirty-day leaves in Mustangs training camps before rushing back out to wherever AFSOC wanted him next.

Riley's insides tensed as he came to the end of his count. *Thirty-four, thirty-five, thirty-six . . . thirty-seven . . . thirty-eight! Something is definitely happening here,* he thought.

WHOOMPF! The unmistakable sound of a mortar tube echoed through the valley below.

"Incoming!" Riley yelled as he opened fire with his M4 carbine at "boulders" thirty-seven and thirty-eight, causing one to stumble back down the hill and the other to remain permanently where it was.

A flare lit up the night sky as heavy machine-gun fire, rocket-propelled grenades, and small arms rounds targeted Riley's ODA. Riley looked to his left and saw an anticoalition militia approaching from the north, right over Tapia's position. Riley, seeing the size of the enemy force, let off a few more three-shot bursts, then bolted back down to the harbor site.

He took cover in a low ditch and scanned the camp. What he saw was not encouraging. Four of his ODA members were down—two with what looked like some pretty major shrapnel wounds. There was no sign of Tapia anywhere. The rest of his squad was scattered around the camp, pinned under the heavy barrage. One of their patrol Humvees had been hit with an RPG, and the large quantity of ammunition inside was cooking off. This situation was spiraling downward fast.

Movement caught his eye. It was Scott Ross, lying flat behind some empty petrol cans and waving to catch Riley's attention. Using hand signals, Ross indicated that his com was down and pointed back toward the second patrol vehicle.

Riley looked in the direction Ross was pointing and saw their salvation. Off to his left, about fifteen meters away, an MK19 automatic grenade launcher was mounted on its low tripod. Riley quickly signaled back to Ross to provide full-automatic cover fire, then rocketed out from safety and across the dirt. He almost made it. Something hit him in the hip, spinning him counterclockwise in midair.

He landed hard, gasping for air. As he tried to get up, a mixture of stinging and deep, throbbing pain dropped him down flat. He knew his men desperately needed him, but he couldn't move. Helplessness quickly overwhelmed him. *Lord, I can't stay down, but I don't know if I can get up! Give me what I need! Please, give me what I need!*

Ross was shouting at him, but the surrounding noise made it impossible for Riley to make out the words. Without the Mark 19, their chances were bleak.

Mustering all the strength he had left, Riley began pulling himself the rest of the way to the weapon. Bullets danced all around him, kicking up puffs of dirt into his face and clanging against the nearby Humvee. With each grab of the rocky ground, his adrenaline increased. Finally, the endorphins began to get the best of the pain, and Riley was able to get his feet under him. He stumbled forward, launched himself behind the Mark 19, and let loose.

It took him just under a minute and a half to empty the ammunition can of sixty grenades. The sound was deafening, and the explosions from the shells hitting the enemy positions lit up the night. Riley knew from experience that there was nothing to do but fall back in the face of that kind of fire, which was exactly what the enemy militia did. But RPGs and mortar rounds kept dropping into the camp.

Riley signaled for Ross to come and load another can of ammo on the Mark 19. Then he half ran, half staggered over to what remained of his ODA. The rest of his team huddled around him and he took a quick head count. Besides Ross, there were Dawkins, Logan, Murphy, Posada, and Li. *Not good.* They would be outnumbered if a second wave came.

"Posada, contact the command-and-control nodes in the rear and request immediate close air support and a medical-evacuation flight."

"Yes, sir!"

Riley drew his team close. "Okay, men, we have two options. We dig in here and try to hold off another attack, or we surprise them while they're regrouping."

"Tell ya what, Pach," said Kim "Tommy" Li, a man with an itchy trigger finger and way too many tattoos, "if there's gonna be target practice going on here, I'd rather be the shooter than the bull's-eye."

Riley laid out his plan. "Okay, then, here's how it's going to work: I'm guessing they'll feint another attack from the north, but their main force will come from the east, because that's where the Mark 19 is. They know that if they don't take the Mark out, they're toast. So, Murphy and Li, I want you to belly out to those boulders twenty meters north to meet their feint. Logan, you and Ross remount the Mark on the Humvee and get her ready to go head-to-head with their onrush. Dawkins, you and I'll hit the east security post. When you all hear us start firing, circle the Humvee around east; then everyone open up with everything and blow the snot out of these desert rats. Got it?"

An excited mixture of "Yes, sir" and "Yeah, boy" was heard from the men.

"Excellent! Posada, sweeten up our coordinates with command."

"You got it, Pach," Posada said as he pounded away on his Toughbook—a nearly indestructible laptop computer perfect for use in combat.

"We've got five of our guys down, with at least one probably out—that's unacceptable. Let's make 'em pay." Riley locked eyes with each member of his team and tried to draw from them the same courage he was attempting to instill. "Dawkins, don't wait for me to hit that security post with you! Ready . . . go, go, go!!"

Skeeter Dawkins was a good old boy from Mississippi. Fiercely loyal to Riley, there were several times when he had to be pulled off of fellow team members who he thought had disrespected their lieutenant. He was big, strong, fast, and knew only two words when under fire: *Yes* and *sir*.

Dawkins ran out ahead and was already in position by the time Riley got there and dropped next to him with a grunt of pain. Sixty meters out, Riley could see between forty and fifty well-armed enemy militia members prepping for another attack. "I'm guessing they're not done with us yet, Skeet."

"Yes, sir." It sounded more like *Yeah, zir*.

"Looks like they'll be feinting inside while rolling a flank around left. Must be boring being so predictable."

"Yes, sir."

The two men lay silently for a minute, watching the preparations of their enemies. Riley turned to look at the empty sky behind them. "Sure would like to see that air support come in right about now."

"Mmm."

"Skeet, anyone ever tell you that you ain't much of a conversationalist?" It was hard not to slip into a Mississippi drawl when talking with Skeeter.

Skeeter grinned. "Yes, sir."

The random actions of the enemy force suddenly coalesced into an organized forward movement.

"Looks like the Afghani welcome wagon's rolling again."

"Yes, sir."

"Skeeter Dawkins, you gonna let any of those boys through here?"

Skeeter turned to Riley. He looked genuinely hurt at his lieutenant's attempt to force an expansion of his vocabulary.

Riley laughed. Nothing like feigned confidence to hide what you're really feeling. "Don't you worry, airman. Just make sure you give them a gen-u-ine Mississippi welcome."

Skeeter smiled. "Yes, sir!"

Riley could hear the muffled sound of the Humvee starting up as he and Skeeter readied their M4s. Red dots from each of their M68 Close Combat Optics landed nose level on the first two attackers. Their fingers hugged the triggers.

The sudden whine of two Apache helicopters halted Riley's counterattack. The 30 mm cannons mounted on either side of the choppers strafed the enemy force. The ensuing carnage was hard to watch. One life after another was snuffed out in rapid succession.

When the last bad guy stopped moving, the Apaches turned and headed back to where they'd come from. Skeeter pulled Riley to his feet and helped him down the hill. Pain crashed through Riley's hip, and his left leg buckled. Kim Li rushed over and slipped himself under Riley's other arm.

"Well, Pach, it was a good plan," Li laughed. "Guess I'll have to take my target practice elsewhere."

Riley knew it was just Li's adrenaline talking, but he still had a hard time not laying into him. Too much blood had been spilled and too many screams filled the night air to be joking about killing just now.

Back at the harbor site, an MH-53 Pave Low was just dropping in to evacuate the team. Riley was eased onto a stretcher and carried the rest of the way. As he was lifted onto the helicopter with the two dead and five injured, football was the furthest thing from his mind.

Riley Covington's hand shot out, clicking the alarm to Off just before the numbers shifted to 5:30 a.m. This was a game Riley played against the clock every morning, trying to wake up as close as he could to his alarm time without having to hear the obnoxious chirp. He was pretty good at it too. His days at the United States Air Force Academy had ingrained in him a sense of time that most people would find borderline compulsive.

He tossed his down comforter off and slowly swung his body out of bed, feeling the cold hardwood floor under his feet. The firmness of his mattress could be manually adjusted, and for the two days after each game, his bumps and bruises forced him to put the setting at "way soft."

Moving to the window, he pulled the drapes back, and instantly the room filled with white light. The sun wasn't up yet, but the reflection of the moon on the fresh snow made Riley squint. *Why would anyone want to live anywhere else?* he mused. He had always loved the Colorado winter—the frost on the windows, the muted sounds caused by a blanket of snow, the feel of a cold house in the morning while you're still warm under the blankets.

CHAPTER

ONE

Feeling invigorated, he padded into the kitchen, flicked on Fox News, and began to assemble the ingredients for his daily breakfast shake—a simple concoction of protein powder, soy milk, whey, and frozen berries. As the blender whirred to life, Riley read the crawl at the bottom of the television screen.

HOMICIDE BOMBER IN NETANYA, ISRAEL, KILLS FOUR AND WOUNDS SEVENTEEN.

Riley's anger flashed. This was the fifth bombing in the past two weeks. What was the matter with these people? Didn't they care whom they killed? Didn't they know that these women and children had nothing to do with their war?

As he stewed on this, his mind drifted back to a conversation he'd had with Tim Clayton, the senior pastor of Parker Hills Community Church, his home church when he could attend.

"I'm sick and tired of hearing people say we need to have compassion for these murderers and understand their belief system," Riley had said the day a Palestinian bomber had killed fourteen people on a bus in Haifa.

"No one can make you love anyone, Riley," Pastor Tim countered. "But keep in mind that these people are caught up in one of the greatest lies ever perpetrated on mankind—the lie that it is worth killing others for your beliefs. These people need our prayers, they need our pity, and they need the power of our nation to try to stop them before they throw their lives away like this."

"I'm with you on your last point," Riley responded. "They need to feel a serious U.S. smackdown. But, Tim, you haven't seen what I've seen. You haven't seen your buddies lying in pieces in front of you. You haven't seen the children mangled by the screws and ball bearings from some terrorist wacko's bomb. I'm sorry, but pity's something I really have a hard time with right now."

"I understand," Tim had said gently. "Maybe because I haven't seen it, I can keep more of an objective viewpoint. I just know that the moment after these men—and women now—detonate their bombs, they've got a huge surprise waiting for them."

Riley's brain knew Tim was right. Convincing his heart was a different matter. *I gotta mull this over a different time. I've got work to do.*

He chugged the purple liquid right out of the blender—no use dirtying a glass—then moved back through the bedroom and into the bathroom, where he cranked the shower to full blast. Fifteen minutes steaming up the glass stall would work out the kinks in his body and leave him ready to start another day.

Riley felt great, especially for fourteen weeks into a PFL season as a starting linebacker. He had always taken care of himself physically—even as a cadet at the Academy—and it paid off this late in the season. While other guys' bodies were starting to break down, he was still at the top of his game. He knew that he was living an American dream—a dream that could disappear with one good hit or one wrong step—so he did everything he could to make the best of it.

///////////////////////

After his role in Operation Enduring Freedom, Riley had been unsure what would be next for him. He could have had a very promising career as an officer in AFSOC. He knew how to lead men and was able to garner their respect through his example. Besides that, the military was in his blood. His father had been a navy man in Vietnam, and his grandfather had flown an F-86 in Korea, chalking up seven MiGs to his credit. Riley's choice to try for the Air Force Academy in Colorado Springs rather than the Naval Academy in Annapolis had led to all sorts of good-natured ribbing of his dad by his grandpa. Holidays with the family had never been the same again.

Although he knew the military was an honorable profession, Riley still had that Pro Football League dream. He'd been on leave on draft day, and he could still feel the incredible tension he experienced while sitting in his parents' living room. The talk on ESPN was whether any team would pick this year's Butkus Award winner, since, like all Academy graduates, he had a five-year military commitment hanging over his head. As the picks progressed, it was hard for him not to get disheartened.

All the pundits said Riley had the skills to be a first rounder, but he'd begun to wonder if the specter of mandatory military service was just too much for most PFL teams. Riley's dad kept feeding him words of encouragement, and his mom kept feeding him lemon pound cake. Half a day and three-quarters of a cake later, he finally heard his name called in the third round. The cheers in the Draft Central auditorium could only be matched by the screams in that little house. To be chosen in the PFL draft and to be chosen by the Colorado Mustangs—what could be better than that?

The selection had been a definite risk for the organization, but they felt it was worth it if they could bag someone with Riley's playing potential. Of course, both Riley and the team would have to wait. Riley had no problem with serving out his commitment. He was more than willing to fight for his country—die for it if necessary.

And he had come fairly close to doing just that. The bullet he had taken during the firefight back in the Bagram Valley in Afghanistan had entered just above his hip. It had chipped a bone and caused a lot of bleeding, but thanks to the quick medical evacuation and the incredible medical team at Ramstein Air Base in Germany, the only lingering issue he had was a dull ache when the weather turned.

After returning from Germany, Riley had been called to his commanding officer's desk. The CO had looked up directly at Riley. "Covington, I brought you in here to make you an offer I hope you won't take. The higher-ups want me to give you the ludicrous choice of opting out of the rest of your full-time service commitment to the United States Air Force so you can go play in the Pro Football League. You'd stay in the reserves, and we'd have you in the off-season until your time's up. Now, I've seen you lead men, and I've seen you save lives. I think it would be a shame for you to give up the chance to make a lasting difference for this country so that you could go play some kids' game. But, hey, that's the choice I'm told I have to offer you. You've got twenty-four hours. Dismissed."

Riley had struggled with the choice as he walked back down the willow-lined street to his quarters. A lot of what his CO had said was right. Would choosing the PFL be taking the easier and less meaningful way out? But he could still make a difference in many people's lives playing football, right? And he certainly wouldn't be the first guy to follow such a path.

The precedent for a professional athlete opting out of military obligations had been set after the first Gulf War. Chad Hennings had returned a war hero after having flown A-10 Warthogs during the liberation of Kuwait. Although he had a long commitment still awaiting him, the air force believed he would serve them better in a public-relations role. It turned out to be a great decision; Chad had taken the opportunity to help lead his football team to three championships during the nineties.

Once the door was opened, others had stepped through. Steve Russ and Chris Gizzi both served full-time for a couple of years after the Academy, then completed the bulk of their service in the reserves during the summers while spending most of the year playing professional ball.

Riley wrestled with the decision through the night. He had made a commitment to the air force, and he did not take that lightly. The guys of his squad depended on his leadership, yet to a man they told him he would be a complete idiot not to jump at this opportunity. Still, he held back.

Finally, early the next morning, a three-way call had come from his dad and grandpa.

"God has given you the abilities and the opportunity to do something that few people have a chance to do," Grandpa Covington had said. "Obviously, He's got something special in mind for you."

"Riles," his dad said, "you know that whatever decision you make, we'll be proud of you. We're much more concerned about who you are than what you do."

By the time Riley hung up the phone, it was like a weight had been lifted from his shoulders. He finally felt free to pursue his dream. Why it was so important to get the go-ahead from these two men, he couldn't say. Maybe he wanted their affirmation, maybe he wanted their wisdom, or maybe it was just plain old respect for their opinion. All he knew was that their words were the key that opened the door to his PFL career. Six months later, he said his final good-byes to full-time air force life.

Riley chuckled to himself as he thought about the final party his squad had thrown for him before he left AFSOC. He had never seen so much alcohol in his life. While he nursed his Diet Coke, his guys gave speeches that became more syrupy and less coherent as the night wore on. Skeeter Dawkins gave him a tribute that stretched out for a record eighteen words, and Kim Li actually cried during his fourth toast of the evening. The party had officially ended with last call at 2 a.m., but Riley had spent until four thirty driving his men home.

Two weeks after that, he was running onto the Mustangs' practice field at the Inverness Training Center.

/////////////////////////

Riley shut off the water and climbed out of the shower.

As he got dressed, he glanced over at the Purple Heart and Silver Star his mom had framed for him and insisted he keep hanging in his home. This wall was the most out-of-the-way place that Riley could hang them while still honoring his mom's request. Riley Covington had been called a hero, but he was uncomfortable with that label. He had simply carried out his mission the way he'd been trained—nothing more, nothing less. It was his duty as an officer in the United States Air Force. Riley had acted as the natural-born leader he was, and now he hoped to use that leadership to take his team into the play-offs.

He went out into the garage and hopped into the black Denali he had bought used from one of the defensive ends who didn't make the cut last year. As he backed the truck out, the tires crunching through new snow, he thought about the next two weeks. The team had started out the season slowly, but they were charging hard at the end, winning seven out of the last eight games. If they could win these last two games, they were assured a wild card berth.

Riley was quickly becoming one of the key leaders of the defensive squad. The other guys were watching him, both on and off the field, and he knew he had to set the example for passion and hard work. He had no doubt that he was up for the challenge. *Let them see your focus. Let them see your work ethic. Let them see your integrity. Be the first on the field and the last off.*

Ultimately, it wasn't that different from his role as a second lieutenant.

The Yoo-hoo and Diet Mountain Dew Code Red blended together as they were poured into the cup, forming a frothing concoction the color of moderately underdone roast beef. *Cherry chocolate nectar of the gods,* Scott Ross thought as he threw out the empties.

It had been ten months since Scott had made the transition from AFSOC to Homeland Security, but already he had created a name for himself as a top communications analyst. His ability to tie together seemingly random pieces of information was almost eerie. "It's as simple as playing connect the dots," he liked to say, "only without the numbers."

Scott grabbed a handful of ice from the drawer and added the cubes to his concoction. Three weeks ago, he had stayed after hours to insulate the bottom drawer of his workstation at the counterterrorism division (CTD) of Homeland Security. He had dropped in some coils from a small refrigerator left over from a long-ago failed attempt at dorm life, then cranked the setting up to high and let it cool overnight. The next morning he'd stocked his new minibar with the ingredients needed to create his cherished brew, dropping ice in a specially designed rear compartment. This was just one of Scott's ways of "sticking it to the man"—"the man" being the guy who refused to stock the vending machines with Yoo-hoo.

Even before the firefight in the Bagram Valley had left him bloodied and dazed, Scott had known that military life wasn't for him. It was way too structured. The only reason he had joined the air force to begin with was that he had burned his bridges at two different colleges, and home was not a place anyone would want to go back to.

He had grown up as an unusual kid—odd, some might, and did, say—in central New York. He was extremely intelligent but had struggled with what one of his teachers had termed a "focus deficiency." Unfortunately, his parents had been too wrapped up with their own addictions to get him the help he needed.

When he reached high school, his creative energies had started taking on a more destructive nature. That was when he met Mr. Pinkerton, the head librarian at the Fulton Public Library, where Scott spent much of his time devouring books like *The Anarchist Cookbook* and *The Big Book of Mischief*. Mr. Pinkerton had steered him to the classics—Milton, Dickens, Dostoyevsky—and to the sciences—Einstein, Hawking, *National Geographic*, and anything having to do with mathematics and statistics. Eventually, Mr. Pinkerton had become Scott's mentor—a relationship that had lasted several years. But while the older man had greatly expanded Scott's mind, he couldn't do much with his authority issues, which expressed themselves by his barely graduating high school and later receiving invitations to leave both the University at Albany and Adirondack Community College.

Strangely enough, Scott had thrived in the air force. He seemed to do much better when there were no choices offered to him than when he had the option to do something stupid. He completed the Special Forces training with flying colors and quickly rose to the rank of staff sergeant. But even with all his success, he'd known his military career would not last long. The air force had taught him discipline and focus and how to live with purpose. But his need for independence, combined with the extreme difficulty of getting Yoo-hoo in Afghanistan, cemented his decision to accept the employment offer presented to him by the Department of Homeland Security.

"Hey, Scott, check this out," fellow analyst Tara Walsh called.

Scott grabbed his drink and moved to her workstation. "What's up?" he asked as he leaned over her shoulder.

"Oh, gag!" she cried, pushing the cup away from her face. "I asked you not to bring that stuff over here. It leaves a lingering odor like five-day-old birthday party."

"Sorry," he said as he quickly chugged the drink and set the cup on her desk.

"Oh, great. Now it's five-day-old birthday party mixed with two-hour-old Egg McMuffin. Just keep your head turned when you breathe. So, anyway, I was sent up these strings of chatter, and they reminded me of what you were talking about in our briefing this morning. Check out these key phrases." Tara laid summaries of two intercepted phone calls and one e-mail on her desk. She circled each phrase with a red felt-tip pen as she said it. "'Hand of Allah' here, here, and here; 'heart of capitalism' here and here; and 'Allah controls the weather' here, here, and here."

Immediately Scott's brain kicked into high gear. All animation disappeared from his face, and his eyes became vacant as words and phrases flashed into his mind and were either kept or discarded—an interview from last week, a report from yesterday morning, an intercepted satellite phone call from back in October—bits and pieces flowing in and being flushed out. Hypotheses and theories were built up and shot down, but out of the wreckage would emerge other possibilities. Tara, like Scott's other coworkers, had learned that when he drifted to this mysterious place in his head, it was best to just stand there, shut up, and wait.

A few months ago Scott had been asked to describe the analytical processing his brain went through so that others could be trained in it. The invitation had caused Scott to flash back to the eighth-grade algebra class that had led to his expulsion from Fulton Junior High School. He had gotten all the answers right on his midterm but found it impossible to show the steps he had taken to figure them out. He had been called in to see Principal Stansfield, who wouldn't believe Scott's pleas of honesty. The principal had called him a cheater and accused him of stealing the test ahead of time. This had caused Scott to make the slight error in judgment of hurling a decorative lead-framed picture of Stansfield's wife and two lovely daughters through a glass window, accidentally hitting the school nurse in the forehead as she was on her way back from lunch. "No thanks," he had told the trainers. "I'll just do what I do best and let you guys who have nothing better to do train the newbies."

"Where's my cup?" he cried, suddenly returning from his trance. Glancing around, he spotted his oversize maroon mug with the gold letters spelling out "University at Albany: The Path to Success Starts Here" slowly rubbing off its side. Then he remembered his little chugfest. "Okay, never mind. Now, follow my train of thought here. 'Hand of Allah' has hit at least thirteen places in the last week that I can think of with the occurrences crescendoing up to today. 'Weather' obviously means inclement weather can either affect the implementation of the action or the number of casualties—I'm leaning toward the latter. I still can't figure out the 'heart of capitalism.' Is it a financial center like Wall Street or maybe a manufacturing area? It's got to be someplace with a real possibility of a major storm system shutting down or at least slowing the operation. We've got to put more time into this, but every indication I'm getting, Tara, is that the 'hand of Allah' is big and it is imminent."

"Do you think we have enough to take this to Porter?" Tara asked. Division chief Stanley Porter was notorious for ripping to shreds analysts who wasted his time. Countless were the times that Scott had left the DC's office pondering the ways he could cause his boss the greatest amount of physical pain while leaving the fewest visible marks.

"I don't think we have a choice," Scott replied. "Give me fifteen more minutes to connect the dots; then we'll enter the belly of the beast."

As he walked back to his workstation, he became more and more unsettled. The feeling he had in the pit of his stomach was the same one he had experienced many times in Afghanistan. Unfortunately, whenever it came on, nothing good ever followed.

FRIDAY, DECEMBER 19
NORTH CENTRAL UNITED STATES

"I am so cold!" Abdel al-Hasani told his older brother, Aamir. "How do people live here? I'm wearing three layers of clothing, and I'm still chilled to the bone."

"Don't worry, Brother. Soon enough, you will be luxuriating in a perfect world with a perfect climate surrounded by perfect women."

"That truly will be amazing. However, even though I know we're promised seventy-two of those perfect women, I would be content with just seven—as long as they all looked like Areej, the daughter of Abdullah the butcher."

"Ah, one Areej for each day of the week," Aamir laughed. "You are a discriminating man, Abdel."

Ten days ago, the brothers had flown from Riyadh to Paris, where a car and fake passports had been awaiting them in the northeastern suburb of Clichy-sous-Bois. They had then driven to Zurich, where they had boarded a Swiss International flight to Winnipeg with a stop in Toronto. Renting a car with their new Canadian passports was not a problem, nor was crossing the border from Fort Frances, Ontario, to International Falls, Minnesota. They had continued to their destination city, where they found an envelope taped under a car parked in space D-136 of the international airport's west parking garage. The envelope contained a list of instructions and five keys. This began a scavenger hunt of sorts for Aamir and Abdel. They visited the bus terminal, the train station, two Mail Boxes Etc. stores, and the trunk of a 1988 Buick LeSabre. At each location, the locker or mailbox or trunk contained an identical gym bag, which they transferred to their car.

Now they were in their room at the Days Inn, carefully working with the contents of these bags. The men sat beside their beds, each of which had been covered with a tarp. On each tarp were thirty-five pounds of C-4, a vest with multiple pouches, and several boxes of large ball bearings. The brothers were forming solid cylinders of the plastic explosive. When they completed four of these cylinders, they would tape them together and place them in a pouch. In a mesh outer pocket that spanned the length of each pouch, each brother had already deposited dozens of ball bearings that would become deadly projectiles when the bombs exploded.

As Abdel molded the cold, gray material, he began thinking again of the moment these explosives would shred his body. Most of the time he was able to shut out that part of his task, but every now and then reality slipped in. He closed his eyes and felt the impact of the explosion. He heard the ricochets of the ball bearings. He smelled the smoke and the blood. His hands began to shake.

Abdel's mind drifted back two weeks to the humiliating day when he made his martyr's video. With his *shemagh* wrapped around his head and cascading over his shoulders, he had stood there awkwardly holding an AK-47 and mumbling his way through a script that had been handed to him ten seconds before the tape started rolling. Never a good reader, it had taken him three attempts to finally get all the words right.

Aamir's performance had been quite different. Abdel's older brother was so confident, so defiant of the Western world, so determined to take this course of action. Aamir had spat out his words with hatred, even embellishing the script. He was a true believer.

What I simply think, Aamir knows. But . . . but what if he's wrong?

"Brother, are you sure we're doing the right thing? I mean, is there no other way to accomplish our goals than by this act?"

Instantly, Aamir's hand connected hard with Abdel's cheek, knocking the younger brother to the ground.

"Never say that again! Do you hear me? Never! We have been chosen for a great honor, a monumental task. There are others around this very city right now who will join us in this strike. They will not back down like cowards. You have a responsibility to carry out your mission. For this you have been created. You have a responsibility to Allah, to your family, to the Cause, to your fellow martyrs, and to me!" He glared down at his brother, then picked him up by the front of his shirt and deposited him back on his chair. He gently placed his hand on Abdel's face. "Soon all this will be over. We will have struck the Great Satan a tremendous blow. And while they try to put the pieces of their decadent country back together, we will be *shahids*—martyrs, guaranteed a place in paradise."

Abdel just stared at Aamir until his brother finally took his hand away. Then he turned away without a word, picked up some more C-4, and began his work again. Aamir was right. If he didn't go through with this, he was a dead man anyway, and that same fate would probably extend to his family as well. *Allah, I do this for you. Make me like Aamir. Give me the confidence I lack.* Allahu akbar!

/ /

Scott knocked on the division chief's door.

"Make it quick!" came the reply.

Scott gave Tara a momentary grin, and they walked into the lion's den together.

The two analysts couldn't have made a more opposite pair. Tara looked like she had just stepped off the cover of *Vogue*. Her perfectly blushed cheekbones matched her perfectly shadowed eyes, which offset her perfectly painted lips—all of which were framed by perfectly coiffed, shoulder-length blonde hair. She wore a dark blue Dana Buchman pantsuit and a pair of Kate Spade pumps, both of which she had saved up for and still could only afford once they had made their migration to Nordstrom Rack.

Scott, on the other hand, had a goatee that was double the length of his No. 2–razored hair, and the Yoo-hoo combos were just starting to show on his waist—hence his switch to *Diet* Code Red. He was making his own particular fashion statement today with jeans that were tattered at the cuffs, flip-flops, and a T-shirt from Blue Öyster Cult's '78 North American tour.

Stanley Porter glanced up from his desk, saw Scott's T-shirt, and shook his head. "Ross, you idiot, you weren't even alive in 1978."

"I know, Chief, but my dad left me this shirt in his will. I take it out each year on this day to commemorate the anniversary of his death."

Scott heard Tara stifle a laugh; she knew he had worn the same shirt three days ago. Porter eyed him carefully, clearly trying to decide whether Scott was being serious or insubordinate. Finally the chief waved his hand. "So, tell me what you've got."

Scott untangled the web of information he and Tara had accumulated. "This whole 'Allah controls the weather' thing threw me for a while. Then I heard about that Yemeni guy that North Central Division picked up last night cruising south through the Iron Range in northern Minnesota. That's when things began to click. I'll bet you pesos to pieholes that dude has something to do with this."

"Have you talked to NCD yet to figure out if this 'dude' has talked?" Porter asked.

Tara jumped in. "The guy's name is Mohsin Kurshumi. I just spoke with Jim Hicks, head of ops for the NCD. He was standing right outside of Kurshumi's interrogation room while he was talking to me. He said they are still in the process of actively persuading Kurshumi to talk."

"Okay. Walsh, get back on the phone with Hicks. Tell him we don't have the luxury of asking nicely with this dirtbag. Ross, I want a full written report on my desk in fifteen minutes. Go!" Porter turned away from them and grabbed his phone.

As Tara and Scott headed for the door, they were stopped short by the DC's voice. "Hey! Nice work, you two."

They couldn't help but smile. Hearing a compliment from Stanley Porter's lips was about as rare as seeing a tie around Scott Ross's neck—both usually came out only at weddings and funerals.

Robert Taylor had just enough time to swivel his chair toward his computer screen before the phone pulled him back again. It had been this way ever since he had arrived at the Colorado Mustangs' training facility in Inverness at 6 a.m. Judging by his full voice mail in-box, the phone had been ringing through the entire night.

Taylor was in his eighth year with the Mustangs, and he still hadn't completely adjusted to the frenzy. This wasn't quite how his profs had portrayed it when he was taking his public-relations courses at the University of Colorado. *Set a goal, make a plan, PERT-chart it out. Yeah, right!* This was complete insanity. The national media attention generated by the Mustangs' recent success was overwhelming, and Taylor knew it was only going to get worse during the next couple of weeks.

He grabbed the receiver. "Colorado Mustangs Public Relations, this is Robert," he said, already thinking through possible ways to get whoever it was on the other end off the phone.

"Hey, Bob, this is Steve Growe, PFL Network. Are you busy?"

"Not at all, Steve, I'm just kicking back with

my feet up on the desk, eating a bagel, and sipping my coffee. What do you think? I have over 250 player interview requests, and the team is about to head to meetings and film breakdown, which means I have less than ten minutes to get down to the locker room and drop the requests in their lockers."

"Don't most of them just throw those requests right into the trash?"

"Yeah, thanks for reminding me. It does wonders for my job satisfaction. Anyway, what do you need?"

"Listen; I'm sorry to throw this at you, but my boss is telling me we have to get White, Ricci, and Washington right after they come off the field today. We'd also love to get Riley Covington live if you can pull it off for me."

"Sure thing. How about I get you the pope while I'm at it? Or maybe you want a shot at the O-line?" Taylor knew it would probably be a whole lot easier to set up an interview with the head of the Catholic Church than with the Mustangs' offensive line, who were notoriously closemouthed during the season. "You guys don't ask much, do you?"

"Sorry, Bob."

"You know I can't promise anything, but I'll see what I can do. Covington usually does what he can, but there are over twenty requests for him alone."

"That's why we want him; he's the real deal. ESPN is announcing the All Star roster later today and he's a lock for it this year. Help me out, and I'll owe you one."

"Yeah, yeah. I've heard that one before. I'll call you later."

Taylor hung up and darted out the door, leaving the phone ringing behind him. *White I can get,* he thought, *and Ricci's a lock. Not a chance with Washington; he's in "game mode." And Covington? Covington would give you the shirt off his back. The problem is he's only got so many shirts.*

/////////////////////////

Riley bounced up and down on the practice field, trying to get his circulation going. It was another beautiful December Colorado day—

the sun was shining, the temperature was in the low fifties, and all around the snow was just beginning to melt off—all around, that is, except for where Riley was standing. The heating coils under the turf of the east practice field ensured that the snow never had a chance to build up.

Riley closed his eyes and turned his face toward the sun, feeling its warmth on his skin. He used these brief moments of peace to center himself before everything broke loose again.

The training facility was a madhouse today. The press was everywhere. The players were tense. The coaches were unforgiving. The focus and the mental preparation needed to make it through the next two weeks before the play-offs were taking their toll on everyone.

There was a certain grind that took place in the PFL toward the end of the season. It was sort of a *Groundhog Day* feeling where every day was the same. When certain situations came along and shattered that equilibrium, everyone got out of sorts.

The Colorado Mustangs were experiencing one of those situations. With all the pressure to make it into the postseason, it was as if the play-offs had come two weeks early. The Mustangs on the field all knew the importance of each play, and each was haunted by the "what have you done for me lately" mentality of the fans and the organization that signed their checks.

"Riley, Riley!" a voice called to him, interrupting his calm.

Turning toward his name, he realized too late that it was coming from the long row of reporters, photographers, and videographers who lined the pavement alongside the field.

Seeing him look over, the reporters erupted into calls of "Covington, over here!" and—from the ones who pretended to be buddies of the players—"Pach, my man, this way!"

Riley gave them a smile and a nod, then turned his face back up to the sun. *Burton will run them off soon enough.* Roy Burton, the head coach of the Mustangs, was known for keeping his practices closed to the media.

The final few guys ran out onto the practice field, making sure they weren't late.

"Coach, just two more getting their ankles taped," one of the trainers yelled across the field.

"It's up to them," Coach Burton called back, not looking up from his clipboard.

At the pro level, there was never any screaming or yelling if someone was late to practice. Instead, the next morning, latecomers found freshly printed $1,500 fine notifications on Colorado Mustang letterhead sitting in their lockers. The fines had a way of getting a guy's attention quickly, and repeat offenders were rare.

"If you're not early, you're late," defensive end Micah Pittman muttered to Riley, causing laughter from a few other players around them.

The horn signaling the beginning of practice echoed around the facility just before rookie wide receiver Jamal White darted from the building.

"Got him!" about half the team called out. White didn't think it was funny as he finished tucking in his jersey. He glared at the veteran players whose tapings had caused him to be late.

The taping system in the PFL would certainly not pass ACLU muster. The taping order was purely based on seniority. Rookies had to make sure they got to practice and to games early, because it didn't matter how long they had been waiting; when a veteran player came in, he moved right to the front of the line. A guy could be next in line for forty-five minutes and not make any progress. Many rookies, including Jamal White today, learned this $1,500 lesson the hard way.

"All right, guys, let's get better today. We know what we have to get done, so let's get it done," Coach Burton bellowed.

The players slid into their routine quickly, beginning the warm-up phase of practice with a "pat-'n'-go" session. All running backs, wide receivers, and tight ends slowly jogged downfield, and each caught a lazy pass from one of the quarterbacks. No hits, no real exertion—this was just to limber up the body.

Looking over from the defensive drills at the south end of the practice field, Riley watched tight end Sal Ricci catch an easy toss from starting quarterback Randy Meyer. Ricci had really been feeling the pressure these past few weeks. Riley knew that in addition to wanting to do his best for his team, Ricci felt the eyes of all Italy on his back.

Joining the Mustangs had been the final step in a meteoric rise for Salvatore Ricci. Coming up through the Italian Football League—which Ricci had to constantly remind people was not called the "Italian Soccer League"—Ricci had been a big reason why A. C. Milan had taken the 2003–04 *Serie A* division championship. When Ricci was approached by the Hamburg Donnerkatzen of the International American Football League, he had been apprehensive. He knew how to use his body and his feet; hands were not something he was accustomed to using. But he was a natural athlete, and soon, scouts from PFL teams began showing up at his games. He knew then that it was only a matter of time before he "jumped the pond." Two years ago the Colorado Mustangs had drafted him away from the IAFL.

Ricci seemed to be enjoying America, but it was clear to Riley that the Italian still didn't feel like he fully fit into the culture. Everything here moved at such a faster pace than it did in Europe. But whenever Sal complained about the pace of life in America, Riley reminded him of his whirlwind romance with Megan Unruh. Sal had met Megan when she was doing a newspaper story on him for the *Denver Post*. Four weeks after they met, they were married. Then nine months to the day from their wedding night, Alessandra Bianca Ricci was born.

Since the Italian's start with the Mustangs, PFL viewership in Italy had skyrocketed. To add to that pressure, Ricci had told his teammates he had been visited last week by a representative of the Italian president. The gentleman, in his exquisite black suit that probably had cost the equivalent of Ricci's signing bonus, told him that after the "inevitable Mustang PFL Cup victory," the president of Italy wanted to entertain him at his personal residence. On top of that, Riley had read that the Italian government planned to declare a national "Salvatore Ricci Day."

After the pat-'n'-go came about ten minutes of stretches. Then the players transitioned to the installation period, reviewing their assignments for this week's game plan. Riley listened closely as Rex Texeira, the linebackers coach, went over the play shifts that had been specifically designed for this Sunday's game against the Bay Area Bandits.

The Bandits' quarterback liked to drop a few steps back from the center, then roll out before throwing a pass. That meant that

Riley and his right-side counterpart, Keith Simmons, were going to be doing a lot of blitzing.

"If the QB steps out of that pocket, I want him to see your faces," Texeira said.

"You got it, Tex-Rex," Riley replied. "Hey, Simmons, you feel like upping it to seventy-five-per for this week?" At the beginning of the season, Riley and Simmons had devised a little incentive program for keeping their game up. For each tackle that Simmons got, Riley would donate fifty dollars to the Denver Boys' Home. Simmons would donate the same amount for each of Riley's tackles.

"It's your checkbook, big spender," Simmons said. "Better start limbering up your writing hand, 'cause I'm feeling fast and mean."

After ten minutes of focusing on the Xs and Os of the upcoming game, the team began a seven-on-seven session. During this drill, plays were run at full speed but with no offensive or defensive linemen involved. Everyone was going all out today. Randy Meyer was rocketing passes in, making it extremely difficult for the defensive backfield to get a hand on the ball.

Soon the offense started to get a little mouthy. After a particularly nice short pattern catch, Sal Ricci tossed the ball to Riley.

"Just wanted you to remember what the ball felt like," Ricci taunted.

Sal may have been one of Riley's closest friends, but this linebacker didn't take that kind of trash talk from anyone. *Time for this Euro to be welcomed back to reality,* Riley thought as he forced a smile at his buddy.

As they lined up for the next play, Riley drew a bead on Ricci. The ball was snapped and Ricci came right toward Riley, who watched him intently, looking for anything that would tip off his direction. *There it is!* Riley had seen Ricci's eyes take a quick glance to his left to see if his lane was clear. Riley shot to his right a step before Ricci, grabbing the ball just before it reached the tight end's hands and running it back into the end zone.

As Riley jogged back to his huddle, he tossed the ball to Ricci. "How do you say *payback* in Italian?" he laughed.

Ricci shook his head, grinning. "What did I do wrong this time?"

"It's your eyes, Reech. You're going to follow your pattern whether the lane is open or not. By looking first, all you're doing is making sure someone will be there waiting for you."

"Got it. Thanks, Pach," Ricci said.

A while later the coaches pulled the full squads to the main field for team drills. By this point in the practice session, the players were expected to be performing at "game-time speed" and to thoroughly know the game plan and their assignments. Every move was captured by the "eye in the sky," a name used by the players for the multiangled film shot by the team's video department from a crane over the practice field. After practice, every step would be analyzed by coaches during position meetings to ensure proper technique. Any mistakes would evoke the wrath of the coaching staff. Perfection was not only expected but demanded.

The team ran sixteen plays of full-team, full-speed, full-contact football. Then special teams came on to attempt some game-pace kicks and punts. This allowed the rest of the team time to strip off their pads. From here on out, the offense and defense would alternate every five to eight plays, working on everything from two-minute drills to nickel packages to short-yardage situations.

"Hey, Riley, you've made sure those rookie linebackers have the limo ready for you tonight, right?" Chris Gorkowski, one of the veteran offensive linemen, asked as he pulled his shoulder pads over his head.

"Yeah, I've got everything covered."

"Well, you'll have to drink something other than Diet Coke to get that tab up over five thousand dollars, choirboy," Gorkowski joked. Everyone on the team knew Riley wasn't a drinker.

It had become a tradition for the rookies to take all the veterans out on the town to the most expensive restaurant in the city once a year. The vets would run the bill up as high as they could and leave the rookies to pay the tab.

"Don't worry about us linebackers. You just make sure you linemen leave some food for the rest of us."

Riley really had no desire to go. He had agreed to the evening primarily to hang out with Ricci and to make sure nobody got too far out of line. As practice ended and Riley headed toward the pressroom, he knew that wading through the interviews that were waiting for him was only the beginning of what promised to be a very long night.

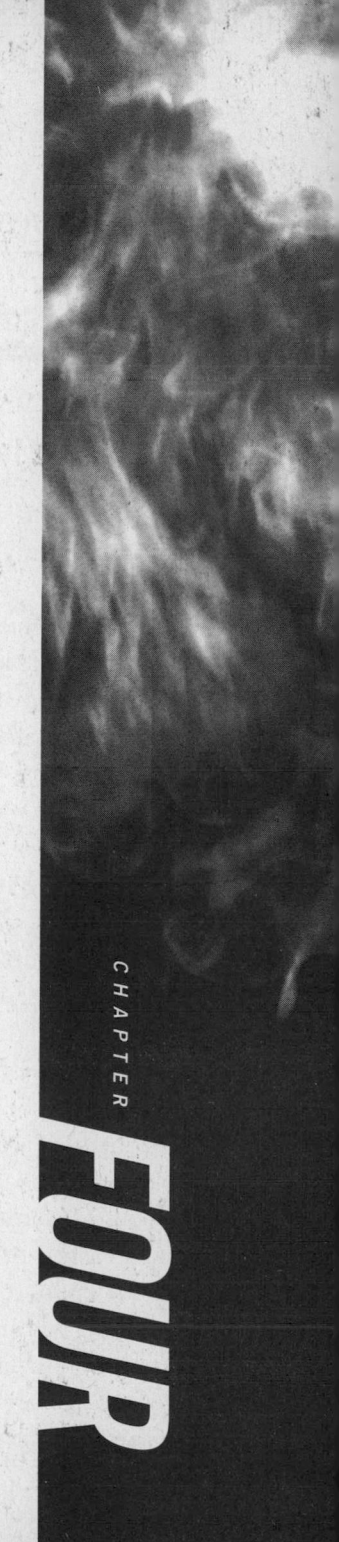

CHAPTER

FOUR

FRIDAY, DECEMBER 19
CTD NORTH CENTRAL DIVISION
HEADQUARTERS
MINNEAPOLIS, MINNESOTA

Jim Hicks sat straddling Mohsin Kurshumi. His forehead was pressed hard against the other man's forehead, tilting the Yemeni's head back at a seventy-five–degree angle and pushing it hard against the top corner of the chair.

Hicks's right hand held the tie of the interpreter, who had vainly tried to remove himself from the interrogation when he saw the violent turn it was taking. The agent's left hand held the MKIII combat knife he had kept from his days as a Navy SEAL. The tip of the blade was about a half inch through the skin behind the prisoner's chin and was gradually making progress as Hicks slowly twisted the blade left, then right, then left, then right. Blood trickled down the cold metal and between Hicks's fingers. Kurshumi had stopped screaming when he realized that each time he did, it just drove the blade in a little deeper.

When Hicks could finally see raw, animal fear in the man's eyes, he knew he had him.

He gave the interpreter's tie a hard yank, adding a third sweaty head to the private confab. "Mr.

Mazari, please be so kind as to tell Mr. Kurshumi that the cameras in this room have unfortunately malfunctioned. That means there's nobody who's going to know exactly what happens in here."

The interpreter gave a simultaneous translation to the prisoner, whose eyes grew bigger as he realized where this conversation was going.

The blade kept twisting. "Tell him that he will not be my first 'accidental' kill, but I've a good mind to make him my slowest. And if you would, Mr. Mazari, tell him that if he thinks I'm worried about you saying anything . . . well, after what's gone on in here already this afternoon, I think there's a good chance that I'm the only one who's going to walk out of this room in one piece." Hicks turned his head slightly toward the interpreter and gave a subtle wink that seemed to say, *Don't worry about it.* However, the accompanying grin said, *I haven't quite made up my mind.*

"I want to know the who, the what, the where, and the when," Hicks continued. "And I want to know NOW!" Kurshumi's eyes squinted in pain as the knife finally pushed through the bottom of his mouth. The point prodded his tongue into action like a spur to the flank of a horse.

Ten minutes later, Hicks left the interrogation room and hurried down the sterile white corridor. Driving open the door to the men's room with his shoulder, he dropped to his knees in the first stall and vomited up lunch, breakfast, and last night's dinner. This wasn't the first act of "persuasion" he had been involved in. But he prayed it would be his last.

He slowly pushed himself to his feet and steadied himself as he wiped his bloody handprint off the white plastic toilet seat. At the sink, he tried to wash all traces of Mohsin Kurshumi off his hands— soaping, then resoaping, digging under his fingernails, and scouring the quicks. Hicks lifted water to his mouth to rinse out the aftertaste and splashed the cool wetness on his face to calm himself. Adjusting the knobs to hot, he picked his knife off the counter and began scrubbing it, starting with the handle and working his way down the blade, working at it long after he knew it was clean.

As he watched the water cascading off the metal and swirling down the drain, Hicks knew the hardest part still awaited him. Gathering up all his willpower, he slowly raised his head until he met his own eyes in the mirror.

The empty gaze registered deep down in his gut. Long ago he had resigned himself to the belief that the ends justified the means when hundreds, if not thousands, of lives were at stake. Yet acting on that belief had cost him countless sleepless nights and countless nightmares when he did sleep. He had lost two marriages, and now he felt he was gradually losing his soul. *Don't let the monster eat you alive,* he told his reflection. *You did what had to be done. Never forget that! You did what had to be done.* The longer he looked in his eyes, however, the less convinced he became of his words.

The ring of his cell phone saved him from more soul searching and snapped him back to tough-guy mode. "Hicks," he answered.

"Hicks, this is Scott Ross down in Midwest Division. You talked to my colleague Tara Walsh a couple of times earlier today. We heard you had some success with Mr. Yemen-guy, and I was hoping to get a heads-up on any information he may have given."

"Yeah, Ross, Tara said you'd be calling. The boys who were listening in on the interrogation should be getting you a transcript soon, but let me give you the highlights. Kurshumi was on his way toward Minneapolis, where he was supposed to locate a green Toyota Highlander with Michigan plates in the parking lot of a Byerly's in St. Louis Park. In the wheel well of this car would be an envelope with instructions and keys. All indications are that he was going to pick up items to make an explosive belt as part of a coordinated suicide attack."

"Of course! 'Allah controls the weather!' I thought they *didn't* want bad weather, because it would keep people in their homes. Instead, they *do* want it cold and nasty so that they can put as much clothing on their bodies as possible to disguise themselves and their vests to help . . . Wait a second, did you say 'suicide attack'—as in a Palestinian-blows-up-the-bus kind of suicide attack?"

"Unfortunately, that's exactly what we're looking at. We've sent people out to gather the stuff that Kurshumi was meant to collect. I'm guessing their scavenger hunt will turn up between thirty and forty pounds of explosives, a vest or belt, and a projectile of some sort."

"I can't believe it's finally happening here," Scott said.

Hicks knew what he meant. Ever since 9/11, the evidence had pointed to the inevitability of just this sort of attack. However, there was a huge emotional leap separating theory from reality.

"So," Scott continued, "how many are there, and where and when are they planning to hit?"

"I wish I had better news here, but this guy doesn't seem to know any details. He's just an expendable pawn on a need-to-know. All he could tell me was that the attack is scheduled for tomorrow. This evening, he was supposed to call a number that he carried with him, but when he got pulled over, he swallowed that number without looking at it. That's all we've got right now."

"C'mon, man, you know we need more than that! We've got some psychos out there who want to blow a whole load of bolts or bearings or screws or something through a bunch of American bodies tomorrow, and all you can tell me is that someone's going to do it somewhere sometime? Are you sure you got everything out of Kurshumi? Can anyone else up there take a shot at him?"

Hicks gave his anger time to vent through his grip on his cell phone before he answered. "I'm going to chalk that question up to your youthfulness, Mr. Ross, and to your enthusiasm, which I highly suggest you get under control. Believe me when I tell you that there is nothing Kurshumi knows that he did not tell us. Do you understand?"

"I understand. . . . It's just that this is a really nasty game, and I feel like we're playing in the dark."

"Welcome to counterterrorism, Mr. Ross. Now, I've got work to do." Hicks flipped the phone closed and cocked his arm back, then stopped himself just before pitching a strike against the aqua blue tile wall. *Little punk sits behind a computer screen all day and then tells me how to do my job? The only blood he's ever had on his hands was probably from his own nose.*

With effort, he got himself back under control. Glancing in the mirror one more time, he quickly turned his eyes away. *You've got work to do, son,* he thought as he burst out the door to head back to his team. *Enjoy your self-loathing on your own time.*

Abdel eased the blasting cap into the final cylinder of C-4. Although he had practiced this countless times while training in Pakistan, he still felt nervous sliding the triggering device into the plastic explosive. There was finality to the action, as if engaging a lock for which he had no key. *Click! Your fate is sealed. Your destiny awaits.*

Aamir's hand clamped down on his shoulder, startling him. "Can you feel it, Abdel? We truly are the most blessed among men. Think about what this means. Most people live and die in insignificance. But we have been given a chance to achieve immortality. The names of the great martyr brothers Aamir and Abdel al-Hasani will be venerated for generations in story and song. Think of the honor that will be bestowed upon our family. Think of the financial security Father and Mother will experience the rest of their lives. Think of the smile of Allah and the joy of the Prophet as they witness our victory, achieved in their names."

Abdel stared at his brother. He still hadn't forgiven Aamir for striking him earlier. He had spoken only what words were necessary since the incident. As he listened to his brother's voice drone on and on, he wondered whom his brother was really trying to convince. *Does he truly believe the words he's saying? I know that I once did. I wonder if I still do.*

When Aamir finally finished his soliloquy, Abdel shook himself loose from his brother's grip and walked to his jacket, which was hanging over a chair. Ripping open the Velcro, he reached into the front pocket and pulled out a small, very sharp folding knife. As he walked back to his brother, the snap of the opening blade broke the silence of the room. He reached up and grabbed the top of Aamir's T-shirt, then brought the knife up and with three quick cuts sliced off the front of the shirt's thin collar.

When Abdel opened the double layer of material, a small roll of paper fell out into his hand. The paper had been loosely sewn into the shirt in a way that combined security with easy access. The garment had then been given to Aamir with the instructions to wear it under his clothes at all times and to not remove the paper until 6 p.m. the night before the attack. The only deviation allowed was if he was in danger of being caught, at which time he was to rip off the collar and swallow the enclosed information.

Abdel gently unrolled the paper, revealing ten neatly printed digits. He dropped the small strip into Aamir's hand. "It's time to make the call."

Aamir pulled a disposable cell phone out of his pocket. They had paid cash for the phone at a Wal-Mart last night and had not even had to show ID to acquire their minutes.

Aamir dialed the number, then simply said, "The hand is poised to strike." The older brother scribbled quickly in Arabic as he listened to the voice on the other end. When the line went dead, he placed the cell phone in the waste can next to the television and pounded it to pieces with the lug wrench from their car, wasting twenty-eight of their original thirty T-Mobile To Go minutes.

Aamir popped the strip of paper into his mouth and spoke to his brother as he chewed. "The plan is beautiful. We will strike America a blow it will not soon forget. Tomorrow, we will leave—"

Abdel put his hand up, interrupting his brother. "Please, not today. I can't handle any more today. Tomorrow, Aamir . . . please . . . after sunrise prayer . . . you can tell me what to do then." He grabbed a chair, placed it in a corner of the room, and sat with his head in his hands. He could feel the eyes of his brother on him, but he didn't look up.

Is this fear? Is it doubt? I was so sure at camp in Pakistan. I was so sure back home in Riyadh. Why am I struggling so much now? Is this really what you want, Allah? You know I will do anything for you.

Abdel remained stationary as the room settled into darkness. At some point in the evening, his brother asked him if he wanted to join him for some dinner. He responded with a weak wave of his hand. The hotel door closed with a click as his brother left, then clicked again when he returned.

Abdel heard the sounds of Aamir quietly getting undressed and slipping into bed. Soon his brother's familiar soft snore drifted across the room, a sound that had been part of Abdel's life for as long as he could remember. He wasn't sure when he finally fell asleep, but when he woke up the next morning his back and neck were stiff and his forehead was red from the hard pillows of his hands.

Scott Ross had assembled his primary team of five in a conference room when the call came from Jim Hicks. He tossed his phone to Tara, telling her that he and Hicks were "relationally challenged."

She listened for a minute, then tossed the closed phone back to Scott. "They've collected all the materials that Kurshumi was supposed to pick up—a vest, thirty-five pounds of C-4, and three boxes of 5 mm ball bearings. We've got tonight to figure this thing out, because tomorrow things are going to get really ugly really fast."

"So we know the what and the when. If we can figure out the where, then we'll have a better chance of nailing the who," Scott observed.

"You sound like an Abbott and Costello routine," said former teen hacker Evie Cline.

"Oh, I don't know," added MIT grad Virgil Hernandez.

"Third base!" the rest called out. The rest, that is, except for Tara, who often felt like the only one in this group who had actually broken out on the other side of puberty.

"Okay, gang, let's reel it in. Tara's giving us the eye again," Scott said. "So we're missing something here. Let's start from the top. I really think that the key to this whole thing has to be the 'heart of capitalism.' Evie, you checked out the financial areas of the Twin Cities. Anything stand out to you?"

"They've got a federal reserve bank, but it's just one of twelve around the country. It's nothing that would make a huge statement."

"Joey, you checked out manufacturing. Can you give me anything?"

"Nothing that would make me stand up and say, 'Wow.'" Joey Williamson was the only member of the group besides Scott not to have a degree from a prestigious university.

"Virgil, you checked to see if there were any big meetings or conventions in the Twin Cities."

"There's not much of anything. Not many trades schedule their conventions the week before Christmas."

"Right. And, Tara, you were checking on . . . Wait a second— back up. It's the week before Christmas?" Without a wife, kids, or parents, Scott tended not to notice holidays.

"Sorry," Hernandez said, "am I being politically incorrect? We're also right in the middle of Hanukkah and a couple of weeks away from Kwanzaa, if you'd prefer."

Scott ignored Hernandez and put his hand up, signaling for everyone to be quiet. After two solid minutes of silence that seemed like an eternity to the highly caffeinated, attention-challenged team, he turned to Tara. "We've got them! The heart of capitalism. It's Christmas! Greedy kids, plastic cards melting from the friction, useless junk flying off the shelves! That's got to be it! What's the biggest shopping area in the Twin Cities?"

Tara didn't answer; she was already dialing Jim Hicks's number. When he answered the phone, she said, "Jim, Tara; we've got it. 'The heart of capitalism'—it's the mall. They're going after the Mall of America!"

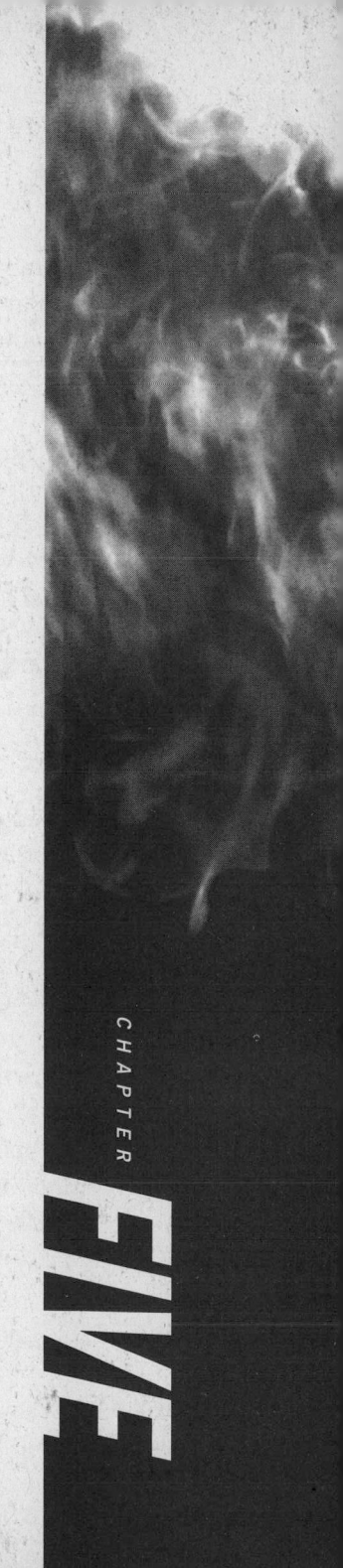

Riley jogged out of the training facility after finishing his live interview with the PFL Network.
The cold night air hit him full force, catching the
breath in his lungs. A weather system had moved
in during the afternoon and dropped the wind
chill below freezing. *Fifties today and twenties
tonight. You want to know Colorado weather? Flip
a coin.*

Quickly he zipped up his leather bomber
jacket the rest of the way and shoved his hands
deep in the pockets. He wanted to smack himself
when he thought of the toasty nubuck service
gloves that he had just picked up at REI but were
currently sitting in the bag on his dresser back
home.

When practice ended around 3:30 p.m., most
of the players had spent time lifting weights before
going to position meetings. After the linebackers'
meeting, Riley had quickly cleaned himself up for
his interviews. Robert Taylor had given the go-
ahead to KCNC, KUSA, and Fox Sports for taped
conversations, after which Riley was scheduled for
a five-minute live shot with PFL Network.

CHAPTER

FIVE

Each reporter was given a ten-minute slot to set up equipment, do the interview, tear down, and be out the door. The room was big enough for the video crews to get creative with the lighting, which always seemed to take up the bulk of the prep time. Riley sat down on a stool in front of a large black curtain and tried to manufacture excitement. But by the third time he heard the same questions, Riley was having a hard time keeping his answers fresh and his armpits dry. Repetition and heat—that was the glamour of a PFL player interview.

Finally, with the live shot done, he bolted out the door. It was 7:15—only five minutes later than Taylor had promised he'd be finished.

When Riley got to the parking lot, he couldn't help but laugh. Every Hummer limousine in the Denver metro area must have been lined up there, stretching from the maintenance garage, past the Mustangs store, and out onto Inverness Boulevard. There were white ones, black ones, and one that was bright yellow. *I hope these rookies have been saving their money,* he thought as he looked for the linebackers' limo.

He spotted first-year man Garrett Widnall five cars down, waving to him and holding the door open. Widnall had been a rookie free agent who had barely made the team. It was one thing to be a big fish in a little pond at Division II Humboldt State. Now Widnall was swimming with the sharks, and it was still a toss-up as to whether he would get eaten alive. Riley knew the evening's festivities would hit the kid's wallet hard. He decided that he would pull him aside tonight and talk through some sort of financial arrangement with him.

Passing by vehicle after vehicle, he could feel the deep bass from the Hummers' sound systems rattling his insides. *Lord, please blow my limo's speakers before I get there.* Suddenly, something caught his ear. *What in the world is that? Opera?*

A center window in the behemoth next to him slid down, and Sal Ricci stuck his head out with a big grin.

Anticipating Riley's question, Ricci said, "It's Andrea Bocelli— my gift from the boys for getting offensive player of the week." Ricci had been awarded that title after last Sunday's game against the

Pittsburgh Miners in which he had racked up 178 yards receiving and caught 2 touchdown passes, one for 85 yards.

"You must be loving that."

"Well, not exactly." Ricci leaned back from the window so that Riley could look in. Toward the back of the limo, a trio of wide receivers was doing an impersonation of the Three Tenors—singing into bottles of Michelob. Judging by the number of empties on the floor of the vehicle, these weren't their first microphones, and this wasn't their first song. While they sang with great passion, their goal seemed to be focused more on volume than pitch. Riley grimaced.

"And check out Watkins," Ricci said, jabbing his thumb toward the opposite side of the limo by the bar. Jerrod Watkins, fifth-year tight end out of Central Michigan, was swaying back and forth while making some very strange noises with his mouth and hands. "He calls it operatic beat box."

"I didn't know that was possible."

"It's not. I do believe it's going to be a long ride to Del Frisco's."

Laughing, Riley pulled himself back out of the window and made his way down to his position's limo.

"What's up, Jacks?" he said to Garrett Widnall as he stepped through the door. Widnall's nickname was one of the team's more obscure ones, finding its origin in the Humboldt State mascot.

The rookie climbed in after him. "Hey, Pach. Pretty sweet limo, huh?" Widnall shouted. Evidently Riley's prayer about the blown speakers had gone unheeded.

"Yeah . . . uh, pretty sweet." As Riley looked around, his impression was less of twenty-first-century luxury than of 1970s Huggy Bear.

"And check this out! I had them stock the fridge in the bar with Diet Pepsi for you." Widnall swung the refrigerator door open, proudly displaying its contents.

"Thanks, man. That was very—"

"You stocked it with what?" Keith Simmons interrupted, getting right in Widnall's face. "I didn't just hear you say Diet Pepsi, did I? Boy, don't you know that my man Pach drinks Diet Coke? What's the matter with you?"

Widnall turned to Riley with big, pleading eyes.

"Simm . . . ," Riley warned, trying to defuse the situation.

"When I want to talk to you, Pach, I'll look at you. Now, Rook, get your little Humbone State backside in that building, and don't come out until you find Mr. Covington some Diet Coke! Got it?"

"Sure thing, Simm," Widnall muttered as he scrambled out of the limo.

Simmons stood up through the moon roof and called after him, "And you better hurry up, or I'm ordering three prime ribs tonight and giving two to my dog!" He fell back onto the leather seat laughing. "You see that boy run?"

Riley didn't want to laugh but couldn't help it. Everyone had been on the wrong end of rookie night before, and it was never a pleasant experience. "Just do me a favor tonight, okay? Go easy on Jacks."

"Of course, Pach. I'll treat him like he was my little brother. Man, I hated that punk." Everyone in the Hummer burst out laughing.

I was right, Riley thought. *It's going to be a very long night.*

///////////////////////

Riley watched as Travis Marshall nervously folded and unfolded the thin brown straw that had come with his little four-dollar bottle of Coke. He could almost see the sixth-round offensive tackle out of William and Mary computing the tab in his head and dividing it by the dozen rookies on the team's roster. He had received a $25,000 signing bonus back in July, but after a welcome to the wonderful world of taxes, agent fees, and a down payment on a condo in town, he was probably living paycheck to paycheck. He looked worried, as he should be. The vets were already doing some pretty heavy damage at the restaurant.

"Hey, Travis," Riley said, tapping Marshall on the forehead. "You in there?" Riley, Ricci, and Marshall were sitting in a booth just off the main tables.

"Man, I think I better start filling some doggie bags here, because I don't think I'll be grocery shopping for a few weeks," Marshall replied softly.

"Well, you know you can always raid my refrigerator anytime you need to," Riley offered.

"I'd say the same thing," Ricci said, "but Meg says we can't afford you anymore. Every time you come over for an evening, she's got to plan a trip back to Wild Oats the next day."

Chris Gorkowski slid into the booth next to Riley, pinning him to the wall. "Hey, Marsh, you're not going to finish that, are you?"

Before Marshall had a chance to reply, the veteran center reached over, picked up the younger man's New York strip steak, and bit a chunk out of it the size of lower Manhattan.

"You see what happens, Sal? I warned them about letting Snap here off of his leash," Riley said.

Gorkowski turned to Riley, gave him a full, meaty grin, and slid his enormous bulk even farther into the booth.

"Uncle!" Riley gasped.

"Marsh," Gorkowski continued, the alcohol on his breath causing all three of the men to lean as far away as they could, "me and the boys have been missing you over at the O-line table. We think it's time you came over and sang us a little William and Mary fight song, preferably in the voice of Mary rather than William."

"You can't be serious," Marshall pleaded.

In response, Gorkowski bit off the borough of Brooklyn, dropped what little remained of the steak back onto Marshall's plate, and said, "We'll be waiting."

When the center had gone, Marshall looked at the others with desperation in his eyes. "Riley, Sal, can't you guys do something?" he begged.

Riley laughed. "Well, since the air force took away all my access to heavy artillery, I'm kind of at a loss."

"Just go and get it over with," Ricci said. "It's all part of the game. You should have seen what I had to put up with. At least you came from an American university. I arrived from the Hamburg Donnerkatzen."

"Yes, the mighty Thundercats, widely recognized as the worst club nickname in all of global sports," Riley laughed. "You should have seen it—he's getting all these Lion-O and Panthro and Cheetara references thrown at him, and he's got no clue what anyone's talking about."

"Apparently, we Italians were not quite cultured enough to have the *ThunderCats* cartoon broadcast on *canale cinque*."

But Riley was laughing so hard by now that he didn't even hear Sal. "And then the singing! I think at different times throughout the evening Sal had to sing the Italian national anthem, the German national anthem, the A. C. Milan fight song, *and* the Hamburg Donnerkatzen theme song."

"I didn't realize the Donnerkatzen had a theme song," Marshall said.

"They don't," Ricci responded. "I just made up a song in what the guys thought was German. It was actually mostly Italian with some *ja, ja*s and an *Ach, du lieber* or two mixed in. It's not like they would have known the difference."

"Yeah, and it's a good thing they didn't have an Italian-to-English dictionary handy. From what I remember, most of the song had to do with the lineage of your fellow receivers and their various romantic attachments to barnyard animals." Tears were streaming down Riley's face as he fell sideways into the booth. When he finally caught his breath, he turned back to Marshall and said, "Just go and do it, Marsh. The night will be over soon enough. Besides, these guys are so smashed, they won't remember a thing in the morning."

//////////////////////

The servers scurried around as fast as they could, knowing there would be an enormous tip awaiting them at the end of the night. Riley caught one girl's attention and waved her over.

"Hey . . . uh . . . Anna," he said, reading her name badge, "I was wondering if you could do me a favor. Could you get two New York strip steaks—how did Travis have his steak cooked, Sal? Medium well?—yeah, cooked medium well. Include sides of the chateau potatoes, sautéed mushrooms, and angel hair pasta. Then I want you to box it all up, stick it in a bag, and bring it back here." Riley slipped her two hundred-dollar bills. "You keep the difference. And keep this strictly between us, all right?"

"Yes, sir, Mr. Covington."

Riley saw Ricci grinning at him and shaking his head.

"What? This is probably cheaper than him coming over and raiding my pantry."

"I don't understand you sometimes. What are you hoping to get out of all this nicey-nice stuff you're always doing?"

Riley leaned back in the booth. "I don't do it to get anything out of it. I do it because it's the right thing to do." Seeing that Ricci was still smirking and shaking his head at him, Riley went on. "I don't know how to explain it, Reech. . . . A couple of years back, there was a big fad here in the U.S.—I don't know if you saw anything about it in Germany. Everyone had stuff with the letters *WWJD* on them—bumper stickers, shirts, key chains—anything anyone could make a buck off of, they stuck the letters on it."

"Yeah, I saw some of that stuff. 'What would Jesus do,' right? In Germany, the letters were *WWJT*—'Was würde Jesus tun.'"

"Exactly. For many people it was just a cool saying, something to make them feel spiritual. For me, it's really how I try to live my life."

Ricci scooped out another helping of the spinach supreme from the family-style dish. "I guess that makes sense. You see someone who has a problem, you give them what they need, and, bam! you're one step closer to heaven."

"Not quite, Sal. I don't need to get any steps closer to heaven because of my belief in Jesus Christ. Doing all the good things only—"

Ricci's cell phone interrupted the conversation. He looked at the caller ID, flushed, and then hurriedly said, "Sorry, I have to take this."

Riley watched Ricci walk out of the room. He wondered what could have thrown him off like that. Sal probably received a few dozen phone calls every day. What was it about this one that had made him bolt from the table? Sal's moods were often a little unpredictable, but Riley had always written that off to his friend's being European. *Probably just something going on at home.*

His thoughts were interrupted by a frightening, high-pitched version of Travis Marshall's voice carrying across the room.

*"Oh, we will fight, fight, fight for the Indians
When the Big Green team appears. . . ."*

Ricci slid back into the booth. He seemed a little more composed, but Riley noticed beads of sweat on his forehead.

"That was quick. Everything okay with Megan and Alessandra?"

"What? Oh, Meg? Yeah, no big deal. Alessandra hit her head on the corner of our coffee table. I think Meg just wanted someone to tell her she's not a bad mother."

Riley eyed his friend. The Italian's mind was clearly a thousand miles away.

When Marshall finally finished his fight song and escaped back to Riley's booth, Gorkowski made his way up on top of the linemen's table, his left foot planted squarely in the middle of a mound of potatoes au gratin. "Can I have your attention, dear friends and teammates," he slurred. "In honor of our beloved dozen rookies who are paying for this feast, I would like to propose a toast. I hold in my hand a bottle of Macallan 1964 single malt scotch, which I would like to pass around. It is a most exquisite beverage, as it should be for $2,500 a bottle. I would like to thank you boys for—whoops!"

A collective gasp sounded around the room as the bottle "accidentally" dropped to the table and shattered. "Oh my," the All-Pro center teased. "Me and my butterfingers. Well, you know us linemen—we're not supposed to hold anything."

Everyone burst into laughter—everyone except the rookies. They were too busy doing mental mathematical gymnastics with the numbers 12 and 2,500. The conversation kicked up again as the dessert cart was brought around and each table ordered one of everything. Ricci remained subdued, so Riley and Marshall did most of the talking.

"You know, where I grew up they called this pudding," the rookie offensive lineman said, looking down at the crème brûlée. "Here, they burn it, give it a French name, and charge $8.95 a pop."

Riley laughed. "Well, when I was growing up, most of our cuisine came from the kitchen of a world-renowned culinary master—the great Chef Boyardee." Out of the corner of his eye, he saw Anna, the waitress, trying to get his attention. She was holding up a large bag. Riley made an attempt at a meaningful look and a nod toward Marshall.

"Hey, what's that all about, Riley?" Marshall asked, turning to look back. "You siccing Gorkowski on me again?"

"Way to blow the surprise," Riley said to Marshall. He signaled for Anna to come to the table.

She presented the bag to the shocked lineman. Marshall rifled through the sack, opening everything up and devouring the smells. "I don't believe this. Who does this kind of stuff, Pach?"

"Hey, anything to keep you out of my kitchen."

Mercifully, the night was coming to an end. As everyone piled out of the restaurant, Riley caught up with Garrett Widnall. Together they worked out a deal for him to cover Widnall's portion of the night's expenses with payback coming out of the anticipated play-off bonuses.

"Thanks, Pach. You saved my skin tonight."

"You just make sure you do your part to get us into the post-season, or else you'll be working it off this spring mowing my lawn or painting my house or sanitizing my garbage cans or polishing my car or rubbing my feet or all of the above."

"Rubbing your feet, huh? Maybe we need to rethink the terms of our arrangement," Widnall laughed.

/////////////////////

Driving home that night, Riley couldn't get Ricci's abrupt change of mood out of his mind. He knew that the man had some secrets. Asking him about his past was like asking Ebenezer Scrooge for the PIN to his checking account. He couldn't count the number of times he had tried to delve into Ricci's history, and within five minutes his friend would find a way to turn the conversation around so they were talking about Riley again. The news agencies had given the basics about his childhood in an Italian orphanage and his gradual rise to national attention, but as he thought about it, Riley realized he knew little more about his friend than anyone with Internet access might know.

Glancing down at the seat next to him, he saw the blue glow of his cell phone and debated whether he should give Ricci a call. He picked up the phone, tossed it a couple of times in his hand, then set it back down. *There's a fine line between trying to help and prying. I'll catch up with him tomorrow on the plane.*

Finally arriving home four hours past his usual bedtime, Riley tossed his keys, which went sliding across the granite countertop in his kitchen and into the sink. He punched a button on his phone that automatically dialed his voice mail, then put the receiver on speaker.

A call from his mom wanting to talk. Another call from his mom. A call from Robert Taylor asking if he'd come in a half hour early to do a video interview with ESPN. A call from his dad wanting to know if he knew his mom wanted to talk.

Riley hung up the phone, stretched, and moved toward the bedroom. He dropped his clothes onto the hardwood, set his alarm, and climbed under his comforter. Just before turning off his bedside lamp, he spotted the bag with the gloves on his dresser. He willed himself back out of bed, grabbed the gloves, retrieved his keys from the sink, and set them both by the garage door. As he slid back under the covers and closed his eyes, the last thing he heard in his head as he drifted off to sleep was a strange falsetto voice serenading him:

We'll have a touchdown, touchdown, Indians!
And raise the Green and Gold!

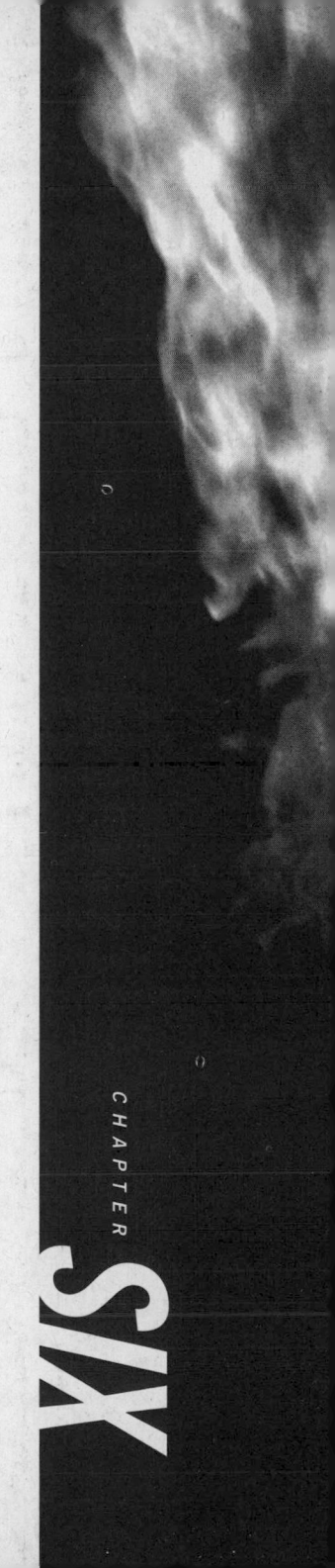

"I can't believe those idiots aren't going to shut down the mall," Scott Ross said as he threw his half-full bottle of Yoo-hoo Lite into the trash can, swearing he would never again touch that perversion of perfection. His head was still spinning from the whirlwind trip that had brought him from discovery of the Mall of America as the likely target: grabbing his always-packed bag, hopping a CTD jet with Tara Walsh, flying through much of the night, and finally making their way to the North Central Division headquarters in downtown Minneapolis. "Don't they realize what's about to go down?"

"Their exact words were, 'We're not going to shut down the mall during one of the biggest shopping weekends of the year because of some guy's hunch,'" a disgusted Jim Hicks responded. "We've even taken it to the governor, who—spineless wonder that he is—backs the mall folks' decision. I can't believe I'd ever long for a return to the days of Jesse Ventura."

CHAPTER

SIX

"Didn't Secretary Moss try to convince them?"

"Come on, you've been around long enough to understand Moss. He only likes to scare people when he needs more funding for Homeland Security."

"Well, isn't that just ducky? We can't get backed by the wuss *or* the weasel," Scott grumbled, sitting down on the corner of Hicks's desk that just happened to hold the remaining half of the man's onion bagel.

Hicks laughed as Scott contorted himself, trying to cleanse his posterior regions of cream cheese. "Let me tell you what I need from you, Ross. I need names. I need faces. I need anything I can get that will help me pick out the needles that are looking to blow up the rest of the haystack."

"Believe me, we're working on it as hard as we can. Tara's on the phone right now with my team back home. They're processing through the facial pics that our cameras snapped at all the border crossings in Minnesota, North Dakota, and Montana. We're filtering first on Canadian rental cars, based on the vehicle what's-his-Yemeni-name was driving."

"Kurshumi."

"Gesundheit," Scott said, providing his own rim shot.

Hicks's glare made it clear that he felt the time for jokes was past.

"You know, Jim, with that evil eye, you and Tara are going to get along just fine. So, anyway, we're starting with the rental cars; then we're adding a little dose of racial profiling—*that's our little secret*," he whispered with a conspiratorial wink. "We're running all those pics through our facial recognition blender and hoping something comes out of the mix. Do we have any idea how many evildoers we're looking for?"

Hicks shook his head. "No clue. Kurshumi was really information-deprived."

"When we get you the faces, what's your plan at the mall?"

"We've been able to talk the governor into securing us fifty cops—just enough to cover his backside in case this thing does go down. I've brought in the CTD ops teams from Northeastern Division and Western Division, plus the folks you brought along. That gives us sixty-six agents. Even with that many good guys on site, we still don't stand a chance without more info."

"Keep the faith," Scott encouraged as he carefully checked the corner of the desk before he sat down again. "We'll give you something. They don't make them any better than my gang."

SATURDAY, DECEMBER 20
NORTH CENTRAL UNITED STATES
7:10 A.M. CST

Aamir and Abdel al-Hasani prayed with their hands cupped at their chests, then wiped them across their faces before rising from their knees. *Fajr*—the sunrise time of prayer—was now complete.

The blessed words still echoed in Abdel's mind. *All greetings, blessings, and good acts are from you, my Lord. . . . O Allah, be gracious unto Muhammad and the people of Muhammad.* The thought struck him that today would be the first day in many years that he would complete only one of the five required daily prayers of the *salat*. Hopefully the next time he spoke to Allah it would be face-to-face. Then he could affirm to him in person that he was the only God, and that Muhammad was his prophet.

"Are you ready, mighty warrior?" his brother asked.

"I will be there with you on earth and in heaven, Aamir. That's all I can say."

"Are you still having doubts about—?"

"Stop!" Abdel thrust his hand in front of his brother's face—a clear sign of disrespect, but he didn't care. "Don't say any more. I told you I would be there with you. Leave it at that! Now, let's prepare ourselves."

Abdel pretended he couldn't see Aamir's darkening face as he crossed the room to where the vests were stored. *I'm just frightened,* he told himself. *There's nothing wrong with that. Even Muhammad was frightened after Gabriel first visited him.* As he walked back carrying the first of the vests, he reassured Aamir, "I love you, my brother. There is no one else I would rather be entering glory with than you."

Abdel briefly met his brother's eyes, then quickly looked away as Aamir took the vest from him.

"Turn around," Aamir softly commanded him. Abdel obeyed, and Aamir lowered the dark green vest over his head. The nylon material rested on the new white T-shirt that covered Abdel's upper body, which, along with the rest of his body, had been shaved completely hairless during a ritual cleansing process they had both participated in prior to their predawn prayer. Aamir reached around to the Velcro straps in the front and pulled them tight around Abdel's back.

In the closet hung a red and green flannel shirt that Aamir now brought over. While Abdel held the detonator in his hand, his older brother helped him slide his arms through the sleeves. He was very careful not to snag the long wire that connected to the vest. Before buttoning the cuffs, Aamir used surgical tape to attach the detonator to Abdel's forearm. They would cut the tape prior to walking into the mall.

As Abdel repeated the same process with Aamir, the silence became heavier. Both men were lost in their own thoughts. Abdel visualized the plan over and over. He thought through all the possible contingencies. What would they do if they were stopped at the doors? What if one of their compatriots failed to complete his mission? What if he froze?

"All good acts are from you, my Lord," says our prayer. Is this a good act? Or could what I'm doing actually be wrong? The ninth sura of the Koran says, "Fight them; Allah will punish them by your hands and bring them to disgrace" and "Fight those who do not believe in Allah, nor in the latter day, nor do they prohibit what Allah and his apostle have prohibited, nor follow the religion of truth." We do not have the power to fight them with tanks and planes, so we use what we have. Is that not just?

Again the sound of the ball bearings and the screams of the people drowned out his thoughts. The smell of blood filled his nose. He closed his eyes and saw the bodies of children—innocents. *But are they really innocent? Will they not grow up to be infidels?* Again he saw the tiny faces covered in blood. *Yes, they will probably grow up to be infidels, but for now . . .*

Aamir's grunt at the pull of the tape on the sensitive skin of his recently shaved arm snapped Abdel back to reality. *My course is set. My destiny awaits me. Allah, if what I am doing is right, give us success. If what I am doing is wrong, please forgive me.* Abdel looked into his brother's eyes, and this time he held his gaze.

"JIM!" Scott Ross's voice rang through the cubicles and echoed into the offices on the outer rim of the second-floor CTD headquarters.

"Haven't you ever heard of intercoms?" Jim Hicks grumbled as he came running to the workstation Scott had taken over. He couldn't help taking a glance at the striking Tara Walsh standing right behind Scott.

"I didn't know where you were," Scott absentmindedly apologized.

"Yeah, who would have ever expected me to be in my office?"

"I tried to tell him," Tara said.

"Okay, okay," Scott said. "Just shut up and listen. Tara and my team came through! We've got names, and we've got faces!" Scott stared at Hicks, waiting for a reaction. After ten seconds things got uncomfortable.

"Are you going to tell me or what?" Hicks growled.

For a moment, Scott's mind flashed through many of the "or what" responses that were available to him. He mentally selected one that had to do with Hicks's eternal destiny, very hot places, and French Canadians, allowing it to blend into his internal monologue. A slight grin at the corners of his mouth was the only evidence of what for Scott was a very rapid and very satisfying exercise.

Scott spoke as Tara passed pictures to Hicks. "We've got four names. Each one may or may not be involved. Iskandar Bogra from Pakistan. . . . Here's your boy, Kurshumi. . . . And the last two bring an interesting twist—Aamir and Abdel al-Hasani, Saudi brothers who first popped onto our radar screen at a bad-guy training camp in Pakistan."

"Have we seen anything of these men since the border crossing?"

"You ask the right questions, my friend," Scott said, picking up more photographs from his desk. "Here are two pictures taken within four hours of each other. Do you recognize the guys? Here's Mr. Bogra, and here's brother Aamir. Now for the punch line: these were both taken at the Hawthorne Avenue bus station right here in

Minneapolis. If I'm not mistaken, the Hawthorne station is where you found one of Kurshumi's packages."

Hicks hit the intercom and called the ops teams together for a briefing in five minutes. Looking at Scott and Tara, he said, "Thanks, you two. You may have just saved a lot of lives."

He turned to go back to his office, but Scott grabbed his arm. "Jim, I want in on the op."

Hicks's face took on a condescending air. "I hate to burst your bubble, sport, but this isn't like shooting pellets at the birds in Granddaddy's backyard. Go back to your computer screen and let the big boys handle ops. This is real war with real bullets and real blood."

"I hate to burst *your* bubble, *sport*," Scott spat out as he tightened his grip on Hicks's arm just enough to make him wince. "I spent six years with AFSOC, two of them hunting *hajjis* in Afghanistan. I've drawn blood and I've lost blood, and the only reason I'm still standing here today is that I drew more than I lost. I found these guys, so let me finish the hunt!"

Hicks and Scott locked eyes, both waiting to see if the other would flinch. Finally Hicks shook his arm free and said, "Air force special ops, huh? I thought you guys were just glorified weathermen."

"Why don't you try me and find out."

The older man smiled, then chuckled. "Pretty rough talk for a guy with a pooch," he said, patting Scott's stomach. "Okay, c'mon, tough guy. We'll get you geared up."

Scott smirked to himself as he followed Jim down the hallway. From what he had heard of the man, he might have been the first person to have caused Jim Hicks to back down since before the Nixon administration.

SATURDAY, DECEMBER 20
MALL OF AMERICA
BLOOMINGTON, MINNESOTA
3:20 P.M. CST

The wait since gearing up this morning had been terribly long. But now that they had arrived, Abdel felt a surge of excitement and destiny. A thin layer of ice crackled under the tires as Aamir pulled the rented Dodge Stratus into a space in the south surface parking lot at the Mall of America. Snow was falling, and the wind was blowing. *Allah truly does control the weather,* Abdel thought as he wrapped his dark blue knit scarf around his face.

He undid the snap on the sleeve of his jacket and waited for Aamir to cut the tape. The scissors had been sitting on the dash, and the cold metal touching his skin sent an icy surge of adrenaline through his body. When it was done, he held the small red-button-topped cylinder in his left hand. He then mirrored the process with his brother, cutting the layers of white tape, being very careful not to catch skin.

Only one thing was left to be done. Inside Aamir's shirt, Abdel felt a small metal box attached to the hidden vest. He gently flicked a toggle switch on the box, arming the vest. Aamir did the same to his.

"Remember, we will part ways at the escalators," Aamir reviewed. "You will go to the fourth floor and position yourself by the escalator across from the cinema. I will get in line at the Timberland Twister roller coaster. At exactly 3:30, I will go to be with Allah. Thirty seconds later, one of our brothers will join me from the second floor. Thirty seconds after that, you come to meet me in heaven. Together, we will watch from on high as the last martyr joins us from the entrance to the east parking garage. Abdel, my dear brother, remain strong and show no mercy to those who deserve no mercy. And, whatever you do, when you hear the first blast, don't look down; it will only steal your courage."

Their final hug was extraordinarily long. Neither brother wanted to let go of the other for the last time. Finally, after looking in each other's eyes, they separated. They zipped their jackets, pulled on their gloves, and stepped out into the icy black slush. Together they crunched their way from the car. There was no need to lock the doors.

/////////////////////

Scott Ross's bladder was screaming. He was really beginning to question the wisdom of having taken up a position next to Healthy

Express. In his hand was his third mango smoothie since arriving here just before 10 a.m. That was about five and a half hours ago. He shifted his legs back and forth, trying to ease the pressure. Across the way, he could see Jim Hicks standing in the window of American Eagle Outfitters. He knew that if he asked for a potty break, he could pretty much kiss any respect from Mr. Navy SEAL good-bye.

Although police or CTD agents were covering the many entrances to the mall, Scott had picked the south entrance on a logical hunch. It was one of the four main entrances, which would allow the perps to blend with the heavy foot traffic. He knew they wouldn't be coming in from the east or west parking garages; the protection from the elements that the parking garages provided would go directly against their desire to bundle up as much as possible. The decision for south over north had basically come down to his preference for smoothies from Healthy Express over frozen desserts from Freshens Yogurt. *I guess too much frozen yogurt could have created a whole different set of problems.*

/////////////////////

Sweat poured down Abdel's face and froze on his cheeks as the two brothers approached the entrance. His whole body was on edge. A sudden commotion to his right caught his attention. His thumb shifted to the detonator button. Looking over, he saw an older lady sprawled out on the sidewalk, bags spread all around her. A man was leaning over her, trying to help her back up.

"Easy," Abdel heard his brother say softly to him.

They waited for the doors to clear; then Aamir held the door and the two men entered.

The blast of hot air was almost disorienting when coming in from the frigid outside. The scents of peppermint, cinnamon, and popcorn filled Abdel's senses. He automatically assessed the situation. It wasn't the moving people he was concerned about; it was the stationary ones—people who could be watching for them. But as he scanned the surrounding areas, all he saw were a few teenage girls talking on their cell phones, a scruffy-looking guy in a trench coat hanging out at the juice bar, a family dividing up their cash, and singles and couples passing by, carrying bags of expensive, worthless junk out to their cars. *They're the lucky ones,* Abdel thought. *They made it out alive. But look at the thousands of people who won't be so lucky.*

///////////////////////

All Scott's old AFSOC training was coming back to him: his body control, his mental focus, his ability to rapidly process a potential target to know whether to move in or to stand down. *It's too bad old Pach isn't here for this. He'd be—*

Suddenly his heart froze at the same time his adrenaline spiked. Walking right toward him, unwrapping a blue scarf from his face, was Abdel al-Hasani. The taller man next to him had to be his brother.

He brought his smoothie to his mouth and spoke around his straw into the comm system on his wrist. "Boss, I've got the al-Hasani brothers."

Scott saw Hicks look his way; then he deliberately shifted his eyes to where he could still see the al-Hasani brothers, knowing Hicks would follow his gaze.

A moment later Scott heard Hicks's voice in his earpiece. "Everyone on comm, this is Hicks. Only essential chatter. All teams high alert. We've got a visual on the al-Hasani brothers. Four Team and Six Team, get ready to follow up our takedown. Everyone else, find any others."

Scott locked eyes with Hicks across the corridor and again heard Hicks's voice, this time directed only to him. "Okay, easy does it, Weatherman. If these guys suspect anything, it's all over."

Slowly, the two men slipped out after their prey.

///////////////////////

As the brothers bumped and pushed their way through the crowds, the detonator Abdel carried felt heavier and heavier. The pressure of his grip increased to keep the cylinder from slipping out of his shaky, sweaty hand. He carried it as he'd been taught, with his thumb next to the button but not on it—too big a chance for an accident. This attack was perfectly planned to cause the greatest amount of terror among the shoppers in the mall . . . and the people of America. It wouldn't do for the bombs to go off too early.

What was that? The trench coat man is moving. Abdel's thumb instinctively twitched. *Steady. They can't know we're here. Just keep it together.* The man seemed to be looking straight ahead. *Relax. He doesn't even notice me. Why should he?*

///////////////////////

Jim Hicks walked out the door of American Eagle and slid in purposefully behind the larger of the two brothers. *Come on, Aamir, give me an opening,* he thought. He glanced to his left and saw Scott gradually shifting his course to come up behind Abdel. *Not bad moves for a flyboy.*

As the two men slowly followed the brothers through the bustling crowd, Hicks's mind raced. He had no doubt that the hand buried deep in a pocket of the terrorist's parka held a detonating device. How to separate the device from the hand without the bomb going off was the seemingly impossible question.

Hicks looked ahead and saw an escalator. *Going up will make it even harder for the snipers to get a clear shot. We gotta move fast. Think!*

He shot a glance toward Scott. As he did, he saw Aamir give his brother's arm a squeeze, then break right, skirting the escalator. Hicks followed him, while Scott stayed with the younger man. Quickly glancing at Scott boarding the escalator immediately behind Abdel, he thought, *Why'd I let a rookie in on this? If he takes him down too soon, the commotion will cause this guy to detonate. Patience, Weatherman. Patience.*

///////////////////////

Aamir al-Hasani knew that clutching his brother's arm just before they split up had been against the rules they had established, but he couldn't help it. The pride he had in his brother and in his family was overwhelming. He glanced one last time at his brother going up the escalator, but instead his eyes locked with the man behind Abdel. *Isn't he the man in the trench coat from the juice store?*

Aamir saw something in the man's eyes—recognition. *He knows who we are! The plan's been betrayed!* His thumb moved over the red button. *Allah, this isn't the plan, but I must do it now!*

Throwing open his jacket, he yelled at the top of his lungs, "Allahu ak—"

///////////////////////

Hicks saw Aamir look up at Scott and knew that he had been made. But he also realized that the detonator was now out in the open. He had just seconds to act. "Code red! My guy! Take the shot! Take the shot!"

A CTD sniper who had been following Aamir with his crosshairs and half depressing the trigger of his M24 SWS eased his finger back the rest of the way. The 7.62 mm round exited the barrel of the rifle traveling at 2,800 feet per second and a tiny fraction of a second later exploded the head of Aamir al-Hasani.

///////////////////////

As they reached the top of the escalator, Scott saw what was happening on the ground level, but the noise of the mall had kept Aamir's cry from Abdel's ears. However, the surrounding din would not drown out the screams of the mall patrons when they recognized what had just happened.

Instinctively, Scott acted. He slid his knife out of the sheath in the small of his back, grabbed Abdel's left arm, and drove the ASEK's five-inch blade deep into the man's armpit. That moment of shock was all Scott needed to pull Abdel's hand out of his pocket and sweep his legs out from under him. Then, pulling the blade out, Scott shifted it to his other hand and drove it through the back of Abdel's wrist and into the wood of a bench. The detonator dropped to the ground.

///////////////////////

Hicks dove for Aamir's lifeless left hand and removed the detonator, acting more out of instinct than need. Quickly glancing up the escalator, he saw that Abdel was down, and his left hand was pinned to a wooden bench with a combat knife. Scott was leaning over the younger brother with a handgun pressed to his forehead. "LOCK DOWN! LOCK DOWN!" Hicks commanded into his comm, giving the order for all entrances to be closed. He was grateful to see Six Team converging on Scott's position.

People were screaming and running all around him. Hicks pulled out the neck chain holding his badge just so no one would get the wrong idea about what was happening and try something foolish.

Suddenly, Hicks's insides churned, and the glass all around him shook. An instant later a deafening noise assaulted his ears. Hicks looked up at Scott, but the explosion was too distant to have come from Abdel.

Hicks ran in the direction the shock wave had come from as Scott bounded down the up escalator and jumped over the handrail from eight steps up. Getting through the mass of panicked people was nearly impossible. Parents were searching for their children in the amusement park. Others were running and pushing, trying to get to the parking garages. Here and there were individuals and small groups who, stunned by the mayhem, just sat down, unsure of what to do.

Finally they made it to the other side of the mall. The frigid air hit them in the face even before they cleared the now glassless doors of the north entrance. Spotting smoke fifty yards into the parking lot, they pushed through the screaming crowd of people and continued their sprint.

The nearer they came to the blast site, the greater the damage they saw. Car windows were shattered all around them. Some higher-profile vehicles had large round holes punched into the sheet metal. When they arrived at ground zero, Hicks held up his CTD badge.

As he surveyed the site, his mind flashed back to the carnage he had seen in Desert Storm. Surrounding them were blasted-out cars—most smoking, a few still burning as agents tried to put out the flames with fire extinguishers that had been pulled from the entrance to the mall. Flashing blue and red lights in the distance briefly caught Hicks's eye as emergency vehicles approached. To his right, agents and officers had congregated in two huddles, looking at something on the ground. Blood reddened the snow as it flowed beyond the circles of men.

Hicks grabbed the nearest CTD agent, showed his badge, and leaned in close. "What's going on?" he yelled over the deafening sound of hundreds of car alarms.

"When lockdown was called, about fifteen cops came bursting out the doors, surprising the bejeebers out of some guy who was about to enter. The perp took off running, so two of the officers went after him. He gets out here, holds up his hand, and then vaporizes. Unfortunately, he took the two cops with him."

"Kurshumi, number one," Hicks muttered. "Aamir and Abdel, two and three. This must have been Bogra, which would make him the fourth and, hopefully, last." Turning to Scott, he said, "Do me a favor and get back to Abdel. I want you to oversee the bomb squad getting that vest off of him. And then get him hauled back to CTD for interrogation ASAP."

"You got it." Scott ran back the way he had come.

Hicks stared at the smoke swirling in the cold Minnesota wind. *These guys were just pawns, but they had to have known the chess master. Or at least they've heard of him.* The seeping blood of the slain officers had reached his feet, and he instinctively stepped back. *This can't happen again. This cannot happen again! Not here. Not in America. Abdel knows something and he's going to talk! No matter what I have to do, he will talk!*

Hicks turned and slowly made his way back inside. Although he had helped save thousands of lives, the two dead cops weighed on him. He sensed the direction that the Abdel interview would take. While he walked, he mentally began distancing himself from what he was about to do. However, the weight of the knife belted on his leg was a persistent reminder of the heaviness of the guilt that was strapped to his conscience.

"Where's my chicken? I want my chicken!" Chris Gorkowski, in his usual understated way, was wandering the aisles of the chartered Boeing 767 in search of a bucket of Popeye's. The rookies were expected to bring fried chicken, biscuits, and mashed potatoes and gravy for the veteran players in order to help offset the typical airline food. For the rookie who overlooked his poultry obligations, there was usually awaiting him when he arrived back home a little ritual in which the player was dog-piled by the rest of the team, duct-taped so he couldn't move, and then dumped into the ice tub.

Gorkowski's bulk brushed past Riley Covington, who had settled himself into seats 35H and J for the two-hour flight to San Francisco. Coach Burton had such an intense hatred for the city of Oakland that he refused to stay in a hotel on that side of the bay. So tonight would be spent in downtown San Francisco, and tomorrow morning they would bus across the Bay Bridge to Golden West Stadium.

Riley checked his watch—1:35 p.m. The plane was set to depart in twenty-five minutes.

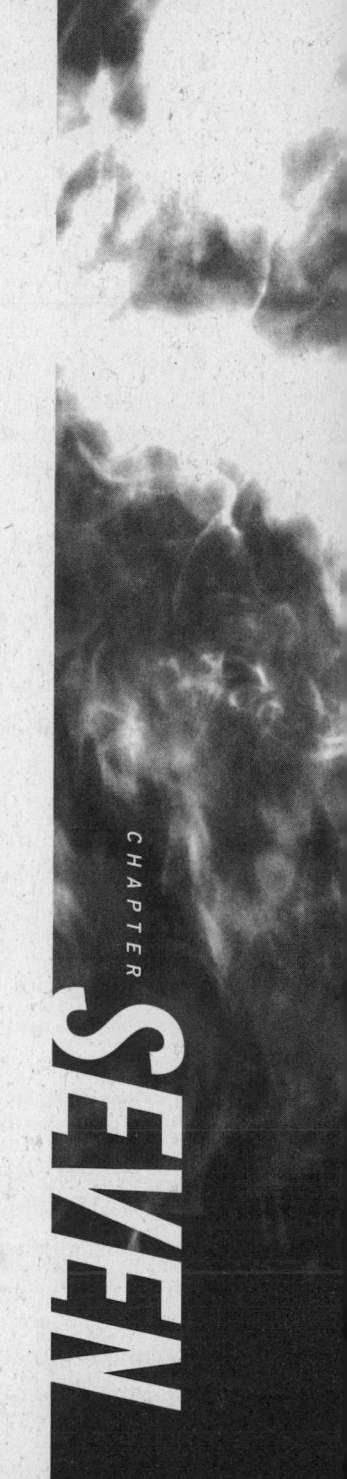

CHAPTER

SEVEN

Slipping earbuds into his ears, Riley toggled his iPod to *A Decade of Steely Dan*, closed his eyes, and absorbed the smooth tones of "Deacon Blues." The players each got two seats to stretch out their large frames, while the coaching staff enjoyed the luxury of first class. The plane was fairly empty now, but it would fill up quickly as the three remaining buses emptied of players, coaches, support staff, media, and the owner's guests. Eventually the plane would take off with more than 150 passengers on board, along with thousands of pounds of game-day gear, medical supplies, and video equipment.

Saturdays were meant to be relaxing days. Everyone involved in special teams gathered at Inverness Training Center at 8:30 a.m. for a review. The rest of the players made their way in by nine for thirty minutes with the position coaches to finalize the game plan and answer any questions.

After these short get-togethers, most of the players went home and packed before returning to Inverness. Some of the players who didn't have family to go back to hung around in the players' lounge playing pinball or Xbox or poker. The buses left promptly at 12:30 p.m. Anyone not there on time was fined five thousand dollars plus the cost of a first-class ticket to wherever the team was playing that week.

At Denver International Airport, the team buses pulled up planeside. Security was cleared with surprising efficiency: tables were set up next to the plane, and ten TSA personnel screened the bags while another ten screened the passengers with the light saber–esque magnetometers. There were no checked bags for the players.

"Hey Nineteen" had just begun gliding into Riley's ears when a voice roused him from his half doze. "Riley Covington to the cockpit, please. The captain would like to speak to you."

Riley grinned. He had a good idea why the captain wanted to see him.

He dropped his iPod into his shirt pocket and began working his way against the human traffic to the front. About halfway up the aisle, he had to squeeze in over Sal Ricci to let some people by. Ricci cursed at him, something Riley had rarely heard him do.

"Sal, you kiss your daughter with that mouth?" Riley asked. Looking down at his friend, Riley saw that he was pale and sweat was on his forehead. "You okay, man? You look stressed."

"I'm sorry, Pach. You know how I hate flying."

"You want me to send Bones back here to give you something to take the edge off?" *Bones* was Ted Bonham, the head of the medical team.

"No, I'm all right. I just need to relax a bit."

Riley pulled his iPod out and dropped it on Ricci's lap. "Put it on Yo-Yo Ma's *Bach: The Six Unaccompanied Cello Suites*, then sit back and close your eyes. If that doesn't take you to your happy place, then you can't get there from here."

Ricci managed a weak smile. "Thanks, Pach. I'll give it a try."

Riley saw a brief opening in the traffic and bolted down the aisle. About ten rows up, he glanced back at Ricci, who was still sitting there ignoring the iPod. *Someday I'll take him up in a Cessna and help him get over his fear. Not too many people are still scared of flying after they hold the yoke of a plane in their hands.*

Finally arriving at the front of the plane, he poked his head into the cockpit. The captain slid his seat back and extended his hand. "Mr. Covington, I'm Mike Flores—Air Force Academy, class of '76. It's a real pleasure to meet you. I've been a fan for a long time."

"Call me Riley. How long did you serve?"

"I put in twenty years, then began flying commercial."

"Well then, it's truly an honor to meet you." He shot a quick glance at the first officer, who was awkwardly trying to stand from his seat.

"Steve Davis. Nice to meet you, Riley."

"Likewise," Riley said as he shook his hand. Then turning back to Captain Flores, he asked, "So, what's up?"

"We were wondering if you'd like to sit in the jump seat for the flight. You're more than welcome."

This was what Riley had been hoping for. Any day he could fly in the cockpit of a big jet like this was a great day for him. "Sure, I'd love it. I do have to take a short position test for Coach Texeira, but I'm sure I can take it up here."

Captian Flores gave him a quizzical look.

"The position test is nothing major, just going over a few Xs and Os. I'd be done in no time."

"Excellent," the captain said. "We have a few things to do, and then we'll be on our way. I know your special ops training required you to pick up your FAA air traffic controller's license. So, if you'd like, you're welcome to handle the communications on the flight."

"You sure about that?" Riley was almost giddy at the prospect.

"Absolutely," the first officer threw in, knowing his workload had been dramatically reduced. Federal aviation regulations were much more lenient with charters. The whole atmosphere of a chartered flight was quite a bit more relaxed. In fact, during takeoff, it was not unusual to have players standing in the aisles or even talking on their cell phones.

The captain handed Riley the mic and said, "From now on, we're United 1918."

"Got it." Riley stretched up to click the cabin communication button. "Ladies, gentlemen, and Mr. Gorkowski, this is Captain Covington. Welcome aboard flight 1918, with nonstop service to San Francisco. At this time, I would like to ask everyone to take their seats and ensure their tray tables and seat backs are in their full upright and locked positions." By this time, some of the good-natured hoots and jeers of the players began reaching the cockpit. "Today we are expecting moderate to severe turbulence on takeoff. Gorkowski, this means Mr. Plane go bump-bump." Riley heard Gorkowski make a reply, but thankfully he couldn't make out the words. "I'll try to keep her steady, but I'm not promising anything. Last time I flew one of these, I had to put her down on a highway outside of Kabul."

Flores and Davis laughed when Riley winked at them. They had stopped their preflight checklist to listen to this little speech. Riley knew the media people in the back of the plane would be scrambling for their notepads to record what was going on up front.

"I'll be back with you shortly," Riley continued, "but for now please give your undivided attention to your flight attendants for our safety demonstration." Then, "accidentally" leaving the mic keyed, he said, "Hey, Captain, now that the announcement is over with, can you remind me which of these pedals down here is the gas and which one's the clutch?" This remark caused at least three players to spit out their drinks, which led to a series of colorful comments from the recipients of the spray.

Captain Flores and First Officer Davis were having a hard time completing their work through the tears in their eyes. "Tell you what," Riley said to them. "I'm going to take my position test out in the cabin while you guys finish up your work."

"That's probably a good idea," Flores agreed, wiping his eyes.

"I certainly don't want to overstep my bounds, but there are a few guys I'd love to mess with back there once we get in the air."

"As long as we aren't breaking any FAA regs, I'd love to hear what you have planned next."

/////////////////////////

Riley made his way back to the coaches and found Rex Texeira. "Hey, Tex-Rex, mind if I knock out that position test?"

Texeira handed over the test without even looking up. Both men knew the test was merely a formality. What made Riley such a great player was that he was not only physically blessed with strength and speed but was also one of the smartest players in the league. He had tremendous instincts, always knew his assignment—often better than the coaches—and never had wasted steps. He usually recognized where the play was going before the snap and routinely disrupted it immediately.

Riley began the examination as the plane took off and quickly breezed through the test; he drew lines to where he was responsible for filling various gaps, he identified the men he was to pick up on pass routes, and he showed the proper zone drops he had to cover. The plane was climbing past fourteen thousand feet when he finished. He walked back to the cockpit, taking a quick detour to look out the galley window and admire the snow-covered Rocky Mountains.

Riley entered the cockpit and leaned between the pilots. "How's everything looking, fellas?"

"Good call on the turbulence," Davis, the copilot, said. "The PIREPs are showing moderate to severe instability all the way to flight level 400."

"All the way to forty thousand feet? Perfect! I think it's about time I address the passengers again," Riley announced with a mischievous smirk.

"Go for it," Davis laughed as he handed Riley the mic.

Riley sat back in the jump seat and crossed his leg over his knee. "Ladies, gentlemen, and Mr. Gorkowski, this is Captain Covington from the flight deck. As you can tell, we are encountering significant chop, and from what the planes ahead of us are saying, it's not going to stop. Give an extra tug on those seat belts—or for you offensive linemen, those seatbelt extensions—and remember the airsick bags are in the seat pockets in front of you. I'll be right back." Again keeping the mic keyed, he asked, "Hey, cool radio, Captain. Does it get FM?"

Riley released the button on the mic and looked to Captain Flores. "Would it be okay to push the Warning button the next time I'm talking to the guys?"

"Well, it's not exactly authorized procedure, but . . . go ahead. I'm enjoying this."

A voice came over the radio. "United 1918, climb—maintain flight level 340."

Riley immediately keyed the mic. "Up to three-four-zero, United 1918." As he released the mic, the plane made another shift right and dropped about a hundred feet, causing Gatorades throughout the plane to fall into laps and aisles. An angry protest came from some now-queasy players.

Switching back to cabin communications, the fake captain said, "Sorry, folks, sometimes I don't know my rudder from my aileron. There're just so many buttons up here." Turning slightly from the mic, he continued, "Hey, Captain, do you have the owner's manual up here? I can't for the life of me remember what this little doo-hickey here does." Just then, the plane hit more turbulence and took another sharp jolt. About this time, some guys were probably beginning to wonder if Riley was still playing or if they had a real situation on their hands.

Coach Burton screamed from his seat in 1A, "Knock it off, Covington!"

But Riley was on a roll. "Hey, Captain, when the elevation thingy says twelve thousand feet, is that from sea level or from the top of the mountains?" As he said that, he reached up and hit a button while keeping the mic on. A computerized voice came over the intercom: "WARNING; WARNING; TERRAIN; PULL UP. . . . WARNING; WARNING; TERRAIN; PULL UP!"

A collective gasp and a few screams could be heard throughout the cabin. With almost perfect timing, the plane hit another air pocket. It rolled a bit left and dropped. After a long, uncomfortable pause, Riley keyed the mic again. "This is Captain Covington. We are now leveling off at thirty-four thousand feet, and I am passing the controls back to Captain Flores. Please enjoy the remainder of your flight."

///////////////////////

As the plane began its descent, the aircraft's FMS computer system printed out a message to the pilots. Captain Flores ripped the small white paper from the printer, scanned the message, and then read it again more slowly. "Take a look at this, Steve."

Davis skimmed it and looked at Flores, speechless. He then handed the paper back to Riley, who read the message:

> *U.S. hit by terrorists at Mall of America*
> *Casualties unknown at this time*
> *All flights proceed as scheduled*

Riley leaned back in the jump seat and stared at the words, hardly able to comprehend them. Another terrorist attack on U.S. soil. He knew from his air force intelligence briefings that another attack had been inevitable. But now that it had actually happened, reality just wouldn't sink in.

"We'd better check with OPs to see how this is going to play out," Flores told Davis.

Riley stood up, still clutching the paper. "Gentlemen, I know things may get busy up here, so I'm gonna head back to my seat. Thanks for letting me hang out with you."

They both wished him well. As Riley exited the cockpit, Davis was already pecking away on the flight computer.

Riley walked back to his seat, getting a fairly even mixture of high fives and glares for his little prank. As he passed Gorkowski's seat, he saw that the veteran had an enormous gravy stain down the front of his tailored yellow shirt and his Emilio Pucci silk tie. "A little baking soda might get that out," Riley suggested with a smile.

"You're a dead man, Covington," the fuming offensive lineman replied.

Riley found his row and fell back into his seat. A few guys came up to him wanting to relive his little joke, but Riley was not in the mood anymore. The military man in him overshadowed the football player. It was times like these that he wondered if he had made the right choice giving up the air force for the PFL.

The Mustangs charter landed without incident at 3:16 p.m. PST in San Francisco. The plane taxied to the four luxury buses and stopped. The players, coaching staff, and guests transferred from their air transportation to their land transportation and were off.

On bus one, Riley was surprised no one had mentioned the attack yet. Several guys had their BlackBerries out and were checking the college football scores. Finally Robert Taylor, the PR man, shouted, "Unbelievable! The Mall of America was bombed!"

A few of the guys at the front of the bus spun around in their seats.

Taylor read the headline from his BlackBerry: "'Suspected Terrorists Attack Crowded Mall of America.' It doesn't seem like they have a lot of information yet."

Sal Ricci made his way to Taylor's row and said, "That's Minneapolis, isn't it? My wife has some old friends there. Can you check a different Web site?"

"That's all I'm seeing on these sites. We'll be at the Hyatt in a few minutes; you can check the news there. In the meantime, let me call some of my network sources." Taylor immediately started dialing numbers, while Ricci stood in the aisle leaning over his shoulder.

Ten minutes later, the buses angled into the roundabout of the hotel behind the blinking lights and sirens of the California Highway Patrol escort. Two hundred or so fans were already yelling and jockeying for position behind the roped-off barricade near the doors.

As the players bounded down the bus stairs one by one, the fans screamed even louder. The PR department surrounded Riley and

Coach Burton and shielded them through the doors of the hotel. As they entered, Riley spotted a guy saying, "Oh, come on, Covington. I came all the way from El Paso. Will you . . . ?"

Riley thought, *Nice try, bud, but I can spot a seller from a mile away*. At first, Riley had found it tough to tell the true fans from the memorabilia peddlers. After a while they become easier to spot with their five footballs to sign or their stack of glossies and ready black Sharpie.

As Riley cruised through the lobby, Taylor caught up with him to let him know PFL Network and NBC wanted interviews. "Robert, give me some time. I want to go see what happened in Minneapolis and then relax for a while. Come get me at six."

Riley turned, grabbed an envelope, and looked inside for his key. The fans' well-wishing screams turned to creative curses as he rounded the corner and quickly headed for the elevator. Riley knew that many in the disgruntled crowd would stay several more hours before they dispersed, hoping they might still get a glimpse of one of their favorite players.

///////////////////////

The players relaxed in their rooms until about 6:00, when they made their way down to the ballroom level and jumped into a private buffet line.

The talk in line and at the tables was split between the attack on the Mall of America and the day's college football scores. Rather than showing news updates from Minnesota, the large TV in the room was tuned to ESPN, which was airing the end of the University of Hawaii's surprise upset over Notre Dame.

While Riley ate, he fielded questions from Garrett Widnall and Travis Marshall, who both wanted a military perspective on what had happened at the mall and what America's response should be.

After an excellent meal of filet mignon, fried chicken, various pastas, and a massive salad bar, the players began filtering out to their position meetings. The coaching staff used these smaller group times to make sure every man knew his assignment.

A special teams meeting followed. Special teams was the black sheep of the team. It was an unspoken but well-known fact that the special teams players' primary responsibility was simply to not mess anything up.

Immediately after the special teams meeting, the offense and defense gathered separately to finalize the game plan. Finally, the entire team met for Coach Burton's pep talk. Then it was off to their respective rooms—no shared rooms for the Colorado Mustangs—until pregame curfew at 11:15 p.m. There wasn't a lot of fooling around or banter by this time. The pressure had already begun to mount in anticipation of a very important game against a bitter division rival.

Jim Hicks entered Interrogation Room 3 and saw
Abdel al-Hasani sitting at a stainless steel table
on a stainless steel chair. The man was shirtless,
his left side heavily bandaged. His left hand was
covered in surgical tape. A handcuff just above
the bandages was connected to a medium-gauge
chain that slipped down through a hole drilled
into the surface of the table and came back up
through an identical hole eighteen inches to the
right of the first, connecting to a cuff on his right
wrist. The only piece of furniture that was not
bolted to the floor was a second chair, which
Hicks now sat in.

Hicks placed his knife on the table just out of
Abdel's reach and said, "Your brother was a foolish man."

Abdel's eyes slowly lifted to Hicks's, then
slipped back down.

The look was not what Hicks had expected.
He prided himself on being able to read the eyes
of those he questioned, and Abdel's stare was
filled with hopelessness mixed with a cry for help.

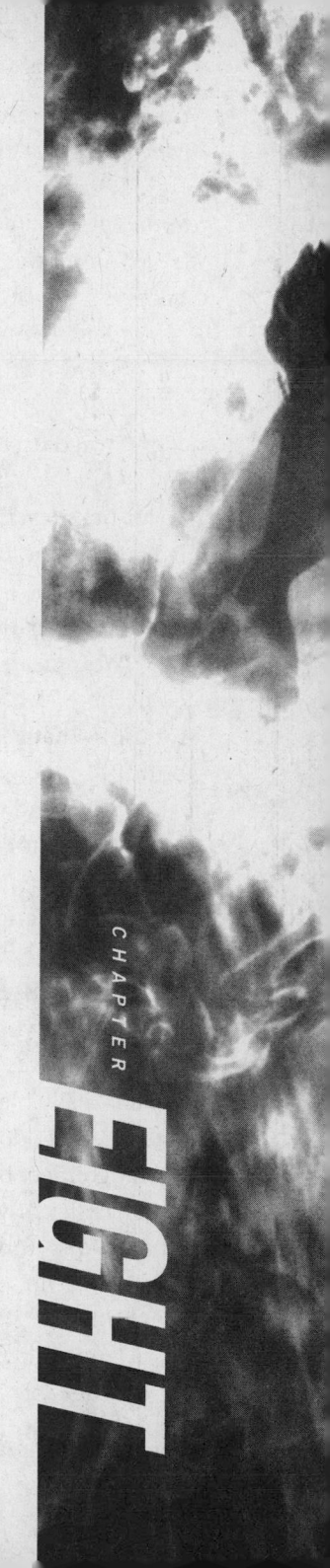

C H A P T E R

EIGHT

Go slow with this one, he thought. *He's dying to talk but needs to be convinced it's okay.*

"I have to admit," Hicks continued, "I admired Aamir's strength and courage. But I don't understand his actions."

"Aamir was a true believer in the Cause," Abdel said, not lifting his eyes from the table.

"And you, Abdel? Are you a true believer in the Cause?"

"I am a true believer in Allah. I am a true believer in the Prophet."

"You didn't answer my question."

Abdel remained silent, his eyes burning a hole in the table.

Hicks reached for the knife, slid it into its sheath, and placed it back on the table. "Your English is very good. Where did you learn it?"

"It was part of my preparation."

"You mean you learned an entire language just so you could come here and blow yourself up? Very impressive, but also very foolish. What a shame to waste a mind like yours on one push of a button."

"My mind was created by Allah and for Allah," Abdel said quietly. "I use it for what he requires of me."

"And this attack—this attempt to rip apart the bodies of innocent women and children—is this what Allah requires of you? Or did someone else ask you to do this?"

Again the eyes, again the look, again the withdrawal.

"Abdel, you are an intelligent man, much smarter than your brother. He was convinced of the lies. He became confused about what is really black and what is really white. But you . . . you always had a seed of doubt, didn't you? You always knew that something didn't connect between your loving Allah and the murder of innocents." Hicks's voice continued to rise as he spoke. "Who did it, Abdel? Who took the Allah of your youth and turned him into a butcher? Who took the beauty of your childhood faith and smeared it with blood? Who convinced you to commit this atrocity? Give me a name, Abdel! I need a name!" Hicks was standing now, leaning across the table.

Abdel sat silently. Thirty seconds passed. One minute passed.

Hicks remained hovering over the man, his hands planted firmly on the table, not a muscle on his body moving. One minute thirty. Two minutes.

Suddenly, Abdel's whole body heaved a massive sigh, as if he was releasing years of doubt and sorrow. Without looking up, in a voice barely audible, Abdel al-Hasani uttered one word: "Hakeem."

SATURDAY, DECEMBER 20
UNITED STATES

The man unconsciously rubbed the brass medallion between his thumb and index finger. Sometimes he flipped the disk and caught it; sometimes he spun it on a table. But mostly he just rubbed it. It was like a reminder deep down in his pocket, an aid to help him think.

The medallion was a disk about the size of a half dollar. Around the rim of its front was etched the same word in seven different languages: onore, honneur, честь, honor, الشرف, Ehre, τιμή. In the middle of the medallion were engraved three daggers, handles set equidistant, their tips touching in the center. The daggers were barely visible after so many years of rubbing. The reverse side was blank.

The brass disk had not always been a medallion. Before being melted down and re-created, it had been a 7.62 mm cartridge allegedly removed from an unexpended AK-47 clip that had been fired by Saddam Hussein—a gift for a small boy from his uncle.

Hakeem Qasim sat brooding at the desk in the dark hotel room. Even after all these years, he could still detect the slight odor of the brass as he rubbed it. The only light in his room came from CNN, long since muted. The government was remaining tight-lipped about the attack on the Mall of America, so the news channels had exhausted their facts on the failed terrorist attempt hours ago. Until new information broke, they were just filling time with stories like the girl with the big hat who worked in the third-floor Hot Dog on a Stick who had confessed to staring in shock as the liquid rolled back and forth in the slushie machines immediately after the explosion.

This was to be the beginning of my revenge, Hakeem thought.

Much had occurred in Hakeem's life since the murder of his

family. Two days after the surgical strike on Uncle Ali, he had gone to live with his mother's brother, Ibrahim, in Ramadi. He had taken nothing with him; all his possessions had been destroyed in the explosion except the clothes he wore and the bullet on its chain around his neck.

Hakeem had met Uncle Ibrahim only once before. Ibrahim was known to have connections to the Cause—an Iraq-based international terrorist organization focused on dealing justice to imperial America and Western Europe. Because of that, Hakeem's mother had insisted that her family keep their distance. But now, in this orphaned boy, Ibrahim had seen an opportunity to create a weapon potentially more powerful than anything the Cause had stashed in its secret arsenals in the southern al-Hajarah desert. He saw a chance to create a mole.

So before Hakeem's physical and emotional wounds had had a chance to heal, Uncle Ibrahim introduced him to a man simply known as al-'Aqran—the Scorpion. Each day this mysterious man spoke to Hakeem about revenge and about the importance of family honor. He talked about the boy's place in the Cause. He sermonized about the evils of America, the virtue of patience, and the glory of a martyr's death.

"Your day will come, Hakeem," al-'Aqran had told him, "the day that you bring honor back to the name of your father. Satan's great puppet, Bush of America, took your family, your future, and your honor. He wanted your uncle Ali, but did he care whom else he slaughtered? Did he care about your life or the lives of your mother and father? No, they were nothing—throwaway lives, dung.

"But while you wait for your revenge, you have a challenging task ahead of you, young warrior. You must become one of them. You must live like them, talk like them, drink like them, fornicate like them. . . . Ah, I see by your face that you worry. Don't, for Allah knows your motives. He knows your heart. You must take a career and excel. You must take a wife and have children. You must appear exactly as one of them.

"However, you will be living with a secret—a purpose no one will know about. People will look at you and see one of them, but you will not be one of them. You will live in the decadence of the imperialist society, and when the time is right, you will help destroy that society. Those who have humbled you and your name will themselves be humbled by your hand, young Hakeem, by your hand. The honor of your family depends upon you."

When he wasn't being indoctrinated into al-'Aqran's hatred of the West, Hakeem was learning languages, cultures, and the intricacies of bomb making. This intense education continued for two years.

One day the Scorpion came to the boy and abruptly removed the AK-47 cartridge from around Hakeem's neck. Three days later, he presented the medallion to the boy. "For your life ahead, you cannot carry with you something as conspicuous as the gift your uncle Ali gave to you. So I have recast it in a form that can stay with you forever and always remind you of who you truly are."

The next morning, they had left Ramadi. After a journey of many weeks, twelve-year-old Hakeem found himself alone, abandoned at the gate of a monastery.

For the next fourteen years, Hakeem had lived as another person. The only links he kept to his former life were his medallion and his deep-seated hatred. Al-'Aqran had told him that someday he would be contacted, and then his revenge could begin. The contact had come ten months ago. Since that time Hakeem had lived a double life, doing his job while he prepared to destroy his society, loving his family even as he prepared to abandon them.

In less than ten days, the double life would end. He would once again be fully Hakeem, son of Mustapha Qasim, nephew of Ali Qasim, soldier of the Cause, hand of vengeance! He would bring America to her knees and restore honor to the family of Qasim.

But the first step in that restoration had not gone as planned.

He picked up the remote control and flipped through the cable news stations. Each channel seemed to rub his failure in his face, doing nothing to help his dark mood. He flung the remote across the room, where it shattered against the wall.

How could they have disgraced me and the Cause like this? The plan I created was so detailed! I'd worked on it for years, hoping for the opportunity to unleash it! The training of these fools was supposed to have been perfect. My contacts promised me. This was to be the beginning of a new era of terror in America! This was to be the beginning of my revenge! Instead, it's another misstep—another black eye to the Cause.

He held the brass disk in front of his eyes. It glowed blue from the television. He could faintly see the well-worn daggers—one for Father, one for Mother, one for Uncle Ali.

Uncle, I once promised you that when I was called upon, I would fight the Great Satan. I have waited many years to avenge my family. I have been very patient for my retribution in your name. Forgive me, Uncle, for my failure in this first attack. I promise you that in nine days, I will restore honor to the Qasim name!

Riley awoke from his dream with a start. *That's one thing about war,* he thought. *You can get it out of your days, but you can never get it out of your nights.* He shook his head, trying to get the images out of his mind, as if his brain were an overgrown Etch A Sketch. He glanced over at the clock—6:52 a.m.

Through his open curtains he could see that dawn had just begun to break. Not that the sun stood much of a chance in this weather. San Francisco was a beautiful city most of the year, but these overcast, drizzly December days were enough to put chills in any man's bones.

Riley put on his hotel robe and walked to the window. Through the gray he could make out the Golden Gate Bridge, and closer to him was the island prison of Alcatraz. This was the same view he'd had the last two times he was here. He had always wanted to drive the bridge and tour the prison, but the only times he'd been in the city had been for football—not a lot of free time to sightsee. *Some summer I'll come back, rent a convertible, and cruise the California coast from Napa all the*

CHAPTER

NINE

way to San Diego. Maybe it'll be for my honeymoon, he mused. *Although, I guess finding a girlfriend first would help.*

The "whole marriage thing" was a common discussion/sore spot between Riley's mother and himself. The conversation always seemed to boil down to his mom not understanding how someone who was as great a catch as her son could still be single.

"When are you going to settle down and start a family? Your father and I want to be able to hold our grandkids on our laps without fear of breaking a hip! And don't tell me you can't find anyone. The girls have got to be falling all over you," his mother would say.

"Yeah, but not the kind of girls I'm looking for," would be his reply.

His fame, his odd schedule of PFL and off-season air force reserves, and his general ineptitude with women all combined to make his chances of ever having a meaningful relationship with a young lady about equivalent to the Detroit Wildcats' chances of ever having a meaningful relationship with the PFL Cup.

The cold dampness seemed to seep through the window, causing him to involuntarily shiver. Grabbing the remote control, he turned on Fox News to see if there were any further developments from the Mall of America attack.

As he sat on the edge of the bed, the 7 a.m. wake-up call came. He automatically picked up the receiver of the phone and dropped it back down, never taking his eyes off the screen. The graphic for FOX NEWS ALERT rolled onto the screen along with its accompanying sound effect. The talking head gave a quick intro and then threw it to Greg Peterson live on-site in Bloomington, Minnesota.

> *"The mood in the Twin Cities is somber today as people come to grips with the realization that suicide bombing has come to America. The FBI, Homeland Security, and local police are all declining to comment when it comes to details of the attack on the Mall of America. Through witnesses, we have learned that there were three attackers. One was subdued by law enforcement officials inside the mall; another was killed, also in the mall; and the third detonated his device in the north parking lot, which you can see behind me now. The police are keeping a*

wide perimeter, but we are told that at least fifty cars sustained damage from projectiles, and countless others lost windows and windshields during the blast.

"The two officers killed during the attack—twelve-year veteran Jonathan Weems and rookie Wesley Katagi—were both members of the Bloomington Police Department. Although the mall is closed today, people have been flocking to a make-shift memorial for the two slain officers just outside the mall property at 24th Avenue South and Lindau Lane. There they have been leaving flowers, cards, and other tokens of love and appreciation for the sacrifice these brave men made. Also, early word is out that a fund is being established for people to help the two widows and five children that are left behind. Back to you, Karen."

Riley turned the TV off and hopped into the shower. *I wonder if Pastor Tim is rethinking his pity for these terrorists.*

At 7:25, he finished packing his bag and headed downstairs to the team meeting rooms for the chapel service. The chapel service was an important part of game day for quite a few players—though not always for the same reasons. Some attended chapel as part of their pregame superstition, and others came because they figured it was a good way to get God on their side for the day. But most came because worship was an important part of their faith, and chapel was the closest thing to church they could get on a game-day Sunday.

As Riley entered the hotel conference room, there were about fifteen other players scattered around in comfortable black swivel chairs. The mood was very somber; a few players conversed in low whispers, but otherwise the room was silent. This was not out of reverence, Riley knew, but out of nervousness for the day's game. Everyone was already on edge. Riley nodded to a few players, shook hands with Walter Washburne, the Mustangs' team chaplain, and took a seat next to Travis Marshall.

Washburne began the service with a recap of the mall attack. He spoke of the two officers who had been killed—men who had sacrificed themselves for others, who had died for something they believed in.

Then he began talking about the terrorists—also men willing to die for something they believed in.

Heads came up at this point. *Where's he going with this?* Riley wondered.

Washburne continued, "The sad thing is that these men were willing to die for a lie. They believed the Koran tells them to kill those who don't agree with them. Maybe it does and maybe it doesn't—I'm not an expert in the Koran or in Islam. However, I know I've heard plenty of Muslims say that their beliefs don't include this kind of evil. Whether it does or not, these men believed it did, and they put their lives on the line for their beliefs.

"In Philippians 1:21, Paul the apostle writes, 'For to me, to live is Christ and to die is gain.' Like these brave police officers and like these deluded murderers, Paul realized something. His life wasn't about himself. This is one of the toughest things for anyone to learn, especially a professional athlete who constantly has praise heaped upon him. People around you are always saying, 'It's all about you! It's all about you!' A football player who is able to pick up a team photo and not look for himself first is a rarity. For any of you to be able to take your eyes off yourselves and put them on someone else is nothing short of a miracle.

"But some of you have had that miracle happen in your lives. Some of you have realized that this life is not about you but about Christ. You are living for others. That's where the difference is between those brave policemen and those cowardly terrorists: the terrorists were only willing to die for their beliefs; the policemen lived out their beliefs every day until their lives were taken from them.

"Paul knew that dying was the easy part—it meant heaven for him. Living for Christ is the hard part—daily putting yourself second and others first. Let me encourage you, men, to keep your lives in perspective. It's not about you. It's about what you can do for God and for those He puts in your path."

Washburne finished with a prayer for the families of the slain policemen. The men slowly grabbed their bags and filtered out of the room. Riley and Travis waited behind for the chaplain, who followed after gathering up his things.

"Good words today, Chap," Marshall said as they made their way down to the team meal.

"Thanks, Travis. You think anyone really heard what I said today?" Washburne was a realist, and he knew that game day was not necessarily the best time to try to effect major life change.

"Well, you were given the opportunity to preach it, and you took it. The rest is up to God," Riley offered.

They walked into the large ballroom and right up to the buffet. There was a huge assortment of breakfast foods and high-carb pastas, along with a large tray of steaks. At the end of the buffet was an omelet bar, where Marshall headed after picking up a couple of different kinds of sausages. Many players were too nervous to eat much before a game, so they just grabbed a piece of toast and some orange juice. Riley made himself a peanut butter and jelly sandwich, then sat down at a table and quietly ate his spartan breakfast.

After the meal, Riley, Ricci, Marshall, and Garrett Widnall headed toward the buses for the forty-five–minute trip across the bay into Oakland. The men quickly slipped out through the lobby door and up the stairs of the bus as frenzied fans reached out, trying to touch the players. Most of the guys already had their iPods playing and seemed to be gazing into a far-off land. Ricci slipped into the seat next to Riley. No one said a word.

The players prepared for games in various ways, but there was one general unspoken rule: no one talked on the buses. This allowed each man to prepare mentally for the game. For most, it had been this way ever since high school, and with each new level of play, the rule never changed.

At some unspoken signal, four motorcycle cops eased out of the hotel driveway with sirens and lights blazing, and the first two buses began following them. The other two buses would follow shortly after with the rest of the team, the coaches, and the staff.

Riley tried to keep his mind on the game, but his thoughts kept wandering back to chapel. *I don't understand what the terrorists are thinking. I never have. I have to admit that they certainly are committed . . . or desperate. Or maybe, like Walter said, they've simply found a higher—though completely delusional—calling.*

Riley was pulled out of his thoughts by a car driving next to the bus. The vehicle was filled with people dressed in black, and every person in the car had both their middle fingers extended up toward Riley—every person except for the driver, who wisely kept one hand on the steering wheel. One of the motorcycle cops saw this and quickly took action, moving the car away from the bus. *These Bay Area fans are nothing but class.* Riley laughed softly to himself.

The closer they got to Golden West Stadium in Oakland, the worse the atmosphere became. It seemed as if they were driving into a sea of black and silver. All around them were people with their faces painted and wearing all sorts of pirate garb, spiked accessories, and skeleton masks. Everyone they passed seemed to want to use their fingers to emphatically assure the players on the buses that they thought they were number one. Even the parking-lot security guards cussed at them and flipped them off.

Some of the players in the back of the bus began to laugh. "Hey, check out old granny over there. I'm not sure what that gesture means, but whatever it is certainly seems like it could lead to infertility," Keith Simmons hollered, as he egged her on by beating the bus window. He was clearly breaking the code of silence, but no one minded since he was saying exactly what everyone else was thinking.

The bus negotiated the crowded parking lot and turned down a long ramp that led into the bowels of the stadium. Security guards swarmed the bus, and a German shepherd began sniffing the off-loaded bags. The players quickly grabbed their belongings and followed the team equipment managers to the visitors' locker room.

As the guys found their lockers, they began their various routines. Some immediately got their ankles taped. Some were worked on by the team massage therapist. Some grabbed hot packs and began loosening tight muscles. Some walked directly onto the playing field to see how the footing would be. Some simply sat in front of their lockers staring at the floor.

As time went on, the tension only increased. Many of the players watched the early game between Boston and Florida on the monitors mounted high in the corners of the locker room. A few players wandered from the training room to the equipment room to the locker room in an endless circuit. Others rode stationary bikes, then sprawled out on the floor and began stretching. A player's pregame routine was like his fingerprints; you never found another one exactly like it.

Usually, once the players were dressed, they would walk onto the field for a light jog. Often they would throw the ball around and get a general feel for what the conditions were like.

After Riley got his ankles taped and slipped on his football pants, he walked down the tunnel and out onto the field. As he exited the tunnel, he could smell the barbecue from the concessions. *That smell always reminds me of summer.* His thoughts were interrupted by Bandits supporters who had gathered next to the tunnel. Expletives flew from the fans, less than five feet away. Riley walked past them with a smirk and a small wave, never lifting his eyes from the ground.

He walked to the south side of the field, where there were some more very vocal fans—one group right behind the uprights and another group about thirty rows up. This higher group was focusing their invectives on Mustangs kicker Tory Girchwood.

"Wow, Girch," Riley said, "I didn't know that about your mom."

"Pach, you ever want to take a shot back? You know, something that might shut them up just a bit?"

"What exactly did you have in mind, my young friend?"

Girchwood merely smiled and picked up a ball.

"Are you thinking what I think you're thinking, Mr. Girchwood?" Riley asked in mock surprise.

With a wink, the kicker turned and punted a rocket from the 20 yard line up toward the second group of fans. The ball sailed just over that group and, looking like a laser-guided missile, spiraled directly into the chest of a particularly foul fan who had been cussing his way down the stadium steps. The ball knocked the wind out of the man and drenched him with his fresh 32-ounce Bud Light. The stunned Bandits faithful looked at the man—one of their own who had been brought to his knees. Then they looked down at Girchwood, who was standing there with a huge smile on his face, surrounded by players who were doubled over laughing. Suddenly the Bandits fans broke into a huge cheer and began chanting his name: "Girchwood! Girchwood!"

When Riley could catch his breath, he said, "Congratulations, Girch! You're an honorary Bandit!"

Girchwood simply stood there smiling.

Riley meandered back into the locker room to throw on his shoulder pads and jersey. It was almost time for the entire team to take the field for pregame warm-ups. While the warm-up routine looked like it was specially designed to accomplish something important, it was really just a way to stay loose and to expend a little of the nervous energy. The team was on the field for about thirty minutes before heading back past the angry mob and into the locker room.

Upon entering the locker room, many of the players grabbed towels from the trainers. Riley snagged a towel, swung by the Gatorade table, downed an eight-ounce cup in one motion, and headed for his locker. Other than the occasional sound from the bathroom of a nerves-induced heave followed by a quick flush, the room was eerily silent.

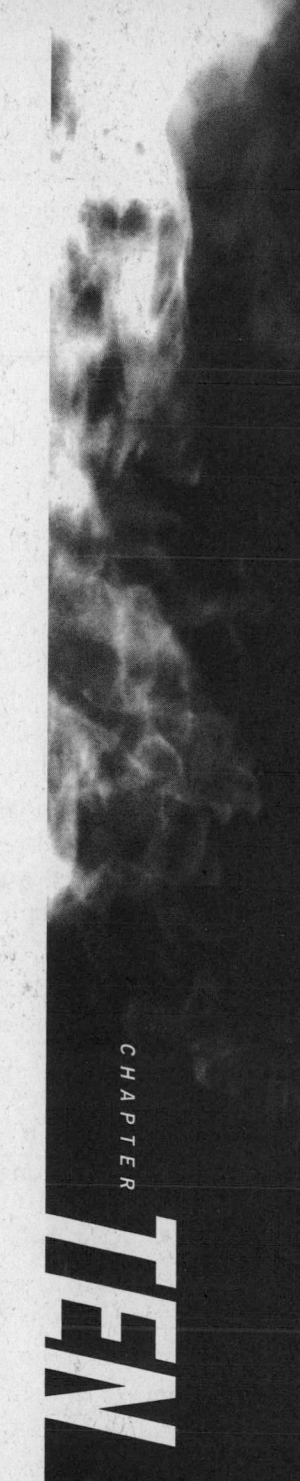

Hakeem's body was where his superiors expected him to be, but his mind was far from his job. He dwelled not on the responsibilities of his occupation but on the double life he had been forced to lead for so long. But his duplicity was nearing its end. *This facade will be the first casualty when the hammer comes down.*

To any of his coworkers who happened to glance his way, Hakeem looked studious, deep in thought. As he sat with his head bowed, his mind went back to the previous night.

Hakeem had attached a small Sony Handycam to a tripod. He put on gloves prior to opening the case for the mini DVD-R. After snapping the disc into the camera, he waited while it formatted. Then he had twisted the viewing screen so that it was facing the front. Placing a floor lamp directly behind his chair, he sat with the remote control in his hand. He looked closely at the screen to make sure there was nothing but darkness on his face. Satisfied, he took a deep breath, pressed Record on the remote, and began speaking in a voice and accent he had been practicing for the past eight years.

CHAPTER

TEN

"People of America, I am the voice of your pain today. I planned and executed this attack. I am Hakeem Qasim. I am the Cheetah. I am the Hammer.

"What do I fight for? I fight for the Cause. What is the Cause? It is a movement that you and your government created with your imperialist policies. You claimed Arab lands as your own. You came to steal our oil. You imported your decadent culture and tried to steal our souls. That is why the Cause is made up of warriors from many nations. That is why all Islam is against you. That is why you cannot stand up to our onslaught. We will wear you down. We will break you.

"Why do I fight? It's simple. *You* came to my country. *You* attacked my people. *You* killed my family. Do you expect me to accept that from you? Do you expect my people to lie down as you and your Western allies take turns with us, one after another? No! Look now! The victim is holding a dagger. The victim has drawn blood. You thought you had beaten us down, but you have failed. We are still standing, and we still have much fight in us.

"We realize that we do not have the firepower to defeat you on the battlefield. So we will use the most powerful weapon we have—ourselves. Like the Intifada to the occupying Zionists, we will be the spike through your boot. Over time, we will decimate you. We will dissect you limb by limb, piece by piece. No place is safe for you anymore! Let me repeat that so you fully understand. No . . . place . . . is . . . safe!

"I have told you my name, and I have told you my purpose. But who am I really? I am your neighbor. I am your friend. I am your coworker. I am your husband. I stand with you in the elevator thinking about how to kill you. I ride with you on the bus dreaming about detonation. I sit with you on the plane, in church, at the movie theater.

"You think that I am you, but you are mistaken. My greatest desire is to bring pain to your comfortable world—pain like I felt when you stole my family from me. Some of us in the Cause fight for Allah; some of us fight for ideology; some of us fight for revenge; some of us fight for honor. But we all fight. And we will not stop until your streets run red.

"So tomorrow, when you get on your train or your plane or your bus, maybe you will see me and you will wonder what's in that briefcase I'm holding. Maybe when you're stuck in traffic, you will see me in the car beside you and you will wonder what's on the seat next to me. Or maybe when you enter your church or your synagogue or even your mosque—for you milquetoast Muslims—you will see me and you will wonder what I have strapped to my chest.

"Hear me! This will happen again . . . and again . . . and again. There is a new reality for you. The days of *Pax Americana* are gone."

Hakeem reviewed all this in his mind while outwardly he appeared serene and composed. Though the attack next week would be deadly, he knew that when the video he had created was released after the attack, it would have a much more far-reaching effect. *Sow seeds of distrust. Create fear. If you poke the sleeping devil just right, he will wake up and devour himself looking for the offender.*

Now that Hakeem had taken a night to think through his performance, he was even more anxious for the final hour to come. Eight days seemed like such a long time. *I've waited over a decade and a half for this. I can wait a few more days.* For now, he had to try to focus. Any deviation in his cover now, and the whole plan could collapse in pieces around him.

SUNDAY, DECEMBER 21
CTD NORTH CENTRAL DIVISION HEADQUARTERS
MINNEAPOLIS, MINNESOTA

"It's good to see you drinking a man's drink," Jim Hicks said to Scott Ross as they sat down at Hicks's desk, each with a fresh cup of coffee in his hand.

"That's only because I haven't been out of this building for the past eighteen hours."

"You should get some sleep. Maybe it'd help you—"

The look from Scott stopped Hicks midsentence.

"Never mind. I should have known. You know, Weatherman, you and I are a lot alike. You just don't have the twenty years of having your soul sucked out of you yet."

"Golly, Jim, it's a wonder CTD doesn't have you in the recruitment department. 'Join CTD. See the world. Lose your soul!'"

Hicks laughed as he reached into his drawer and pulled out a bottle of Baileys Irish Cream. "You want a little shot for your coffee?"

"No thanks, man. I learned long ago that for me one shot leads to another, which leads to another, which leads to another, and pretty soon I'd be up on your desk dancing the one-man *lambada*."

"The *lambada*, huh? Isn't that the forbidden dance?"

"*Sí, pero necesito bailar.*"

"Nice try, Weatherman, but the *lambada* was a Brazilian dance, not Spanish. I know that because my second wife was from São Paulo."

"My bad. *Sim, mas mim necessite dançar.*"

Hicks stared at Scott; then he laughed as he stretched back in his chair and kicked his feet up on his desk. "You are a strange one, son. Now, let's go back over what we've got for a fourth time so that when the higher-ups ask, I can use some word other than *diddly-squat*."

"Okay," Scott began, leaning back into the same position as Hicks. "We've got the name 'Hakeem,' and from what you learned in your follow-up conversations with Abdel, we know this Hakeem is going to be coordinating more attacks. Abdel said that there had always been rumors in the Cause of some mole or sleeper known only by the name Hakeem, who would one day rise up and inflict great pain upon the West."

"Hold up there a second," Hicks said. "You know, that's one thing that struck me. As Abdel was walking me through his story, he mentioned Hakeem a few times. Each time it was while he was talking about his own recruitment or training. At first he mentioned the rumor of Hakeem in relation to attacking the West. But toward the end, he mentioned him twice in relation to America. That happened all three times I had him tell his story. Was that just semantics, you think?"

"Could be. Or it could be that Hakeem's focus has narrowed." Scott paused and looked away for a moment. "If it did narrow, then why? Maybe because of the second Gulf War—although Abdel was recruited after it started. Maybe because of a focus shift in the Cause itself."

"Yeah, maybe . . . maybe. Or maybe the mole moved. Maybe Hakeem was based in Europe but always wanted to move to America. Then, when he got his chance, he took it."

"That's a lot of maybes, but I'm tracking with you. If you're right, then we're looking for some sort of businessman or professional, like a doctor or maybe an IT guy. If he was just some everyday worker bee, he could have come over anytime. But his power is in his position. So when the opportunity came for his position to move, he came with it." Scott whipped out his phone and hit speed-dial two. Three rings later, Tara Walsh answered. Tara had reluctantly flown home last night to head the efforts of the team. "Tara, did they bump you up to first class like I asked them to?"

"Would have been tough for them to do, since, as you well know, I flew home on our Gulfstream."

"True, true. But I still think you deserve the finer things."

"I'm flattered. Now, if you don't mind, we're kind of busy here."

"Always business with you. Look, I want you to pull Virgil and Joey out of whatever they're doing and set them to researching European businessmen and professionals who have moved to the States in the last three years."

Tara's loud and long reaction to the request caused Scott to cover the mouthpiece of the phone and say to Hicks with a grin, "Apparently she feels our parameters are a bit wide."

Then back to Tara: "There now, do you feel better? So, pull Virgil and Joey out of whatever they're doing and set them to researching European businessmen and professionals who moved here in the last three years, starting with any that might be of Middle Eastern extraction. Okay? . . . Yeah, but . . . yeah, but . . . yeah, I know. Just try. . . . Okay, good-bye. . . . Thanks. . . . Good-bye. . . ." Finally he closed the cover to the phone.

"She said she's thrilled to help out in any way she can," Scott said as he eyed the Baileys longingly.

"Praying in the showers! Praying in the showers!" Chaplain Walter Washburne yelled.

About twenty men slowly rose from the seats in front of their lockers and made their way to the large shower area for a pregame prayer. The players knelt, held hands, and bowed their heads. Washburne prayed, "Lord, thank You for these men and the opportunity You've given them to use their gifts today. Protect them from the other players but especially from these fans."

A small chuckle went through the group.

"This stadium is the mission field to which You have called these men today. So give them the courage of David, the wisdom of Solomon, the strength of Samson, and the integrity of Daniel. Whatever happens here today with the game, help these men to be able to walk out of here with their heads held high. We ask that Your will be done in all things. Amen."

Most of the guys rose and made their way back toward their lockers. Some remained on their knees, silently praying on their own. For many, this was one of the hardest times—getting up to

CHAPTER

ELEVEN

face the reality of game day. As long as they remained down on their knees, they couldn't make mistakes and they couldn't get hurt. Anticipation of the coming events played havoc with all of the players' emotions, and each handled it in his own way.

Silence overtook the locker room again. The defensive linemen passed around an ammonia strip designed to wake the dead. The overwhelming smell cleared the sinuses and brought complete focus. As the strip passed from hand to hand, it left each man with tears pouring down his face and an overwhelming desire to go out and hurt people.

The offensive linemen were dealing with their own pregame tension. They knew that they were only noticed when they failed and the quarterback got smacked. Center Chris Gorkowski's nerves were beginning to get the best of him. He grabbed a towel off the floor and began to make convulsive noises into it.

"Get that little demon out, Snap!" All-Pro fullback Marius Washington blurted through the silence. "C'mon, get it out!"

That was all the trigger Gorkowski needed. After relieving himself of the morning's breakfast buffet, he threw the towel on the ground. The lineman grabbed his helmet, leaped to his feet, and screamed, "WOOOOOOOO-HOOOOOOOOO!"

Coach Burton yelled, "Bring it up!"

The guys huddled around him.

"I'd like nothing more than to embarrass this team in their own backyard. We all know they embarrass themselves enough. Just make sure each and every one of you leaves it all on the field today!"

Burton then led the team in the Lord's Prayer, which for most was more a ritual of superstition than sincerity.

At the end of the prayer, the team ran out the door, through the tunnel, and onto the field. They were greeted with the thunderous sound of seventy thousand boos from the Bandit Nation. Most of the players ignored it, but a few played to the crowd, dancing around and waving their arms, trying to get them to yell even louder.

The Mustangs ran across the field to their sideline, where they set up camp and waited for the Bandits to take the field.

As the first Bandit emerged from the tunnel, the boos turned to wild cheers. The sound was deafening as the players sprinted onto the field to AC/DC's "Back in Black."

A few minutes later, the Mustangs' team captains—quarterback Randy Meyer, defensive end Micah Pittman, and Riley—met with the Bandits' captains at midfield for the coin toss. The players all shook hands, and Riley took a couple seconds to say a few words to his old air force teammate, Bandits cornerback Alex McNeill. The coin tossed, Meyer called heads, and it landed tails, causing the crowd to burst again into an ear-splitting cheer. The Bandits chose to receive, and the captains went back to their sidelines to the jeering of the fans and the growing odor of stale beer.

Coach Burton walked down to where the defense was waiting. "Hey, fellas, just play your game and be patient. They *will* make a mistake."

At 0–14, the Bandits would be playing hard for a number of reasons. First, they had no desire to go into the record books as the first team to go winless in a season since the 1976 expansion Tampa Bay Tarpons. That was back when there were only fourteen games in a season, so the Bandits had already tied that woeful record. The other reason they were playing hard was their rivalry with the Mustangs. There was simply too much history and too much hatred between these two teams for either franchise to lie down for the other.

For as far back as most fans could remember, there had been loathing between these two clubs. If you asked ten Mustangs fans, you'd probably get ten different answers as to why that hatred existed. Some still despised the Bandits' ex-coach-turned-announcer Jim Madison. Others took their aggressions out against the reign of ancient, tyrannical owner Arthur Drake. Still others were offended at the team's bouncing from Oakland to Los Angeles and back to Oakland. And the Bandits fans each had their own reasons to hate the Mustangs. Ultimately, the rivalry had taken on an existence all its own. It didn't need a plausible explanation; it just *was*. The players felt it too. That's why, no matter the record, anytime the Mustangs and Bandits played, the outcome could go either way.

The game started at a quick pace. The Bandits began with their hurry-up offense, trying to catch the Mustangs off guard. Six plays into the drive, the Bandits were already past midfield. Riley was getting frustrated, and his frustration turned to anger when he missed the key tackle on one, two, three plays in a row by just a step or two.

The Bandits drove all the way to the Mustangs' 10 yard line. It was third and five. The Bandits quarterback took the snap and dropped back a few steps. Riley held his zone. Suddenly he saw the quarterback's eyes flash to the tight end. Riley broke on the ball, swung at it, and missed. As he fell to the ground, he heard a roar from the crowd as the tight end pulled in the ball at the goal line for a touchdown.

Riley slammed his fist into the ground, then popped back up. After the extra point, the defense ran off the field to regroup. Most of the coaches were yelling, "Keep your heads up!" and "That's okay, fellas; just keep battling!" Riley was irritated at the way the game had begun, but he knew there was a lot of football still to play.

The sideline phones began to erupt almost immediately. On one of them, defensive end LeMonjello (pronounced *Le-MAHN-jel-lo*, and don't you dare say it wrong!) Fredericks was getting some feedback from the defensive line coach. LeMonjello was affectionately known by his teammates as "Jiggly," after the tasty kids' treat. Coach Cox must have said something that Jiggly disagreed with, because he grabbed the phone with his enormous hands and ripped it off its mount. He held the phone up toward the coach's box and yelled, "Coach this!" He slammed the phone into the trash can behind the bench and dropped himself back onto his seat. Almost immediately empty space opened on both sides of Fredericks's huge frame. Apparently the rest of the guys on the bench felt it best to give Jiggly a little space.

/////////////////////

Sal Ricci jogged onto the field with the rest of the Mustangs' offense after the kickoff. He waited in the huddle for the play call, then took his place on the end of the line of scrimmage. He knew there was no way he would hear the snap count with all the noise in the stadium, so he didn't bother straining his ears to hear Randy Meyer's shouts. Instead he watched for the telltale tightening of Gorkowski's hands that indicated he was about to snap the ball. The instant he saw the ball fly back into Meyer's hands, Ricci shot forward, meeting the defensive end's jam head-on before spinning away and taking off on his route.

The play was a scissors pattern that had Ricci crossing midfield. His eyes were on Meyer as he ran, but out of his peripheral vision he saw a linebacker bearing down on him. Slightly altering his course, he went on the inside of the umpire, causing the linebacker to plow over the unsuspecting official and send both of them sprawling. Three steps later Meyer had the ball in Ricci's hand. Ricci looked downfield only to see three very large black-shirted Bandits in his path. He juked past the first defender, but the next two sandwiched him between their foul-smelling jerseys and brought him to the ground.

The hit was jarring, but what really hurt was the thumb jab in the trachea, courtesy of one of the Bandits lying on top of him. Ricci got up coughing but tried his best not to let the pain show. Trotting back to his own side of scrimmage, he picked at the turf lodged in his helmet, while calls of "good job" and "nice catch" from his teammates surrounded him.

The pain in Ricci's throat was starting to subside as he leaned into the huddle.

"Nice pattern, Reech," Meyer said. "Way to use the umpire as a pick."

"If he's in the field of play . . ." Ricci laughed.

"Okay, good start. Let's keep it going!" Meyer continued. "West Right Tiger Left Nineteen Handoff Release! Break!"

Ricci's brain quickly deciphered the code. The Tiger Left package meant there would be two tight ends. Sure enough, Fuchs, the second tight end, was quickly stepping to the left side of the line with him. Fuchs placed himself just off the left tackle, and Ricci stood behind him. Ricci's role was to motion right. If he saw that the linebacker read the handoff and was on the ball, he would take him out. If not, he would block the first man he came to.

Meyer started the call, and Ricci began moving; then everything burst into activity. Ricci saw the linebacker racing to the point where the handoff would be made. Ricci launched himself at the

Bandit's upper body, but the defender was anticipating him and rolled off the block. Ricci went down, then heard the crack of linebacker forcibly meeting with halfback. That quickly, he went from hero to goat. When Ricci jogged toward the sidelines for the third down play, Coach Burton was waiting to tell him what he thought of his blocking skills.

When Ricci finally made it past the head coach, the tight ends coach was waiting to give the second chorus to Burton's song. That lasted another full minute, until mercifully, the Mustangs got a first down, and Ricci escaped back onto the field.

The next five plays netted thirty-four yards and two first downs. It was second and fifteen after a dropped pass and a false-start penalty. As Ricci got set on the line of scrimmage, he knew the ball was coming his way. Here was his chance to redeem himself. Gorkowski snapped the ball, and Randy Meyer dropped two steps back and threw a rocket right at Ricci. The tight end reached for the pass, but the ball bounced off his numbers. The defending cornerback was there, ready to make the tackle, but when the ball popped up, he caught the deflection instead and ran it back for a touchdown. The extra-point try soared between the uprights, and just like that, the Bandits were up 14–0.

Ricci looked toward the sidelines and saw Coach Burton staring right at him. There was no place to run, no place to hide. He knew that whatever Burton was going to say to him was exactly what tens of thousands of people were this very moment shouting at him through their television sets. He took a deep breath, then ran to face the music.

/////////////////////

Riley Covington knew the Mustangs desperately needed this game. At 9–5, their play-off chances were touch and go. It was one of those "you control your own destiny" moments. If the Mustangs lost here, there would only be one last meaningless game before their offseason.

The game had gone back and forth through the rest of the first three quarters. Neither team had been able to do much with the ball, but the Mustangs had slowly built up 10 points to make the score 14–10. Now, with three minutes to go in the fourth quarter, the Bandits had the ball and were trying to eat up the clock. One more first down would effectively end the game.

It was third down and seven. The quarterback took the snap. He dropped back and prepared to pass. Riley was blitzing up the middle when he realized that the QB was going to throw a screen pass to the fullback. Digging his cleats into the turf, Riley stopped his forward progress and began backpedaling as quickly as he could. When the quarterback released the ball, Riley was off balance, but he still managed to leap backward and snag the tip of the ball with his finger. The ball deflected enough to miss the fullback and drop into the arms of Mustangs safety Danie Colson. Colson raced down the field and high-stepped it into the end zone. He spun the ball on the ground and did his famous "hoodaman" dance around it—a celebration perfectly timed at just under five seconds to avoid the unsportsmanlike conduct call. By the time he finished his dance, his teammates were on top of him. He waded through the group until he found Riley and gave him a bone-crushing hug.

Coach Burton met Riley and Colson as they were coming off the field. Colson still had the ball in his hands. Burton had almost lost his voice from screaming all afternoon. "I told you guys," he croaked. "I told you. Just be patient and they'll make a mistake. They're the Bandits; that's what they do."

Girchwood slammed in the extra point, taking the last gasp out of the Bandits faithful. Now at least half of the continuous stream of verbal abuse was directed against their own team. The Bandits had one more chance but couldn't get anything going against the swarming Mustangs defense. They went four and out, and the Mustangs kneeled out the rest of the time.

The media rushed onto the field with their microphones, cameras, and tape recorders as the players went out to meet each other. Despite the rivalry, most of the guys congratulated each other and wished the opposing players well. Riley joined a small group made up of both Bandits and Mustangs at the 50 yard line for a postgame prayer. The Bandits chaplain thanked God for protecting the players, while reporters and cameramen waited impatiently. When the prayer was complete, Riley was instantly assaulted with cameras and microphones stuck right in his face. He tried to keep a smile and answer some questions, but he was exhausted.

When Robert Taylor saw what was happening, he quickly jumped into the mix. "Riley's gotta go. Sorry, fellas," Taylor said.

Taylor kept his arm around Riley as they both jogged off the field. When they entered the tunnel, some Bandits fans took their parting shots at the Covington family tree. Police were standing nearby to make sure that it was only words pelting the players. Riley smirked at Taylor after one particularly foul insult. "If my mama really did that, I don't think Daddy'd be too happy."

They walked through the double doors and into the visitors' locker room. Many of the guys were hugging each other and giving high fives. The coaches and the management were walking from locker to locker, congratulating everyone. Riley went up to give Ricci a quick hug, but Ricci just held up his fist for Riley to tap with his own and said, "Good game, Pach," then turned back to his locker.

Coach Burton called the team together for his postgame speech. "Men, I'm proud of your effort. It's tough to go into someone else's backyard and come out with a win. My hat's off to you today. One more and we're in the play-offs. Enjoy your day off tomorrow."

At that pronouncement, the team cheered. Often a football player's Monday had a lot to do with the team's Sunday. A victory meant a day off from practice with only a required workout. A defeat meant a workout, two and a half hours of unpleasant meetings, then ten back-to-back hundred-yard sprints for the whole team.

Coach Burton finished with the Lord's Prayer, and the players jumped up from their knees and headed for their lockers.

As Riley wiggled out of his uniform and pads, he noticed a familiar smell beginning to permeate the room. The postgame locker room odor was something that all veteran ball players were used to, though for the novice it could be quite overwhelming. There was always an underlying rank stink—mostly sweat mixed with doses of whatever else might come out of a body during its various stress-related processes. After a loss, the stench sometimes seemed overpowering. But after a win, the locker room had the smelly pungency of victory. Today, the steam that clouded up eyeglasses and camera lenses didn't seem quite so bothersome; the humid heat that flattened fabric of any kind against skin seemed a little less sticky. The piles of equipment and wads of tape strewn across the floor seemed a little less hazardous. Victory made everything and everyone more beautiful.

The media were finally allowed in, and there was a mad rush to the lockers. Riley answered the same questions seven times before he was able to break free and hit the showers.

After dressing, the players packed their bags, grabbed a sack lunch and a Gatorade or soda, and hopped on the bus. Finally, the players were able to sit back, relax, and enjoy the win on their way back to Denver.

Police escorted the four buses out of Golden West Stadium and all the way to the Oakland airport. The team went through the regular security process, then boarded the plane and grabbed their seats for the two-hour flight to Denver.

It was a raucous scene on the United charter 1918. The cabin microphone was put to use quite a few times by a number of players. In comparison to Riley's microphone usage on the trip out, these players demonstrated much less complexity in their vocabularies and much more alcohol in their systems. Everyone was exhausted by the time the plane landed in Denver at 9:25 p.m.

After exiting the plane, the players boarded buses to take them to Inverness. When Riley saw his Denali in the player parking lot, all he could think of was home, bed, and sleeping in as late as he could manage in the morning.

"Merry Christmas to you," Michael Goff sang as he opened the back door to his house. He had just returned home from another twelve-hour shift as a security guard at Sky Ridge Medical Center. The smell of homemade meatballs filled the kitchen—a smell so good it almost diverted him from his mission.

He caught his wife's eyes as she turned from the stove and gave him a curious look.

Michael gave her a wink and continued his song. "Merry Christmas to you." He moved into the living room, where his eight-year-old son, Kevin, was playing Madden football on the Xbox—as usual, Kevin's team was the Mustangs. "Merry Christmas, dear Kevster," Michael sang with much flair as he positioned himself between his son and the television.

"Dad, you're in the way. Besides, Christmas isn't for two more days," Kevin scolded. But even as he halfheartedly complained, he was clearly intrigued by the look on his father's face.

"Merry Christmas toooooo yoooooooouuuuuuuu." Michael dropped to his knees, pulled two tickets out of his parka, and waved them in front of his son's face.

CHAPTER

TWELVE

"Are those . . . are those Mustangs tickets?"

"No, Kev, they're for Disney On Ice. I hear they're doing the princess tour. What do you think, you knucklehead?"

Kevin dove for the tickets, snatching them out of his dad's hand. The colorful background was a scene of Randy Meyer wearing an old orange jersey and throwing a perfect spiral. He ran his finger over the raised lettering. "'*Colorado Mustangs vs. Baltimore Predators. Monday, December 29. 6:30 p.m.*' Dad, these are the real thing!"

"Oh, are they? Sorry, I must have picked up the wrong ones."

Kevin suddenly spun the tickets to the ground and began his best impersonation of Danie Colson. He cocked his arms to his side, thrust out his chest, and began moving in a circle in what could best be described as a chicken walk. "Hoodaman?" he called out.

"Yoodaman!" his father answered.

"Hoodaman?"

"Yoodaman!"

"Hoodaman?"

"Yoodaman!"

They fell into each other's arms, laughing.

"Dad, you're the most awesome dad ever! How'd you do it?"

"Well, it's like this," Michael began to explain as he dropped onto his beat-up La-Z-Boy and lifted Kevin onto his lap. "I called up Coach Burton, and I said, 'Yo, Burt, my kid's the biggest Mustangs fan on the face of the earth. We need tickets to the Monday night game. So fork 'em over, or do I have to come down there and give you a signature Goff smackdown?' Half an hour later these came by special courier."

"Yeah, right," Kevin laughed and gave his dad another big hug. "Hey, let's go tell Mom!"

They began a chant of "Go, Mustangs! Go, Mustangs!" and formed a mini conga line. They danced their way into the kitchen, where Marti Goff, who had heard everything in the small house, feigned shock and surprise when Kevin waved the tickets at her. She joined the conga line behind her husband as it snaked through the kitchen and down the hall to the bedrooms.

"So, how'd you swing that?" Marti whispered over Michael's shoulder.

"Larry Gervin had these two tickets he was looking to trade away. In exchange, I promised to cover his shifts on Christmas and New Year's Eve."

Marti slapped his arm. "You're going to be gone Christmas?" Then, after a few seconds, she leaned forward and gave him a kiss on the side of his neck. "You're a good dad, Michael Goff. . . . Go, Mustangs! Go, Mustangs! Go, Mustangs!"

TUESDAY, DECEMBER 23
DENVER, COLORADO

Todd Penner stepped out of Trice Jewelers and into his 1986 Oldsmobile Cutlass. He had just paid the second-to-last installment on the layaway he had stashed in the vaults of the jewelry store. Walking the steps of Platte River Stadium with his tray of drinks at next Monday night's Mustangs game should net him enough in tips to finally take the ring home. For now, home for this twenty-year-old was still Mom and Dad's. But the ring—that precious circle of gold with its microscopic diamond chip ensconced firmly in its center— that ring was for her. The one. Sweet Jamie.

As he got into the car, he could still smell the remnants of the Chick-fil-A combo he had scarfed on his way here. *Food's great, but it takes a week to get the smell out,* Todd thought. He took a swig of his large Dr Pepper (really the primary reason he went to Chick-fil-A to begin with) and successfully started up the car—not necessarily a given considering the 236k on the odometer of the vehicle that his friends affectionately referred to as "La Bomba." *True, it may be a bomb, but it gets me where I need to go . . . usually.*

Back to Jamie—sweet Jamie—the girl he had been "dating" since sixth grade. At that time, dating meant hanging out together at church youth group and sitting together for lunch at West Middle School. There had certainly been some rough times in their relationship as they had both grown up at their own pace. But love overcame all odds, and eight years later Todd was ready to make things permanent.

He had the proposal all planned out. On New Year's Day (a perfect day for a new start), he would drive her up to Red Rocks

Amphitheatre. That was their special spot. They had seen concerts there by everyone from Kelly Clarkson (her choice) to Evanescence (his choice). The best concert of all, though, was back in 2003 when they spent an evening listening to James Taylor. Sure, he was possibly older than the rock formations themselves, but he was a favorite with each set of their parents. Thus, both Todd and Jamie had grown up on JT's music. The summer night had been perfect, with thunderstorms way out to the east providing a light show to accompany the legend's exquisite voice. It was an evening they would tell their grandkids about.

Todd's plan was to sit Jamie down on the very spot where they had sat that magical night. He would get down on one knee, profess his eternal and undying love for her—*Is "eternal and undying" a redundancy?* he wondered—and ask her to be his wife. Although he was fairly sure of her answer, the thought of doing it both thrilled and terrified him.

He clicked on his AM radio and tuned it to 950. Sports analyst Jim Rome was on a tirade about the pitiful Bandits and their choke against the Mustangs on Sunday. That had been an awesome game! He had watched it at home, squished on a sectional with his two younger brothers and his younger sister—the sister being the most rabid Mustangs fan of all the siblings. For the past three years, she had handily won the family fantasy football league. The popcorn had been flying when Colson ran that interception back. *One more game, Mustangs; just one more game!*

After a twenty-minute drive, Todd pulled into the main parking lot at Arapahoe Community College—his last stop before heading to his job waiting tables at Chili's. There was a problem with his spring schedule, and the three phone calls he'd made to the registrar's office had not accomplished a thing. These next months were very important to Todd, because if he could get through this semester at ACC as well as he had made it through his last three, he could potentially enter Metropolitan State College next fall with a scholarship. And he knew that a scholarship was probably the only way he could afford Metro—even with the College Opportunity Fund stipend.

Jamie's and his plan was to work hard at school for two more years. Then he would have his business degree from Metro, and she would have her BFA in 3-D graphics and animation with a minor in computer science from CU Denver—her parents had committed to fund her education through the bachelor level. After that, her artistic and Web skills would combine with his entrepreneurial spirit and business savvy, and they would slowly build what would ultimately become a thriving company. At least that's how it looked in the business plan he had created for his small business management class last semester.

Todd knew that things would probably not work out as smoothly as they looked on paper. However, he also knew that no trial could bring them down, as long as he and Jamie faced it together.

TUESDAY, DECEMBER 23
ARVADA, COLORADO

Carol Marks walked her final piano student to the door and waved at the child's parents, who were waiting out in the car. "Good job, Eric," she called out as the nine-year-old ran to the driveway. "Maybe next week we can get you to sing along as you play." *Fat chance,* she laughed to herself. *After nearly four decades of teaching, this boy's got to be the most stubborn student I've had yet.*

She often wondered if it was time to take down her teaching shingle. With her husband's salary, she didn't need the aggravation of grumpy kids and surly parents anymore. But there was still something about it that she loved. She loved experiencing those "aha" moments with the students when something new clicked in their young minds. She loved witnessing the joy of a great performance at the yearly recitals. She loved seeing the wonder in the eyes of the kids as they opened themselves up to new musical adventures—*Yeah, all except for Eric!*

Although her love for teaching was the main reason she kept doing it, there was a secondary reason, too: the income from the lessons helped fund a Marks family addiction. For the past thirty or so years, Carol and her husband, Paul, had been Mustangs season ticket holders—not an inexpensive undertaking.

They'd started out with four tickets in 1977, a season that had seen Marc Warmuth at quarterback, rookie head coach Gary Lewis at the helm, and the mighty Red Scare defense destroying all those who took them on. Although the Mustangs were embarrassed in the PFL Cup that year by the Texas Outlaws, Paul and Carol had been hooked. Every year since then, they'd scrimped and saved to keep their tickets.

Over time they had gotten to know the people in the seats around them. Soon, four of the families began getting together outside of the football games. The ladies even gave their little group a name—the Buckaroos—which caused much groaning among the men.

As the years went on, they had watched each other's families begin to grow and then spread out across the country. There was even a marriage between the Markses' eldest son and another couple's daughter.

The group's conversations had gradually moved from children to grandchildren. Their pregame tailgating increasingly included items listed as "low-cal" and "fat free." There had been two heart attacks and a cancer scare, but through it all the Buckaroos held together.

The move to Platte River Stadium created a temporary crisis among this happy band of four families. They were determined to keep their gang from falling apart. So together they had gone and scouted out the new stadium. And together they had put in for their new seats—the Markses only putting in for two now, since the kids were out of the house and starting families of their own. And now, even after three decades together, the group met for every game, either at the stadium for home games or at one of the family homes for away games.

That was the other reason Carol continued teaching piano. Her parents were gone, her kids were out of the house, and she didn't want to take the chance of losing more family. Quite a few times over the years, she and Paul had helped supplement the cost of tickets for other members so they could stay together. Sure, Carol loved the Mustangs, but the real reason she went to the games was to see the Buckaroos.

Riley eased his Denali to the curb outside the Ricci residence in Canterberry Crossing, a subdivision in Parker. Off to his left he could see a group of four men teeing off on Black Bear Golf Course. *Either they're single, or they have very understanding wives,* he thought.

He grabbed some packages from the passenger seat, then went around to the liftgate. There, protected in a shallow box, was his offering for the Christmas feast—brown bag apple pie (his mom's recipe with the slight modification of a store-bought crust).

After Riley had left the air force, his mom had taken a day and taught him how to make one main course (pepper steak—*steak au poivre,* if he really wanted to impress), one side dish (green-bean casserole), and one dessert (apple pie). Mom reasoned that with these three recipes under his belt, he would always be prepared to bring something whenever he was invited to someone's house. *Good thinking, Mom, as long as I'm not invited to the same place twice.*

He scooped up the pie, wrangled the liftgate closed, and walked up the path.

CHAPTER

THIRTEEN

Before he even had a chance to ring the bell, Sal Ricci opened the door. "Welcome!" Ricci said as he took the packages from his friend's hand. Then he called over his shoulder, "Riley's here, babe."

Riley pressed Lock twice on his key fob and followed Ricci in.

The smell of Christmas filled the air—the woodsy scent of a beautifully decorated fir tree, the cinnamon and clove fragrance of potpourri, the rich, thick smells coming from the kitchen, the . . . *Whew, what is that smell?* Riley looked down to see nine-month-old Alessandra preparing to crawl up his leg.

"Sorry, bud. I think she needs a change," Ricci said, scooping his daughter up.

"What have you been feeding that poor kid? Pork rinds and broccoli?" Riley called after him. He sought refuge for his nose in the kitchen, where Megan was busy preparing the feast. "Merry Christmas, Meg. It smells wonderful in here."

She put her spoon down and gave Riley a hug. "Welcome, Riley. It's great to have you with us today. Wow, what is this?" she asked, taking the pie from his hand. "Is this homemade?"

"Yep—exactly like Mom used to make. But do me a favor—next year ask me to bring a side dish."

"Sure thing," she said, giving him a curious look. "What happened to my husband?"

"Alessandra had a toxic leak. It's funny; I remember when you were pregnant. Sal said he would never change a diaper."

"True, and for the first months it was all I could do to get him to change her. But recently, he jumps at the chance to change every diaper. It seems like every waking moment he's playing with her or just staring at her." She stopped for a moment, then looked Riley in the eyes. "You're Sal's closest friend on the team. Have you seen anything different about him lately?"

"Different how?"

"I don't know. I guess I'd say he seems edgier than usual. He says it's because of the pressure at the end of the season, but I think it has to be more than that. One moment he's wonderful, and the next moment he bites my head off about something; then the next moment he's staring off into space." Megan paused and looked down. When she looked back up at him, there were tears in her eyes. "Would you . . . would you tell me if he was having an affair?"

"After I got through beating him to a pulp, yeah, I'd tell you—or at least I'd make sure that he told you. But I don't think you have to worry about that. I would be truly shocked if he were messing around on you, Meg. I've seen the same stuff you have, but I see it all around the locker room. Everyone is on edge."

"You don't seem to be."

"Well, that's because I'm an extreme introvert who suppresses my feelings of angst until they reach a boiling point, finally finding a violent outlet on the playing field."

"Impressive. You've been talking to the sports psychologist," Megan said with a relieved laugh.

"Watching *Dr. Phil*, actually. Seriously, I'll talk with Sal today and try to find out what's going on."

"Thanks, Riley." She gave him another hug as Ricci came in with Alessandra.

"What's-a happening-a here? Are you a-messing with-a my girl?"

Riley laughed. "Sal, for being Italian, you have the worst fake Italian accent in the world. You sound like a junior high production of *The Godfather*."

"Well, let's-a sitta at the table. Or am I-a gonna hafta make-a you an offer you can't-a refuse?" They all laughed as they sat, including Alessandra, who had no clue what was being said but apparently knew that her daddy was the funniest man in the world.

THURSDAY, DECEMBER 25
CTD NORTH CENTRAL DIVISION HEADQUARTERS
MINNEAPOLIS, MINNESOTA

Scott Ross saw it as soon as he walked into Jim Hicks's office. Sitting on Hicks's desk was a case of Yoo-hoo.

"Merry Christmas," Hicks said.

"Jim, I'm touched."

"Now don't go all sappy on me. I was getting tired of all your complaining, and . . . well, I appreciate all the hard work you've put in over the past few days. Let's leave it at that."

"Not even a Christmas hug to go with it?"

Hicks glared at Scott.

"Well, thank you anyways. And, just so you know that I didn't forget about you this yuletide season . . ." Scott reached into his coat and pulled out a magazine with a little red bow stuck on its front cover.

Hicks took it from him. "Wow, *Guns & Ammo*. Exactly what I've always wanted."

"Take a look. It's the January issue!"

Hicks couldn't help but smile. "Scott, you're like the son I'm glad I never had."

"Thanks, Pop. So, I'm assuming by your being here that you have no pressing family obligations."

Hicks shook his head. "No, I stopped having family obligations three years ago when my second wife divorced me."

"How'd that happen?" Scott asked as he cracked open his first Yoo-hoo bottle of the day. He offered one to Hicks, who quickly declined with a grimace on his face.

"Listen, Scott, I appreciate your feigned interest and all, but I'm not really into talking about myself."

"Believe me, I understand. But I was thinking, you know, it being Christmas and all. What the heck. We could even do it quid pro quo—you know, like in *Silence of the Lambs*. 'A census taker once tried to test me. I ate his liver with some fava beans and a nice Chianti,'" Scott said in his best Anthony Hopkins impersonation, finishing with the skin-crawling slurping sound.

Hicks thought for a moment, then said, "Why not? Okay, I've told you about my divorces. Quid pro quo. Where's your family? Why aren't you with Mom and Dad?"

"First of all, 'told you about my divorces' is a little strong for what you've said thus far. But if it will make you feel better, I guess I can launch first. My parents were addicts. Coke, horse, meth—you name it, they took it. There was this one Christmas when I was eight—my parents sent me into a house to score some chiva for them. I heard yelling and screaming as I walked up. I tried to turn around, but my parents wouldn't let me back in the car without the dope. So I went back and knocked. No one answered the door.

I walked in, and the smell in the house nearly bowled me over. It wasn't until years later when I was with AFSOC that I recognized what that smell was. It was death, hanging big-time in that house.

"So anyway, I look around and see this big nasty-looking guy, hair in a ponytail and all tatted up—I can still see him like he was right in this room. He was standing over his old lady. She was pretty bloodied up by this time. This guy sees me, and before I have a chance to tell him why I'm there, he crosses the room and plants his fist right on my cheek. He knocked out a tooth. I'm lucky he didn't break my jaw. Then he grabs a handful of my hair and a handful of my pants, carries me to the open door, and literally tosses me out onto the sidewalk and slams the door behind him.

"So I'm all scraped up and bleeding. I go crying and limping up to my parents' car. My dad rolls down the window and asks if I got the chiva. When I tried to explain what had happened, he flies out of the car, smacks the other side of my jaw, grabs the money from my hand, and drives off with my mom. I walked two and a half miles to get home that day. Needless to say, Santa forgot to leave anything under the tree that year." Scott downed the rest of his Yoo-hoo and chucked the empty a little harder than he intended into the stainless steel waste can.

"Are your folks still alive?"

"I don't know, and I can't say as I care. Don't get me wrong; I don't hate them. I probably should, but I can't. They were addicted. Nothing was more important than feeding the monkey. That's why I rarely drink, and I don't smoke or do anything like that. I've seen what the monkey can do, and I don't want any part of it."

They were both quiet for a few minutes.

Finally, Scott broke the silence. "You know, I don't think I've ever told anyone that story before."

"So, how'd you come from that home to what you are today? A lot of folks would have used that as an excuse for wasting their lives and living off the government."

"It was one man who did it—one man who changed my life. And believe it or not, he was a librarian—Mr. Pinkerton. Funny, after all these years I still don't know his first name. He saw something in me—potential, he said. He took the time to let me know that just because my parents were trash, I didn't have to be. He helped me believe in myself. He helped me get through school and then directed me toward the air force after I botched college. Without him stepping in, I hate to think where I'd be now."

"You still in contact with him?"

"Nah, he died when I was in Afghanistan. I couldn't even go to his funeral. When I heard he was gone, that was one of the hardest days of my life. . . . So, buddy, quid pro quo. Let's hear about you."

Hicks reached into his desk and pulled out a tumbler and a small bottle of Jack Daniel's Gentleman Jack. He tilted the bottle toward Scott, who waved it off. After pouring himself two fingers, Hicks began. "My story's not pretty either, but for a different reason. You took something screwed up and made it good. I took something good and screwed it up—royally. . . . You sure you want to hear about this?"

"I'm all ears," Scott said, twisting the cap off another Yoo-hoo and kicking his feet up on the desk.

"Well, you asked for it. Without going into too many details, I got married right before heading up to RTC for boot camp. We were both eighteen and stupid, and family planning was certainly not on my mind at the time. I'm seven weeks in when I get a call from my wife, who says she's pregnant. All I could do is think of the situation in terms of me. *It's too soon. I'm just starting my career. How can I raise a kid? We're too young.* All that junk went through my mind. So I tell her, 'Baby, this isn't a good time for us to start a family. Why don't you get—I can't even remember her best friend's name now—why don't you get your best friend to drive you over to Planned Parenthood and get it taken care of?'

"Well, my wife had a conniption over that. I yelled at her; she yelled at me. I told her that I was the man of the house and that if she wasn't going to listen to me, she might as well go back home to her mom and dad—which she did. Mom and Dad thought I was the devil anyway, and they promptly had the marriage annulled. So I guess technically I had one annulment and one divorce. Seven months later, I'm at SEAL training. I hear through the grapevine that she's had a girl—named her Tyler after her brother. Go figure."

"You ever see Tyler?"

"Yeah, once. Kelly—I guess I never told you her name—Kelly got remarried a few years later. She and her husband settled down in Omaha. One time I get an extended leave. I find out where Kelly's living, drive out to Omaha, and stake out the house. It's about 3:30 in the afternoon and I see this twelve-year-old girl come walking down the street. I would have recognized her anywhere—looked exactly like pictures I've seen of my dad at that age, only with beautiful, long brown hair. So, anyway, she comes down the street, walks into her house, and I drive off."

"You never said anything to her?"

"What am I going to say? 'Hey, sweetheart. I'm the father who wanted you dead. Glad to see you're still alive and kicking.' I'm not even sure she knows I exist. Probably better that way. I'm sure she's got kids of her own by now. Kelly's husband seemed like a good, white-bread kind of guy. Gave Kelly and Tyler a good, stable home—a heck of a lot better than I could have given them."

"And what about the second wife?"

A big smile spread across Hicks's face. "Ah, Marina. I truly thought she was my second chance. I met her about eight years ago. We had a whirlwind romance, and I married her three months later."

"Sounds like a good start. What happened?"

"9/11 happened. This job happened. When CTD was created as a response to the attack, it became my life. I wanted to find every little Prophet worshiper who even had a passing thought about hurting America. I wanted to find them and make them pay, practically and tangibly. I spent more and more time on the job. I became consumed. When I did go home, I took my job with me. I guess I wasn't easy to live with, and finally Marina had enough. One night, she let me have it—laid out all her frustrations. I snapped and hit her. Only time it ever happened, but once was enough. She was gone. I can't say that I blame her; I deserved it. In fact, the only reason I have a career right now is that she didn't call the cops even though she had every right to. She was and is a great woman. Her biggest mistake was getting mixed up with me." Hicks looked distant for a moment, then refocused on Scott. "So, what do you think of me now, Weatherman?"

Scott turned his eyes to the desk and didn't answer right away. When he did speak, he kept his eyes down. "There was something

Mr. Pinkerton used to say to me when I blew it big-time. I think it was a quote from somewhere in the Bible. He'd say, 'Putting the past behind, I press on toward the goal.'" He turned his eyes up to Hicks. "That's the only way I've been able to forgive myself for some of the junk I've done in my life. Friend, I think we both have a lot of 'putting the past behind' to do."

They stared at each other for a moment. Then Scott said, "You sure you don't want that Christmas hug?"

Hicks laughed. "Shut up and take that box of liquid mud out of my office."

///////////////////////

After the Christmas feast was consumed, Megan Ricci said, "Sweetheart, why don't you and Riley go into the living room to digest. Alessandra and I will take care of the dishes."

"It's hard to pass up an offer like that," Ricci replied. As the men got up from the table, Megan gave Riley a quick wink and a nod toward her husband.

Great, Riley thought, *Meg got it all worked out, but now I have no idea what I'm going to say to Sal.*

The two men entered the living room and settled into a couple of overstuffed leather chairs. The smell of the expensive cowhide filled the air.

"So, let's have it," Ricci said.

"What do you mean?"

"Whatever you and Meg were conspiring about. That wink meant that either the two of you have some secret romance going on—which is so not you—or she wants you to talk to me about something."

"Well, now that you mention it," Riley responded, trying to regain his footing in the conversation, "there is something I've been wanting to talk to you about for a week or so now. You haven't been yourself lately, Reech. You've been moody; you ripped me a new one on the plane; you've isolated yourself from me and Travis and Garrett; and I gotta say, you played Sunday like your mind was anywhere but in the game."

As Riley watched, Ricci's expression shifted from neutral to anger to profound sadness and back to neutral. Ricci sighed. "I appreciate your concern. Truly I do. I guess I'm just really feeling the pressure. It was never like this in Europe."

Riley, relieved that it was what he thought it was, said, "You're taking the game too seriously. Sure, you want to do your best. Sure, there's tons of pressure. But you know what? If we lose, you'll still get up the next day. You'll still have a wife who loves you. You'll still have a daughter who thinks you're the greatest thing since sliced focaccia. The things that matter will still be here."

Rather than cheer Ricci up, Riley's words seemed to darken his mood. Finally he said, "Riley, I want you to promise me something."

"Sure, buddy. Whatever you need, you know you only have to ask."

"No, I'm serious. I need you to swear to me."

"Of course, Sal. What is it?"

"I want you to swear to me that if anything ever happens to me, you'll take care of Meg and Alessandra."

"C'mon," Riley laughed, "those Predator DBs are big, but they're not that big."

But Ricci wasn't laughing. "Swear it to me, Riley. If anything ever happens to me, I need to know that my girls are taken care of."

"Sal, I give you my word," Riley said somberly. "You never have to worry about Meg or Alessandra."

"Thanks. I know you're probably wondering what that was all about," Ricci said, giving a little self-deprecating chuckle. "I've been having these dreams—strange, ugly dreams. I guess they've got me a little shaken. You know Italians—we can never shake the feeling that a nightmare is actually someone from the other side warning us that something really bad is about to happen." He laughed and finished his sentence with ghostly sounds. "Hey, isn't there a game on right now?" His hand encircled the television remote, and he pressed the red On button.

What was that all about? Riley wondered.

The discussion had certainly taken an unexpected turn. Now, as he looked intently at his friend, something told Riley that this conversation was far from over.

Riley drove away from the Inverness hotel at 7:30
a.m. His day was open until 2:00 that afternoon,
when he needed to be back at the hotel for chapel
and the pregame meal, then to drive himself to
the stadium, arriving no later than 3:30.

One of the things that made Monday night
games at home so great was the same thing that
made Monday night games away so terrible. For
both home and away games, all the players spent
the night at the hotel. However, when they were
at home, they could leave the hotel anytime after
6:30 a.m. and spend the morning doing whatever
they wanted to do. At away games, the players
were stuck in the hotel all day.

Riley had a loose schedule for the day. He
was on his way right now to meet his friend Mike
Robertson at the Kiowa Creek Sporting Club to
shoot some clays. He was fairly certain this wasn't
on Coach Burton's list of approved activities, but
it sure helped relieve some of the pressure on a
late game day.

Riley liked to get out shooting at least once
a week. Because Robertson worked at the club,
Riley was able to shoot all the typical guns he
owned plus a few of the "atypical" ones that had
happened to find their way into his collection—

CHAPTER

FOURTEEN

usually gifts from his old AFSOC buddies. For shooting trap today, Riley had snagged his 12-gauge Perazzi MX2000 with its over-under barrel and beautifully made custom stock. But he also brought along his compact Glock 19 9 mm—midnight black with ten in the clip. And, just for fun, he packed his Crimson Trace laser that attached to the top of the Glock for some pinpoint target practice.

Later, he had designs on the best pastrami sandwich in town at the New York Deli News with Pastor Tim, and sometime in between he had to take Alessandra Ricci's Christmas present back. Sal and Meg had been very gracious when their nine-month-old girl pulled open the box and yanked out the size 3 Little Mermaid dress that Riley had picked up at The Disney Store. "The others just looked so small," he had explained. Meg offered to exchange it, but Riley insisted on doing it himself—more out of embarrassment than anything else.

Ricci had been like a different person at the team dinner last night. All the surliness was gone, and he was back to his old self. He had even arranged for a dish of lemon Jell-O with a little whipped cream happy face on it to be delivered to LeMonjello Fredericks. The big lineman's threats almost got the name of the culprit out of the poor waiter who delivered it, but the second fifty-dollar bill that Ricci had promised him if he survived LeMonjello's assault was enough incentive to cause temporary amnesia.

Although Riley tried not to think too much about the game, it was never far from his mind. The Predators' passing game was good, but their running game was great. Their lead halfback, James Anderson, had the size of Jerome Bettis and the speed and cutting ability of Barry Sanders. Riley knew that whatever the ultimate outcome of the game, he was going to be exhausted and in pain. At least when all was said and done tonight, he could hop into his truck and drive home. There was nothing worse than a long flight back to Denver when you were too sore to even sit.

MONDAY, DECEMBER 29
UNITED STATES

The faint metallic smell from the warming brass reached his nose. Hakeem sat at his desk, nervously rubbing the disk between his fingers. All the plans had been made. His men knew their roles, and he expected that they had been ritually purified by now. His own part was ready to go—checked and rechecked and re-rechecked over the past few days.

He held up the disk and read the word that was engraved on it in seven languages—*honor. That's what today is about—restoring my family's honor. Who did this to you, America? The family of Qasim! Never forget that name. And even if you try to erase it from your memory, I'll make sure you are reminded.*

Hakeem reached into his bag and brought out a hammer and a narrow awl. Getting down on the floor, he placed the tip of the awl at the exact point where the three daggers met. With one strong, well-placed hit of the hammer, the awl punctured the brass disk right through the middle. Hakeem then reached back into his bag and brought out a new fourteen-karat gold chain and threaded it through the hole. Placing the chain over his head, he stood and looked in the mirror. *There, the symbol of your honor is back over your heart where it belongs—where Uncle Ali originally intended it to be.*

After admiring the necklace for a minute, he tucked it under his shirt, feeling its weight against the pillow of hair on his chest. Everything was ready. All that was left to do now was wait.

MONDAY, DECEMBER 29
AURORA, COLORADO

"Are you ready for some football?" Marti and Kevin Goff called from the back bedroom.

"Yes, I'm ready. I've been ready for the last half hour!" Michael called back. It had actually only been twenty minutes since he had gotten home from work, but for those twenty minutes he had been forced to stay in the living room. This meant that he could neither change out of his work uniform nor take care of an even more pressing need, since both bathrooms were down the hall in the "forbidden" area.

"We said, 'Are you ready for some football?'" Marti and Kevin called out together.

"Yes, I'm ready for some football! Please give me some football! Seriously, I'm so ready for some football—and I better get it soon or else I'm going to be ready for some paper towels."

Marti came walking out from the back rooms. Michael shot her a pleading look.

"I know, I know," she said with a mischievous look on her face. "Ladies and gentlemen, it gives me great honor to introduce to you . . . Kevin Michael Goff, world's greatest Mustangs fan."

Michael and Marti started clapping and cheering. Kevin came running down the hall and leaped into the living room. Michael stopped clapping, stared with his mouth hanging open, then fell on the floor in hysterics. Kevin was shirtless, and exactly half of his body from forehead down to waistline was painted orange and half was painted blue—although what had looked blue in the store was tending toward purple on the body. Then, smack-dab in the middle—painted in brilliant white—was the letter *M*. Kevin was dancing and flexing his little eight-year-old muscles, all the while chanting, "Go, Mustangs! Go, Mustangs! Go, Mustangs!"

Michael laughed so hard that the earlier serious problem quickly became an emergency. He stumbled past Kevin and Marti—laughing all the way down the hall and into the bathroom.

When he came back out, Kevin gave a yell and struck an Incredible Hulk pose. Michael lost it all over again.

"He desperately wants to hug you, but I told him he couldn't because he's still wet," Marti told her husband.

"Oh, Kev, you're killing me," Michael said, slowly regaining control. "You look half Oompa-Loompa and half Violet Beauregarde. And why is there only an *M*? Shouldn't you have done *CM* for Colorado Mustangs?"

"Didn't need to."

"And just why didn't you need to?" Michael asked, fearful of what the answer was going to be.

"'Cause someone else is going to be the *C*."

"Are you talking about Mom? Because I didn't get her a ticket, and it wouldn't be proper for her to go shirtless at the stadium anyway."

"I'm not talking about Mom. I'm talking about the person who's taking me to the game."

"You couldn't be talking about the person who's taking you to the game, because *I'm* the person taking you to the game, and there is no way this side of a presidential proclamation that I am going to go out in forty-degree weather and take off my shirt."

"C'mon, Dad. Please. Maybe we'll even get on TV."

"Yeah, c'mon, Dad," Marti joined in. "Your son's not scared of a little cold."

"True, my dear. But our son is not scared of my chain saw either, so I need to be scared of it for him and encourage him not to do anything dumb. That's what parents do, O love of my life; they encourage their children not to do stupid things. And even as I'm standing here trying to reason with you, I'm realizing that there is absolutely no chance of me winning this argument, so I might as well give in now while I still have a scrap of dignity left—dignity that will be stripped away from me tonight the moment I remove my shirt from my colorful body."

"So, is that a yes, Dad?"

"That's a yes, Son."

Kevin ran to hug his dad, remembered his wet paint, and instead renewed his dancing, now chanting, "Go, Dad! Go, Dad! Go, Dad!"

Marti motioned for Michael to follow her back to the "paint room." "Tell you what," she told him over her shoulder, "if you let me paint this on you now, I promise to help wash it off tonight."

"Hmm, suddenly body paint doesn't seem like such a bad idea. . . ."

MONDAY, DECEMBER 29
PLATTE RIVER STADIUM
DENVER, COLORADO

The temperature had dropped to thirty-six degrees, and a light mist hung in the air. Not necessarily the perfect temperature for tailgating, but traditions must be kept. The four couples—the Markses, Rawlinses, Newmans, and Ashtons—met in their usual place in a small parking lot just off the 21st Avenue exit. They had been doing this for so many years that they had the setup down to a science.

One corner of an awning was attached to the top of Paul and Carol Marks's Suburban, with the other connected to a corner of the shell on Doug and Abby Rawlins's Dodge Ram pickup. The awning was long enough to fit eight chairs and a barbecue, which the Rawlinses brought each week in the back of their truck. The only element that varied was the food. There were eight home games every season, so each couple was responsible for bringing the meat two times.

This week promised to be an experience. Andy and Liv Newman, always the adventurous couple in the group, had recently bought Steven Raichlen's *The Barbecue! Bible* and were anxious to try out some recipes. This week they brought *evapi*—a Bosnian burger recipe that blended beef, pork, and lamb with various ethnic spices. Carol was excited about trying it out, but Paul grumbled to Gil Ashton about how no one seemed to be able to just bring brats soaked in beer anymore.

When the barbecue was finally heating up and everyone had a cup of Carol's spiced cider in their gloved hands, Doug Rawlins spoke up. "Well, Buckaroos, we've got an announcement to make. With Doug Jr., Jim, and Kelly all living around Phoenix now, and with my retirement last year, Abby and I have been deciding what we want to be now that we're all grown-up. The answer that we both came up with is that more than anything we want to be grandparents."

As Carol listened, her eyes began to tear up. *Please don't say it, Doug; please don't.*

Doug's own voice was starting to crack a bit. "We've got three kids, three kids-in-law, and seven grandkids down there, and up here all we have is you. Now, don't . . . please, don't get me wrong. You all were the whole reason why this was a hard decision to make. But family's family. I want my grandkids to know their granddad. I want to be a part of their lives. So . . . this will be our last game, fellow Buckaroos. We're both so sorry."

A chorus of "Don't be sorry" and "Of course you have to go" and "We'd make the same decision" came from everyone—except for Carol. She stood with her back to the others as she fiddled with the thermoses that held the cider.

Abby walked up and put her hand on Carol's gently trembling shoulder. "Carol, are you okay with this?"

Carol turned and burst into tears. "Of course I'm not okay with it, but . . . but . . . well, hang it all, it's the right thing to do. Oh, Abby, I'm going to miss you guys so much." She fell into her friend's arms, and they both cried together.

After a few minutes, Carol looked up and saw that everyone was silently staring at them. "Well, don't just stand there, Buckaroos. This is our last game before two of our members ride off into the sunset. Let's make tonight a shindig we'll never forget!"

//////////////////////////

"C'mon, Manny, let me have the hot chocolate. You know when it gets like this no one's going to be buying Cokes. This is beer and chocolate weather."

When Todd Penner had arrived at Platte River Stadium and discovered that he was scheduled to tote around cold drinks, he saw his hopes of getting the ring out of layaway fading. He knew the way things worked, and "cold drinks" was not where he wanted to be.

Todd gave his biggest smile. "Please, boss, I need the money. I'm using the tips to get Jamie's ring. Do it as a favor to me." He saw that he was getting nowhere, so he clasped his hands together, batted his eyelashes, and added, "Better yet, Manny, don't do it for me; do it in the name of true love."

Manny's resolve never stood a chance. Todd had been too good a worker for too long, and the boss broke into laughter at this performance. "Okay, lover-boy, you can have hot chocolate. But careful on the whipped cream—you go through twice the cans that everyone else does."

"What can I say?" Todd responded, still batting his eyelashes. "I like my chocolate extra sweet."

"Get out of here, you freak, before I change my mind."

Todd was totally stoked when he left the room. All his plans were coming together. As he walked across the ramp, his mind went back to his clandestine meeting with Jamie's dad yesterday. They had met at the Starbucks in Arapahoe Crossing; Todd offered to buy.

"In that case, I think I'll splurge," Brian Starling had said. "Order me a venti caramel macchiato."

"Sure thing, Mr. Starling." Todd turned to the menu board, mentally comparing what he saw with what he knew was in his wallet. He said to the barista, "The gentleman will have a venti caramel macchiato . . . and make mine a tall drip coffee." Then, turning back to Jamie's dad, he said, "Go ahead and have a seat, sir, and I'll bring the drinks over."

As he waited for the drinks, he went over his spiel again in his head. It had taken him half the night to process through exactly what he should say. He felt he had put together a fairly persuasive presentation—even alliterating his main points: facts, figures, future, and faith. The drinks came, and with them came the moment of truth.

Sitting down across the table, Todd began, "Mr. Starling . . ."

"Satchmo."

"Okay . . . uh . . . Satchmo."

"No, the music playing in the background. 'What a Wonderful World' by Louis Armstrong, also known as Satchmo. One of my favorite songs."

"Yeah, it's definitely a great song. Do you want me to wait to talk until it's over?"

"No, go ahead," Brian said.

Todd couldn't be sure, but he thought he saw the man hiding a smile behind his coffee cup. "Thanks. Okay. Well, sir, Jamie and I have known each other for a long time now. . . ."

"I know, Todd. I was there."

When Todd had called Mr. Starling to request this meeting, he assumed Jamie's dad probably had at least a strong hunch about its purpose. But so far, this was turning out to be more difficult than he'd anticipated.

"Right. Stupid me. Of course you were there. So you know that I've known Jamie for a long time. I've also had strong feelings for—"

"Strong feelings, huh? You know, Todd, I have strong feelings for my wife's meat loaf. Do you consider my daughter on the same level as my wife's meat loaf?"

"No, of course not. I mean, don't get me wrong, I do have strong feelings for Mrs. Starling's meat loaf—it's incredible and all. But what I'm trying to say is that I've loved Jamie for a long time." Todd paused for a moment, doing his best to regroup. *Okay, "facts" is not going so well, and I can't even remember what "figures" was about. Time to wow him with the future.*

Todd opened his leather business portfolio—a graduation gift from his high school accounting teacher—and pulled out a copy of his and Jamie's business plan. "If you'll look here, Mr. Starling, you'll see the plan we've created to make sure we can be financially self-sufficient. And not just self-sufficient but prosperous. If you'll look at this ten-year graph . . ."

"Todd, stop, please." Brian was laughing now. "Listen, are you going to take care of my daughter?"

"Of course, sir. It's all right here, if you'll just look at—"

"Will you love her with all your heart your whole life?"

"With all my heart."

"And do you understand that if you ever do anything to hurt my daughter—physically or emotionally—I will cause you pain? And not just the oh-that-stung-a-little-bit-but-I'm-fine-now kind of pain, but the oh-Lord-just-take-me-home-'cause-I-don't-want-to-live-any-more kind of pain. The kind of pain that will make your unborn great-grandchildren scream out. The kind of pain that will cause old women on the street to have great pity upon you until they hear what you've done to my daughter, at which point they will beat you with their walkers, then kick you when you're down. The kind of pain that the government—"

"Mr. Starling? I think I get the picture."

"Good. Then put the graph away and ask me what it is that you brought me here to ask."

"Sure, of course." Todd cleared his throat. "Mr. Starling, will you give me permission to ask your daughter for her hand in marriage?"

Brian looked Todd in the eye and said, "Son, I can think of no man I would rather see Jamie spend the rest of her life with than you. You have not only my permission but my blessing. I pray that

God will give you two the years of joy that He's given to Jamie's mom and me."

As Todd remembered his future father-in-law's words, tears came to his eyes. He slipped the belt for the loaded hot chocolate tray over his head, looked at the single can of whipped cream, and called out, "Better give me a second can." *Forget what Manny says. Life is too good to skimp. Tonight, we let the whipped cream flow!*

The first quarter and a half went well for the Mustangs. The Baltimore Predators had come into the game ranked second in their division, so both teams were battling hard for a play-off spot. But as the game went on, it became apparent that Colorado had some of the "Monday night magic" going on. In the first quarter, Randy Meyer threw two touchdown passes, both over 30 yards and both to Antwon Thatch, who was known for his perfectly executed routes. Tory Girchwood tacked on a 43-yard field goal six minutes into the second quarter.

The defense had also been on fire, holding the Predators to just 36 yards in the first quarter. The one time Baltimore running back James Anderson broke loose for the end zone, he was caught from behind by Keith Simmons, who stripped the ball as he brought him down and then recovered the fumble. Later, Riley picked off a tipped pass, giving the Mustangs a +2 in the turnover column.

Halfway through the second quarter, the score was 17–0, and the Mustangs had all the momentum. The game had the makings of a blowout. But

CHAPTER

FIFTEEN

Riley knew all too well not to take any victory for granted. In week three, the Mustangs had been in the same situation against the San Diego Thunder. The defense had let its guard down, and that game had ended in a humiliating Thunder comeback victory.

Riley, as the middle linebacker, gave the call in the huddle. "Okay, guys, keep it burning. Don't forget these guys are good. Forty-four Cover Three Sky—Forty-four Cover Three Sky! Break!"

Forty-four gave the formation—four linemen and four linebackers. Typically the Mustangs ran a 4–3 formation, but Coach Burton, expecting a handoff to Anderson, had added an extra linebacker. The rest of the play call directed each player to cover his proper gap in the offensive line.

The Predators approached the line of scrimmage. Riley, seeing the tight end go to the left side of the line, called out "Leo! Leo!" The call of "Leo" echoed throughout the defense. Everybody tensed. Riley homed in on the quarterback as he gave the call.

"Blue Eighty-nine! Blue Eighty-nine! Go!" Holguin, the Mustangs' right end, launched himself into the Predators' line, then realized that no one else had moved. Whistles blew and flags went in the air. Everyone stood and walked back to their huddles.

Riley watched the sideline as he walked. He saw Coach Burton say something behind his hand to the defensive coordinator, who then signaled a play to Riley. Riley nodded, then jogged to the huddle.

When the defense had gathered around Riley, he reached across and gave Holguin a light slap on the helmet. "That's what I'm talking about, Hulk! Keep it focused!"

"Won't happen again, Pach," Holguin replied.

"Okay, Crank Jet Forty-four Mike Box Cover One—Crank Jet Forty-four Mike Box Cover One! Break!"

As they ran back to the line, Riley knew that this run coverage play had him covering the "A" gap, to the left side of the center. Burton was betting on another run up the middle, and Riley's job was to sprint to that gap and kill it.

As the Predators lined up, Riley saw that the tight end had moved to the other side. "Rex! Rex!" The rest of the defense followed his lead.

"Red Sixty-five! Red Sixty-five! Go! Go! *Go!*" The ball snapped, and Riley shot to his gap. He saw the quarterback lodge the ball in Anderson's hands and saw the halfback come straight for his hole. Just before they met, Riley felt a leg whip catch him down low, sending him falling to the ground. He caught Anderson's jersey enough to slow him down before Simmons came flying in, placing his helmet right on the running back's hands.

The ball flew into the air, bounced once, then landed immediately in front of Riley. Riley tucked the ball under his body just as five fully loaded cement trucks dropped onto him—at least that's how his brain deciphered the sensation. Hands began reaching under him for the ball. But those weren't the hands he was concerned about. The first of the two that disturbed him was reaching under his face mask. A thumb was in his left nostril, and the rest of the fingers were digging for sockets. The second hand of concern delivered a third punch to an area of his body that no man wants to have assaulted in any way. This punch was enough for Riley to momentarily lose his grip on the ball, which he felt quickly slide from underneath him. Just like that, what should have been the third turnover became an offensive fumble recovery.

After everyone unpiled from him, Riley rolled over and lay there until Simmons came and pulled him up. He slowly made his way back to the huddle, trying to catch his breath. When he got there, the defensive coordinator signaled in the call. Riley turned to his teammates and said in a shrill falsetto, "Forty-four Strong Safety . . ." He cleared his throat while the rest of the guys laughed. "And that, my dear boys, is why we never forget our hard plastic friends. Okay, Forty-four Strong Safety Delta Box Three Zone—Forty-four Strong Safety Delta Box Three Zone! Break!"

It was third and 11 for the Predators on their own 38 yard line, facing the south end zone. Both teams came out of their huddles.

The game clock ticked down: 7:05, 7:04, 7:03.

///////////////////////

Todd Penner knew he had a sale. He was walking section 530 and working his way south when he saw some crazy guy and his kid whip off the blanket they had been huddled under, revealing their fully painted bodies. They started screaming and dancing around as all the folks around them cheered them on. *That's a kid who desperately needs some hot chocolate,* Todd thought.

When he finally made his way down the stairs next to the colorful duo, he said, "You two interested in a little warming up?"

"Good call," the dad answered. "We'll take two."

"You look like a kid who likes whipped cream," Todd said to the boy.

"You betcha!"

"All right, two chocolates—one with super massive mongo amounts of whipped cream—coming right up." *Gotta work the tips,* Todd thought as he lifted the belt off of his neck and set the tray down on the steps.

/////////////////////

Carol was doing her best to enjoy the game, but her mind was far away from the stadium. She had purposely sat on the far end of the line of eight seats so she could process. She tried to pretend the reason she was so quiet was that she was really into the game.

Sure, there will still be three couples left. And it isn't like Paul and I haven't discussed this very eventuality umpteen times. But the reality of it actually happening is like a slap in the face. Why couldn't they just be snowbirds living half the time here and half in Arizona? Well, that makes a lot of sense, you goose—if they were here for Mustangs season, they would be spending winters here and summers in Arizona. Oh, why am I even worrying about this? What's done is done.

"Hey, Carol, great game, huh?" Abby Rawlins called down to her.

"They're my Mustangs!" Carol replied, forcing herself to give the biggest smile that her face could fake.

/////////////////////

When the game clock indicated 6:30 left in the second quarter, the man sitting in seat 102-4A slowly reached into his coat, pulled out a thin wire attached to a 6.3 mm plug, and connected it to a jack that was just barely visible in the tip of a football—a ball that had been on his lap the entire game.

As the digital numbers on the giant clock across from his seat passed 6:15, he toggled a small switch on the cylinder in his left pocket, arming the device.

At 6:05, he stood and turned his back to the field and yelled to the people around him, "I am the Cause! May Allah have his retribution! Allahu Akhbar!"

As the spectators within hearing distance reacted with fear and shock, the man pressed down on a button set in the top of the cylinder.

In a split second, an electrical signal was sent through a wire into the center of the football, triggering the blasting cap, which had plenty of power to set off a reaction in the surrounding explosive. The football exploded.

The detonation sent a shock wave filled with ball bearings tearing through the man's body and shooting out in every direction. The man, along with everyone within twenty feet of him, was immediately ripped into small pieces. Even beyond twenty feet, the ball bearings continued to shred flesh as the shock wave scrambled internal organs. As the distance grew greater, the shock wave became less deadly, but there was no stopping the ball bearings. The deadly projectiles continued to fly until something—or someone—intercepted their path.

///////////////////////

Riley and Keith Simmons reached to slap hands as they did before each play. As their hands met, Riley heard a whistling sound and, at the same time, saw Simmons's eyes grow wide. A concussive shock wave slammed against Riley's abdomen—a feeling he hadn't experienced since the mortars dropping in the Bagram Valley. Then the sound of an explosion overpowered the deafening crowd noise.

Riley's military instincts kicked in immediately. He dropped to a crouch and scanned the stadium for the source of the blast. What he saw rocked him to the core.

Out of the corner of his eye, he saw Simmons fall to the ground holding his left thigh—red beginning to stain the white of his uniform pants. At least three other Mustangs were down.

Smoke was pouring out of section 102. It looked as though everyone within a thirty-foot radius of the blast's epicenter had been killed instantly. Seats and debris littered the area, along with massive amounts of blood.

The crowd of seventy-two thousand stood in stunned silence.

/ /

The second man was gratified to hear the explosion. It had begun! Allah had finally brought his wrath again to the shores of the Great Satan. Never again would anyone in this country feel safe.

The first explosion had taken place in the first level, where everyone in the stadium could see it. It had gotten everyone's attention, which was its purpose. The purpose of the second explosion was to create mass confusion and get people moving. Thus, the second man's position was in the top deck, across the stadium from the first explosion.

After the first blast, the second man began counting. When he reached fifteen, he stood and slid sideways onto the stairs. He faced the crowd and began shouting the words he had been practicing for weeks.

/ /

Todd Penner was shaking the whipped cream can when he heard a roar that he had heard only once before—when he and his dad were fishing the Bear Creek Lake and a bolt of lightning had hit about twenty-five feet away from them. Instinctively, Todd looked up at the sky for a thunderhead, then realized that they were much more likely to face a blizzard than a rainstorm this time of year. Then he saw the smoke in the lower section across the stadium.

Todd stood looking at the scene of destruction, too horrified to move. The tray of hot chocolate lay at his feet. The silence of the crowd was eerie. Suddenly, a man began yelling. The speaker was on the steps about four rows down. Todd heard something about an American and wrath, but that was all he could make out. The man was facing the section to Todd's right and was holding both arms up as he spoke. In one hand was a football. Todd couldn't see what was in the other, but the poised thumb gave a pretty good indication of what it might be.

Without thinking about what he was doing, Todd bent down, picked up his tray, and let the hot chocolate fly. The nearly full tray hit the man in the neck and right shoulder, causing him to go sprawling backward and the ball to go flying out of his hand. Screams of surprise and pain came from the people surrounding the man as the hot liquid splashed onto their hands and faces. The man tumbled down the steps and crashed face-first into the metal guardrail.

///////////////////////

As Riley crouched on the 30 yard line, the crowd finally reacted to the explosion. It was as if a switch had suddenly been thrown, and pandemonium broke loose. People were screaming and holding on to wounds all across the playing field and as far as three sections over in the stands from where the bomb had gone off. Everywhere, people began fighting and pushing for the exits. Players ran toward the tunnels.

Riley ran to Simmons to check his wound, but the linebacker was already starting to lift himself up.

"I'm okay," Simmons yelled over the noise.

"Can you get yourself off the field?"

When Simmons nodded, Riley pointed him to the side tunnel and gave him a push. Simmons joined the stream of people rushing to get under the stadium, while Riley began scanning the crowd again.

The initial surprise of the attack was being overtaken by anger. The anger soon progressed to rage. After the attack at the Mall of America, Riley had no doubt who was behind this. *You better hide deep in your caves, you cowards! Even if it's the last thing I do, I swear I'll hunt you down!*

///////////////////////

Todd ran down the steps toward the man he had hit with the tray of hot chocolate, though he had no idea what he was going to do when he got there. But before Todd could reach him, the terrorist was pounced on by a bald man with a salt-and-pepper goatee who had crawled his way over a row of people, leaving two bloody noses and a black eye in his path.

"Police!" the man yelled at Todd as he drove the would-be bomber's face into the guardrail one more time, causing a horrible crunching noise that Todd heard even above the screams and curses filling the air around him. As the off-duty cop whipped out some handcuffs, a massive wave of people came rushing down the steps. The smell from the first blast was just beginning to reach their noses.

"C'mon, kid," the cop yelled to Todd. He lifted the bomber up and shoved him against the railing. He stood tight against the man's right side and pulled Todd up against his left. "Hold tight and don't move!" It was a command Todd couldn't help but obey as the crowd slammed itself against him, driving the air out of his lungs.

Lord, Todd prayed, *help me breathe. Please, just help me breathe!*

/////////////////////

The third man waited for the second explosion, but it never came.

He fought against panic. He had been trained for this very eventuality. He knew that the second explosion was to be fifteen seconds after the first, and the third—his—was to be thirty seconds after that.

He had been sitting in section 107 and was now caught up in the flow of people who were trying to escape to the concourse. His count had only reached thirty-seven, but he was in danger of being sucked into the tunnel. That wouldn't do, because this explosion was designed to be seen by all. He raised his football up in one hand and the detonator in the other.

"Allahu Akbar!" he yelled and in a split second wiped out 122 lives, including his own.

/////////////////////

After Riley got control of his growing rage, he began moving through the two teams, yelling, "Out the side tunnel! Get into the locker room!"

Most followed his instructions until the second explosion, after which everything became complete bedlam. Fans began pouring over the railings, not realizing how far the drop onto the field was. Some got back up and limped off. Others appeared to break bones in the fall and, after a few dozen more dropped on top of them, never got up again.

Riley ran toward the Mustangs' sideline. He had no clue what he was doing; he just let his instinct guide him. Most of the players had already fled, but a few sat frozen on the benches.

Riley dropped in front of one player, who had put his helmet back on for protection. "Chris! Chris!"

"What? Oh, hey, Riley," Chris Gorkowski answered. He had obviously drifted off to some happier place far from the devastation in the stadium.

"Chris, you gotta get up and get out of here!"

"Nah, Riley. I was thinking that I'm probably fine right here."

Riley slapped the side of Gorkowski's helmet—probably harder than he needed to—then grabbed the offensive lineman's face mask. "Listen to me, you big idiot! You have to get to the locker room! Now! See Skid and Bama over there?" Riley twisted the big center's helmet toward the two other players who were sitting on the bench, then twisted it back to face himself. "You're going to get those two out of here! Got it? Anything happens to them, I'm taking it out on you!" Riley gave Gorkowski's helmet one final neck-jarring slap and ran off.

When he looked back, he saw Gorkowski with a handful of both players' jerseys, yanking them off the bench and dragging them toward the locker room. Riley began working his way back to the center of the field, but it was getting harder to move as more and more terrified people flocked to the grass.

As he looked around, he saw people stacked up at each exit from the field—players and fans alike. He felt the rage building up again. *Get ahold of yourself! You're no good to anyone if you lose control!* Riley put his shoulder down and drove himself through the crowd.

///////////////////////

Carol Marks couldn't believe what she was seeing. After the first blast across the field, the eight Buckaroos had remained frozen in their seats like everyone else. Then, as if on some inaudible cue, the whole crowd of people moved at once toward the small tunnels that would take them to the concourse and out of harm's way. The four couples were nine rows down from the exit and were quickly swept into the wave of humanity.

What little control and order had existed were destroyed with the second blast. The crowd took on a life of its own. Paul and Carol had been seated in the center of the row and held tight to each other's hand, determined not to get separated. The other three couples were swallowed by the crowd as soon as they hit the steps.

Doug Rawlins turned around as he was being pushed toward the tunnel and mouthed the words *Meet at the cars! Meet at the cars!*

Paul gave a thumbs-up in response.

At last, Paul and Carol made it to the aisle. But as soon as they hit it, Paul was wrenched away. Carol screamed and stretched for his hand, but he was already out of reach. Paul was yelling back to her, "Just go with the flow, babe! Meet me at the car!"

Carol felt a hit from behind that nearly took her breath away as she was forced into the flow. Her sixty-year-old legs were having a hard time keeping up the pace. A couple of times she stumbled on the steps, but the mass of people was so tight that she had nowhere to fall. Finally she reached the top of the stairs and was funneled into the narrow tunnel.

As Carol entered, her foot hit something soft yet solid. This time when she stumbled, there was more space in front of her, and she went down. While she was falling, she realized what she had tripped on. And as she landed, she realized that she was about to find herself in the same situation as the person whose body had sent her tumbling. Immediately she tried to lift herself up, but a foot in the center of her back pushed her down again, forcing the air out of her lungs.

That first foot was followed by another and another. She struggled to get air, but the continuous flow of feet on her back and her head made it impossible. She tried to scream, but there was nothing there. Her arms were pinned underneath her as she squirmed her body back and forth.

A Sorel Caribou boot landing on her temple put an end to her movement. Darkness began in her peripheral vision and quickly moved toward the center. Her last thought as she faded away was *So this is what it feels like to die.*

As soon as people started moving, Michael Goff scooped Kevin into his arms and looked for a chance to enter the human river.

Kevin was crying. "What's happening, Daddy?" He always slipped back to *Daddy* when he was scared.

"I don't know, sport. Just hold tight. Got it? Lock those arms around me, and give my neck the strongest Hulk hug you've ever given."

The resulting squeeze almost threw Michael's neck out of alignment, but he didn't care. As long as he was in pain, he knew that Kevin was safe.

Michael forced his way into the aisle and down the steps. People were screaming all around him. Then he heard the second blast. *Gotta keep a cool head. Down the steps, out to the concourse. Skip the escalator— that'll be a death trap with this crowd. Ride the wave down the ramps.* "I'm gonna get us out of here, sweetheart. Daddy's got you."

The force of the crowd was overwhelming. Michael had little control over where he was going. But since everyone was heading the direction he wanted to go, he stopped trying to fight the flow and went with it instead.

The crowd pressed through the entrance to the tunnel. Michael could see people ahead stepping over some obstacles. He thought they must be backpacks that people had accidentally dropped until he stepped on one. The "Ohhh" from below him as his foot fell told him exactly what he was stepping on. He desperately wanted to reach down and help the person he had just walked over, but before he could, he was out the tunnel and into the mass of people in the concourse.

The fourth man was exhausted after being pushed, jostled, and cursed at for the past three minutes. He had been sitting in section 120 and had allowed himself to get caught up with the wave of people. While going through the narrow tunnel to the concourse, he was gratified to feel the give of several bodies beneath his feet.

When he heard the first explosion, he had started the timer on his digital watch. A moment of fear had gripped him when the second man hadn't completed his mission as planned. But when he heard a second blast from the lower deck, he knew that Allah's plan would continue in spite of the one man's failure.

As he looked around, all he could see was people—tightly packed, fish in a barrel. Exactly what they had hoped for. He reached the place where the ramps spilled out to ground level. It was time.

He managed to squeeze his arm up from the press of bodies and watched the stopwatch reach 3:30. Knowing he would never be able to get the football over his head, he cried out, "I am the Cause! Die, infidels! Allahu Akbar!"

Then he pressed the red button on his detonator and joined the flood of souls rushing to meet their Maker.

/////////////////////

Michael was nearing the ramp when he heard another explosion directly below. Suddenly the forward momentum of the mass going down the ramp was halted by another mass trying to escape the new blast by going back up. The resulting collision of two immovable forces snapped bones and crushed the life out of scores of people on the seam.

The pressure against his back was almost unbearable, and Michael joined in the chorus of "Go back! Go back!" Finally the momentum of the crowd shifted and the flow started toward the next ramp along the concourse.

"Keep hanging on, sport!" Michael yelled into his son's ear.

"I'm scared, Daddy!"

"I know, baby. I'll get you home. You're doing an awesome job holding on!"

/////////////////////

The fifth man had never entered the stadium. He had been spending his time pacing back and forth in front of the bronze sculpture of five mustang stallions, a mare, and a colt. He couldn't see the game clock from his vantage point, so he had just waited nervously for the first explosion. He was wound so tight that when the blast finally reached his ear, he lost control of his bladder.

He started his digital stopwatch and waited.

Soon people began pouring out of the stadium and running past him. He fought not to get swept into the crowd and positioned himself directly in front of the giant sculpture, in the only pocket free of people. Soon it would be his turn. His job was to get the fleeing people to turn back toward the stadium and into each other.

He kept checking his stopwatch, knowing without thinking about it that he was watching the final countdown of his life.

When the bomb went off at 3:30, he knew his time was short. He stared at the increasing numbers—3:58, 3:59, 4:00.

He stepped out from behind his shelter and shouted, knowing that no one would hear, "I am the Cause! Allahu Akbar!"

The power of the blast knocked the sculpture from its foundation, and the sound of the ball bearings against the bronze was like a thousand marbles being dropped into the bottom of a metal trash can. The giant horses tumbled onto the crowd, but when they landed, they hurt no one. Everyone around was already dead.

///////////////////////

The sound of another explosion echoed through the stadium, this one from much farther away. The resulting surge of the crowd again almost knocked Kevin's dad off his feet.

This can't be happening, Kevin thought. *I've got to be dreaming.*

Kevin looked back over his dad's shoulder, watching the people pushing and shoving. As he scanned the faces, he locked eyes with one particular man a few feet away. The man smiled at Kevin, and Kevin weakly smiled back. Then, as he watched, the man raised a football into the air with one hand and a cylindrical object with his other. After clearing his throat, the man shouted, "Hear me, America! I am the Cause! *Allahu Akbar!*"

With one last nod to Kevin, the man's thumb depressed the red button on the detonator.

Kevin didn't feel the shock wave, nor did he see the result of the hundreds of ball bearings exploding from under the leather shell of the football, completely wiping out everyone and everything in a fifty-foot diameter.

///////////////////////

Another explosion shook the stadium as Riley spotted Ricci with his hands pressed to the side of Predators running back James Anderson. Riley ran up to him. "Sal, get to the locker room!"

"Can't. Anderson's going to bleed to death if I go."

"Yeah, and you may die if you stay. I'll keep him from bleeding out."

"I'm not going to leave you here!"

"Sal, you've got a wife and kid! Now get out of here!" Riley drove his shoulder against Ricci, knocking him out of his crouch. Riley's hands reached into Anderson's torn, bloody jersey, found the wound, and pressed down to try to stop the bleeding.

"Riley, you call me when this is done! Let me know you're okay! You hear me? Call as soon as you can!"

"Get out of here!" Riley watched as Ricci ran toward the exit by the field manager's office and melded into the flow of people. *No, Sal! Why didn't you go to the locker room?*

He looked back down at Anderson. "Hold on, Jim! Help's coming, buddy!" But even as he said the words, Riley knew that Anderson's time was short. He had seen this kind of wound before, and it never turned out well.

Riley looked around. Tears came to his eyes as he saw the destruction. Smoke poured from all over the stadium. Most of the seats were cleared out by now, revealing the carnage. Body parts were all over. Scattered here and there were people unlucky enough to have been hit by a stray ball bearing. Many family members were holding these dead and wounded, sobbing and calling out for help.

Riley couldn't believe this was happening here in the United States—in Denver, Colorado! He hadn't seen this kind of mass destruction even in the military. So many dead; so many suffering.

And here he was with his hands inside another man's body, trying to keep him alive.

Riley had little doubt as to who was behind this attack—the same group of Arab fascists who were behind so many other things that were wrong in this world. *Lord, I don't know if this is a good prayer or not, but make these murderers pay! Make them feel the same kind of terror they've—*

Another explosion shook the stadium with the accompanying slam of a shock wave and the whistling of ball bearings. One of the trainers five feet from Riley cried out and dropped to the ground. *That one was close,* he thought as he looked around for the source of the blast.

When he spotted it, his heart sank. *Sal!* The entire crowd that had been trying to force its way into the tunnel next to the field manager's office was gone—evaporated, shredded, shattered. There was absolutely no movement anywhere around the exit.

"Saaaaaaal! No, not you, Sal! Saaaaaaal!"

As Riley cried out, he felt Anderson's heart stop beating under his fingers. "Forget you, Jim! You are not going to die!"

All the control he had been struggling so hard to maintain was lost. Riley yanked Anderson's helmet off, then violently pulled the man's shoulder pads over his head. He began CPR on the running back—thirty compressions, two breaths, thirty compressions, two breaths.

"I'm not going to let you die, Jim! You hear me? You will not die!"

Thirty compressions, two breaths, thirty compressions, two breaths. Riley continued the pattern, not stopping until a couple of cops pulled him off—long after the attack had ended and long after James Anderson's soul had left his body forever.

MONDAY, DECEMBER 29
MINNEAPOLIS, MINNESOTA

The tinny sound of a personalized ring tone playing Blue Öyster Cult's "Don't Fear the Reaper" emanated from Scott Ross's cell phone, filling the backseat of the taxi and letting him know that Jim Hicks was trying to get hold of him. When Scott had played the ring tone for Hicks earlier in the week, the older man had seemed less than enthused about being identified with the reaper. However, it seemed that Hicks spent much of his life being less than enthused about things, so Scott didn't worry much about his opinion.

Scott was about ten minutes away from the Minneapolis-St. Paul International Airport. He had booked a late-night flight back home to St. Louis after he and Hicks had agreed that Scott's presence might be needed to spur his team on a little bit. Five days had passed since any significant progress had been made, and Tara Walsh was getting unbearable on the phone. "Sounds like Daddy needs to get home and give the kids a talking-to," was Hicks's comment to Scott after the last phone conversation he had with the "overworked beauty queen."

Scott fumbled for his cell, in the process spilling his Yoo-hoo on the taxi's backseat. He quickly mopped up the mess with the corner of his canvas jacket before the driver could see.

"Yeah, Jim," he finally said, only to hear dead air on the other end of the line. He quickly hit Send twice to call back the missed number.

"Sorry, Jim, I was trying to find my phone and—"

"Shut up and listen! Tell your driver to turn around and take you to Holman Field in downtown St. Paul."

"Why? What's going on?"

"Do it first; then ask questions."

Scott mumbled something about Hicks and a wildebeest, then gave the driver the instructions. When he got back on the phone with Hicks, he said, "Okay, *mein führer*, it's done. You going to tell me what this is all about?"

"We've been hit again, Weatherman, and this one's bad. Platte River Stadium in Denver during *Monday Night Football*. At least four bombs and maybe as many as seven—the details are still coming in. Don't know the casualties yet, but it's going to be well into the four digits."

"No, don't tell me that, man!" Scott felt suddenly dizzy, and the Yoo-hoo soured in his stomach. Despite the cold, he cracked the window to get some air blowing on his face. After a few moments, he managed to ask, "Were any players hurt?"

"Why, are you worried about your fantasy team?"

Scott didn't even hear the sarcastic answer. "Were any Mustangs players hurt?"

"I didn't know you were such a fan."

"Jim! Answer me or I will personally lodge that phone in your throat! I need to know about Riley—Riley Covington, my old lieutenant. He plays linebacker for the Mustangs. I told you about him."

"Yeah, you're right; you did. Sorry, Scott, I didn't even make the connection. Listen, buddy, I know some players are down, but I don't know who or what condition they're in. Just get to Holman Field as quickly as you can. I've got one of our Gulfstreams waiting to take us to the scene."

Scott hung up, then leaned forward. "Listen, buddy," he said to the taxi driver. "I need to be at Holman fast—like, immediately."

He reached into his back pocket and pulled out his wallet. "I've got forty bucks here for you if you can get me there within fifteen minutes. But I'm going to subtract a dollar every time the speedometer drops below seventy-five miles per hour. Got it?" Scott also promised a full presidential pardon for any speeding tickets the driver might get along the way and was surprised that the man actually seemed to believe him.

When they finally arrived at the airfield, Scott paid the driver the fare plus a thirty-seven-dollar tip.

MONDAY, DECEMBER 29
INVERNESS TRAINING CENTER
ENGLEWOOD, COLORADO

Riley sat in front of his locker at Inverness Training Center. The uninjured Mustangs players had been loaded onto buses at the stadium twenty minutes after the attack and five minutes after the Predators had boarded their own buses, presumably to go back to their hotel. The Mustangs were now on lockdown in the practice facility until all the players and staff had been questioned and cleared by the authorities.

Inverness was a beehive of activity. Federal, state, and local authorities were all wanting their turns with the players. Members of the media had been admitted into the facility but then tucked away in the amphitheater-style conference room usually reserved for full-team meetings. Despite close supervision on the reporters, some had still managed to sneak out to go prowling for information.

Outside the facility, hordes of fans and well-wishers were already crowding the snowy streets, overflowing the parking lots at the training facility and the corporate center next door.

Word was that six Mustangs had been hospitalized and eight were missing. One of the missing was Sal Ricci. Riley had no clue what the Predators' casualties were—although he knew too well of at least one dead. He had wanted to stay at the stadium to help, but the option had not been given to him. So he sat at his locker, his mood ranging from rage to despair.

He looked up to see Travis Marshall tentatively approaching him. "Hey, Pach? Pach?"

Riley didn't say anything, but he assumed the look in his eyes was sending a clear message that he didn't want conversation.

Marshall visibly mustered his strength and pressed on. "I was just thinking that it might feel good for you to take a shower. I mean, you're still in your uniform and you're . . . well, you're covered in blood, man, which can't be good. And the steam—maybe it can help clear your head."

Part of Riley wanted to explode at Marshall, and for a second he thought he might. But then the darkness softened, and he let out a long sigh. "Yeah, you're right." Riley shook his head. "I still can't believe it."

"You and me both, Pach. You and me both."

"Did you ask around about Sal for me?" Riley asked hopefully.

"Yeah. Still no word."

Riley slowly nodded. "Well, keep an ear out. I've got three messages from Meg on my phone. I've got to call her back, but I have no clue what to say."

"Take a shower. Think it through. Something will come to you."

Riley stood up and pulled off his jersey and pads. The jersey had begun to stiffen from the blood. The same was true of his pants, and he gratefully dropped them in one of the large hampers.

As soon as he did, one of the FBI counterterrorism agents came and snatched the bloody uniform up. "Evidence," he said.

"Knock yourself out," Riley replied and walked out the back of the locker room and into the showers. He turned the shower on as hot as he could take it and stood under the water. He watched as the clean water hit his body, cascaded off, and ran brown down the drain.

Sal! Where are you, man? You've got a wife who loves you and a little girl who . . . who . . .

A stifled sob burst from Riley, but it was all he would allow himself. He began slowly pounding on the tile of the shower wall. As his anger built once more against the orchestrators of the day's tragedy, the speed and intensity of the blows gradually increased.

I'm coming to get you! I don't know who you are or where you live, but I'm coming. I'll smoke you out of your rat-hole cave or I'll sneak into your house in the middle of the night. I'm going to find you—and you will pay!

Riley stopped pounding and leaned with both his fists against the wall. *Lord, where were You? You could so easily have stopped this. It would have taken nothing for You to . . . to do something. And now what do I say to Meg? I don't understand it, Lord. And I don't understand You!*

Riley slammed off the water, grabbed a towel, and went back to his locker. As he was buttoning up his shirt, he spotted a man coming toward him.

He was the perfect stereotype of a G-man—dark suit, dark tie, white shirt, shoes shined to a blinding glare. Riley half expected him to say that he had been sent by J. Edgar Hoover himself.

"Mr. Covington? I'm agent Pat Kimminau of the FBI. We're going to need to question you in a little bit here, but first I have a couple of things to tell you. First, there's a Scott Ross from Homeland Security Counterterrorism Division who called for you while you were in the shower. He's on his way to Denver and wants to see you. He asked if you would be available to meet with him."

"Scott's coming? Yeah, of course. Tell him I'll be around."

"Second, we've found Sal Ricci. I . . . he's . . . I'm sorry, Mr. Covington."

Riley kept his stone face for the agent, but inside part of his heart broke. "Tell me."

"Well, he was right where you said he might be—over by the turf manager's office. Truthfully, there wasn't much left of anyone around that area. Sorry; I don't mean to sound callous."

Riley indicated for him to continue with a nod of his head.

"We found enough of his jersey and pads to positively identify his presence. The ME will have to confirm it with DNA testing, but that could take months. The scene is . . ." The agent paused, clearly worried that the graphic description might be too much for the athlete to stomach.

Riley looked up, silently imploring him to say it and get it over with.

"Well, it's a mess, and it's gonna be difficult to separate the tissue of the victims. I'm sorry, Mr. Covington."

Riley remained quiet for a moment, trying to keep control of his voice. "Has anyone called his wife yet?"

"No. We were told that you had requested to call her if we confirmed the worst."

"Yeah, okay," Riley said, mentally drifting away from the conversation. "Thanks."

"If there's anything else we can—"

"No. Fine. Thanks." Riley dismissed the agent with an absent-minded wave of his hand. His thoughts were completely with what he was going to say to Meg. *How do you tell a woman that her whole life has just fallen apart?*

"Riley . . . hey, Pach."

Riley looked up. Travis Marshall was back with Garrett Widnall and a couple of other players.

Marshall had tears in his eyes. He continued, "We heard about Sal. I know you're planning on calling Meg. We were wondering if we could pray with you before you do."

"Yeah, sure; thanks."

They all gathered around Riley and laid their hands on his shoulders. Marshall began praying, but Riley was only half listening. His sorrow and rage were becoming more defined now—his sorrow taking on the faces of Meg and Alessandra. His rage was less defined, but whoever the shadowed face belonged to, he was wearing a *dishdasha* and had a *smagh* folded on his head.

Riley knew he should be paying attention to the prayers, but his heart wasn't in it. He patiently endured the men's words and was relieved to hear the final *amen*.

"Thanks, guys; I really appreciate it," he said to them, forcing a smile as they each said their "Anything you need, let me know" and "Just holler; I'm only two lockers down" to him.

Riley picked up his cell phone and stared at it, rehearsing in his mind what he was going to say. He could feel a bunch of eyes on him, so he moved into the taping area and leaned against one of the tables.

Part of him wanted to abdicate the responsibility and leave the notification to the police. That would be so much easier.

As he stood there, his eyes wandered to the words printed on a large plaque on the taping room wall: "You can easily judge the character of a man by how he treats those who can do nothing for him." *Meg can do nothing for me right now,* he thought, *but I can probably do a lot for her—starting with allowing her to hear about Sal from a friend instead of from a stranger. But what in the world do I say?*

He was so intent in his thoughts that when the phone started vibrating in his hand, he almost dropped it. He looked at the caller ID—*Sal Home.* He drew in a deep breath and answered.

MONDAY, DECEMBER 29
PARKER, COLORADO

The last hour had been a nightmare for Meg Ricci. She had been watching the game when the broadcast had suddenly cut out. An ESPN logo appeared on the screen, and Meg assumed that they were having technical difficulties. She reached for another freshly laundered baby blanket to fold as the picture cut back in, showing ESPN studios.

"Ladies and gentlemen, we have word that there has been an explosion of some sort in Platte River Stadium. The report is that it took place somewhere in the . . . Wait . . . I'm just getting information that there has been a second explosion. By all indications, this appears to be an intentional attack. . . ."

The blanket Meg held floated to the floor. Her eyes locked on the television screen, but she no longer heard the words that were being said. Panic began welling up in her. Her breath was getting faster and faster. She could feel a scream building inside her, but it couldn't find an outlet. She reached for the remote but then pulled her hand back. She reached for the telephone but couldn't think of whom to call.

The phone rang, releasing the scream that was in her. She lunged for the cordless, knocking over her stack of neatly folded blankets. Picking up the receiver, she couldn't think of what to say.

"Meg? Meg, are you there, baby?" It was Meg's mom, calling from Fort Collins.

"Mom? Did you hear? Were you watching the game?"

"Yes, honey. Dad and I were watching. Are you okay?"

"Mom, what about Sal? What should I do?"

"Sweetheart, this is Dad. Don't do anything; we're on our way. We'll be there in an hour."

"Dad, I don't know what to do. Should I go to the stadium?"

"Meg, listen to me. Stay right where you are. We're coming, and we'll figure it out when we get there. Promise me you won't go anywhere."

"Okay, Daddy. But hurry. Please hurry!"

Her mom took the phone back. "Meg, we'll have our cell phone on. Call us with any updates. I love you, sweetie."

"I love you, too, Mom."

As Meg hung up the phone, the pounding on the front door finally registered. She ran to the door and opened it. Her neighbor Jill Walton came bursting in and wrapped her arms around Meg's neck. Meg immediately broke down into gut-wrenching sobs.

After several minutes, Meg allowed Jill to lead her to the couch. "Oh, Jill, I'm so scared."

"Of course you are. Have you been able to talk to anyone yet?"

"Only my folks."

"Well, let's just start dialing until we get ahold of someone. I'm sure everyone's okay."

"You're probably right. But I need to talk to Sal. I've got to hear his voice."

Jill picked up the phone and passed it to her friend. "I'm going to go make some tea. You start calling."

Two cups of tea later, Meg was still dialing. The TV continued to give reports, and she alternated between wanting to hear more information from the news channels and muting the announcer when the updates became too overwhelming. Her fear kept increasing as time went on. "Why doesn't anyone answer? I've tried Sal. I've tried Riley. I've tried the main Mustangs number." A small cry came from upstairs. "Oh, that's Aly. I'll be back in a minute."

"Stay right where you are. Let me go check on her. You keep dialing those numbers."

"Thanks, Jill." As her friend went to the stairs, Meg hit speed dial 1.

After four rings, Sal's voice came on. *"Hey, it's me. Leave a message."*

Meg hung up and hit speed dial 5, praying that maybe Riley would pick up.

After two rings, Riley answered. "Hey, Meg."

///////////////////////

"Riley, thank heaven you're all right! I've been trying you and Sal all night! Is Sal with you? Can you put him on the phone?"

Riley started to speak, then stopped. Finally he said, "Meg, I . . . well . . . Meg, Sal's gone."

"He's already on his way home? Why wouldn't he have called me back? That's so—"

"Meg, that's not what I—"

"—typical of—"

"Meg, stop!"

The silence on Meg's end of the phone was broken only by a barely audible "Oh no."

///////////////////////

Please don't say it, Riley, Meg silently pleaded. *Please don't say it!*

"Meg . . . Sal's dead. I . . . he . . . It was the last of the bombs. He didn't even feel it coming. Oh, Meg, I'm so sorry."

Meg dropped to her knees. The phone fell on the floor, knocking the batteries out of the back. Her sobs started long and soft and gradually increased in speed and intensity.

Jill, who was carrying Alessandra down the stairs, saw Meg, saw the phone, and ran to her friend. She put the baby on the floor nearby and enveloped Meg in her arms.

Alessandra crawled to the disabled phone and picked up one of the batteries. She examined it, then noticed her mama and Jill crying. She watched them for a few moments, and then she began to cry too.

/////////////////////

Riley tried calling Meg back, but she didn't answer. He left a message saying that he would call again in a few hours and would like to stop by.

As he stood leaning on the taping bench, the darkness that he had been descending into got deeper. And as that darkness led him further and further down, he willingly followed.

TUESDAY, DECEMBER 30
FEDERAL BUREAU OF INVESTIGATION,
   DENVER FIELD OFFICE
DENVER, COLORADO

The failed bomber sat in the chair and stared at
his reflection with his one eye that was not quite
swollen shut.

The entire left side of the man's face was dis-
figured by multiple fractures from when the off-
duty Denver policeman had slammed his face into
the metal railing. The cotton wadding in his nose
forced him to breathe through his mouth, which
he noisily did. His hands and feet were firmly
cuffed to the chair on which he sat.

On the other side of the two-way mirror stood
Jim Hicks, Scott Ross, and Division Chief Stanley
Porter. The DC was in his usual foul mood and had
already chewed Scott out for wearing Birkenstock
sandals on the job—especially in the middle of
winter. They were waiting for the arrival of the
interpreter, and with each minute that passed,
Porter's mood grew visibly darker.

Finally the door swung open and a woman
walked in.

Scott waited for Porter to launch into her,
but Hicks beat him to the punch.

"Khadi! How you doing? I haven't seen you since . . . when?"

"Two years ago in Nicosia. You were going in, and I was coming out."

"You're exactly right! Good to see you."

"Good to see you, too," Khadi replied, turning her attention to the other men.

Hicks made the introductions. "Khadijah Faroughi, this is Midwest Division Chief Stanley Porter."

"We've met," Porter said, ignoring Khadi's outstretched hand.

"Charmed," Khadi said, pulling her hand back and turning toward Scott.

"And this is Scott Ross," Hicks continued, "best analyst I've ever come across and not too bad on the ops side either."

Scott couldn't immediately place the woman's name, but he was sure he'd heard it before. In any case, he had not been able to take his eyes off Khadi from the moment she'd walked through the door. A classic Persian beauty, her brown eyes and jet-black hair richly offset her light olive skin.

Scott quickly determined that this was a woman he wanted to get to know better. "Faroughi. That's Iranian, isn't it?" Scott held out his hand and gave her his biggest smile.

Khadi apparently was used to getting this reaction from guys. She gave Scott's hand a quick, formal shake, then looked at Hicks. "Wow, Jim, you said this one was quick," she said sarcastically. Then, looking at Scott's feet, she said, "Cute sandals. The wool socks are a particularly nice touch."

Scott felt his face redden, and for one of the first times in his life he had nothing to say.

Suddenly Khadi's name clicked into place in Scott's mind, and a mischevious grin spread across his face. "Wait a second . . . Khadi . . . You're 'Khadi with a *D*'! I've heard about you. Don't worry; I'll be super-extra sure not to call you Katie—like, with a *t*. Rumor is a guy once lost a limb making that mistake!"

This time it was Khadi's turn to redden. She started to say something, then turned instead to Hicks.

"Well," Hicks said, "since we're all through spreading the love, let me get you caught up on the situation. We've got exactly one suspect. He was taken down by a kid with a tray of hot chocolate just before he could detonate his bomb. We've got the kid in another room."

"Must have been a pretty full tray by the looks of him," Khadi said.

"Most of what you see there was done by an enthusiastic off-duty member of the DPD. Our meds stitched up his head and lip, but I don't think they were overly concerned about future scarring."

"Has he talked yet?"

"No, we'll be the first professionals to speak to him."

"Well, let's do it," Khadi said, moving toward the door.

"Hold it!" Porter's voice came booming across the room. "We're going to set some ground rules before you take a step in there."

"Ground rules?" Hicks shot back. "*You* are going to give *me* ground rules? Tell you what—I've got some ground rules for you. How about you keep your little rules to yourself and let me do my job?"

"Listen, bruiser, I saw how you 'did your job' with Kurshumi. Thanks to you, we're going to have to bury him so deep inside of Gitmo that he'll only see the light of day every other Ramadan!"

"So he got a little cut. It'll make it easier for him to sip his cider through a straw. We got the information, didn't we?"

"Yeah, we sure did. But this ain't 'Nam, and this boy ain't Charlie. The rules are different now, and I'm the one who's making them. And my rule number one is this: you are not going into that room with that knife strapped to your leg."

Hicks advanced on Porter until they were nose-to-nose. "Are you going to take it from me?"

"Back off, Hicks, or I'll bust you down so far you'll be shining Ross's shoes—if he'd ever wear them."

Hicks held Porter's eyes long enough to make his point; then he took a step back.

Porter held out his hand. "No knifey, no talkey."

Hicks slowly bent over and pulled the MKIII from its sheath. As he straightened up, he locked eyes with Porter again. Then, in a swift movement, he brought the blade rushing down toward Porter's hand. At the last second, he rotated the knife and slammed the grip into the waiting flesh.

Porter never even flinched.

Hicks moved toward the door. "Let's go, Khadi."

"One more thing," Porter called out.

Hicks wheeled around. "What now? You want my belt? my keys?"

"No, I want you to take Ross in with you. Consider him my little monitor. Ross, if anything gets out of hand, I'm holding you personally responsible."

Scott saw Hicks decide it was senseless to argue anymore.

Hicks sighed. "Fine. C'mon, Weatherman. Looks like you're going to learn the fine art of persuasion."

TUESDAY, DECEMBER 30
I-25, SOUTHERN COLORADO

Oneness. Wholeness. Completeness. With the first explosion that had rocked Platte River Stadium, Hakeem's doppelgänger had died. Now he was free to live as a single, united person. The elation he felt was almost more than he could stand.

He rolled down the car window and let the 75 mph arctic blast hit him full in the face. He yelled out into the darkness, "I am Hakeem Qasim, from the honorable family of Qasim! Fear me! Fear my family! Fear my people!"

Quickly the rushing air became too much for him, and he rolled the window back up, switched on the heated seats, and cranked the heater to full blast. He laughed at his impetuousness. More emotions than he knew what to do with.

He felt the brass coin hanging from his neck, now icy to the touch. *Uncle, I have done it! Thank you for giving me the strength to take revenge.*

The late-model Lexus RX 350 hummed southward along I-25. The SUV was the last luxury he had allowed himself from his old life. His only disappointment was that the man who had kept it for him the three weeks since he had bought it had been a smoker. But Hakeem had a hard time feeling any anger. Five hours ago, the man had become *shahid*—the third of the seven martyrs at Platte River Stadium.

But there weren't seven martyrs, were there? Hakeem cursed

the second man, whose bomb had failed to go off. If he had been a coward or had been killed before completing his mission, Hakeem hoped Allah would deal with him terribly. If he had been caught, then it could mean trouble. Either way, Hakeem knew he had better keep watching his back.

He saw another mile marker and calculated the time till he arrived in Las Cruces, New Mexico, at just under four hours. There he would look for the Holiday Inn Express on South Valley Drive. After parking, some "friends" would approach him, give him a forged American passport, and then usher him across the border into Mexico. This was the only part of the plan that made him nervous—mainly because it was the only part of the plan that was out of his control.

Once in Mexico, Hakeem would be taken south to Mexico City. There he would use another forged passport—this one from the *Estados Unidos Mexicanos*—to board a flight across the ocean to where he would receive a hero's welcome. He couldn't wait to get home and reexperience his youth—the taste of the food his mother had cooked, the smell of the men after a long day's work, the feel of a prayer rug under his knees.

Hakeem knew the celebration would be short-lived. His goal was not to go back and live a hero's life. He was only going back to reconnect and regroup. Soon it would be time to return to America; there was still work to be done here.

/////////////////////////

Hicks, Scott, and Khadi stood in the hall outside the door to the interrogation room.

"Remind me to scratch Porter off my Christmas list," Hicks grumbled.

"Yeah; like I warned you, he's a class-A horse's . . . uh . . . patoot," Scott said, changing course midsentence on Khadi's behalf.

For her part, Khadi did nothing to acknowledge Scott's act of gallantry.

Scott continued. "Obviously, Porter and the higher-ups want no new marks on this guy. Probably so they can splash his picture across the media outlets like a prize trout on the cover of *Field & Stream*. So, since I'm obviously new to this, is this a situation where you would consider something like waterboarding?"

"Could be," Hick replied. "But I'm not in the mood for the mess. I've got something else in mind. It's a little process I learned from Amos Tsarfati, a friend of mine in the Mossad. I spent a few weeks with him not long ago on a sort of technique exchange program. You ever heard of 'shaking'?"

"Shaking?" Khadi jumped in. "Isn't that dangerous? I remember some Palestinian guy getting killed during a shaking. As a result, the Israeli Supreme Court banned it. It's been out of their playbook since '99."

"Has it? Guess Amos didn't get the memo."

"I've heard of shaking, but I guess I'm not sure exactly what it means," Scott said. He wasn't thrilled about the direction things seemed to be heading.

"What does it sound like?" Hicks asked.

"Like grabbing hold of someone and shaking him," Scott answered.

"Bingo!"

"But can just shaking a person really get him to talk?"

"Trust me, when I'm done this guy won't be talking—he'll be singing. Khadi, I want you right next to me, so you don't miss a word he might mutter. Weatherman, you find a corner and enjoy the show."

As they walked through the door, Khadi gave an inquisitive look to Scott. "Weatherman?"

"It's a long story."

Hicks strode across the room, sat on the corner of the table, and pushed the prisoner's chair back with his foot. He stared at the would-be martyr for more than a minute. The man defiantly stared back. Then Hicks uttered one word: *"Al-Hazz?"*

Scott recognized the Arabic term for "shaking," and he saw a brief flash of fear in the prisoner's eyes. Almost immediately, the man regained his composure.

Hicks leaned closer until he was less than a foot away from the man's face. *"Al-Hazz?"*

This time the man tried to spit his defiance into Hicks's face, but his mouth was so swollen that it mostly dropped on his chin.

Hicks merely smiled and nodded. "*Al-Hazz* it is." He stood and grabbed the man's collar. He called back to Scott while Khadi gave a simultaneous interpretation to the prisoner, "Mr. Ross, the goal of *al-Hazz* is to shake long enough that it causes severe pain but not so long that it causes lethal intracranial bleeding. It's a fine line that admittedly I've never quite gotten the hang of."

Hicks began violently shaking the man backward and forward. The man's head flopped like a rag doll's. Hicks continued to shake him for fifteen seconds, and then abruptly stopped. The man's brain, however, continued its movement for another moment. That, combined with the damage already done to his face and head, caused the man to scream out in pain.

"Who is your contact?" Hicks yelled in the man's face as Khadi translated the words in his ear.

The man gradually got control of himself, but his head continued lolling up and down. Slowly, he raised his eyes to meet Hicks's. Again he futilely tried to spit in Hicks's face.

Hicks grabbed the man's collar and began shaking him again. This time the man's screams began early on and continued far beyond the twenty seconds of violence.

"Who is your contact?" Hicks repeated.

Now when he tried spitting, the terrorist could only weakly puff out air.

Hicks grabbed the man's face in his right hand, making sure that his thumb pressed hard into the man's shattered left cheek. "You're going to tell me what I want to know. It's simply a question of how much you're going to make me work."

Scott shifted from one foot to the other as he watched this from his little corner of the room. He wasn't squeamish. Less than two weeks ago he had pinned a man's hand to a bench with his knife. He knew there were things that needed to be done to get this all-important information. But that didn't mean he needed to stand here and watch it. Just because he was going to eat a burger didn't mean he needed to watch them slaughter the cow. He slipped out the door and began walking down the hallway.

Porter stepped out of the viewing room and yelled after him, "Ross, get back here! I told you to stay in that room!"

Scott had had it. He was finished watching Hicks torture the suspect. He needed some air, and no amount of yelling or threatening was going to make him turn around. Over his shoulder, he displayed a hand gesture that expressed his disagreement with Porter's suggestion. He regretted it immediately, but there was no taking it back. He continued walking, slowly picking up his pace, until he burst through the front door.

Immediately frost built up on his mustache from his breath as he tilted his head into the falling snow. The icy air bit his flesh and constricted his lungs. He stood there not moving for a long time as the snow fell through the straps on his sandals, coating his socks.

When he could stand the cold no longer, he walked back inside, certain he was about to face the wrath of a very angry man.

CHAPTER EIGHTEEN

TUESDAY, DECEMBER 30
PARKER, COLORADO

The taxi driver waited to take off until the front door was open and Riley had turned around to wave—an unexpected gesture from a cabbie at 2:30 a.m.

Riley hadn't trusted himself to drive home after everything he had been through, but he hadn't wanted to get involved in a discussion with a cabdriver about the day's events, either. The guy had been very compassionate about what had happened and seemed genuinely concerned about how the players were doing. Riley had given only monosyllabic responses to the man's questions, doing his best to show the driver that he wasn't interested in a conversation. He tried to convince himself that he was blowing the guy off because he was too tired to talk. But deep down, Riley knew his interest in communication had died as soon as he saw the name on the driver's cab license—Hassan Muhammed.

Riley dragged himself through the house. Every muscle in his body ached, and his head pounded from exhaustion. Still, he knew it would be a while before he was able to fall asleep.

Walking into his great room, Riley flipped

a switch on the wall that ignited his fireplace, then dropped into his favorite recliner. The coolness of the leather against his skin briefly eased the tension in his body. He reached for the phone to get his messages, then thought better of it and grabbed the television remote instead. He figured all the people that he needed to talk to he had already contacted—Mom and Dad, Grandpa, Pastor Tim, and Meg—and the rest of the messages would just be media. About an hour ago, Meg's dad had called Riley's cell phone to tell him that she was sleeping with the help of a sedative; he had promised Riley an update in the morning.

Riley pointed the remote at the television, then put it back down without turning the TV on. All the stations would be carrying stories on the attack. As much as he wanted the details of what had happened, he knew he wasn't ready yet.

He stared at the flames, wishing for the hundredth time that he had installed a wood-burning fireplace instead of this gas one. The pale glow of the blue flame did absolutely nothing to lighten his mood.

The question that dominated his mind was, what could he do about what happened tonight? He hadn't asked to be drawn into this fight. In fact, he had left the Air Force Special Operations Command so he wouldn't have to fight anymore. His days of ringing ears and dodging projectiles were supposed to be over.

But now they had brought the fight back to him. They attacked his people. They killed his friend.

How many children had been orphaned today? How many people died? How many would be crippled or in pain for the rest of their lives? All because one group of deluded terrorists wanted to make a point!

Lord, where were You? You know I always try to trust You. I want to believe that You're in control. And then something like this happens, and what am I supposed to think? One bomb after another after another—and the screams! Oh, God, the screams . . . Listen, I know that You are there—I do. I mean, this doesn't make me doubt Your existence. I've seen too much evidence of You in my own life. In Afghanistan alone, You proved Yourself over and over. But . . . I don't know . . . I guess this whole thing really makes me question Your character. I mean, c'mon, Lord, You saw what

happened! You saw the disembodied souls flying up out of that stadium!
One move from You, and it would have been done, over with, or it never
even would have happened to begin with. Pastor Tim would tell me that
You were there, that You've got a plan, that You'll work everything out. I
guess deep down I believe that . . . but honestly, I'm not ready to go down
that deep yet. I'm sorry, Lord; I know You say that vengeance is Yours, but
right now I'm ready to get a piece of that action.

Riley got up and walked to his finished basement. All along the
walls were trophies from various hunting trips—a moose, a gemsbok,
a blue wildebeest, and various other horned and antlered animals.
In the corner stood an eight-foot brown bear, an unexpected visitor
Riley had encountered while hunting elk in Wyoming.

Beyond the far end of the room lay a second, smaller room,
which contained a large safe. Riley now opened that safe to reveal
his collection of large and small firearms.

His eyes moved across the various shotguns and hunting rifles.
Then they settled on the M4 carbine—a going-away present from
his alpha team. "In case you ever need it," they had laughed. He
reached in and lifted the assault rifle from its rack. As it always did,
the lightness of the weapon surprised him. How could so much killing power be compacted into five and a half pounds of metal? He
spotted a loaded clip but left it untouched. *Let's not get carried away,*
Kemosabe.

Riley carried the rifle back into the trophy room and sat down
on an overstuffed chair, placing the weapon across his lap. It was
hard to weigh his options when he didn't know what all his options
were. He was still in the air force reserves and could easily re-up with
them. However, the chances of his getting assigned to hunt these
killers down were just this side of nonexistent, going that route.

He could go off on his own trying to track these people. But
that, too, was a less-than-brilliant idea. He could see the headlines
now: "Vigilante Linebacker Sentenced to Life in Prison for Killing
Wrong Man at 7-Eleven."

There had to be a way. He hadn't picked this fight, but after
what they had done, there was no way he was going to turn the
other cheek.

Riley leaned his head back and let his mind wander to the

moment when he would find the man responsible for this attack. He had him pressed against a wall with a knife to his throat. The man was begging for mercy. Riley pushed the blade up against the man's neck and—

RING! RING!

Riley awoke and stumbled to the bar to grab the phone, grumbling about people calling in the middle of the night. Then he glanced at the atomic clock hanging on the wall—10:30 a.m. *I've been asleep seven hours,* he thought.

Looking at the caller ID, Riley saw that it was his grandpa's cell phone. "Hey, Gramps," he answered. "How're you doing?"

"I'd be doing a lot better if you'd open your front door and let me in. I've been knocking for five minutes, and my saggy old backside is about to get frostbitten—heaven knows that wouldn't be a pretty sight."

TUESDAY, DECEMBER 30
FEDERAL BUREAU OF INVESTIGATION, DENVER FIELD OFFICE
DENVER, COLORADO

Scott was prepared for a shredding. You couldn't give your division chief—especially one like Stanley Porter—the single-finger salute and expect to waltz back in like nothing had happened.

Sure enough, Porter was waiting for him in the hall as he walked toward the interrogation rooms.

"Listen, Stan," Scott started, "I—"

"First of all, shut up. And second of all, it has been and always will be Mr. Porter to you. Third, I've got something I need you to do. Down in IR-110 we've got the hot chocolate kid. I'm not going to send Hicks down there, because he'd probably slice the kid's lips off or give him a full metal colonoscopy. You're . . . *odd* enough that you might be able to make a connection with him. Find out everything he saw and get me a full report. I'm going to stay here and make sure that your friend doesn't start attaching electrical wires to various parts of this guy's body."

"Yes, sir. I'd be glad to go talk with him. Thank you, sir."

"Listen, Ross, we all have times when this job gets to us. I understand that. But just so you know, if you ever again do what you just did to me, I will personally snap that finger off your hand, dip it in ink, and use it to sign your exit papers. You understand?"

"Understood, sir. It won't happen again."

Scott turned and walked down the hall, trying to get the image of Porter's threat out of his mind. He quickly ducked into the break room and grabbed a few of the Yoo-hoo bottles he had stashed away upon arrival, then stepped into a viewing room.

Inside the room, a female CTD agent whose name Scott couldn't remember was talking to an FBI agent. Scott interrupted their conversation. "Hey, I'm Scott Ross. DC Porter sent me down to talk with the kid. What can you tell me about him?"

The CTD agent gave Scott a visual once-over and answered in a bored voice, "His name is Todd Penner. Twenty years old. No record. Scared to death. He's a little banged up from the ordeal."

As she spoke, Scott checked Todd out through the two-way mirror. He was fidgeting, and his eyes kept darting around the room.

"Kid's got *nice guy* written all over his worried face," Scott said. "Either of you take the time to tell him he's not in trouble?"

"We were told not to say anything to him until someone came to talk to him."

"Brilliant," Scott said sarcastically. "Did you at least offer him some coffee?"

"How could we do that, sir," the CTD countered in the same tone, "without talking to him?"

"Great point, agent. Way to think out of the box. The kid's a hero, and you let him sit there thinking he's going to prison. That's using the old noggin." Scott walked out of the room shaking his head.

He paused for a moment outside the door to the interrogation room in order to change his demeanor. Then he burst through the door and addressed Todd like he had just stumbled across a long-lost friend. "Todd! How you doing, buddy? Name's Scott Ross." Scott shook Todd's hand, then reached into one of the leg pockets of his cargo pants, pulled out a Yoo-hoo, and dropped it on the table in front of the surprised kid. He then grabbed a second bottle out of the other side pocket, cracked it open, plopped down in the opposite chair, kicked his feet up on the table, and tilted his chair back.

"So, Todd, how does it feel to be a hero?"

"Really, Mr. Ross, I didn't know what I was doing. I didn't mean to hurt . . . How does it feel to be a what?"

"A hero—and it's Scott."

"I thought I was in trouble, sitting in this room for so long."

Scott glared at the two-way mirror as Todd's eyes welled up with relief.

Todd twisted the cap off his Yoo-hoo and chugged about half of it down before coming up for air. "I figured I was being charged with assault with a deadly weapon or something."

Scott laughed. "Yeah, I've tasted stadium hot chocolate—I can see your point. What made you think of chucking that thing at the dude's head?"

"I have no clue. It was either instinct or God. Hey, Mr. Ross—Scott—is there any way I could let my parents know that I'm okay?"

"You mean they haven't allowed you to phone home?" Scott quickly slid his cell phone across the table. "Your parents have to be worried sick. Take all the time you need."

Todd grabbed the phone and punched in a number. It barely had time to ring before it was picked up on the other end. "Dad? . . . Yeah, I know. I'm so sorry. . . . No, I'm fine; I'm fine. . . . No, really. . . . Yeah, it was, Dad—absolutely terrible, unbelievable. . . . I'm in a questioning room at some government building. . . . No, I don't know how long I'll be here."

Scott again glared at the unseen faces beyond the glass.

"Dad, will you let Jamie know I'm all right? . . . She was? How long ago did she leave? . . . Well, if you could call her, I'd appreciate it. By the way, Dad, they're calling me a hero. . . . This government guy. He comes in and says, 'How does it feel to be a hero?' . . . Well, I probably can't get into it right now; I should probably go. But I'll tell you all about it later. . . . Yeah, I can hear them in the background."

Todd laughed at something—probably the cheering of his family that Scott could hear all the way across the room.

"Tell them I said to go to bed—it's a school night. . . . Thanks, Dad; I love you, too. Tell the same to Mom and to Jamie. . . . Bye."

Scott remained staring at the glass another minute while he heard Todd blow his nose and expel a couple of deep breaths, trying to regain composure. Finally Todd said, "Thanks, Mr. Ross."

"Hey, buddy, no problem. I'm sorry it took so long. The fam had to be scared to death."

"Oh, man! They were terrified."

"So, who's Jamie?"

"Jamie? She's the girl I'm going to ask to marry me in a few days."

"Really? Congratulations! That's awesome."

"Thanks. She's pretty incredible."

"So, Todd, is it all right if we get back to you giving the bad guy a cocoa beaning upside the head? You feeling up to talking?"

"Sure, sure, Mr. Ross—Scott. Like I said, I don't know what made me throw the tray. I heard the first explosion, and everyone around me was completely quiet. Like we were all trying to figure out what happened."

"What made you notice the bomber?"

"I don't know. I think it was because he was the only person who was looking the wrong way—you know, up at the crowd instead of down toward the field. Then the guy holds up a football in one hand and something else in the other. What freaked me out was that there was a wire connecting the thing in the one hand to the football."

"A wire to the football? Interesting. . . . Did he say anything?"

"Yeah, he did. I've been sitting here trying to piece together what he said. It was something like, 'America' . . . uh . . . 'America, because I've come to your' something—'stores' or 'shores,' I think. Then he said something like, 'Prepare to meet the wrath of . . .' And that's when the tray hit him. Scott, are you okay? Mr. Ross?"

But Scott waved him silent. His mind had slipped into the zone. The terrorist's statement made no sense—'because I've come to your shores.' He processed the statement, mentally comparing it to other code words and chatter he had picked up. Nothing. *Run through the statement again—'because I've come to your shores.' C'mon, what's missing? An accent! Try it with an accent—'because I've come to your shores.' Be-cause. Be cause. The Cause.*

"Todd, are you sure of the words? Could he have said something like, 'The Cause has come to your shores'?"

"Sure, I guess. I was a little wigged out."

"Dude, you're awesome! They'll be throwing parades for you! I gotta go talk with some folks. I'm sure we'll get you out of here soon." Scott reached deep into his cargo pockets again and pulled out another Yoo-hoo, sliding it across the table. "Is there anything else I can get you while you're waiting?"

"Well, I didn't really want to mention it again. I know so many other people are really hurting. But I'm thinking I should have somebody look at this." Todd lifted his shirt revealing an entire left side that was black and blue. "I think I busted a few ribs when the crowd was pushing down on us. I should probably make sure nothing inside is messed up."

"Did you tell anyone else about this?"

"Well, yeah, the lady who brought me in here. She said that I could talk to a medical person after I'd been debriefed."

Scott looked toward the two-way glass, his face a mixture of anger and disgust. "Two minutes! That's the amount of time you have to get a doctor in here. You understand?" Turning back to Todd, he said, "I'm so sorry, buddy. We'll get someone in here right away. I gotta go, but I'll be back to check on you when I can. You all right here?"

"Yeah. Thanks, Scott."

Scott burst out the door and headed down the hallway toward the other interrogation room. Suddenly, Hicks bolted out of the other door. They met halfway between the two rooms, and both said in unison, "It's the Cause!"

/////////////////////

Riley ran upstairs and hurriedly turned the locks on the front door. "Grandpa, I am so sorry. I fell asleep in the basement and didn't hear a thing."

His grandpa didn't answer at first. Then with a wry look he

nodded toward Riley's left side. "You being a little overcautious there, son?"

Riley looked down and gave an embarrassed grin. Without thinking about it, he had slung the M4 over his shoulder before running to open the door. "You know those media types. Gotta find ways to discourage them." He slid the rifle off and set it by the doorway, then gave his grandpa a huge hug. He ushered him into the great room, which was now well heated from the fire that Riley had left on all night, and settled him into his recliner. "Coffee?"

"You gotta ask an air force man if he wants coffee?"

Riley laughed as he went into the kitchen to put on a pot of Costa Rican Tarrazu. "So, what are you doing here, Gramps?"

"Well, your dad and I talked, and we figured that after what happened, you'd have revenge on your mind. We thought it best that one of us come out to talk with you. I drew the assignment—him being a navy guy and all."

Riley stood in the kitchen and leaned on the cold granite of his center island. "You looking to talk . . . or to talk me out of it?"

"Just talk, son; just talk. I learned long ago that I couldn't talk you or your dad out of anything. So, your wandering around strapped with an M4 makes me think that we weren't too far off in our assessment."

"Grandpa, I've never seen anything like it—not in Afghanistan, not anywhere. I had my hands inside a guy's body trying to stop the bleeding *as he died*. And the worst part? I know somewhere people are dancing and celebrating what happened last night. What would you do? I mean, if you still had a chance to make these murderers pay, could you stay home?"

Grandpa took a few moments to sort through what he was going to say. Finally he looked Riley in the eye. "Can't say as I could, Riley. I've told you before that I'm much less concerned about what you do than I am with what's in your heart. If you go after these guys out of hatred or revenge, it'll eventually tear you up inside."

Riley walked over with two cups of thick, black coffee—no time to dainty up your joe in the field.

"Mmmm, strong stuff," Grandpa said appreciatively.

"I remember what you always said: 'It's not coffee unless you can stand a spoon in it.'" Together they chuckled softly. "Listen, I know that what's in my heart is not good right now. But if hate is what it takes to get me motivated to get back in the game, then so be it."

They both sat silently, looking at the floor and sipping their coffee.

Finally, Riley broke the silence. "I know, I know. That's messed-up thinking. It's just . . . where was God last night? Where was He when people were getting blown to pieces and getting trampled? Where was He when I sent Sal away to his death? Why didn't He stop me from killing my best friend? I mean, what kind of God is that? Where's His love? Where's His compassion? Where's His power?"

Grandpa took a minute before answering, then said, "Riley, I learned long ago that there're two kinds of people in this world. One kind looks at the circumstances and lets them define God. The other kind looks at God and lets Him define the circumstances. What do you *know* to be true about God?"

"I hear you. God and I had this conversation about seven hours ago."

Again silence.

"What do you think I should do, Grandpa?"

"What do *you* think you should do?"

Riley heaved a big sigh. "I think I need to get my heart right. Then I think I need to find out what I can do to help bring these murderers down."

"Spoken like a true Covington, son."

TUESDAY, DECEMBER 30
FEDERAL BUREAU OF INVESTIGATION,
    DENVER FIELD OFFICE
DENVER, COLORADO

"Does Porter know about this?" Scott Ross asked Jim Hicks. The simultaneous discovery of the Cause being at the root of the attacks had both men excited and anxious to tell somebody.

"No. Seems he left the viewing room about ten minutes ago when Secretary Moss arrived."

"The Secretary of Homeland Security is here? Yeah, I guess this would be big enough to get the weasel out of his cushy office." Scott grabbed a passing agent. "Any idea where the SHS and the DC are holed up?"

"Main conference room." Scott's expectant stare prompted the man to continue. "Okay, you know the main war room you passed as you came to the interrogation area? It's right in the middle of that."

"Gotcha. Thanks." Turning to Hicks, Scott said, "Well, shall we?"

Hicks gave his affirmation with his feet.

"I'll take that as a yes," Scott muttered, hurrying after him.

They entered the war room and found the

conference room just where the agent had said. It was a large box-like structure in the center of a busy, open space filled with ringing telephones and low-walled cubicles. There was only one door into the conference room, and two dark-suited Secret Service agents were positioned in front of it.

Hicks approached the door with Scott in tow. "Jim Hicks, CTD," he said, showing his badge. "This is Scott Ross, also with CTD. We need to see Secretary Moss."

"One moment, please," said the agent on the left, who then proceeded to whisper something into his wrist comm.

Ten seconds later, the door buzzed open and a very impatient Hicks entered with Scott close behind.

The light in the room was slightly dimmed, and a large flat-screen television was visible—turned on but blank at the moment—in an open cabinet to their left. Standing perpendicular before them was a long conference table surrounded by large, soft swivel chairs. Eight of the chairs were filled. Scott recognized a few of their occupants from Internet pictures, including Secretary of Homeland Security Dwayne Moss, who sat at the head of the table, and Undersecretary Gregory Blackmon to his right. Stanley Porter was seated to Moss's left. Also present were FBI Director Edward Castillo, Western District CTD Chief Patty Wallace, and three other people whom Scott didn't know.

Without waiting to be introduced, Scott blurted out, "Mr. Secretary, we've figured out the organization behind this attack! It's a terrorist group called the Cause!"

"They already know," said Hicks, who had been staring at the blank television since they walked in.

Scott felt the heat of embarrassment flush through his body.

Hicks continued, "You guys got a tape, didn't you?"

"Actually, it's a mini-DVD," Undersecretary Blackmon said. "It was sent to Jeff Eitzen at the local CBS affiliate."

"Oh, great. Have they aired it yet, Mr. Secretary?" Hicks asked.

Secretary Moss paused for a moment as if taken aback at being addressed directly by an agent. Finally he replied, "No, not yet, Agent Hicks—or is it Ross?"

"Hicks," the senior agent answered.

Scott already despised the man for his condescending manner.

"Hicks it is. I have managed to secure for us, Agent Hicks, a twelve-hour buffer by promising that this local anchor will get first shot at breaking the story," the secretary said in a tone that made it seem like his accomplishment was approaching the magnitude of the Treaty of Versailles.

"Great work, Mr. Secretary; score one for us," said Hicks, whose sarcastic tone drew a sharp look from Porter.

Secretary Moss, who after years of various elected and appointed offices had trained himself to hear only what he wanted to hear, replied, "Thank you. Now, would you like to view the video?"

Hicks and Scott answered by taking two chairs at the far end of the table from the rest of the group and facing the television. Undersecretary Blackmon pressed Play on the remote. A silhouetted figure appeared from the chest up on the screen. After a moment, he began:

"People of America, I am the voice of your pain today. I planned and I executed this attack. I am Hakeem Qasim. I am the Cheetah. I am the Hammer."

Scott felt himself shudder when he heard the name Hakeem. The guy they had been hoping to find had instead found them. As the words went on, Scott listened with half his brain, while the other half went into process mode.

First, the setting—judging by the furniture, it was obviously a hotel room. The quality of the lamp in the background and of the desk next to the man showed that it was not just a Motel 6 this guy was staying in. He had been careful about not leaving anything on the desk, and he had covered the one visible print on the wall with a sheet. It looked like there might be a bit of a pattern on the walls that, with work, could be brought out.

Second, the man himself—his silhouette didn't show anything outstanding. He seemed to be a well-built individual—someone who took care of himself. Close-cropped hair with no hat or headdress of any kind. The ridges at his sleeves and collar indicated that he was wearing a T-shirt. The man was very careful in his words and pronunciations. However, a slip here and there told Scott that English was not his first language. He affected a straight nonregional American accent.

But something's not completely kosher with his accent, Scott thought. *It's extremely well practiced and extremely well executed . . . but . . . but a different feel's coming through. What is it? It's not Middle Eastern—not Arabic-based. It's more . . . European. But not like the growing-up-in-England-or-part-of-the-U.K. kind of highbrow accent. It's more of a center-continent, English-as-a-second-language feel. C'mon, what's the country? Work your way top down: It's not Scandinavian. It's not Germanic. It's not French . . . or is it? It's got the romantic feel, but it's not pure French. It's not—*

A hand on his shoulder shook Scott from his thoughts. He looked up and saw that the video was over and everyone's eyes were on him. Porter was glaring at him, and Secretary Moss had a bemused look on his face. For the second time since walking in, Scott's face reddened.

Hicks, who had shaken Scott out of his reverie, said, "The secretary asked what you make of the recording."

"Right . . . sorry. Well, good luck getting anything from the room, except possibly doing major enhancement on the wallpaper. But even that would probably only give us the chain of hotels the guy recorded in—NIH."

"NIH?" Undersecretary Blackmon asked.

"Sorry, needle-in-haystack. A lot of work for little payback—although we could get lucky. Occasionally, a hotel chain will go with something regional. But when they do, the pattern is rarely so subtle."

"Go on," the secretary said.

"Okay, the guy's not American, though he's trying hard to sound like he is. He's also not Arabic—but then again, that name . . . Hakeem Qasim. Well, if he is Arabic, that part of his life is way in the past. I think he's southern European—Iberian, southeastern French, non-Germanic Swiss, possibly even all the way across the mid-states to Turkey—although Turkic is probably too harsh.

"He inadvertently gave us the benefit of having the lamp offset to his right, which allows us a little more detail in appearance. Short, tight hair—probably razored. When he turned slightly right, you can see that he is clean-shaven. The roll of his shoulders shows that the guy works out. When you balance him in proportion to the furniture, he stands six-two to six-three. And judging by the timbre of his voice, I would put his age at twenty-five to thirty-five—max of forty."

"Wonderful; that narrows our suspect list down to five digits," the secretary complained, drawing glares from Hicks and Scott. Even Porter, who knew good analysis when he heard it and recognized a stuffed suit when he saw one, shot him an angry look.

Porter jumped in. "What can you tell us about the Cause? I know that's the group that Abdel al-Hasani and the rest of his gang at the Mall of America were part of."

"Well . . . ," Scott began.

"If I may, Scott," Khadi Faroughi said, lightly touching his arm—a touch that rocketed through his whole body. She must have slipped in unnoticed during the viewing of the video.

Scott nodded for her to take the floor, and she continued. "When I wrote my master's thesis five years ago, I focused on up-and-coming expatriate terrorist organizations—in other words, groups that are actually leaving the Middle East and basing themselves in heavily Muslim populations in the West. At that time, the Cause only warranted about four paragraphs. But since then, their chatter has grown exponentially to the point that they have been considered one of the second-tier players. I think in these last two weeks, they've forced themselves into first tier."

"What's their issue?" Porter asked.

"The organization grew up in the late eighties, then really expanded during the first Iraqi conflict. It's a revenge/honor–based philosophy: the West hit us, so we're going to hit back harder. Because of the Iraqi–Ba'ath tie-in, they're not all radical Islamists. You do have plenty of religious fanatics, but you also have a lot of angry people who just want to hit back to restore family honor. It's basically a hodgepodge of ticked-off Arabs—'You want to kill Americans? Have we got a bomb for you!' That kind of thing."

"Okay, okay, enough," Secretary Moss said, waving his arms in an attempt to bring a halt to the discussion. "What I want to know is what you're going to do about it."

"Well, Mr. Secretary," Hicks answered, "so we don't bore you with any more details, let me tell you what I want to do. I want to put together two teams—teams that will be able to operate freely without having to ask permission."

"Black ops," Porter said.

"Black ops. We'll probably be doing some things that no one will want to know about, let alone take credit for. I'll send one team to Italy, because—correct me if I'm wrong, Khadi—that's where the Cause has one of their main operation bases."

Khadi nodded.

Hicks continued, "I'll be taking the second team to Paris."

"Paris? What, do you think the French are behind this?" Secretary Moss asked.

"No, sir," Hicks replied.

Scott marveled at the older agent's ability to keep to himself the snide comment he undoubtedly wanted to make about how this idiot could have been put in charge of anything, let alone something as important as national security.

Hicks continued, "Both Abdel al-Hasani and our new guy traveled through the suburbs of Paris on their way stateside. In 1998, the International Civil Aviation Organization mandated that all plastic explosives have a taggant, or identifier—usually some chemical that gradually evaporates out of the explosive material that allows dogs to smell it or machines to pick it up. When the lab boys examine that undetonated football, I think they'll find the explosives are loaded with French detection taggants."

"You're saying that these bombers carted their explosives all the way here from France?" the undersecretary asked. "Why not just make them here?"

Khadi responded, "We don't think their infrastructure is that strong here in the States yet. Abdel al-Hasani told us that although he was supplied with all the materials, he and his brother had to make up their own vests. The sophistication of the football bomb was something that probably had to be put together elsewhere. Agent Hicks is guessing the Paris suburbs because of our guys' travel itineraries."

"And you agree?" Moss asked, looking first at Khadi and then at Scott, who both nodded.

"So they've got a bunch of explosive footballs. How'd they get them from France to here?"

"Probably chartered a plane, landed in Mexico, and paid a coyote to bring them across the border," FBI Director Castillo answered.

"Precisely," Hicks said.

Porter spoke up. "Okay, Hicks, it sounds like you're leading team two. Whom do you recommend to lead team one?"

"I'm trusting that team to Ross." Hicks turned to Scott. "What do you think? Can you handle it?"

"Jim, I'm totally in on the team, but I'm more of an intel guy who knows how to handle a gun—"

"And a knife," Hicks added.

"Yeah, and a knife. I'll take lead on the team, but I need someone else for the operations side."

"I've got some great ops men, but they're pretty hard-core. I'm not sure how they'll do with your . . . idiosyncrasies. You got anyone specific in mind?"

"Actually, I do. But it's way out of the box." Then turning to Secretary Moss, Scott said, "I guess that's why they call it 'black ops.'"

"Well . . . as long as it doesn't take too much time to set up. I've got to be on a plane in—"

"We'll take care of whatever needs to be done," Porter interrupted. To Hicks and Scott, he said, "You boys have got carte blanche on this, so make it work. If you mess it up, we never had this conversation."

Hakeem awoke with a jolt as the pickup truck in which he was riding left the main road and the ancient suspension emitted a noisy protest. At first he was totally disoriented, and he fought the urge to panic. Slowly, his environment started to make sense to him—all except for the bumpy road.

He was stretched out in a tight area behind the bench seat of the pickup and beneath a canvas tarp, the goatish smell of which reminded him of his childhood. He was cramped, bruised, and claustrophobic, but he did not yet move, straining instead to hear the hushed conversation between the driver and his companion. The two were whispering conspiratorially, and one of them let out a low, gravelly chuckle.

He had met the two men—who identified themselves as Miguel and Miguel—in Las Cruces, New Mexico. An hour after setting out, they had pulled the old pickup truck to the side of the road and used hand motions to indicate that they wanted Hakeem to hide himself behind the seat.

At first the two men in front of him had been loud enough in their conversation to keep Hakeem from falling asleep, and he had remained alert as

CHAPTER

TWENTY

they approached the Mexican border crossing. Judging by the distance from Las Cruces, Hakeem guessed that they had bypassed the direct route south to El Paso and Juarez, instead taking a southwesterly course through Columbus, New Mexico. As they approached the checkpoint, one of the Miguels had said in broken English, "Now border. Shhhh."

Crossing the border had proved to be easier than Hakeem had expected. Every muscle of his body was tense as he tightly gripped the small Smith & Wesson 4013 pistol that the hairier of the two Miguels had missed in his cursory frisking, hidden as it was in a very uncomfortable region in which to tuck a gun. He had heard a heavy rapping on the glass and a squeak as the window was cranked down. Voices, a little laughter—*Is that a good sign?*—then silence for two minutes and forty-three seconds by Hakeem's count. Finally, voices again, the squeak of the window going back up, and a metallic grind as the driving Miguel searched to find a gear—any gear—in which to begin some forward momentum in the pickup.

Now, as the two in front whispered, Hakeem remained quiet under the tarp and decided to wait and see how things would play out. He still held the pistol, which he now slid under his belt in the small of his back, making sure that the tail of his heavy flannel shirt covered the weapon.

A few minutes later, the truck slowed to a stop. The doors opened, and there was some rattling around. Then the tarp was yanked off Hakeem, and hairy Miguel said, "Amigo" and reached his hand out. Hakeem took the man's hand—noticing the clamminess of his palm—and allowed himself to be pulled from his hiding place and onto the dirt. His legs buckled under him as the circulation began to flow to his lower extremities. Miguel let go of his hand and stepped back.

The crisp morning desert air felt invigorating after hours under the tarp, and the first light of dawn softly illuminating the desolate landscape almost made Hakeem's surroundings seem picturesque. The only thing that broke the beauty of the moment was the AK-47 that Miguel 2 was pointing at Hakeem.

Hairy Miguel laughed as he shook a Marlboro out of a crumpled pack and lit it with a small novelty lighter shaped like a grenade. He slipped the pack and the lighter back into his shirt pocket, then reached into the front of his pants and pulled out an old Colt .38 snubby.

"Don't worry, amigo, our intent is not to hurt you. . . . Ah, I see by your face that you are surprised I speak English. It seems there is more to me than meets the eye, eh? Maybe I am not so stupid as you think. Maybe I am more than a simple chauffeur. Is that what you thought I was? Just a chauffeur?"

Hakeem didn't answer. He stood with his hands locked behind his head, staring at the man as he waved his gun around.

"So, you do not feel like talking? It's okay. You don't need to talk; you just need to listen. Me and Miguel—we had a little discussion while you were sleeping. We think that it might be time for a little renegotiation of our deal."

"To force renegotiation in the middle of a job is not an honorable thing," Hakeem said.

"Maybe it's true; maybe it's true. However, honor is a luxury that comes at too high a price for a coyote. A coyote must eat whenever he can and as much as he can, because he never knows how long it will be until his next meal."

"Great, a philosopher. Fine. Tell me how much it's going to cost me," Hakeem said as he slowly lowered his right hand to get the wallet from his back pocket.

"Cut to the chase," hairy Miguel laughed. "That's what we like, eh, Miguel?"

When Miguel 2 smiled and turned to nod at his partner, Hakeem saw his moment. In a smooth, swift motion that he had practiced countless times over the past years in front of a mirror, he grabbed the .40 cal from his back, swung the weapon up, and pulled the trigger twice. The first round went into Miguel 2's chest, and the second entered his skull just under his left eye. While Miguel 2 was still crumpling to the ground, Hakeem leveled the pistol at hairy Miguel's face.

Seeing the gun, the man immediately dropped to the ground and began pleading for his life.

"Don't worry, friend, my intent is not to hurt you," Hakeem said in perfect Castilian Spanish. "Ah, I see by your face that you are surprised I speak Spanish. It seems there is more to *me* than meets the eye."

"Please, sir! Don't kill me! I will give you all of your money back and take you the rest of the way. Please don't kill me!"

"I said I don't plan to harm you . . . yet. And you will keep the money I have given you. I belong to an honorable people, and we pay what is due."

"I am so sorry, sir. You truly are honorable. I never would have done this had I known the kind of man you are. In fact, Fabián forced me to renegotiate. I didn't want to, but he—"

"Fabián? Is that his real name?"

"Yes, sir. Fabián Ramón Guerrero."

"And what is yours?"

"I am Valentín Joaquín de Herrera. And you are . . . ?"

"Tired of listening to you. Toss your gun toward me."

The coyote obeyed.

"Now, take out your other gun and throw it toward me."

"But, sir, I have no other gun!" the man protested.

"Adios," Hakeem said. He increased pressure on the trigger.

"Wait, wait!" Valentín reached deep into the front pocket of his cargo pants and brought out an ancient Colt Pocket Hammerless. The grip was wrapped with duct tape, and it looked like firing it would be more dangerous to the one holding the weapon than the one at whom it was pointed.

"That's better. Now, do you have anything else that might be harmful to me—knives, box cutters, really sharp sticks? Before you answer, I want you to know that in a few moments I am going to have you strip down to nothing, and if I find that you were holding out on me at all, I will put two bullets into your stomach and watch you slowly bleed to death."

Valentín's hands dove into his pockets and brought out a utility blade, two ice picks, and one set of brass knuckles with the tops of the third and fourth rings broken out. He then began unbuttoning his shirt.

"No, wait," Hakeem called out. "Seeing you undressed is an image that might possibly plague me for the rest of my life. Leave everything on the ground and get back in the truck. And don't try to run. I am the Cheetah, and I will surely catch you."

"Yes, sir. Of course, sir." Valentín ran to the truck and jumped in through the driver's door.

Hakeem slowly walked around the back of the truck. As soon as he was sure the coyote couldn't see him, he began shaking all over. He had killed a man—pointed a gun, pulled the trigger, and lodged a bullet in a person's brain. His knees felt weak.

But this was ridiculous! Hadn't he just been responsible for the deaths of hundreds, if not thousands, of people? Yes, but this was the first time he had pulled the trigger himself. This was the first time he had directly caused a body to topple to the ground.

Do I feel remorse? No. Would I do anything differently? No. Then why am I shaking? If it's not fear and it's not remorse, then what is it? Maybe it's adrenaline. That's got to be it. It's excitement. Another step in making me the avenger my destiny says that I am. I have been blooded! Oh, Uncle, if you could see me now!

The shaking subsided, but the energy did not. It continued to well up inside him. Hakeem laughed, and then he slammed his fist into the side of the truck. Finally he drew in as much of the early morning air as he could and let out an ear-shattering howl at the sunrise.

THURSDAY, JANUARY 1
FEDERAL BUREAU OF INVESTIGATION,
    DENVER FIELD OFFICE
DENVER, COLORADO

It had been twenty minutes since Riley had passed through the second set of security clearances, and he was starting to get a bit antsy. Although the lounge area had soft chairs, it did not seem a place in which one was meant to get comfortable. There was no reading material on the end tables, and there were no prints on the walls. The only decorative items of any kind were a large aquarium at the front of the room and an old television that still had knobs on the front.

Riley began pacing across the room, rehearsing for the fiftieth time the words he was going to say when the door to the inner sanctum opened. He kept finding his concentration broken by the smack of the air bubbles trapped under the poorly laid vinyl flooring with every other step he took. In an effort to drown out that incredibly irritating sound, on his next pass to the front of the room Riley twisted the On/Volume knob of the television.

The tinny voice of a female reporter sounded through the twenty-year-old speakers: ". . . and

CHAPTER

TWENTY-ONE

Baltimore, around the country, and around the world are still reeling as they try to cope with Monday night's attack at Platte River Stadium."

Riley turned toward the TV as the picture cut to a man with an American flag bandanna wrapped around his head and riding leathers covering the rest of his body. "This is what we get for letting them A-rabs in the country to begin with! They want a fight? I say we press the button and give the whole Middle East a nuclear shower!"

A quick camera change brought another face to the screen— a twentysomething with an eyebrow ring and a Rage Against the Machine T-shirt. "What do we expect? We've been pushing our imperialistic agenda against the oil-producing countries of the Middle East for decades. Should we be surprised when they fight back? This one's on you, Mr. President!"

Another cut landed in an office, which, judging by the enormous number of books stacked on and around the desk, belonged to an academic. A font at the bottom of the screen identified the bespectacled gentleman as Dr. Martin Vatsaas, PhD, Distinguished Professor of Behavioral Science, University of Colorado at Boulder. "People will try to cope with this tragedy however they best can. Some will blame; others will lash out. Many will huddle with friends and family, trying to process the events of Monday night. I think the reactions will be very similar to the aftermath of 9/11. We can expect to see this country experience a temporary unification—socially and politically. We can also expect to see violence against people of Middle Eastern descent rise dramatically."

The picture switched back to the network reporter standing outside of Platte River Stadium. "Not surprisingly, PFL fans across the nation have had mixed reactions to the announcement that the owners of the Colorado Mustangs and the Baltimore Predators have offered to forfeit Monday night's game in order to, quote, 'let our players, our staff, and our fans begin the healing process.' They also believe that this will, quote, 'allow the Pro Football League the best potential for carrying on with this year's PFL Cup tournament.' Eli Boermann, commissioner of the PFL, issued a statement offering his condolences and gratitude to the football clubs and the cities of Denver and Baltimore.

"As I stand here, hundreds of people surround me, and thousands of flowers, stuffed animals, candles, and cards surround the fence of Platte River Stadium. Prayers are being said and tears are being shed for the almost two thousand people who died as the people of Denver try to find answers to this tragedy. This is Marcia Roland, ABC News."

Riley twisted the television off and turned to discover that he was no longer alone in the lounge. Another man, who apparently had slipped in while Riley's attention was focused on the TV, was now sitting across the small room from him. The man looked to be in his early twenties and wore a lined jean jacket and a skullcap imprinted with the number *100* surrounded by a broken circle. The two gave each other a quick nod.

Riley took a chair and hoped—too late—not to be recognized. Unfortunately, it seemed like the young man had already come to the realization that he was sharing the room with a Colorado Mustang, which was the last thing Riley wanted to deal with. The man kept glancing from his worn paperback copy of *A Time to Kill* and was looking like he was trying to get up enough nerve to say something. Riley watched him from the corner of his eye. Typically he was fine with fans introducing themselves or saying something to him. But he had way too much on his mind today to have to try to be friendly. The pain of the attack and of losing his best friend had not diminished much in the last few days.

The guy seemed to get his nerve up and began to rise, but Riley beat him to the punch and quickly stood and walked to the aquarium.

The young man sat back down.

Riley spent the next fifteen minutes looking into the aquarium before finally coming to the conclusion that it was totally devoid of any marine life.

Finally the door flew open, and Scott Ross came bounding in, throwing his arms around Riley. "Pach! I'm so sorry I kept you waiting!"

"No problem," Riley replied as they separated. "I was just admiring the fish tank."

"Yeah, isn't that an odd thing? They tell me some people will spend fifteen minutes staring at that thing before they realize there's no fish in there. Imagine that."

"Yeah, who'da thunk?" Riley said, quickly scanning around to see if there were cameras that had been monitoring him.

Scott looked behind Riley and said, "Hey, Todd! I heard they were bringing you back in. Riley, I want you to meet a genuine hero. Riley Covington, this is Todd Penner. Todd, Riley."

"Todd Penner? The hot chocolate guy?" Riley walked across the room, inwardly kicking himself for having snubbed him. He stuck out his hand. "It's a pleasure to meet you."

Todd shook his hand and seemed to struggle to find the right words to say. "Thanks. . . . I mean . . . I only did what anyone else would do."

"No, actually you did what seventy thousand other fans couldn't or didn't do. Thanks. . . . Truly, man, thanks." Riley finally let go of Todd's hand as Scott walked over.

"Well, Todd, now that you've had the excitement of meeting the incomparable Riley Covington, you need to promise me that you won't tell anyone that you saw him here."

Todd looked surprised for a moment; then he gave a faint smile and said, "That's fine, Mr. Ross. If there's one thing I've learned over these past few days, it's to never ask why."

"Thanks, bud. C'mon, Riley."

Riley gave Todd's hand one final shake before he and Scott walked out of the room together.

"So, Scott, it's been what, three years?"

"Sounds about right. Tell you what, Pach, I really want to catch up with you, but we need to talk business first. Then you can tell me what it's like being Mr. All-Star." Scott held a second set of doors open for Riley, and the two of them headed down to a bank of conference rooms. "First, I want to tell you how sorry I am about what happened Monday night. I've heard stories about what you personally went through. You holding up okay?"

"Yeah. The whole experience has brought back some tough memories, though."

"I bet."

As they walked, Riley ran his mind through the little speech he had prepared to give to Scott. But he had neither the mood nor the desire to do anything except cut to the chase. "Scott, I want back in. I don't know how to do it, and I don't know who to talk to, but I've got to get back in."

"Why?"

"Why?" Riley said, thrown by the question. "Why do you think? They just blew up our stadium! We had nineteen hundred people blown apart or trampled to death! They put thirty-five hundred more into the hospital! What do you mean 'why'?"

"Let me rephrase the question. Why you?"

The question stopped Riley, and he stood trying to think how to answer Scott. *What do I say—rage, anger, hatred, a desire for vengeance? Why am I really here? Because I want to cut the heart out of the people who ripped the heart out of me?*

He slowly began walking again. "I don't know, Scott," he said softly. "I guess . . . I guess I don't want to be on the outside looking in. These people came into my house, they went after my people, they killed my best friend, and now . . . I guess I want to return the favor. When you called me to come down here for questioning, I thought . . . well, whatever—I needed to give it a shot."

Scott had stopped in front of a conference room door. He had that trademark Scott Ross grin on his face—sort of an "I-know-what-Santa's-going-to-bring-you-for-Christmas-but-I'm-not-telling-you-yet" look. As he opened the door, he said, "Pach, I think you're going to like what you're about to hear."

Riley followed Scott into the room. Inside was a long table from which two people were standing up to greet the newcomers.

Scott made the introductions. "Riley Covington, this is Khadi Faroughi. She's a CTD agent who is fluent in Arabic and knows the counterterrorism business inside and out."

As Khadi and Riley shook hands, he noticed that although her hand felt fragile and was cold from being in the climate-controlled conference room, her grip was as strong as any man's he knew.

"Mr. Covington, I'm so sorry about what you've gone through. I can't imagine what these past three days have been like for you."

"Thanks, Katie."

"That's Kha-DI—with a *D*," Scott interrupted with a barely suppressed smile.

Khadi glared at him.

"And this is Jim Hicks. He's the head of our operation."

Riley gave the customary shake to Hicks, but one word in Scott's introduction had started his mind racing. He turned to Scott. "*Our* operation?"

Hicks broke in before Scott had a chance to answer. "Mr. Covington, why don't you have a seat?"

As Riley and the others sat, Hicks continued. "I'm going to cut to the chase here and then let Khadi fill you in on all the details later. The people who were responsible for the attack on the Mall of America are the same ones who masterminded the attack at Platte River Stadium. We know a bit about who they are and a bit more about where they come from. We have been authorized by the secretary of Homeland Security to form two off-the-record teams—black ops, you might call them—to go and hunt these people down. I'm leading one of the teams. Scott's got the other one but needs someone to head up the operations side. For some reason, he's got you in mind for this position.

"Now, personally, I think it's insanity to bring in some prettyboy PFL player who's three years out of his military service to head an ops team. And I've spent the better part of the last two days trying to convince Scott of that. However, he's sure that you're the guy. Even though Europe is very different from Afghanistan. Even though you're used to straight military ops, not undercover. Even though you've got a personal stake in this and you'll probably let your emotions cloud your judgment. Even though—"

"Jim," Scott interrupted, "we've been through this. You don't know Riley; I do. You've gotta trust me on this one."

Hicks heaved a big sigh and turned back to Riley. "Scott's an odd duck, but he is rarely, if ever, wrong. So, although it goes against all my better judgment, I'm giving you the green light to be part of this team."

Riley sat staring at the table. There were so many emotions coursing through him—appreciation to Scott for believing in him; anger and wounded pride because of Hicks's words; excitement, fear, and a bit of "what-are-you-getting-yourself-into" as he thought of what might be ahead of him.

Finally he looked up. "Okay, Mr. Hicks. Pretty Boy's got some questions before he says yes or no. First, you said Scott's leading the team, but then I heard you say it's insanity to bring me in to head it. Which is it?"

"The team is mine, Pach," Scott answered. "You follow my lead on where we're heading and on intel gathering. I, in turn, will follow your lead when it comes to extractions and the actual placing of bullets into the bodies of others."

"Extractions? You mean like people-snatching?"

Hicks answered, "There are a few people we really would like to talk to who probably won't be too fired up to talk to us. So by *extraction* we mean you grab them and then convince them to tell us what we want to know."

"Convince them. Like show them both sides of the issue and hope they choose correctly? Or are you talking about the 'attach-electrodes-and-crank-up-the-juice' kind of convincing?"

"Guess what, Mr. Covington?" Hicks exploded. "In case you hadn't noticed, it's a rough, nasty world out there! If you don't have the—"

"Listen, Hicks," Riley shot back, "I need to know what kind of operation I'm looking at and what my parameters are! All you've done since I walked into this room is doubt Scott and dog me! So unless you're going to start contributing something to this conversation other than questioning my abilities, feel free to pull yourself out of it."

Hicks was on his feet. "Son, I was running ops back when you were skinning up your knees pretending to be Joe Montana with a Nerf football in your backyard! And remember one more thing: I am in charge of this whole operation! So I will contribute to this conversation whatever I think I need to contribute to this conversation! You understand?"

Riley stood abruptly, his chair clattering backward across the floor behind him. But before he had a chance to respond, Khadi spoke up. "Whoa, whoa, whoa. Come on, guys. We've all been through a lot this past week. Let's slow it down a bit, okay?"

The two men stared at each other a moment longer, then sat back down.

Scott, who appeared to be enjoying the show, reached into his cargo pants and pulled out two Yoo-hoos. He offered one to Riley, who rejected it with a curt wave. So he opened both for himself.

"Who all is going to be on this team?" Riley asked.

Scott got his big grin again. "You remember *Blues Brothers*? 'We're getting the band back together'? Well, since 'we're on a mission from God,'" Scott said, vainly attempting a Dan Aykroyd impersonation, "I thought we should get our old team back together."

"What . . . you mean Skeeter and Li and Logan and all those guys?" Riley asked, excitement beginning to build in him.

"Yep, all except for Murphy. He's some Wall Street suit now and isn't interested in getting dirty anymore."

"No surprise there. Only guy I know who would spoon the grounds out of his coffee before he drank it."

"Yeah, remember how he used to carefully lay out his MREs? Like he was getting ready to dine at the Ritz-Carlton?"

Hicks cut in, "As much as I'd love to hear you guys take a walk down memory lane, I've got work to do. So, Mr. Covington, is it yes or no?"

Riley didn't answer right away. He looked at the table for a moment and considered the magnitude of the decision he was about to make. But he already knew what his answer would be. It was why he had come here in the first place. He slowly began nodding well before he looked up and quietly answered, "Yes, Mr. Hicks. It's a definite yes."

"Swell," Hicks said, shaking his head as he stood up, tapped his papers into a neat stack, and walked toward the door. "Weatherman's going to come with me for some more planning. I'm leaving Khadi with you. She'll fill you in on what's happened so far and who it is we're dealing with. I suggest you pay close attention to her."

Scott got up to follow Hicks. He put his hand on Riley's shoulder. "I'll catch up with you later, Pach. You may want to let your family know you won't be seeing them for a while. Of course, you can't tell them who, why, or where."

"Of course. Thanks, Scott," Riley said, standing to shake his friend's hand.

Scott smiled and nodded, then walked out of the room. A moment later, he stuck his head back in. "And, Riley, don't forget— it's Khadi . . . you know . . . with a *d*." Then he quickly ducked out before there was any chance for a response.

CHAPTER

TWENTY-TWO

THURSDAY, JANUARY 1
FEDERAL BUREAU OF INVESTIGATION,
    DENVER FIELD OFFICE
DENVER, COLORADO

Riley and Khadi stood up from the table and stretched. They had been poring over history, facts, and figures for the past three hours straight. Riley's brain was about at bursting level, and he was sure Khadi must be tired of talking.

"How are you doing so far?" she asked him.

"Well, I have to admit it's a whole lot of information to absorb in such a short amount of time."

"And it's not done yet. But I could see you starting to zone out toward the end."

"Sorry about that. I guess it's been a long day—for all of us. Tell you what; you lead me to the commissary, and I'll spring for a Diet Coke."

Khadi laughed. "Your military background is definitely kicking in. Around here we call a commissary a 'break room.' And if you don't mind, I'll take a coffee instead."

As they walked down the hall, Khadi said, "Hadn't you better call Grandpa Covington and tell him you won't be home for dinner?"

"No, Grandpa's used to taking care of . . . Wait, how'd you know he was at my house?"

"We're CTD," Khadi said in a mysterious voice. "We know all and see all."

Riley laughed quietly. "Next time I see one of those black helicopters hovering over my house, I'll know who it is."

Khadi smiled briefly, then said, "Riley, I need to ask you something—especially since I'm going to be part of your team."

"Shoot."

"I don't know you very well, but I hear so much in your voice—anger, pain, sorrow. I hope I'm not being too presumptuous here. . . . I guess I need to know that you're going to be able to keep all that in check and not let your emotions get the best of you on the field."

They entered the deserted break room and discovered that someone had put an empty carafe back in the coffeemaker. Riley started fixing another pot. "Hope you like it strong. My dad always told me that coffee isn't coffee unless it's strong enough to put hair on your—" he stopped short as he caught her eye—"uh, unless it's really, really strong."

"Don't worry; I'm Persian. We serve our coffee with toothpicks."

Riley sat down on a hard, blue plastic chair across from Khadi and used a napkin to wipe powdered sugar from the table between them. They both sat silently while Riley formulated his answer to Khadi's concerns.

Finally he said, "Scott wasn't my first number two in Afghanistan. His predecessor was a guy named Tony Werschky—very Polish, very Brooklyn. Tony was a great guy, unbelievably good at what he did. Two weeks in-country, we were out doing a scouting patrol. Tony's telling me for the two hundredth time about his little son, Alex, back home, when—*pop!*—a sniper's bullet hits him flush in the face. It was the first time I had ever seen anyone killed, let alone someone right next to me.

"I was so shocked, so angry, that I wanted to take off after the shooter right then and there. What stopped me was knowing that I had the rest of my team with me. If I did something stupid, they could all very well end up like Tony. So we reconned the area, set a plan, and ended up taking out the shooter and three of his friends with none of my other guys even getting a scratch."

Riley paused for a moment, wondering why he was opening up so much to this woman he had just met. Maybe it was that she was so easy to talk to. Or maybe it was that he needed to talk to someone—anyone.

He pressed on. "On Monday night, the bad guys took my best friend from me. I spent yesterday evening with his widow—a wonderful woman whose whole world is completely shattered. And then there's his beautiful baby daughter, sweet little Alessandra. She's still trying to figure out why Daddy hasn't come home."

Riley stopped briefly so he could get control of his rising emotion. "And what kills me is . . . is knowing that this same scene is taking place all over Denver. And it will continue to take place until these people are stopped. So, yes, I'm angry about this. Yes, I want revenge. But, no, I will not let it cloud my judgment, and I will not let it cause me to sacrifice my team."

"Fair enough," Khadi said. "That's all I needed to hear."

Silence overtook them again.

Finally Riley spoke up. "So, what about you? I've poured my guts out. Your turn. What brought you here?"

"You mean, what's a nice Iranian girl like me doing in a job like this?"

"Yeah, something like that. I'm interested in your story."

Khadi picked up a coffee stirrer that had hidden itself behind the napkin dispenser on their table. She kept her eyes on the narrow red piece of plastic as she slowly twisted and untwisted it around her left index finger.

"My parents are from Iran. My dad was a surgeon there. In the late seventies, he saw the way the winds were blowing, so he packed up my mom—who was pregnant with me—and my two brothers and moved to Arlington, Virginia. That was November 1978—two months before the shah fled.

"My dad was able to establish himself in Virginia—first in the Muslim community, then in the wider medical community. I grew up a bit of a spoiled rich kid. My dad saw what was happening, and when I was fifteen, he gave me a talking-to that changed my life. He basically said that God has given us one life to live and that he wasn't going to see his daughter waste hers. I took that night to evaluate my life, and believe it or not, I agreed with him. So I dumped a bunch of my friends and started taking school seriously."

Riley glanced over his shoulder and saw that the pot was full. He got up and grabbed two mugs. He filled one all the way but left plenty of room to the top in the other. "Cream and sugar?"

"You insult me."

Riley grinned and filled the second mug the rest of the way. He placed the cup in front of Khadi and sat back down.

Khadi blew on her coffee and took a tentative sip. "Wow—I can feel the hair sprouting already."

Riley opened his mouth to reply, then found he had absolutely nothing to say. He shook his head. This girl was definitely different from any others he had met before.

Khadi picked the coffee stirrer back up and continued her story. "Anyway, I worked hard and was accepted into West Point. I loved the whole counterintelligence field, so when I graduated, I was branched into military intelligence as a 35 Echo—that's army counterintelligence. Stop me if I get too much into my résumé."

"No, please go on."

"I spent ten months in picturesque Fort Huachuca, Arizona—six months in MIOBC and another four at 35E school. From there I was recruited for detached service by Homeland Security because of my TS security clearance and placed into the new Counterterrorism Division. The rest, as they say, is history."

"And what do you do now?"

"I'll tell you after your security clearance comes through."

Riley chuckled, and they both stared at their coffee mugs for a minute.

Finally Riley grinned and asked, "So, what's with this whole 'Khadi with a *D*' thing? I saw your reaction to Scott."

Khadi groaned. "This is not a very flattering story."

Riley simply smiled and waited.

"Fine. Growing up, I was always Khadijah—named after the Prophet Muhammad's first wife. She was a wealthy business-woman who married the Prophet, even though he was fifteen years younger. Khadijah supported Muhammad financially while he spread the faith, so of course there is great respect for her in Islam. As a result, even though all my friends had nicknames—Carrie, Suze, Nance, Tam—my parents wouldn't hear of my being called anything but my full name, which to me always sounded so . . . so . . ."

"Ethnic?"

"Yeah, maybe. Or maybe it's just that it was so different from everyone else. Anyway, I was Khadijah my whole life until West Point. When I got there, I thought, 'Here's my chance!' But rather than have some shortened form of my first name, I became . . ."

"Faroughi."

"Bingo!"

"Didn't help too much on the whole ethnic front, huh?"

"Not exactly. I was Faroughi or Farougee or Garfooey or Fargoofy or any other of a list of name botches throughout West Point and until I arrived here at CTD. Finally, I figured here was my chance, so I started introducing myself as Khadi. It was very exciting, but I quickly found that there was one drawback."

"'Katie.'"

"Right. And in my typical over-the-top fashion, rather than letting it go, I began correcting everyone who mispronounced my name—'That's Khadi, with a *d*.'"

"Big mistake."

"Oh yeah. Soon I was no longer Khadi *or* Katie. I became 'Khadi-with-a-*D*'—sometimes shortened to Khadi-wad."

"Nothing pretty about that," Riley said, instantly wishing he hadn't.

"Why, thank you. But you're right. So, about a year ago I finally clued into the fact that I would be 'Khadi with a *D*' as long as I let it bother me. So now . . ."

"Now you let people pronounce it however they want. Good move."

"Yeah. And when anyone . . . well, maybe anyone except for Scott, who for some reason just gets on my nerves—"

"It's a gift." Riley grinned.

"—when anyone jumps on me about being 'Khadi with a *D*,' I

try to deflect it with a joke or something. You know, 'Call me anything you like; just don't call me late for afternoon prayers.'"

Riley laughed. "You know, that raises another question—and again, if I'm prying too much, let me know. How did your parents feel about their daughter leaving her roots and joining up with the American government?"

The stirrer stopped its movement, and Khadi looked up at Riley. "I guess I don't understand the question—leaving my roots how?"

There was a defensive note in Khadi's voice that should have waved a yellow flag.

Riley, being male, ignored the warning signs and plowed ahead. "I mean, leaving your Persian heritage and your Muslim beliefs to join the American military."

"What makes you think that I am any less Persian or any less Muslim because I work for the American government?"

"I guess I'm having a hard time seeing how a Muslim could be trusted with state security in a time like this."

Khadi's face darkened. "Can't be trusted? So is it somehow antithetical in your mind that someone who worships Allah can despise the evil people who carried out the Mall of America bombing or Monday night's attack? You might be surprised to find out that not all Muslim women were hitching up their burkas and dancing in the streets after 9/11."

"No, you're right. You're right," Riley said, holding his hands up in surrender. "That was a stupid thing to say. I just . . . I mean, I thought . . . You know, I'm going to shut up now."

"Probably a good choice," Khadi said into her coffee cup.

They sat there without speaking for a few more minutes. Then Riley took their mugs and rinsed them out, leaving them in the sink, and they walked silently back to the conference room to begin Educating Riley—Session Two.

TWENTY-THREE

THURSDAY, JANUARY 8
EUROPE

Oh, the smells! Those incredible smells! The people were warm and welcoming, the flavors were rich, the music was celebratory, and the mood was festive. But those thick, dizzying smells—pomegranate soup, *timman*, *lis-san el qua-thi*, and *kubba* with its lamb and cumin and saffron and limes. Those smells were what carried Hakeem away—carried him back to a time when he was just a boy.

Kubba had been his mother's specialty. He remembered working next to her, crumbling the bread, then mashing it together with the saffron rice. She would hold his hands as they rolled out little wet disks. Her arms would be on either side of him, and her body would be pressed against his. He remembered the love and security of that close contact. With no picture of her, he was having a harder time remembering her face as the years passed. But even if a thousand years went by, he could never forget her feel.

He would place a spoonful of the lamb mixture onto the bread and rice combination, and his mother would expertly roll small torpedoes to deep-fry. The rest of the day he would find himself unconsciously bringing his hands to his nose, inhaling the scent of the spices that were imbedded in his skin.

Hakeem was surprised to find tears in his eyes. This was the first time he had cried for his mother since the week after she had been taken from him. He quickly brought out his handkerchief and blew his nose, then laughed to those around him, wafting his hands toward his face to indicate that it was the pungent aroma of the cooking making his eyes water.

Everyone laughed with him.

The people here were still a little unsure what to make of Hakeem Qasim and his Westernized manners. But they knew one thing was true: this man was a hero. And they were going to do whatever it took to show their respect and admiration for him.

Hakeem had been picked up at the airport last night by some new friends and driven to the home where he was now staying. The house and surrounding neighborhood reminded him very much of an upscale part of Baghdad not far from his childhood home.

Whenever an expatriate community plants itself in a new country without taking on any of the host country's culture, the neighborhood quickly develops the characteristics of the homeland. This was certainly the case in this little European enclave.

Hakeem had slept through the night, the morning, and into the afternoon. When he had finally awakened, it was to the sweet smell of cardamom tea with its generous dose of sugar at the bottom and a large piece of freshly baked *um ali*—a wonderful pastry dessert with pistachios, almonds, and cinnamon. These had been placed on the nightstand next to his bed. That was six hours ago, two hours prior to the beginning of this feast—a feast that showed no signs of abating anytime soon.

There were at least thirty people spread throughout the home. Everyone was congratulating him and giving him gifts. He hadn't realized how rusty his Arabic had become over the years, but all were willing to accommodate him by speaking slowly and repeating phrases when needed. His welcome home was everything he had dreamed it would be.

He was speaking with an older man and his son, who was

around Hakeem's age, when a sudden hush fell over the house. All eyes turned toward the front door, where a man stood in the entryway. Hakeem thought the man looked vaguely familiar, but he didn't recognize the burn scars that covered the right half of the man's face and the patch that covered his right eye.

The man scanned the room, and his eye fell on Hakeem. He walked slowly across the floor and stood before the honored guest. Then he spoke. "Hakeem."

At the sound of the man's voice, recognition flooded Hakeem, and he dropped to his knees in front of the man. Next to his father and his uncle Ali, this was the man most responsible for the warrior that Hakeem had become. He had taught Hakeem, trained Hakeem, disciplined Hakeem, prepared Hakeem, and sent Hakeem out into the world as a warrior for honor. This was the man who had created his cherished brass medallion so many years ago. If there was one man still alive whose approval Hakeem craved, it was this man. The Scorpion.

Hakeem bowed his head and said with deep reverence, "Al-'Aqran."

THURSDAY, JANUARY 8
CHIÈVRES AIR BASE
BELGIUM

A sixteen-foot-long moving truck with French lettering on its side pulled up next to the plane moments after the C-37A Gulfstream V touched its wheels down at Chièvres Air Base in Belgium. Quickly, the men of the U.S. Air Force's 309th Airlift Squadron helped Jim Hicks and his team transfer their equipment through the cold, steady rain.

Ten minutes later, the truck was on its way.

Hicks and his number-two man, Jay Kruse, sat up front, while the other six members of the team rode back in the box.

"Predator team, stay sharp," Hicks radioed to the men in back. As a show of respect and as a nod to Riley Covington's participation, Hicks had named the two ops teams after the PFL teams affected by the Platte River Stadium bombings. Hicks's team was designated

Predator team, while the team Scott Ross and Covington led was Mustang team.

Hicks had instructed the men in the rear to set up a mobile surveillance suite as they traveled. By the time they had completed the two-and-a-half-hour trek to Paris, they would be ready to go.

On the drive down, Hicks thought through the past week. He had continued to be impressed by Scott Ross's abilities and even—though he hated to admit—by Riley Covington's.

What was it about Covington that he didn't like? Was it simply the fear that his relative inexperience would get people killed? If it were truly that, Hicks knew he wouldn't have gone along with Scott's plan from the beginning. He wouldn't risk American lives for anyone's feelings. Was it a personality thing? Maybe, but the man seemed like a genuinely decent guy—not the stuck-on-himself football prima donna Hicks had expected.

Am I jealous of the guy? Jim wondered. *Do I want what he's got? But what is it he's got? I don't want his lifestyle. I've got all the junk I need, and as for the spotlight, I much prefer life in the shadows.*

Am I jealous of him and Khadi? I saw the way she was looking at him during our training week—ways I once hoped she'd look at me. But that was a long time ago. She's much more like a daughter than a love interest now. What about Scott? C'mon, how could I be jealous of Riley Covington's relationship with Scott?

A feeling in the pit of his stomach told Hicks that this last possibility might be truer than he had hoped. *Okay, jealous of one guy's relationship with another guy—that's a realm I certainly don't want to delve into.*

But as he drove, he realized that despite their age difference and relatively short acquaintance, he had begun to see Scott as a true friend—something that he had rarely had in his life.

Hicks shook himself out of his introspection as the truck approached the northeastern Paris suburb of Aulnay-sous-Bois, located a little more than eight miles outside of the city center. The revelation that the explosives used in the Platte River Stadium attack had been French had come as no surprise to Hicks. The Parisian suburbs had been a hotbed for disgruntled Arab youth for a generation, and the region's influence and importance in the world of terrorism were rapidly increasing. CIA sources within the Islamic youth movement had indicated with a strong certainty that the base for the Cause in France was in the neighboring communities of Aulnay-sous-Bois, Livry-Gargan, and Clichy-sous-Bois.

The truck turned off Boulevard Charles Floquet and parked at the top of Rue du Commandant Brasseur. The team's target house was on the left side of the street, two from the bottom of the block. Their intelligence indicated that this house was a gathering place for an insurgent group that included two key leaders of the Cause. According to the report, the group was currently meeting in the house along with several soldiers. The strike team's goal was to neutralize the soldiers and remove the leaders to a safe house where they could be held and interrogated.

A week's worth of tension filled each man in the truck; this was the beginning of what they had been called together for.

At Hicks's go-ahead, Jay Kruse slipped in the earbuds of an iPod nano and jumped out of the cab while Hicks joined the rest of the team in back by slipping through a door that had been cut between the back of the driver's cab and the container box. Hicks watched on a monitor as Kruse waved his hand in front of the mini camera that had been hidden in his left earbud, and he banged the side of the truck once as acknowledgment that they were picking up the signal.

Kruse began walking toward the house. The whole team watched his progress on the monitor.

Suddenly the picture was completely obscured by something that as quickly disappeared. Ted Hummel, the team's tech guru, burst out laughing.

"What was that?" Hicks demanded.

"That was the nano, sir," Hummel replied. "Apparently old Kruser just discovered that I loaded the thing with nothing but Jerry Lewis."

Hicks couldn't help laughing with the rest of the team. "Okay, guys, keep focused."

Kruse passed the house without slowing down and came to the end of the block. Everyone in the truck tensed as they watched his next move. If he proceeded straight across Boulevard de l'Hôtel de Ville, it meant everything was clear from his perspective. A left turn meant abort.

Kruse stopped at the corner, looked both ways, and then crossed the street. When he got across, he squatted next to a streetlamp and attempted to stall for time by lighting a cigarette—something that Hicks hoped would take him a while in the misty rain that was falling outside.

Hummel tapped the monitor, and the picture changed from Kruse's live signal to a tiled view of the shots he had just taken of the house. Hicks leaned in and examined the images closely, then tapped the one on the bottom right. Immediately that picture went full screen.

"Okay, we all know our assignments," Hicks said. "Kasay and Johnson, you're with me. Guitiérrez and Musselman, you'll want to watch out when you go around back. This anomaly here—" Hicks pointed to a small shadow protruding from the rear of the house— "could be a bogey. Once we're inside, you guys all know the faces of the ones we want alive. The rest . . . well . . . try to remember we don't want more of an international incident than we're already going to create. But if you see a gun, be sure you shoot first. Check each other out; then let's roll."

Even though these men were professionals, it still paid to be careful. Each man paired off with another and checked the other man's body armor, his weapon, and his communication system. The only one who would be out of communication was Kruse; Hicks didn't want his number-two man to get caught walking around these parts wearing a wire.

Hicks slid back through the makeshift door and into the cab. He put the truck in gear and drove the half block to the target house.

As soon as the truck stopped, the team was out. They were wearing civilian clothes—various shades of dark button-down shirts tucked into loose charcoal pants. Each member wore a fabric mask covering the lower half of his face and carried an FN P90 submachine gun and a MK23 handgun. Four of them also carried two M84 flash-bang grenades.

As Hicks approached the door, he could hear the sounds of

Arabic voices and loud laughter inside. The smell of freshly baked *khubz* warmed his nostrils. So far, their intel seemed right.

They reached their positions—three men in the front of the house, two in back, and one on each side. "Predator Three has one hostile down in back," Hicks heard Guitiérrez say through his comm.

"Copy," Hicks replied.

Hicks had been counting since he left the truck. When he hit twenty, he said, "Go, go, go!"

One team member on each side of the house tossed a flashbang through the windows. A second later came the rapid-fire sound of the four stun grenades. Hicks and the team burst through the doors while the people in the house were still dazed and trying to clear their heads enough to figure out what had just happened.

Hicks, Steve Kasay, and Chris Johnson found themselves in the main room, the center of which held a long table surrounded by eight men.

"Hands up! Get your hands up!" Hicks yelled, knowing the men probably couldn't understand his words but hoping the intensity of his voice would stop them from doing anything stupid. Gunfire erupted from an adjoining room, causing one of the men at the table to reach for the gun that was lying by his right hand. With a quick two-shot burst into the man's chest, Hicks made sure that neither that man nor any of the others would make that mistake again.

"Predator Four has Umari," came a call on Hicks's comm, telling him that Brad Musselman had captured the first of their targets.

"Predator Six's sector is clear," Arsdale said.

That meant that the second target had to be in Hicks's room. The problem was, no one looked right. Hicks shouldered his P90, pulled out his MK23, and pressed it against the forehead of the man nearest him.

"Bazzaz?" Hicks yelled.

The man's eyes were wide, and Hicks could smell him soiling himself.

Hicks cocked back the hammer. "Bazzaz?"

The man slowly lifted his hand and pointed to the head of the table, causing the man sitting there to dive for his gun. Kasay brought the butt of his weapon down hard across the man's forehead, bringing that movement to a halt. Hicks hurried over and lifted the stunned man's head by his blond hair. He held a picture next to his face. "Add a beard and subtract a dye job . . . yep, we have a winner!" He let Bazzaz's head drop back down on the table.

"This is Predator One. We've got Bazzaz!" Hicks yelled into his comm. Then to Kasay he said, "Zip him up!"

So far so good, Hicks thought. With both targets acquired, now it was time to beat a hasty retreat. "Predator Five and Six, get into the main room and secure these bogies," Hicks ordered. "Predator Three and Eight, hold front and back door. All others, back to the nest. I want everyone home in ninety seconds!"

As they ran to the truck, Hicks saw the two captives being carried on the shoulders of his men. Both of them looked terrified, and there was blood running down Bazzaz's cheek from a gash on his forehead.

When Hicks got to the truck, Kruse was already behind the steering wheel, ready to roll. Hicks waited outside the back of the truck—he wouldn't set foot in the vehicle until he knew all his men were safely inside.

A minute later, the other four members of Predator team ran from the house and dove into the rear of the truck. Hicks followed them in and slammed shut the back doors. They all braced themselves as Kruse punched the accelerator.

Hicks looked around the truck and smiled grimly—two prisoners and all eight members of the team accounted for. No good guys hurt.

But then he noticed Kyle Arsdale holding his right arm. There was blood oozing between his fingers.

Arsdale saw Hicks moving toward him and laughed. "Don't worry, boss, it's not deep."

"What happened?" Hicks asked.

"Some grandma—," Ted Hummel began.

"Hey, my arm, my story!" Arsdale said. "There was this elderly lady—"

"Elderly?" Hummel interrupted. "She was ancient—had to be eighty!"

"Yeah, maybe, but she was a spry eighty! Anyway, she's in the kitchen, cutting some lamb for the boys, when we come in. I see her, and she's acting all hurt and stunned. But as soon as I got close, she went all ninja on me! Granny had some skills! I felt bad clocking her, but what else could I do?"

Hicks laughed with the rest of the team, then turned to Carlos Guitiérrez, Predator Three and the team's medic. But before he had a chance to say anything, Guitiérrez reached for his medical kit and said, "I'm on it."

The two prisoners, Hamdi al-Umari and Taha al-Bazzaz, bounced around on the floor against the rear wall of the truck's container box. All the team members were able to steady themselves, but the two prisoners, with their hands zip-tied, bore the brunt of every turn and pothole. Both men were in their late forties and both were directly responsible for supplying the explosives that had killed and wounded thousands in Denver.

Hicks walked over to them and dropped to one knee. Al-Bazzaz had his head down, the blood from his cut dripping on the floor between his thighs.

Al-Umari, on the other hand, was staring defiantly at Hicks. Suddenly he began shouting something in Arabic. Seeing no apparent understanding, he switched to French and finally stilted English. "I . . . laugh . . . their . . . deaths!" He finished by spitting directly into Hicks's face.

One team member swung for the captive, but Hicks deflected the blow. He used his sleeve to slowly wipe the saliva off his face, then smiled and nodded at the prisoner.

Al-Umari apparently misinterpreted this gesture to mean that he could say whatever he wanted—probably thought Hicks's restraint a part of the ridiculous American commitment to free speech. He grinned and said again, "I . . . laugh . . . their . . . deaths!"

As the final word came out, Hicks lunged. His left knee landed with a crunch against al-Umari's ribs. All the man's air shot out of his lungs in an audible burst. Hicks grabbed the terrorist's hair and flung his head back against the side of the truck. His knife was out of its sheath with a metallic ring and instantly was pricking blood from the prisoner's Adam's apple. "As I will laugh at yours," Hicks said in Arabic. "As I will laugh at yours."

He slammed al-Umari's head one more time against the truck, then stood up. He looked at Guitiérrez and, pointing at al-Umari, said, "Stitch him up next. I want them both ready and in their right minds for interrogation when we get to the safe house."

Guitiérrez nodded and turned back to stitching up Arsdale's arm. Hicks went to the front of the truck's box and ducked through the door into the cab. He dropped himself into the passenger seat, stared out the window, and began reviewing his next steps.

TUESDAY, JANUARY 13
A14 MOTORWAY
EAST COAST OF ITALY

It wasn't until four and a half hours into the eight-
hour drive that Riley got his first glimpse of the
Adriatic Sea. After flying through the night, his
team had landed at 6:22 a.m. at Aviano Air Base
outside of Pordenone, Italy. Now Mustang team
was on a five-hundred-mile drive down Italy's
eastern coast to the town of Barletta, located right
at the top of the heel of Italy's boot.

Mustang team, Riley thought as he shook
his head. He appreciated Hicks's honoring the
two football clubs hit in the Platte River Stadium
bombing by naming the ops teams after them. But
he still felt deep down that Hicks's putting him in
charge of ops for Mustang team was more of a dig
than a show of respect.

Riley had been watching for a while for signs
of water, and now, finally, south of Rimini, he
spotted it.

The water along this part of the Adriatic
Riviera was a rich blue, and the sands were white.
It was too cold at this time of year for the beaches
to be busy, but there were still some very large
yachts moored offshore. *You'd have to play in the*

PFL for a long time to afford boats like that, he mused as he tried to look around Skeeter Dawkins for a better view of one enormous craft. The boat was at least two hundred feet long, but it still wasn't easy to see from behind Skeeter's bulk.

It had been a great reunion with his old team: Matt Logan, Kim "Tommy" Li, Skeeter Dawkins, Gilly "Don't Call Me Jilly" Posada, and even Billy Murphy—*Sorry, now that he's on Wall Street it's* William *Murphy*—who, despite his objections, had been called back anyway. Once Uncle Sam had you in his grip, he wasn't always anxious to let go. Murphy was still sulking a bit, but Riley had no doubt the man could be counted on when the bullets started flying.

When the team first gathered ten days ago, Riley had given them one night to celebrate. They had taken full advantage of the evening. It was like old times with the alcohol flowing—even Scott had broken down and nursed a Sam Adams for most of the evening—and Riley sipping on his Diet Coke. That night as the men swapped old and new stories and as Li showed off his latest tattoos and as Scott won money off of other bar patrons by telling them the day of the week they were born based on their age and birthday and as Skeeter did his bizarre trick of flattening the bowl of a spoon onto the bar with just his thumbs, Riley had felt at home. He was friends with his football teammates, but these guys were his "Band of Brothers." Seventy-five percent of the Mustangs he wouldn't trust with his car; these guys he would trust with his life. Even more, he would trust them with his mother's life.

Riley leaned back to look behind Skeeter, who was driving the black Alfa Romeo 159. His eye caught Khadi looking at him. She had been going over the latest intel reports with Scott in the backseat. Riley had nipped the "Khadi with a *D*" thing early on, and since then Scott and Khadi had been getting along much better.

Riley nodded his head slightly toward the water and said, "Beautiful."

Unfortunately, Khadi missed the nod. Color came to her cheeks as Scott's head popped up from his computer screen.

Riley quickly pointed and stammered, "The water . . . see, the sea. I mean, the ocean . . . no, wait, I guess it is a sea—the Adriatic Sea—not even connected to an ocean. Well, not connected unless you follow the Adriatic to the Mediterranean and on to the Atlantic . . ."

"I think you can also get to the Indian Ocean via the Suez Canal," Scott added, grinning.

Riley shot him a look.

Meanwhile, Khadi had turned her head toward the water. "Yes, it is beautiful," she said, then turned back to the file she had been reading.

Riley swiveled and faced out the front of the car. Scott gave a push with his knee into the back of Riley's seat. Glancing over at Skeeter, Riley could see the slightest of grins on the man's narrow face.

"Shut up," he mumbled to the ever-silent man. "Just shut up."

/////////////////////

A half mile back from Riley's car trailed an Iveco Daily cargo van carrying the second half of Mustang team. Li drove, and Murphy and Morgan sat in the cab with him. Gilly Posada was in the back with the equipment.

The other guys had offered to rotate back, but Posada had declined. He preferred the solitude and the darkness. He was a thinker, a strategizer, a planner, and it was hard to get a lot of thinking done within earshot of Li's mouth. This setup gave him eight hours to read reports by flashlight, gather information using one of the team's satellite-linked Toughbook computers, and silently process.

Posada pulled out his GPS tracker and determined exactly where they were. *Two more hours*, he thought. A few weeks ago, while he was stationed at Hurlbert Field in Florida, Italy had been the furthest place from his mind. But then came the attacks, and everything changed.

He thought back to the night he was sitting on his couch with his six-year-old son, Danny, watching *Monday Night Football*. Although it was way past Danny's bedtime, Posada had let him stay up. Next to the Tampa Bay Tarpons, the Mustangs were the boy's favorite team, mostly because Daddy's buddy, Mr. Covington, played for them.

The two were sitting on the couch. Danny wore his knock-around Covington jersey—the signed one was framed and hanging on the wall of his room—and both were trying to clean up the remnants of a recent popcorn fight before Mom came in and discovered the mess.

When the screen had gone to an ESPN logo, Posada had immediately known something was wrong. Then the ESPN studios came on, and the tragic news was announced. As the minutes passed, more and more details poured out. Posada sat mesmerized, his emotions wavering between shock and anger. He changed from one channel to another, trying to get more information.

Then he became aware of a small movement next to him. He looked down and saw Danny. The boy was quietly trembling. Posada's heart sank as he realized his little son had been hearing about all the tragedy and death along with him. He shut off the TV, scooped Danny into his arms, and held him for a long time.

Even now, as he thought of that night and the wet spot that lingered on his shoulder well after he finally put Danny to bed, anger welled up in him. *Try explaining to a six-year-old why someone would want to do something like that.* That night, those terrorists had stolen Danny's innocence. When Posada had left for Denver a week later, the boy was still spending nights in Mom and Dad's bed.

A beep from his laptop drew his attention back to the screen. *Looks like we've got mail,* he thought.

He opened the laptop's Gmail account and saw the new message. It was from prdlvr5280@gmail.com—Hicks's account. The message was addressed to hrslvr5280@gmail.com with a CC to hrslvr5281@gmail.com, Mustang team Toughbooks 1 and 2. Toughbook 2 was Posada's; Scott had Toughbook 1 in the other vehicle.

Hicks had decided early on to keep off the usual communication networks to eliminate any risk of being monitored by friend or foe. He was determined to keep these black ops very black. Sometimes it was easiest to hide out in the open, so most of their communicating was done by innocuous messages sent over free e-mail accounts.

Posada opened the e-mail:

Hey guys,

Fishing's been great here! Caught two big old bass (one smallmouth and one bigmouth) without losing a single fly. :-) Been talking to some of the locals, and they said that fishing hole you were going to try is a great one. You might even find the "mother of all fish" there! LOL!! Well, gonna go drop my line a little more and see what bites. Good luck to you, and don't do anything I wouldn't do. ;-)

Clem

/////////////////////

Scott read the e-mail to everyone in the car. "'Clem'—nice touch," he laughed.

"Yeah," Khadi added, "but I have a hard time picturing Jim typing little smiley faces into his e-mails. He must have gotten another team member to do that."

Scott laughed. "Sounds like Jim thinks we're headed in the right direction. What do you think, Riley?"

Riley only grunted and nodded from the front seat. He could feel Khadi looking at the back of his head, waiting for more of a response. Finally she went back to discussing the e-mail with Scott.

Riley had spent the better part of the last couple of hours beating himself up for even looking at Khadi as a female. She was a team member. She should be treated no differently than any other. *Yeah, but those eyes* . . . It was insanity to let any personal feelings surface on a team like this. Feelings like that got people killed. *Yeah, but that laugh—small when appropriate but not afraid to let it go when the situation is right.*

Besides, she was a Muslim. That was a deal breaker right there. Riley was well aware of what the Bible had to say about marrying someone outside your faith—doing so was asking for tons of trouble. *Yeah, but she loves guns! A girl who loves guns!* This was stupid. What next? Send a little note that read *I like you. Do you like me? Check Yes or No?*

He had to stop this. He was being an idiot. *Yeah, but those eyes. Those deep, brown, lose-yourself-for-a-week-in, rich . . .*

Okay, bonehead, either get into the game or get out of the game. It's a nonstarter, and that's all there is to it.

Riley forced his thoughts to the e-mail. *Mother of all fish*—that meant Hicks had gotten a lead on Hakeem, and Mustang team was heading in the right direction. Riley wondered what he would do when he found the man who was responsible for so much pain in his life and in the lives of so many others. What would happen if it were just one-on-one—no one else watching? Would he bring Hakeem in to face justice, or would he carry out justice on the spot?

A sentence from one of Pastor Tim's sermons popped into his mind: *"Justice comes from God and from those government structures that He puts in authority."* Well, he was working for the government now, wasn't he? *Yeah, but it's been a while since I've been working for God.*

Riley thought back through the events of the past couple of weeks. He knew the circumstances that had put him there were too unusual to write off to chance. *God's got me here for a reason. I'm just not sure I like being confined to His rules.*

They were passing through Campomarino, which put them only two hours away from their destination. From here the team would cut inland a bit before heading back to the coast to Barletta.

The plan was simple. First they would drive through the town, surveilling all their key locations—particularly the al-Arqam mosque. Then they would travel another hour south to the much larger city of Bari, where they would set themselves up in a safe house and plan their next steps.

Things were going to get very busy once they got to Barletta, so Riley decided to try to get a little rest. As he closed his eyes, his mind again drifted over the past few weeks. It was almost surreal, the direction his life had gone. One day his whole focus had been on playing a game, trying to get one team into the play-offs, and a couple of weeks later his whole focus was on trying not to get another team killed.

Part of him missed the old life—carefree, living the PFL dream. But another part of him felt that his existence had taken on a much greater significance.

He thought back to the reaction of the fans and local news media when the PFL team owners had decided to declare the Mustangs-Predators game a tie, thereby eliminating both teams from the play-offs. "Unfair," people had screamed. "A travesty! We were in the lead! It's a slap in the face to those who died!"

Who did the fans think was going to play the game? Two Mustangs were dead, ten were injured, and at least half were emotionally incapable of setting foot on the field again without hours of counseling. The Predators had lost just as many, including their offensive coordinator. Sports fans tended to forget that players were people, not circus animals trained to give them entertainment no matter the circumstances.

No, it wouldn't be hard to leave that world.

As he continued to drift, the face of Alessandra Ricci appeared in the darkness of his mind. *Poor, sweet girl. She'll know only from stories what a stand-up guy her father was. I know she'll always hear that from her mom, but I need to make sure she hears it from me, too. Megan's dad is a good man; they'll be taken care of. But that sweet little girl, growing up without her dad . . .*

Alessandra's face lingering behind his eyes became too much for him, so he sat up and called to the backseat, "Hey, Scott, what else do I need to know about this little hamlet we're going to?"

"Ninety thousand people, very busy port, patron saint is Ruggero of Canne, got a real pretty castle."

"Fascinating," said an underwhelmed Riley.

"Okay, here's something, Mr. Fact-Critic. Think back to military history at your illustrious academy. Do you remember the Battle of Cannae?"

"Yeah . . . it was Hannibal and Carthage against Rome; First Punic War."

"Second Punic War, O great poster child for public education; the first was Hannibal's dad, Hamilcar."

"Continue," Riley said undaunted. He was used to these history lessons from Scott and actually enjoyed them with their lighthearted mocking tone.

Scott closed the lid of his Toughbook, stretched out in the roomy backseat, and locked his hands behind his head. "The Battle of Cannae took place in August of 216 BC, right around where our little town of Barletta would later be founded. Rome marches in with around ninety thousand troops to try to take care of Hannibal once and for all. Lucius and Gaius set up with standard straight line formations, but Hannibal sets up his fifty thousand in a crescent. When the Romans come, the Carthaginians let their center fall back. Rome pursues, Carthage brings the sides around, and—*bam!*— the mighty Roman army is surrounded. Rome has sixty thousand killed—including Gaius—and ten thousand captured. Carthage only loses about seventeen thousand. One of the worst routs and costliest battles in military history."

"Lessons?"

"Always check your periphery, because things aren't always what they seem. Don't let yourself fall into a trap. Word will have gotten here about Jim and the operation in France. They may be waiting for us. Our intel has to be perfect, and we need to run out every possible contingency."

Riley nodded, mentally filing that away for when they laid out their plan of attack. There was no doubt—Scott was good.

"It was Lucius," came a deep voice from the front seat. Everyone's eyes turned toward Skeeter.

"What'd you say, Skeet?" Scott asked.

"Lucius got hisself killed, not Gaius," Skeeter said, never taking his eyes off the road. "That's the public schools of Tunica County, Mississippi, K through 12."

The other three burst out laughing. "You're one strange bug, Skeeter," Scott said, shaking his head.

Tara Walsh despised making the Starbucks run. First of all, she felt it was below her position, particularly since she was the ranking member of the group. But in the egalitarian world of her little think tank, everyone was assigned one day a week to make the run.

The biggest problem wasn't the humiliation; it was all her team's special orders. People in line were not afraid to voice their impatience with her as she verbally stumbled trying to order Virgil Hernandez's venti low-fat caffè vanilla Frappucino, light on the whipped cream with a dash of nutmeg on top or Evie Cline's grande iced Tazo green tea latte with soy milk and light on the ice. Tara never knew how to say the drinks right, and she secretly envied those who rattled off their pretentious-sounding, fifteen-plus-word personalized coffee and tea choices. Couldn't anyone just order normal drinks anymore? Drinks like her standard Two Shots in the Dark, two shots of espresso topped off with dark roast coffee—easy to say, no mess, no fuss.

Balancing a tray of four drinks in one hand

CHAPTER TWENTY-FIVE

and carrying her own cup with the other, Tara planted a quick kick on the door to the "Room of Understanding."

The ROU was designed as a miniature war room, but early on Evie had voiced her concern that "war room" didn't communicate what it was they were really trying to do there. After all, weren't they really trying to prevent wars and bring about world peace and harmony? She had suggested "Love Room," but Tara had quickly vetoed that out of concern that this group of characters might take the name a little too literally while she was out getting coffee. "Room of Understanding" was finally chosen because, according to Evie's reasoning, the purpose of the work done in the room was to gain understanding of various events, thereby bringing greater under-standing among the nations of the world. Tara had fought it, but Scott had said, "It's just a room. Who gives a rip what they call it?"

Joey Williamson opened the door and took the tray from Tara. She saw him look down at her noticeable lack of an accompanying bag that should have been carrying the almond scone he had asked for, but he decided against mentioning it when he saw the dark expression on her face.

The room was large enough to comfortably accommodate five workstations around the perimeter and one large conference table in the middle. All the chairs around the table were unmatched and falling apart, the original chairs having been destroyed dur-ing a series of late-night races through the St. Louis CTD building. Division Chief Porter had told the team that their choices were to either sit on the floor or replace the chairs themselves. So they had scrounged garage sales and the local thrift store to come up with what they now sat in.

As per routine, the team was gathered around the table. Tara sat at the head. The odor her chair gave off when she sat in it always brought the words *sweaty dachshund* to mind. To her left were Virgil Hernandez and Evie Cline. To her right was Joey Williamson. And at the other end was a new guy, a brilliant media and technology analyst who, for some unknown reason, liked to go by the name Gooey.

"Okay, what have you come up with so far this morning?" Tara asked.

Hernandez spoke up first. "Big news is, while you were playing around at Starbucks, we matched a third suspect—Tahir al-Midfai. Iraqi-born, midtwenties. He's the guy who came through Platte River gate 7. We picked him up on a security camera, entering Rome's Fiumicino Airport ten days before the attack. That tells us he didn't fly into the airport, which means he probably originated in Italy. I'll bet you the flowers in the bud vase of Evie's VW that two weeks before the bombing, he was basking in the sun on the beaches of Barletta—or, since it was December, he was doing whatever terrorists do during the winter along the sea."

"When I was a kid in California," Williamson said, "we used to build bonfires on the beach during the winter. We'd roast hot dogs and s'mores and stuff like that."

"Oh, I love s'mores," Evie cried. "I used to make those at Girl Scouts camp—at least I did the year that I made it through the whole two weeks without getting sent home."

Tara just shook her head. A recent commercial campaign flashed in her mind where some poor guy was trying to do his best while working in an office filled with monkeys. "Excuse me . . . excuse me!" she piped in. "I think we may be slightly off track. So, that makes three we've identified—Naji Mahmud, our failed bomber who is now in a coma thanks to the modern-day Einstein who attempted Jim Hicks's shaking technique after Hicks had already gotten the information we needed; Djalal Kazemi, the interesting Iranian connection, now blown to bits; and now this al-Midfai guy. I'm assuming you're running the Fiumicino Airport database against our Platte River database?"

"As we speak," Hernandez assured her.

"So let's recap our bombing order and where things stand for identification. Bomber one—no ID. Why?"

"We've got a good visual on him, but he's not coming up in any databases," Evie said. "He very well might be a one-hit wonder."

"Bomber two—that's Mahmud. Bomber three?"

"That's al-Midfai," Hernandez answered.

"Good. Bomber four?"

"Another mystery date like number one. We have a facial but no match," Evie said.

"Okay, so one and four are unknown. What about five? No ID on him either, right? Come on, our databases can't be that bad," Tara complained.

"It isn't a database issue, Terri," Gooey said, mispronouncing Tara's name for the thirty-second time since joining the team, thus causing Tara to have her thirty-second vision of planting the heel of her boot between his puffy blue eyes. Gooey continued, "It's a camera-angle thing. He was chilling out front of the stadium, and all we got are some nice, framable pictures of the dude's back."

"Thanks . . . Goofy," Tara said, immediately regretting her attempt at a zinger, which for some reason had seemed quite cutting when she'd rehearsed it in her head. Out loud, it just sounded stupid.

The rest of the team rolled their eyes, which was actually a relief to Tara. Enduring an eye-roll meant getting off easy with this bunch.

"So, no five," Tara plowed on. "And what about six? Oh yeah, that's Kazemi. Right?"

"Right-o, Tinkerbell," Hernandez confirmed.

"What? What did you call me?"

"Tinkerbell. Sorry, I thought we were doing Disney names. Didn't you, Mickey?"

"I thought so too, boys and girls," Williamson answered in a falsetto voice. "What about you, Fairy Godmother?"

"Bibbidi-bobbidi-boo," Evie sang.

"I can't believe this," Tara grumbled loudly as she stood up and grabbed her stuff from the table. "I get a bachelor's degree in three years from Hillsdale and a master's from Yale, and here I am stuck in this room with you social miscreants."

As she turned to walk away, Hernandez called out, "Hey, Tink, you forgot number seven."

Tara spun around. "What?" she demanded.

"Bomber number seven. Your list only got through six."

Tara sighed and placed her stuff back on the table. "And what about bomber number seven? What might we have on him?" she asked in slow, measured words.

"Nothing," Gooey answered.

Tara paused before continuing in the same steady pace. "Is

there a possibility of your, maybe . . . I don't know . . . elaborating on your answer a bit, Gooey?"

"Well, Terri, it's like this: There are three cameras that show directly or peripherally that corridor down by the turf guy's office, where the last bomb blew. Not one of them was working that night. Three cameras less than a year old all malfunctioning at once—coincidence?" Gooey leaned across the table and slapped his hand on it as he spoke each of his final three words. "I . . . think . . . not!" Then he triumphantly stood straight up with his hands balled on his hips, staring at the sky in superhero fashion.

The other three burst into applause at this mighty display of detective genius.

"I work with a bunch of idiots," Tara mumbled. Then she said to the team, "I want all those videos reviewed again—every single Platte River tape starting with three hours prior to game time. Those two faceless suspects have to be on there somewhere. And I don't care what database you have to tap into; I want names for both of these guys by the end of the day. Now get to work!"

Tara grabbed her papers from the table again. She walked straight to her desk, dropped the last four caplets from her Extra Strength Tylenol bottle into her hand, and swallowed them dry.

WEDNESDAY, JANUARY 14
BARLETTA, ITALY

The hot wind blew in the big cat's face as he crept through the tall grass of the Namibian plain. A herd of impalas stood two hundred yards ahead. The stealthy feline carefully cut that distance by half. He scanned the herd and picked his victim. Not the smallest but also not the biggest. He wanted to make the effort worthwhile, but he did not want to bite off more trouble than he could chew.

He slowly raised himself into a crouch, his tail end lifting a little higher and wiggling back and forth. Steady . . . steady . . . steady . . . NOW! He bolted across the separation and was two-thirds of the way there before the impalas saw him coming.

Now it was their turn to run. They scattered, trying to confuse him, but he was intent on the single victim he had chosen. The young impala somehow sensed that it was the target. It broke right and made a mad dash for some acacia bushes. Too little, too late.

The cat was within five feet of the animal when something slammed into his side. He let out a yip as he flew sideways and rolled to a halt.

He felt the blood pouring down his fur and knew he'd been shot. This wasn't right! This wasn't how it was supposed to be! Panic set in as he heard footsteps coming toward him. He tried to get up but found he couldn't move—not even to turn his head to see who had shot him. He closed his eyes as pain racked his body. His breathing was rapid and shallow. Then he heard the footsteps stop. He slowly opened his eyes and saw a man in desert camouflage standing above him. On his right arm was a patch of the American flag.

As the wounded cat watched in horror, the soldier raised his rifle, pointed it down at his head, and pulled the trigger.

Hakeem awoke drenched in sweat and nearly hyperventilating. He sat up in his bed and forced himself to take slow, deep breaths.

He had been having the cheetah dreams again ever since arriving in Barletta. The dreams had stopped when his house had been bombed and his family killed so many years ago. Now they were back almost every night, and he loved them. He loved the rush of the hunt and the power of the kill. But tonight, for the first time, his dream had taken an alarming turn.

Hakeem slipped on his pants and walked across the cold cement floor to the hall, taking a blanket from the bed with him. He had been confined to this house and its courtyard ever since arriving in Italy. He couldn't argue with the wisdom of this decision, but it didn't make it any easier. After two weeks here, he was going stir-crazy.

The one solace he had found was up on the tile roof of the three-story house that had become his home. The rooftop gave him a feeling of serenity as he looked down at the city around him. In this morning's darkness the air was chilly and damp from the sea, and Hakeem wrapped the blanket tightly around his body. The Adriatic was much closer to the north, but he still had a more or less unobstructed view toward the eastern seaboard. He turned his face to where the sun would shortly rise as the sky began to lighten.

I'm a different man since coming here, Hakeem thought. *Life among my people, and especially around al-'Aqran, has taken away the lingering effects of living so long in America. I am amazed at how soft I had become. I am ashamed at how I mourned for the people and things I left behind. But no more! My edge has been honed again. My barbs have been sharpened. I now live to die. And the days I have left will be days of honor.*

The darkness continued to disappear, and the soft edges of the buildings around him became more defined. *But what about this dream? I have always been the hunter. Never have I been the prey. What does it mean? Was it just the* quzi *I ate last night? Or, more likely, the four shots of arrack that I drank, chasing the three bottles of Peroni. What are dreams anyway? It's silly to be concerned about them. Dreams are meant to be experienced, sometimes enjoyed, and then dismissed. It won't be long before I am the one standing over the American with the rifle pointed at his head.*

Just then, the first glimpse of orange broke the horizon to the east. Hakeem stood and removed the blanket surrounding him so that his body could absorb the warmth. It was a perfect moment—a connection between heaven and earth. The sun's rays flooded over him, washing away the dream, washing away the past, washing away the doubts. As he stood there, he made a conscious decision to meet from this roof every sunrise that he had left here in Barletta—a number he knew was rapidly diminishing.

CHAPTER TWENTY-SIX

MONDAY, JANUARY 19

BARLETTA, ITALY

For the last six days, Mustang team had made it their lives to know everything there was to know about Via Nazareth—the street that contained both al-Arqam mosque and the house of al-'Aqran. According to the intel from Tara Walsh's group back home, al-'Aqran was the founder and leader of the Cause.

Tara had given Mustang team some good information about this man, and Riley had used the daily hour-long drive to Barletta from the team's base of operations in Bari to review the file. By now he nearly had it memorized.

Al-'Aqran, or "the Scorpion," had been born Abdul Rahman Bey in the Iraqi village of Ar Radwaniyah, just outside of Abu Ghraib. In 1968, at the age of sixteen, Bey had joined the military just months before the bloodless coup that had put Ahmed Hassan al-Bakr and the Ba'athists into power. Saddam Hussein had immediately been made deputy president and had soon become the country's strongman. As with many in the Iraqi military, Bey's loyalty was primarily to Hussein. In 1979, Hussein took power by making accusations of disloyalty in the Ba'ath Party and arresting sixty-eight of its members while they were gathered for a meeting. Bey had been part of the team that executed twenty-two of those arrested.

By 1980, Hussein had become concerned about the radical Shiite influence that was spilling across the border from Iran and its newly installed leader, the Ayatollah Khomeini. These ideas didn't fit well with Hussein's vision of a secular state. So he invaded Iran on September 22, 1980. Captain Bey was part of the invasion force that entered Khuzestan that first day. He spent the next eight years fighting that war to a stalemate.

Tired and disillusioned, Bey had left the military. His loyalty to Saddam never wavered, but he was concerned about the president's judgment and tactics. Iraq was a powerful nation, but it was not powerful enough to win a conventional war in the modern era of treaties and alliances. Much later, Bey had watched with interest, but not surprise, as the Western forces easily toppled Saddam's government during the Occupation of Iraq.

The First Palestinian Intifada in 1987 had greatly intrigued Bey. A small group, outmanned and outgunned, had the boldness to take on the superior occupying Israeli force. But although they had courage, they didn't have enough vision. Rocks were fine; bombs would be better.

That was when the Cause was born and when Abdul Rahman Bey was reborn as al-'Aqran—the Scorpion.

Unfortunately for al-'Aqran, it seemed his vision was greater than his skills; for a decade and a half, the Cause languished in international obscurity. It was during that period that he blew off part of his face while experimenting with explosives. What the counterterrorism community hadn't realized was that what seemed to be incompetence was really just al-'Aqran biding his time while Hakeem, his ace in the hole, was growing in power and significance.

Finally, when the time was right, the Cause had struck. And when they struck, it was not for freedom in Iraq or in belated retaliation for Saddam Hussein's execution. Instead it was to restore the honor of an era gone by. It was to remind the world that not all the Iraqi people were willing to lie down and be America's lapdogs.

Riley closed the file and turned off the reading light in the van. Lord willing, by the end of today, this Scorpion would be in an American cage.

The plan Riley had devised was based on the old football misdirection play—make the opposing team think the action is taking place on one side of the field while you run the ball down the other. Great in concept; difficult in execution.

Al-'Aqran was vulnerable two times each day: when he left his house with his six armed bodyguards to walk to and from the al-Arqam mosque for the morning *Fajr* prayer service, and when he repeated the journey for the afternoon *Asr* service.

At first Riley had thought that this adherence to routine was either die-hard religious devotion or simple foolishness. His opinion changed when the team had spotted three men hidden on the rooftops between the house and the mosque. Each had a Tabuk sniper rifle, and at least one of them had an RPG-7 antitank grenade launcher. Riley had to assume the other two were similarly equipped. What had seemed to be foolish routine was starting to look more like a trap.

There was one other wild card in this deck. Every morning a man appeared on the roof of al-'Aqran's house. Because of where he positioned himself, they could never get a good look at him. He would appear while the sky was still dark and would disappear soon after sunrise. He didn't seem to be armed, but he was still worth keeping an eye on.

A late-model Fiat Punto had been parked for the last three days fifteen feet down and across the street from al-'Aqran's house. Riley had chosen this car to be the diversion. As al-'Aqran was returning from his morning prayers at the mosque, this little Fiat would blow sky-high. The explosion would do three things: First, it would create confusion on the ground. Second, it would draw out the rooftop snipers, who would then be dispatched by Mustang team's own rooftop snipers—Khadi Faroughi and Billy Murphy. Third, the confusion would allow the rest of the team to burst out of the house where they would be hiding along al-'Aqran's route, dispatch the bodyguards, and taser the Scorpion. The team would then carry their prisoner around the building and out back to where the vans were waiting. If all went well, ten minutes after the car blew, they would be on the SS16aa highway cruising back down to Bari.

Scott had sent the surveillance photos of the bodyguards to his crew in the ROU. He had hoped one of them might be Hakeem. But the crack investigation group had been able to identify each guard as long-standing in the European theater, thus making them expendable.

It was 5:13 a.m. when Mustang team's two cargo vans turned down Via Agostino Samuelli, one short block west of Via Nazareth. Matt Logan, the team's demolitions expert, slipped out of the second van and headed toward the parked Fiat while the rest of the team gathered in the rear of the second cargo van.

At 5:25 a.m., they heard three rapid knocks on the rear door, followed by two more. Kim Li opened the door and Logan jumped in.

"Done. A lot of flash, a lot of noise, a lot of smoke, but not a large blast radius. Should be zero collateral damage unless someone is actually in the car. Speaking of which, I also disabled the car's ignition so we don't have anybody driving off in the thing."

"Good work," Riley said. He turned to Khadi and handed her the detonator. "You know what to do. As soon as they're in front of the building, set this thing off. Murph will pop snipers one and two, and you'll catch three." Then he turned to Murphy. "Either one of you misses your target, we're toast. Got it?"

They both nodded, and Khadi gave him a smile.

Khadi was beginning to fit into the team dynamics, and Riley was glad to see it. She would probably never fully understand the loyalty and devotion these men had for each other, but she was a professional. Riley knew his own strength of character, his competency, and his willingness to lead by example all combined with some X-factor to make him a man his teammates would follow to their graves. He didn't expect Khadi to go that far, but he was pleased that she seemed willing to do whatever it took to get the job done.

"Okay, it's time to get in position. You be careful," he said to the two snipers, but his eyes were locked on Khadi's. "Now go."

Murphy and Khadi jumped out of the van, each carrying a case that held an M24 SWS.

Riley stared at the doors as they closed. Was he doing the right thing sending Khadi out to kill someone? It wouldn't be her first time, he knew, and she had been trained to do this. In fact, she had the second highest shooting accuracy on the team—right behind Murphy. She was the right person, but was it the right thing?

His concentration was broken by Scott's voice softly singing, "Riley and Khadi sitting in a tree, k-i-s-s-i—"

The song was interrupted by Skeeter's large hand gently clipping the official team leader on the back of the head. Nervous laughter filled the van.

Riley surveyed the team silently. Wartime created strange relationships. Could there be any other situation with the power to bond together such different personalities and backgrounds? When men struggled together, suffered together, bled together, killed together, and grieved together, a connection was made that often went deeper even than blood.

"Men," Riley said, "when I left this life a few years ago, I thought I had left it for good. When I came back, it wasn't because I sought it out. It sought me out. I was living out my day-to-day just like you guys were. Then these little men with their big bombs came into my life and called me out. Well, since they called, I feel I'm obliged to answer.

"These terrorists took the lives of so many and destroyed the lives of so many others. One of the lives they took was my close friend Sal Ricci. Two of the lives they destroyed were those of his wife, Megan, and his baby daughter, Alessandra." Riley took a picture of Meg and Alessandra out of his pocket and passed it around. "This is to remind you that these men's victims are not just faceless statistics. It's easy to get lost in the numbers of the casualty reports. But when you look at that picture, you're looking at the faces of the victims. And when we go out there this morning and the bullets start flying and the blood starts spilling, remember this woman and this little girl."

They all sat there silently looking at the floor of the van, processing what Riley had said.

Then a quiet voice began singing, "Kumbaya, my Lord, kumba—"

Another Skeeter slap to Scott's head shut down the song.

"Come on, Skeet! You're going to give me a concussion before we even leave the van," Scott said, rubbing the back of his head.

Skeeter feinted like he was going to hit again, causing Scott to flinch. Everyone laughed and then started rechecking their gear.

Like the Predator team, each man carried a P90 submachine gun and a Heckler & Koch handgun. The only additional weapon the Mustang team members had was a Taser X26 holstered to their hips.

It was six o'clock; dawn would break in about fifty minutes. The time had come.

The house they now entered had been chosen because its front was on Via Nazareth and its rear was on Via Agostino Samuelli. It was a long two-story house inhabited by one man in his late fifties and two women whose ages seemed to fall on either side of his. The team had never seen anyone entering or leaving the home before 9 a.m.

Logan, Li, and Scott crept up the stairs to the bedrooms while Riley, Posada, and Skeeter looked around downstairs.

There was some rustling upstairs followed by the sound of glass or ceramic breaking. Then all was quiet again. Riley finished sweeping the first level, then went upstairs. There he found that the three occupants had been bound and gagged and brought into one bedroom. They lay scrunched together on a bed.

"Nice work, guys," he said. "Scott, do your thing. And be nice."

"You got it, Pach."

Scott went over to the three and said, *"Mi dispiace.* (I'm sorry.)"

The three didn't seem to accept his sincerity.

"Non vi faremo del male. (We're not going to hurt you.)"

Again their eyes expressed fear and doubt.

Scott reached over to the fabric that had been used to gag the man and gently pulled it down. The man looked like he wanted to scream but thought better of it when he saw Li fingering his P90. Scott asked him, *"C'è qualcun'altro in casa?* (Is there anyone else in the house?)"

In response, the man let out a flood of angry, fearful words, and Scott quickly replaced the gag.

"What'd he say?" Riley asked.

"He doesn't like your mom."

Riley affected a hurt expression. "He's never even met her."

"Okay, let's try this again," Scott said. *"C'è qualcun'altro in casa?"* He nodded his head up and down and then shook it side to side.

The man shook his head side to side.

"I'd call that a no."

"Good job. Logan, Li, make sure they're secure, then meet us downstairs."

"Shouldn't we bring them down with us? Be a whole lot safer," Logan said.

"No, I don't want them caught in the cross fire in case we have bad guys chasing us. You secure them well enough, and we won't have anything to worry about."

"You got it, Pach," Logan acquiesced.

Downstairs, Skeeter and Posada had taken chairs from the kitchen table and placed them by the front windows. There they settled in for the long waiting game. At one point, there was a flurry of excitement as al-'Aqran and his entourage passed by on their way to the mosque. Riley watched their prey through a slight part in the curtains. This was the man who was ultimately responsible for what had happened at the Mall of America and at Platte River Stadium.

It was all Riley could do to keep himself from putting a bullet in the man's head right then. *All in good time.*

//////////////////////

Khadi looked up the street from her rooftop perch to see if she could spot Murphy. She couldn't, which was good. If she couldn't see him, then chances were the bad guys couldn't either.

From her vantage point, she watched two of these soon-to-be-dead men. Her target was eating breakfast—some kind of nasty-looking sprout sandwich that had been wrapped in wax paper.

She wished things would start soon. The longer she looked at this guy, the more real he was becoming. It was hard to think that this man would shortly be violently killed, and that she would be the one pulling the trigger. No matter what the man had been involved in, stopping a beating heart was not a concept she took lightly.

In spite of her contemplations, she had no doubt that she would go through with it. First of all, the man would not give a second thought about doing the same to her. And most important, her team was counting on her. If she missed her shot, it was very likely that this man would kill one or more of her friends. She was determined that this would not happen. She would not let her team down. She would not let Riley down.

Her attention turned back to the mosque across the street. Suddenly the doors opened and people began filing out. There they were—al-'Aqran and his henchmen.

Henchmen, she thought. *Sounds like a word from* Batman. *Scott must be rubbing off on me.*

The group of men walked slowly down the street, joking back and forth. Al-'Aqran obviously put a lot of confidence in his snipers.

When they were three houses from the detonation point, Khadi stole a glance at her target. She saw that he had picked up his rifle and was watching the group. *There you go, genius. Keep your eyes on your boss instead of your surroundings.*

Two houses away now. Khadi saw the slightest of movements on a rooftop down the street. As she watched, the barrel of Murphy's M24 slowly slid into view.

One house. Khadi's whole body was tense. Her thumb was poised over the detonator button.

Now! Her thumb went down. Up the street a fireball mushroomed into the air, followed by a thunderous noise.

Khadi didn't take time to watch the fireworks. She dropped the detonator, picked up her rifle, and got her target in the sights. Just as they had planned, his attention was on the explosion. Khadi drew in her breath and depressed the trigger. Three hundred fifty feet away, her target dropped out of sight as her bullet found its mark. She dropped the rifle and made her escape toward the vans.

///////////////////////

Hakeem had been eating breakfast when the windows of the kitchen blew in. He ran out the front door, his face and bare feet bleeding from the glass. Across the street, a car was engulfed in flames. Hakeem thought of the snipers and looked up in time to see the head of one of them all but disappear from his body.

He ran back into the house and threw his body against the

doors of the cabinet that held al-'Aqran's guns. The wood shattered against the blow. Hakeem reached in and grabbed an AK-47. As he did, he heard the sound of gunfire outside. He inserted a clip into the automatic weapon and stuffed three more into the waistband of his loose pants. Then he ran back through the broken glass and into the street.

///////////////////////

Riley and Skeeter stood right behind the door so as not to get hit by flying glass. Posada and Scott were outside on the north side of the house, and Li and Logan were on the south side. When the car blew, they all rushed at once. The eyes of the bodyguards were turned toward the explosion, so they never saw the men who put the short bursts of 28 mm rounds into their bodies.

Riley and Skeeter went right for al-'Aqran. The jolt from Riley's Taser dropped the terrorist immediately. Skeeter snatched the man off the pavement and threw him over his shoulder. Quickly, the team scanned the street and saw no one coming toward them. They turned and ran around the house to the vans out back.

As they reached the vehicles, they heard the distinctive clatter of an AK-47. Just then Khadi arrived out of breath from up Via Agostino Samuelli. Skeeter threw al-'Aqran into the rear of the first van, and Khadi and Scott scrambled in with their captive. Logan jumped in the driver's seat as Posada circled around to the other side. Riley, Skeeter, and Li stood outside the van while Riley did a mental head count.

"Murph," Riley said. "Where's Murphy? He should have been here by now!"

They waited for thirty seconds, guns at the ready, watching for Murphy to come between the houses. Finally Riley said, "I'm going after him. Skeeter, Li, you two go with Scott and Khadi. I'll follow you with Murphy in the second van."

"I ain't leaving you, Pach!" Skeeter said.

Riley grabbed the front of the man's shirt. "Skeet!" he yelled. "I don't have time to argue! The team can't afford to lose you, so I am ordering you into that van! Now go!"

Skeeter stood for a moment, glaring at Riley, then dove into the van along with Li.

As Riley ran toward the house, he could hear the sound of tires squealing on asphalt. He went through the back door and crossed to the front of the house. He stopped as he reached the still-open front door and blown-in windows. In the middle of the street, Murphy's twisted body lay in a pool of blood. He must have been hit running across the street from his position.

Riley knew he had to get him, but he also knew that there was someone else out there with a gun—probably more than one by now. As he contemplated his course of action, a footstep crunching glass caught his ear. He spun around in time to see a surprised look of recognition, a rifle butt driving toward his head, and then blackness.

CHAPTER TWENTY-SEVEN

TUESDAY, JANUARY 20
BARI, ITALY

Hicks heard Gilly Posada of the Mustang team radio from the roof of the safe house as the vans that carried Predator team rounded the corner. A minute later, the newcomers barged inside.

It had been twenty hours since Billy Murphy had gone down and Riley Covington had disappeared, and the eight Predator team members had spent all but two of those hours either on a plane or in a van. Hicks was exhausted.

Scott met them inside the door. "Guys, welcome. Jim, thanks for coming so quickly."

"Sure. So what's the status?"

"We've been working like dogs trying to get information. But first, before we get to business, why don't you guys sit at the table? We've got some bread, and Kim's cooked up some Italian sausages."

For the first time Hicks noticed the smell of onion, garlic, and bell pepper that hung heavy in the room. He felt a twinge in his empty stomach but declined the offer with a wave of his hand. "I didn't come here to eat, and I didn't come here to socialize."

"Maybe not," Scott countered, "but you're

going to be an even bigger pain than usual if you don't get some food in you."

Hicks gave in. "Fine, Weatherman, serve the food."

The members of Predator team gathered with him around the scratched table. Hicks sat at the head, then clockwise around the table sat Jay Kruse, Carlos Guitiérrez, Steve Kasay, Chris Johnson, Brad Musselman, Kyle Arsdale, and Ted Hummel.

While the plates were dished out, Hicks scanned the room disapprovingly. It was sparsely furnished and looked like it hadn't had a good spring-cleaning since Mussolini was in power. Li, the one with the tattoos, brought over plates of food and bottles of Italian beer; the Mississippi giant, Skeeter, sat guarding the front door. "Where's Khadi?" Hicks asked Scott.

"She's sleeping in the near bedroom. Logan's crashed over there somewhere too. Gilly's scouting up on the roof."

"What about your prisoner?"

Scott pointed to a dark corner of the large room, where a blanket covered a lumpy shape on the floor. "Mr. Scorpion was getting to be a little too high maintenance, so we shot him up with some happy juice and dropped him in the corner. He should be awake in a couple of hours. So far we haven't been able to get much out of him."

Hicks cut off a piece of sausage and stuffed it in his mouth. The flavor of the sauce was incredible, but the spice of the sausage had him reaching for the bottle of Peroni that Li had placed in front of him.

"Beer at four in the morning? Classy, Jim."

Hicks followed the voice to the bedroom, where Khadi leaned against the doorway. She was still wearing her black outfit from the operation. Her hair was held up with a clip, and she hadn't applied even what little makeup she usually wore. All eating at the table stopped momentarily as everyone took a long look at her. Khadi shifted on her feet uncomfortably, then walked to the kitchen. She grabbed a bottle of Suio sparkling water and sat by Skeeter.

Hicks turned back to his sausage. "Yeah, well, it's four in the afternoon somewhere in the world."

"Pago Pago," Scott said.

"What?" Hicks asked.

"Pago Pago, American Samoa. It's four in the afternoon there."

Hicks just looked at him.

"Hey, sometimes it's a blessing; sometimes it's a curse."

"Yeah, well, what do you say you keep your curse to yourself."

The team ate a little more in silence. Scott walked over to where al-'Aqran was bunched up on the floor. He lifted the blanket to make sure the terrorist leader was still breathing. He was. Scott dropped the covering and returned to the table.

Brad Musselman finally broke the silence. "So, how do we know the football hero isn't dead?"

Everyone in the room tensed at the question, and Skeeter's chair audibly shifted on the wooden floor.

"First of all, the 'football hero' is the operational leader of Mustang team or Mustang Two," Scott said forcefully, "and you'll refer to him and address him with respect accordingly. Understand?"

Musselman waved his fork in a noncommittal gesture.

"Nevertheless, it's still a good question," Scott continued. "The answer is that we don't know for sure. However, we 'borrowed' a witness on his way home from work who told us that there was one dead guy who stayed stretched out on the street until the police came. Obviously, that was Billy. But he also said there was a second guy who was carried out of a house on another man's shoulder. They went into al-'Aqran's house, and our witness didn't see either of them come out again. Our assumption is that if Riley had been killed, he would have been left for the police like Billy was."

"Any thoughts on where he is now?" Steve Kasay asked.

Khadi answered, "About an hour ago, Tara Walsh's contact here—the guy who told us about the mosque and al-'Aqran's house—informed us about three warehouses that members of the Cause have been seen frequenting. Two of them are down by the port, and one is closer to the railroad tracks. We were waiting for you guys to arrive before staking those buildings out for activity. Tara's team is also working on some satellite surveillance. We don't want to move on one of them without being sure that Riley's in there for fear that they'll kill him if we choose wrong."

"I just don't understand how Captain America was fool enough to get himself captured," Musselman said quietly to his plate.

In a flash Skeeter's chair went rattling across the floor and he was racing for the man. Scott intercepted him just as Musselman jumped up to meet Skeeter's onrush.

Hicks rose next, and he raced around the table. "Skeeter, get back to your post! Now!"

Skeeter looked at Scott, who nodded. The big man glared at Musselman, who defiantly returned the stare. Skeeter slowly turned around and found his chair, which was now missing a leg. He threw the broken chair across the room and returned to stand in his place by Khadi.

Hicks watched him all the way.

Musselman chuckled and turned to sit again.

Hicks grabbed him by the shoulder and spun him around. "Did I say sit down?"

Musselman looked surprised. "Well . . . uh . . . no."

"You don't sit down until I tell you to sit down! You want to know how Covington got himself taken? I'll tell you. He was going after one of his men. That's what real soldiers do; they take care of their own. That's what I would do if one of my men was lying in the middle of the street—even . . . you." Hicks accentuated these last two words with his index finger poking hard into Musselman's chest. "And what real men don't do is sit around sipping their beers, criticizing other men's acts of bravery. Do you understand?"

"Yes, sir," Musselman replied.

"I said, do you understand!"

"Yes, sir!"

"Now, sit!"

Musselman dropped into his chair.

Hicks continued, speaking to all who were at the table. "Listen close, because I'm only going to say this once. Effective immediately, there is no Predator team. We are all Mustangs. Do you understand that? We are all Mustang team. Take your assigned number and add eight. If you have a hard time with the math, talk to Scott."

Now he addressed everyone in the room. "We've got a man out there who we've got to assume is alive until proved otherwise. Wherever he is, we will find him—together. And if I see any more of you bickering or fighting, you will find yourselves in two weeks' time gathering sand samples in Somalia. Clear?"

A general murmur of assent answered Hicks.

He turned to Scott. "Get my men rotated into the watch cycle."

"You got it, Jim."

The veteran started back to his place at the head of the table, then stopped and looked at Musselman. "And, Scott, why don't you start right away by putting Brad up on the roof?"

"You got it, Jim," Scott repeated with a smile.

Hicks sat down at the table, took a long swig of his Peroni, and stuffed another bite of the spicy sausage into his mouth.

TUESDAY, JANUARY 20
CTD MIDWEST DIVISION HEADQUARTERS
ST. LOUIS, MISSOURI

The Room of Understanding was in a flurry of activity. That was one thing Tara Walsh appreciated about her little band of misfits: they worked hard, and they were smart. *Guess that's two things,* she thought and smiled to herself.

Each member of the team had given her regular progress updates—all except for Gooey, whom she pretty much left to himself. Hernandez had found out the identity of the fourth bomber—Syamsuddin Ibrahim, an Indonesian from Aceh, which accounted for some of their difficulties in tracking him down. Tara walked over to Hernandez's workstation, where he was continuing to run facial recognition software, searching for a name for bomber one. Hernandez looked up and gave her a quick nod, then went back to what he was doing.

Tara continued toward Evie's desk. About an hour ago, Scott had called and asked that Evie be pulled away from what she had been working on to start searching for satellite images of some buildings in Barletta. Evie had found a multitude of old shots and was now trying to reposition a bird for some real-time pictures.

"Are you having any trouble with permissions for the satellite?" Tara asked.

Evie shook her head. "No, you cleared the path pretty well. I'll let you know if anyone starts raising a stink."

Tara put her hand on Evie's shoulder and then walked around

the conference table to the other side of the room. Joey Williamson was the resident speed-reader at over a thousand words per minute. Tara had asked him to go back over the eyewitnesses' statements to see if anything had been missed. Looking over his shoulder, she watched as his long index finger rapidly traced the lines down the page. *Amazing,* she thought as she reached around him to the dish on his desk that held chocolate-covered espresso beans. She popped a couple into her mouth and then paused.

At the end of the room was Gooey's workstation. It was an unpleasant place for a number of reasons. First of all, Gooey seemed to have some sort of digestion problem, which caused each of them to perpetually burn scented candles at their desks. Second, the place was a pigsty. Papers and trash were spread all around his desk and on the floor. Third, he was as sloppy in his English as he was in his appearance. Every time he spoke to her, she spent most of the conversation mentally correcting his grammar. Basically, what it came down to was that he was the exact opposite of her. Everything she strove to not be, he was.

She crunched down on the espresso beans, letting the taste and aroma fill her senses, then moved toward Gooey's desk. "How's it going, Gooey?"

He answered with a wave of his index finger. "One minute."

Tara began to move away before the aromatic protection of the espresso beans wore off, but Gooey said without turning around, "Seriously, wait. Just one minute."

Tara sighed and prepared for the olfactory assault. She looked at the monitor Gooey was watching. The video was of one of the Platte River gates. Panicked people were streaming out. People were pressed up against the wrought iron bars. Gooey had a bright circle following the head of one particular person. His mouse clicked a button that recorded that segment. "Get everyone around here, Terri. I've got something to show you."

Tara knew that would be a tough sell to her team. "Are you sure it's—?"

"Tara!" Gooey said, as he spun his chair around to face her. Something in his eyes told her that this was important. "Trust me. You're all gonna want to see this."

"Hey, gang!" Tara called out. "Gooey's got something he wants to show us."

A collective groan came from the other three as they stopped what they were doing and walked toward Gooey and Tara. Evie and Hernandez took a detour to Williamson's desk to grab a handful of beans.

Gooey addressed the gathering. "Okay, the big question is how the terrorists got the bombs into the stadium. With all the security, it's remotely possible they could get one or two in. But six? Not gonna happen! There's got to be another way the bomb balls made it in.

"So I've been following Kazemi—the Iranian guy—from the time he went into the gates at Platte River. Here he is going in about two hours before the game. Check him out. He's carrying a souvenir football, and he strolls right past a cop with a bomb dog. Not so much as a tail wag from our canine friend. Conclusion?"

"He doesn't have the bomb yet," Williamson answered, popping another espresso bean into his mouth. "We've seen this. Can you maybe speed things along?"

"Yeah, yeah, yeah. Hang on." The rate of Gooey's words was increasing with his excitement. He used his mouse to forward the timeline until a wide shot of the sidelines came on. "So, how did he get the bomb? This was about an hour and forty-five minutes before game time. Way over in the corner here, Kazemi's leaning over the railing getting his souvenir ball signed. Take a look at who's signing it."

A gasp escaped each of them.

Hernandez said, "I know that number! That's—"

"Yeah, yeah, yeah. And look here."

"That's al-Midfai getting a ball signed," Hernandez said.

"And here."

"That's Mahmud," Evie said.

"And here."

"That's . . . new guy," Williamson said.

"Ibrahim," Hernandez helped him.

"Yeah, Ibrahim," Williamson finished.

"All the bombers got their footballs autographed before the game by the same player. 'But,' you might ask, 'how did souvenir balls magically turn into bomb balls? And if they got the bomb balls signed, why wasn't our friend's name sprawled across the ball that was recovered from Mahmud?' Good questions, grasshoppers. Let's zoom in to the signing process. Here's our favorite player holding a football tucked under his arm and signing someone's shirt. Here he's signing a picture. Now here comes Mahmud, who hands our boy a football. But Mr. Butterfingers accidentally drops it. Now watch carefully . . . there! Presto, change-o. We have a little ball swap. And, good guy that he is, he doesn't forget to sign the new ball."

"He's turned the pen around!" Hernandez called out.

"Yep, he's flipping the pen. I guess he didn't want his name on the bombs on the off chance one of them didn't go off. 'But,' you ask, 'how did our football friend get the bomb balls into the stadium to begin with?'"

Gooey's penchant for asking and answering his own questions was working overtime.

"Here he is walking into the stadium with a couple of other players. Check him out; he's pulling a standard Mustangs ball bag behind him—eight balls rolling right past security. Just like that, we've got our football bomb distribution problem solved. But now for the coop de grass."

Tara held her breath. She couldn't imagine anything being more unbelievable than what they had just seen.

Gooey used his mouse to bring up a new screen with some grainy slow-motion footage. "You guys know about the videos shot by those two Zapruder wannabes by the field manger's office. This is thirty-six seconds prior to detonation. The guy's holding the camera above his head, trying to capture all the freaked-out people. Now, look who slides into the shot at the bottom left. Check out the jersey; check out the pads. . . . It's Mr. Pen Flipper."

"Good find, Gooey," Tara said, "but we all know what happened to him in that tunnel."

"Do we now? Let me zoom tight. Watch our player as he turns back toward the camera."

"Wait! That's not—"

"No, it's not. My friends, meet bomber number seven, all

dressed up like a football player. My guess is that he was hiding away in the field manager's office until the fireworks started."

"But why?" Evic asked. "It makes no sense. I mean, why go through all the trouble of a body double if you're just going to get blown up anyway?"

"Ahhh, the key word being *if*, my young padawan," Gooey answered, fully in his element and wanting to draw out the moment. "*If* you were going to blow yourself up, it would make no sense. But *if* you were not quite ready for your one-way ticket to martyrville but you wanted everyone to *think* you were, then it makes perfect sense. Take a look at this video from gate 5 during the postbomb mass exit. Let me zoom in real close-like to the dude in the overcoat and Mustangs hat. Look familiar?"

Williamson and Hernandez each exhaled matching expletives. Evie just stood there stunned. Tara ran across the room, picked up the phone, and dialed Scott's secure satellite number.

TUESDAY, JANUARY 20
BARLETTA, ITALY

The past thirty-six hours had been a nightmare for Riley—or more precisely, a series of nightmares. Dreams filled with betrayal; dreams filled with heartbreak.

> *Riley is back with the Air Force Special Operations Command. Alpha Team is surrounded. Gunfire pings off the Humvee that is giving him temporary protection. He turns to Scott Ross, his number two, and tells him to order in some air support. But instead of lifting the radio, Scott picks up his Beretta M9, levels it at Riley's head, and with a twisted grin, pulls the trigger.*

Riley half awoke out of that horror into a hazy state. Everything was black; he couldn't move his arms or legs. His body tried to writhe and twist, but the paralysis kept him locked in place. A gutteral yell escaped his mouth. The throbbing in his head was making him sick, as was the salty sweat dripping into his mouth. The chill on his naked upper body caused him to shiver uncontrollably.

Moments passed, and his mind began to

clear. The lack of movement came not from paralysis but from the cords that bound his hands and feet to a chair. The taste in his mouth was not the bitterness of salt but the metallic tang coming from blood that was slowly oozing from where he had bitten his upper lip. His mind rewound, trying to remember how he had gotten to this place.

As he strained to bring clarity to the blurry images in his brain, a door opened and closed. Two sets of footsteps came toward him. Soft Arabic words were exchanged. Riley's whole body tensed. Then he felt a sharp stab into his arm, and his mind swirled back into blackness.

Riley is back at his parents' house. It's Christmas, and earlier in the morning he opened a long package that contained his dream gift—a Crosman 781 pneumatic BB gun. That gift triggered a war that is now taking place on the battlefield of his backyard. For the last three hours, he has been out in the snow, setting up and plinking down his collection of green plastic army men. His boots soaked through a long time ago, and the pain in his toes makes him wince with every step.

"Just one more time and then I'll go in," he tells himself. But before he knows it, he finds himself placing the men back up on the soggy, wooden picnic table—targets for another tiny, copper-plated steel ball.

Riley's post-Christmas morning bliss is suddenly interrupted by a scream from inside the house, followed by two loud pops. Without thinking, Riley runs toward the back door and throws it open. He races through the kitchen without taking off his boots, tracking snow on Mom's squeaky-clean linoleum floor. He runs through the dining room and grabs the end of the banister, using its stability to reverse his direction. He bounds up the stairs two by two. When he reaches his parents' bedroom, he stops abruptly in the doorway.

Riley's mother and father are both lying on the floor, their bodies cocked at strange angles. Standing over them, holding a handgun, is Grandpa Covington. Riley gasps, and the retired airman turns toward him. Grandpa looks at Riley, then nods at his BB gun and smiles. "I'm afraid you're going to have to bring a little more firepower than that, soldier," Riley's childhood hero says as he raises the pistol toward the boy and—

"NO!" Riley screamed as he woke up again. He was shaking all over, and his body was dripping with sweat. "It's only a dream," he muttered to himself. "It's only a dream. It's only a dream."

The effects of the drugs gradually wore off. In the darkness behind his blindfolded eyes, he again tried to rewind the tape in his mind to discern how he had gotten here. He made it to the point of the extraction of al-'Aqran. Everything had gone well, hadn't it? No, there was a problem. Someone—Billy—was missing. He remembered sending the team on its way. . . . Skeeter wasn't happy. . . . Then there was the house . . . Billy's body . . . a sound—what was it?—glass; footsteps crunching glass, and then . . . *Oh no! Please, no!*

The door opened again, and the sound of footsteps echoed in the room—just one set this time. The door closed—a new sound. The footsteps scraped across the cement floor, then stopped. A wooden chair dragged across the hard surface and creaked slightly as someone sat. Silence hung in the air; the only sounds were the visitor's light breathing and Riley's own labored breath.

Time stretched on before Riley finally spoke. "Sal? Sal, is that you?"

The question floated without a reply.

"Sal? How could you do it, man?"

The silence of the visitor was exasperating. Riley's voice began to crescendo with anger and pain. "Answer me, *friend*. How could you do it? Who are you, Sal? What are you?"

A hand grabbed the blindfold and pulled it violently down around Riley's neck.

There, twelve inches from Riley's face, was Sal Ricci. Hate and anger shone in his eyes. "Who am I, *friend*? I am Hakeem Qasim! What am I? I am an Iraqi! I am a child of Allah! I am a predator, and America is my prey!" Hakeem leaped up out of his chair and began pacing around the room.

Riley's head dropped over the back of his chair. The room was spinning. He tried to say something but found that no words would come. All he could manage were short bursts of air. What could he say? What possible words would mean anything in this bizarre parallel universe?

"But Megan . . . Alessandra," he whispered.

Hakeem walked to his chair, turned it around, and straddled it backward. He had regained some of his composure and now seemed almost anxious to speak. But there was still an underlying hiss to his voice. "There is an old Arab proverb: You are in a boat, and your father, your wife, and your child are all drowning. You have room for only one other person. Whom would you save? Not your wife; you can always marry again. Not your child; you can always have more. Would you save your father? Yes. Because you only have one. I have saved my father—or at least I have restored his honor. If it is at the expense of my wife and daughter, so be it."

Riley shook his head in disbelief. "You can't mean that. What's happened to you, Sal?"

His former teammate's closed fist suddenly exploded across Riley's left cheek. "I said my name is Hakeem! Sal is dead."

Riley spit a mouthful of blood onto the cement at the other man's feet and looked at him with disgust. "Whatever. Hakeem will be dead too, soon enough."

Slowly, a heart-chilling smile spread across Hakeem's face. "Right you are, old friend. But I don't think the circumstances of my demise will be quite what you have in mind."

"Come on, Sa—Hakeem. What's left to do? You've restored your family honor. Thousands are dead. The PFL is in shambles."

"The PFL? Oh no, it's not in shambles . . . yet," Hakeem said with that same sickening grin.

"What do you mean 'yet'?" Riley was trying to keep his wits about him, but he felt like he was right on the edge of a downward psychological slide from which he might not be able to recover.

"You know how it is, Riley. No one really cares about the regular season games. They only care about the big ones."

The sick feeling that Riley had in his stomach was now becoming a sharp pain. His voice became pleading. "You can't be serious. . . . Please, man. Leave it alone."

"Leave it alone? Maybe you should be taking your own advice!

Maybe if you'd left it alone you wouldn't be sitting here bleeding all over yourself. What are you even doing here, Riley?"

"I'm tracking down a murderer. I'm hunting for Hakeem the terrorist." Riley paused. Then he added softly, "I'm avenging the death of my best friend."

Silence filled the air.

Hakeem stood up again and circled around Riley. "You weren't supposed to be here, Riley. You're supposed to be back in Colorado, taking care of Meg and Alessandra."

"Funny, I thought that was your job."

A hand came hard across the back of Riley's head, rocking him in the chair. "You forget your place, *old friend*!" Hakeem walked around in front of Riley and slowly shook his head. "Why have you come here? This wasn't supposed to happen."

"Yeah, well, surprise. It did. So are you going to kill me, too?"

Anger flashed in Hakeem's eyes. "I could have put a bullet in the back of your head in that house. And believe me, I'm the only one that's keeping you alive right now."

"What am I supposed to do? Thank you? Hey, I guess Sal's not such a bad guy after all," Riley said sarcastically.

A fist struck Riley's face again. The other man's mouth moved to within inches of his ear, and he hissed, "I said my name is Hakeem."

Riley turned his head and the two men stared nose-to-nose. Blood and saliva filled Riley's mouth. He prepared to spit, then turned at the last moment and shot the bloody liquid to the ground, splashing both their feet.

Hakeem straightened and walked to the single barred window Riley could see at the back of the room. He breathed in deeply, inhaling the salty night air that Riley could catch only a hint of through the scent of the blood coating his face. "I don't understand you, Pach. You go around Afghanistan killing people. You come here to kill people. No one hits harder than you do on the football field. But you're soft on the inside. There is no hate in your eyes. I mean, you've just found out that your best friend has lived a double life and betrayed you. And what do you do? Rather than dishonor him by spitting in his face, you spit on the ground."

"You've dishonored yourself enough already, Sal. You don't need my help," Riley said, the swelling in his cheek causing him to lisp slightly. He noticed that the mention of Sal's name hadn't drawn a swing this time. "You kill out of hate. When I have to kill, I do it out of duty. And I don't kill innocents, only perpetrators."

"Ah, the higher ethics of murder."

"My actions are not murder. Bombing a stadium is murder."

"Then what do you call your actions, O virtuous warrior?"

Riley's temper went over the edge. "You want to know what I call it every time I kill some button-pushing psycho like you? Preventative medicine!"

Hakeem walked back from the window and straddled his chair again. He was chuckling, and Riley knew his temper had cost him an edge.

"That's quite the high road, Riley—'Your killing is bad, but mine is good.'" Hakeem's smile quickly disappeared. "But what do you call it when *your* government blows up a house, and a ten-year-old boy watches his family die in front of him? Was my mother a perpetrator? Was my aunt a perpetrator? Your president wiped out my whole family. Am I supposed to sit back and say, 'Oh, don't worry about it. Accidents do happen'?"

"Get over yourself, Sal. There're a lot of people who have had horrible things happen in their lives, but they don't go turning themselves into a walking mass of C-4."

Hakeem started to reach across to hit Riley again but pulled his arm back and stared at him.

Riley realized his temper was about to cost him any influence he might have on his old friend. He forced himself to dial the rhetoric back a notch. "Listen, I'm sorry you lost your family. I can't imagine what you went through. But this—what you're doing—it's just plain whacked."

"See, there—right there!" Hakeem cried, poking Riley on his bare shoulder. "That's why I say you're soft. If you hit me, I'll hit you back—only harder. *That* is the answer! If I hit you, what do you do? You just sit there and do nothing. Or you look for 'alternatives' or 'understanding.' And please spare me your 'turn the other cheek' drivel."

"Wait a second; get your facts straight! If you hit someone close to me—someone I love—trust me, you won't be doing it again. But if you hit me? Yeah, I'll 'turn the other cheek' or 'take one for the team' or whatever you want to call it."

Hakeem laughed derisively. "Well, I'll tell you what. According to your beliefs, Jesus ended up on the cross because He turned the other cheek. But Muhammad is a warrior; he struck the other cheek. One day Islam will dominate the earth because we fight back. It's the way of the world—the strong take over the weak. Face it—my religion is one of strength; yours, of weakness."

"Your religion? What religion do you have? I've read your file, *Hakeem*. You're a Ba'athist—a worshiper of Saddam Hussein. I've got bad news for you, friend. Your god died at the end of a rope in 2006. Don't go talking to me about religion. You have no more love for Allah than I do."

Color flushed across Hakeem's face, but his voice remained steady. "That's where you're wrong. I'm no Ba'athist. Saddam was a strong leader, but he was not my god. I am a follower of Allah, the one true God. And I am a follower of Muhammad, his prophet. What I do, I do for Islam and in the name of Allah."

Riley gave a bitter laugh at this religious declaration. "Maybe your own twisted brand of Islam. Most Muslims hate what you're doing, but they won't say anything out of fear one of you whack-jobs is going to plant a bomb in their mailbox."

Hakeem dismissed this with a wave of his hand. "Interpretation of the Koran has been watered down in the name of political correctness and world opinion. Tell me, what do these weak vessels do with Surah 5:33, where we are told that the only punishment for those who wage war against Allah and his prophet is that they should be killed or crucified or have their hands and feet chopped off? Why, in Surah 4:74, does Allah promise reward for those who sell this world's life for the hereafter and die fighting for him?

"You look surprised that I can quote from the Holy Book. Well, all those nights in the hotel rooms on the road while you were studying your Gideon Bible, I was learning the true words of the Prophet. That's why I know my calling to be true. I fight the infidel, and I wage jihad against those who try to take what belongs to Allah because that is what I am commanded to do!"

"So, it's a religion of hate."

Hakeem was on his feet again. "You're not listening! It's not a religion of hate! It's a religion that takes care of its own. It's a religion whose followers are commanded to expand its borders. Think about it, Riley. How is it any different than Christianity? What were the Crusades? How many people over the centuries were forced to convert to your supposedly crucified Jesus at the end of a sword?"

"C'mon, Sal, you're smart enough to know that just because someone slaps a cross on their uniform doesn't mean they're on God's team. The difference between you guys and us is that we condemn those who do evil in the name of our God." Riley shifted in his chair to try to get the blood flowing into his legs again. Some words that Pastor Tim had told him a few months ago flooded into his mind, and he said, "We're not trying to force people into some sharia thing. We're not the ones holding the swords anymore. We're trying to do what we should have been doing all along—sacrificing ourselves to show people a better way. That's what Jesus did."

Hakeem laughed mockingly as he paced around the room. "'That's what Jesus did'—oh, please. There you go again with your 'sacrificial Jesus' talk. Did you know that Surah 4 of the Koran makes it perfectly clear that Jesus was not the person crucified on the cross? He was simply a prophet like Moses or Abraham. But you Christians have taken this holy man and turned Him into a god. That is the ultimate blasphemy!"

Riley's temper got the best of him again. "Buddy, your whole life is a blasphemy right now! And just because you point to some Surah, am I supposed to believe it's true? I can point to Philippians 2 and John 19 and 20 that make it clear that Jesus is God and that He died and that He rose again! But what good would it do? No doubt you'll write off those Scriptures just as quickly as I'll write off yours!"

Hakeem circled around, yanked Riley's head back by the hair, and got right in his face. "Yes, I'll write off your Scriptures! I write off anything that is blasphemous! And saying there is more than one god is a blasphemy worthy of death! THERE IS NO GOD BUT ALLAH!"

"Take your hands off me," Riley said slowly, his eyes burning into Hakeem's. The standoff was broken when Hakeem gave Riley's forehead a final push and then walked back to the window.

Riley struggled to control his anger with little success. With each word he spoke, his volume increased. "I'm not getting into some 'Who is God?' argument with you, Sal, because it won't get us anywhere! If I say Jesus, the Father, and the Holy Spirit make up one God, you're still going to hear three gods. So, where do we go from there? And as for your version of Allah—you can keep him! My God lays down His life; your Allah blows up stadiums!"

The fervor of Riley's words echoed off the cement walls. Dust floated around the room's single lightbulb, which hung above their heads.

Hakeem leaned in close to Riley again. "Okay, just for the sake of argument, let's assume that what you say is true. Then you serve a god who lets people kick Him when He's down. Is that really the kind of god you want? As for me, I would rather go it on my own than serve such a wounded puppy of a god. Allah is strong! You know what strength is?" Hakeem placed his fist in front of Riley's face. "This! This is strength!"

Riley waited for Hakeem to remove his hand before he answered. "Unfortunately, like everything else, you've got your definition of strength all backward. It takes a lot more strength to turn the other cheek than it does to strike back. It takes a lot more courage to try to save your enemy than it does to kill him. And it takes a lot more character to forgive than it does to seek revenge."

Hakeem sat down and slid his reversed chair forward until it was inches away from Riley's. He leaned his head forward. "And what about me, Riley? Do you forgive me? And before you answer, let me tell you a little secret: I'm not done yet. I've got one more big party to crash. So, what do you say, pal? Is all forgiven?"

The smell of Hakeem's coffee-laden breath added to the repulsiveness of the choice that stood before Riley. He lowered his head. *Lord, every fiber of my being wants to crush this man's nose with my forehead. But I remember You forgiving the people who crucified You even while You were still hanging on the cross. Help me to do the right thing.*

Slowly, Riley lifted his gaze to meet Hakeem's. "Sal, I forgive you; I truly do. You are a sick, brainwashed man who doesn't have the moral understanding to know that what he's doing is so very wrong. But know this: just because I forgive you doesn't mean that I'm not going to do everything I can to stop you before you hurt anyone else—even if that means putting a bullet in you."

At the last phrase, something registered in Hakeem's eyes—maybe fear, maybe uncertainty. But just that quickly it was gone.

Hakeem burst into laughter as he stood. "Exactly what I would have expected you to say." He walked over to the window again and looked out. The cry of a gull echoed in the silent room. "Riley, your friends have taken our leader and my mentor, al-'Aqran. You are going to be told to make a video to your people suggesting a prisoner swap. Say what you are asked to say. Then, when the video is complete, you are going to be asked by the men holding you for information about your friends' whereabouts and about how many and how well equipped they are. Tell them what they want to know."

Hakeem stepped in front of Riley and looked down at him. "Before tomorrow is over, I will have left Italy to go play my endgame. When I'm gone, I can no longer protect you. I know you. I know your stubbornness. But I advise you to do what they ask of you. Because of my status as a hero, I still hold some sway over them. I can ask them to spare your life, and they will grant me that wish. However, anything short of killing you will be fair game." Hakeem squatted down in front of Riley. "Please, Pach, spare yourself the pain. They're going to break you eventually anyway."

Riley's mouth rose into a weak smile. "Tell your boys that I'll make their video. But as far as telling them anything about my team . . . well, like you said, I guess I'm just a stubborn man."

Hakeem shook his head, then popped up. "So be it." He spun and walked toward the door. When his hand touched the handle, he turned around. "Good-bye, Riley. It has truly been an honor knowing you."

With that, he pulled the door open and exited into the hall. Before the door had a chance to close, a hand stopped it. As it pushed back open, four men wearing black nylon masks came in. One man was carrying a video camera on a tripod. Another man had several sheets of paper, presumably a script for Riley. The third man held a small generator with two protruding cables that ended in copper clips. The fourth man brought in an old, scratched aluminum Louisville Slugger.

The man with the script picked up the chair Hakeem had been sitting in and brought it near where the camera was being set up. He sat down and began shuffling through the papers. When he got them into the proper order, he looked up and said in a heavily accented voice, "Well, Mr. Covington, shall we begin?"

TUESDAY, JANUARY 20
BARI, ITALY

Scott watched as Jim Hicks cleared wood shavings out of the hole he was boring in the kitchen table with his knife. Hicks was on a secure satellite phone conversation with Secretary of Homeland Security Moss, and with every minute that passed, the hole got deeper.

"Yes, but . . . Yes, I know, sir. . . . Well, when you send teams internationally to steal people and blow things up, chances are pretty good that you *will* have international incidents. . . . No, sir, I am not mocking you, but . . . You've got to be kidding! There's no way we can shut down the operation now! Covington is still out there, and we've got to find him. That's not something we can do stateside. . . . No, I am not telling you what to—wait, you know what? Yes, I *am* telling you what to do, and I'm telling you what I am going to do. We are absolutely not leaving here without Riley Covington. So get that out of your mind! Also, I expect you to do everything in your power to retrieve Billy Murphy's body from the Italian authorities. Do you understand? . . . Well, sir, you can do whatever you want to me when I get back stateside. For now, I expect you to do exactly what I've asked. I believe our conversation is over!"

Hicks pressed the End button on the phone with one hand and brought the knife down into the table with the other. "Pompous, stuffed-shirt, windbag, fancy tie–wearing, good-for-nothing . . ."

"So, how'd it go?" Scott asked with a smile.

"The idiot wants to shut us down! Can you believe it? He sends us out, but the moment things get a little bit messy, he wants to cut and run. When I get back, I've got a good mind to—"

"Hold that happy thought," Scott said as he reached to answer his satellite phone. "Ross here. . . . Yes, Mr. Porter. . . . No, sir, we haven't found him yet. . . . Yes, sir, I overheard Jim's side of the conversation. . . . I couldn't agree with you more, sir. . . . Yes, sir, I'll tell him. Thank you, sir."

As Scott hung up the phone, Hicks reached into his pocket and tossed him a handkerchief.

"What's this for?" Scott asked.

"It's to wipe the brown off your nose. I haven't heard that many 'sirs' in one conversation since boot camp."

Scott laughed. "Yeah, well, Porter kind of brings it out of you." As he talked, he went to the refrigerator and pulled out a bottle of sparkling water. Then he reached in and grabbed a bottle of Fabbri 1905 Fantasy in Caffe chocolate syrup. "Anyway, he heard Moss's side of the conversation, so he slipped out to give us a call. He said he knows that Moss is an equine's posterior but wanted me to ask you to try to at least be civil to him while you're ignoring his orders. Then he said to do whatever it took to get Riley back safe."

"Sounds like Porter's a pretty decent guy."

"Yeah, as long as you're doing your job. If I ran the zoo, he'd be the one filling Moss's suit."

Scott sat down at the table and unscrewed the cap from the water bottle. Hicks watched in disgust as Scott chugged about a quarter of it and then filled the empty space with chocolate sauce. He put the cap back on and rapidly shook the bottle. When the contents were as well mixed as thick syrup and sparkling water could get, Scott began the slow process of letting the built-up gas out of the bottle little by little. The first time he had experimented with this concoction, he had forgotten about the whole don't-open-a-shaken-carbonated-beverage thing—not a mistake he was willing to repeat. Scott saw Hicks's appalled look and said, "I agree. It ain't the smooth goodness of Yoo-hoo, but it's the closest I can get over here."

The friends sat silently for a few minutes, each thinking about Riley. Then Scott said, "I'm still trying to get over Tara's phone call about Sal Ricci. It doesn't seem possible that a PFL player is behind the Platte River bombing."

"Yeah, but they have him on video bringing in a full ball bag— right down the tunnel and past the security guard. He even waved to them. They have him swapping out the balls. They have him making his escape."

"I just hope Riley doesn't find out about Sal until he's back with us."

"If he's still alive."

"Shut up, Jim! He's alive! Trust me, he's alive."

Khadi approached the two men and eyed Scott's drink. "Not again, Scott. That stuff is appalling."

"Come on, doesn't the Koran say something about the benefits of a rich, chocolaty soda?"

"No," Khadi replied. "Does the Bible?"

"'Fraid I wouldn't know. But if it doesn't, I think it should. First Chocolonians or something."

Khadi shook her head. "Why can't brilliant people be normal?"

"Thank you, and I don't know. So what brings you to this part of our lovely abode?"

"We just had the changing of the guard on our stakeouts. Still nothing but regular activity in and around Port Building 2 and Train Building. We've seen nothing in or out of Port 1 for nearly twenty hours."

Again silence filled the room. Finally Khadi said softly, "You know, having him out there and not knowing how he is—it's almost more than I can handle."

Hicks slammed his hand down on the table. "We need *something*! Al-'Aqran hasn't given us a thing, no matter how hard I've leaned on him. Our surveillance hasn't given us a thing. Tara's nutcases back at the ROU haven't given us a thing. We've got to get something soon! Otherwise, I swear we're just going to split our team in three and try all of the buildings at once. But without better information, that could be suicide."

Scott's phone rang again. Khadi and Hicks began talking over new options while Scott answered the phone. "Ross here. . . . You're serious? Right up to you? But how . . . ? Not good. . . . Well, it makes sense, unfortunately. Okay, call the rover car to take over surveillance of Train Building, but obviously from a different vantage. You get yourself and your little surprise back here ASAP. And make sure no one follows you. *Capisce?*" He ended the call and put the phone on the table. "Well, I think we may have just gotten our break."

Hicks and Khadi immediately ended their conversation and gave their full attention to Scott.

"It seems that a young man walked up to our surveillance van near Train Building. He said something like, 'You touch me, we kill him. This is your football man.' Then he handed Kim Li and Steve Kasay a vinyl gym bag. Inside the bag is a videotape. I'm betting we've got the makings of some sort of trade for Mr. Scorpion."

"But how did they know our guys were there?" Jim asked.

"I think our contact probably told them," Scott replied.

"Our contact?" Khadi said. "But he's been nothing but loyal. What makes you think that he's the one who gave our position away?"

"Because his head was in the bag with the tape."

///////////////////////

Steve Kasay came into the house through the back door, carrying the videotape. Kim Li followed close behind. Thankfully, they had left the gym bag, along with the rest of its contents, out back. The senders of the video had extended them the courtesy of placing the tape in a plastic bag, which Kasay now deposited into an evidence bag for safekeeping. He handed the tape to a waiting Scott, then went to the sink and began thoroughly scrubbing every wrinkle and crease of his hands.

Khadi, Hicks, Skeeter, and Li gathered around the monitor, while Scott slipped the tape into a high-tech VCR. This machine would convert the analog signal to a digital stream while the tape was playing. When the first pass of the tape was completed, the digital copy would be uploaded and sent to Tara's team in St. Louis for analysis.

Scott pressed Play.

Immediately everyone gasped except Skeeter, who unconsciously broke the glass he was holding in his hand.

The video showed Riley sitting in a dimly lit room, naked except for his boxers. He was tied to his chair, and blood could be seen staining the area where the cords were wrapped around his ankles. He had some obvious bruises to his upper body, and the left side of his face was badly swollen. A thin red line had been sliced across his chest and another down his right side. Two men stood with him, one on each side, their faces covered by black nylon masks. Both wore military fatigues. The man to Riley's left carried a long knife. The man on his right held a piece of paper—a script, Scott thought—in Riley's line of sight.

Riley took a deep breath before he began speaking and winced visibly with the effort.

"My name is Riley Covington. I am an American. I am being held captive by the righteous servants of Allah known as the Cause. In an act of international terrorism, I and my team of American military commandos illegally kidnapped the leader of this peaceful organization. I was captured while performing this hostile act in which many members of the Cause, as well as innocent bystanders, were killed. I deserve to die for this act, but because Allah is merciful, the Cause too will be merciful. They are proposing a prisoner exchange—me for their leader, the guilty for the innocent. Sometime between now and tomorrow night, the righteous leader of the Cause is to be delivered to his home. When that is done, word will be given as to my whereabouts. If he is not delivered before eight o'clock tomorrow night, I will receive the just punishment for my crimes."

At this, the man on Riley's left pulled Riley's head back and held the knife to his throat. Then the screen cut to snow.

In the abrupt silence from the monitor, a new sound was

distinguishable—laughter. It was coming from al-'Aqran's dark corner. It had started out small but had grown louder as the video had continued. Now the prisoner was almost in hysterics.

Hicks looked back at him and said, "Skeeter."

Skeeter walked to al-'Aqran, brought his fist hard against the man's temple, and then covered the newly unconscious man with the tarp.

Scott looked at Khadi and saw she had turned pale. "Khadi, you okay?" he asked.

"I'll be fine. Just go on," she replied, staring down at the floor.

"Those were some pretty harsh words Riley read," Hicks said. "They must be working him over pretty good."

"No doubt, because Riley has to know the way those words could come back in the future to bite him and the government. I'm betting this isn't the only copy of that tape," Kasay said.

Scott was shaking his head. "No, that doesn't sound like Riley. It would take more than some cutting and beating to get him to say those things."

"They aren't just cutting and beating. Did you see the swelling around his nipples? They're using a generator on him too," Hicks pointed out.

"Still—and back me up on this, Skeet and Kim—we've seen Riley in some pretty messed-up situations in Afghanistan. He's used to getting hurt and playing hurt."

"There's hurt, and then there's tortured. It's a big difference, Weatherman. Trust me, I know."

"I hear you; I hear you. It's just . . . I don't know. Riley always seems so in control. He always seems to have a plan. He always moves with a purpose—"

"A purpose!" Kim Li called out. "That's it! Put the tape back on."

Scott rewound the tape partway and then hit Play. "Watch Riley's right thumb," Li said. "See that twitching?"

"Yeah, random twitching is typical during physical duress," Hicks replied.

"Wait a second," Scott jumped in, "that's no random twitching. Short, short, short; short, long—didn't you SEALs ever have to learn Morse code?"

"Actually, we sort of prided ourselves on our post-1940s technology."

Scott ignored Hicks and moved closer to the monitor. "It's hard to see because it's so slight. Kim, Skeet, check me on this. Long, short—that's *N*. Short, long—that's *A*. Short, long, long, short—a *P*—'Nap.' Then an *A* . . . and an *S*. Then an *A* . . . *D* . . . *E*."

The tape went to snow.

"'Nap as a de . . .'—a de-what?" Scott said. *Nap—to sleep—sleeping like a de-mon, a De-nverite, a de-ranged man . . . No, none of that makes sense. C'mon, think! What if it's not "nap"? Or maybe it's not even English!*

"Hey, guys, work with me on this," Scott poured out in a rush. "Maybe Riley knew they'd be watching him, so he signaled in a language other than English."

Khadi tried to get his attention, but he waved her off.

"'Apas' . . . 'aden' . . . 'enapa' . . . 'pasa' . . . That's it! 'Pasa!' He used Spanish! And he must be repeating the message; the video starts and ends in the middle of the cycle. Okay, *pasa* means 'it happens'; *de* is 'of'; but what is *na*? 'It happens of—?'"

"Hey, John Nash." Hicks's voice interrupted his concentration. "I hate to burst your bubble, but it's not 'Pasa de na.' He was signaling 'Pasadena.' So much for your beautiful mind."

The rest of the team all burst out laughing while Scott, red-faced, looked around for a table to crawl under.

"So, Pasadena," Hicks said, reining the group in. "Is there a Pasadena anywhere around here?"

"Maybe . . . but I don't think so," Scott answered, visualizing the area map in his head. "Pasadena has to be some sort of code."

"What if Riley wasn't signaling us where he is?" Khadi offered. "What if he picked up some information?"

"Maybe Pasadena is where the Cause has its U.S. base," Li said.

"Or it could be the site of their next hit," Scott said. "What's in—? The PFL Cup! They're playing the championship game this year in the Rose Bowl!"

"Khadi, get on the horn to Porter and tell him that the Cause is gunning for the PFL Cup," Hicks ordered. "Kasay, Skeeter, Li, I want you guys back out on surveillance. Our time is short, so we have to come up with something now! Scott, you and I are going to get back on that video and—I don't know—discover something!"

Everyone sprung into action. Kasay, Skeeter, and Li bolted out the door. The squeal of their tires could be heard in the house. Khadi was immediately on the phone talking to the St. Louis office. Scott rewound the tape, and he and Hicks began watching it again.

By the third time through, Khadi was off the phone. "Porter's off and running with the info," she said.

Hicks grunted acknowledgment.

"Any luck?" Khadi asked hopefully.

"If we'd had any luck, do you think we'd be watching this again?" Hicks snapped.

"Jim, back off; she's only asking," Scott said. He turned his head toward Khadi. "If you think you can handle seeing Riley like this again, you're welcome to join us."

"Thanks."

Hicks got up and gave her his seat, then made peace by fetching her a bottle of water while he was grabbing another chair.

They watched the tape twice more, evaluating everything from the inflection of words to the placement of several coughs. They looked for anything in the room—the light, the type of chair—that might give evidence to whether it was a port building or a building in the train yard. But everything just seemed so common.

The sixth time through, Scott suddenly reversed the tape and let it run again. Then he reversed it again and let it run.

"What do you see, Weatherman?" Hicks asked.

"I don't know . . . something . . . nothing . . . light maybe. Give me my phone."

Hicks reached over and grabbed Scott's phone from the table.

Scott dialed the ROU number. "Tara, get Gooey on the phone. . . . Hey, Goo, have you run that video through a wave-form yet? . . . Do me a favor, and do it right away. I'll hold."

Scott saw Hicks and Khadi staring at him with blank looks on their faces. "A waveform monitor is a type of oscilloscope that mea-sures the level of a video signal." He saw that the blank looks had not changed. "It measures light fluctuations. I think I'm seeing a regular pattern of slight change in the room's light. I think it might be—Yeah, I'm here, Gooey. . . . Right . . . yeah . . . let me guess—two flashes every twelve seconds. . . . Bingo! Thanks, Gooster; you're the man!"

Scott hung up the phone with a huge grin on his face. "I wasn't sure, but I thought I saw a pattern of barely discernible variations in the lighting on the tape. My guess is that there is a window to the outside somewhere in that room. I wanted Gooey to confirm the timing and the pattern—two flashes every twelve seconds. Out at the end of the port facility stands Molo di Tramontana—a lighthouse, still operational. I want our surveillance teams to confirm this, but I'm pretty sure there is only one building—Port 2—that has a direct line of sight to the lighthouse."

He paused to let the information sink in. Then he added, "Looks like we've got us a target!"

Three ghostly white figures floated on the screen. One appeared to be lying down, and the other two stood slightly behind the first. All were completely unaware of the radar bouncing off their bodies. This rapid, ultrawideband pulsation resonated from an impulse synthetic aperture radar that, like a real-life version of the fictional form of thermal imaging typically shown on television and in the movies, actually allowed one to receive images through walls. This was Ted Hummel's first time employing the system in the field, and he was having way too much fun operating it.

"Tech One," he said into his comm system. For this action, Hummel had been designated as Tech One, and Khadi, who was working with him in the back of the surveillance van, was Tech Two.

"Alpha One, go ahead, Tech One," came Hicks's whispered response.

"Confirm Riley behind window seven; two *hajjis* guarding—I believe beyond a door due to fainter signal. Recommend window five as entry point—four *hajjis* prone, probably sleeping."

Hummel and Khadi had spent the last fifteen minutes radiating the northern wall of the Port 2

CHAPTER

THIRTY

building—the wall receiving the systematic flash of light from the lighthouse. They had spotted three rooms that were occupied but only one room had the signature they were looking for: single occupant with guards.

"Confirm Riley seven; entry five," Hicks repeated.

/////////////////////

With the predawn darkness and their head-to-toe blackness, Hicks and Alpha Team were virtually invisible as they approached the south entrance to the warehouse. They stepped over the body of the guard Hicks had taken out with a laser-aimed, sound-suppressed shot from his M4.

Meanwhile, Delta Team, led by Jay Kruse, was positioning at an entrance on the east side of the building. When both four-man teams were in place, Hicks gave the go-ahead for Sniper Team to move under window seven. Scott Ross, Skeeter Dawkins, and Carlos Guitiérrez ran across the asphalt and ducked under the closed window.

"Sniper in position," Scott reported.

"Okay, let's roll it out," Hicks said. "Tech."

"Check."

"Delta."

"Check."

"Sniper."

"Check."

"Boomer."

"Check," answered demolitions man Matt Logan.

"Okay, on my go . . . three, two, one, GO!"

///////// **ALPHA TEAM** /////////

Gilly Posada fired his Remington 870 Modular Combat shotgun at the hinges of the solid-core door, and Kim Li followed up with a crash from his ram. The door toppled inward. Hicks and Steve Kasay each tossed in a flashbang grenade, then pressed themselves against the outer wall.

BANG!

Immediately following the blast, the four men stack-rushed into the room—Hicks taking point, Li left, Posada right, and Kasay watching behind. A couple of three-round bursts from Hicks neutralized two of the occupants of the room, and a blast from Posada's 870 dropped the third and fourth in rapid succession.

////////// **DELTA TEAM** //////////

Chris Johnson's shotgun and Brad Musselman's ram provided Delta Team with an entrance on the east side of the building. However, when the team followed the flashbangs, they found the entry area empty. Suddenly gunfire burst through a wooden door on the left side of the room and Musselman spun to the ground. Kyle Arsdale impulsively launched a 40 mm grenade into the room. Then, realizing what he had done, he yelled, "Grenade!" The three men dropped to the floor just before they were showered with debris from the Sheetrock walls. When they stood back up, they looked like negatives of themselves—the drywall dust changing their all-black to all-white.

"Arsdale, stay here with Musselman! Johnson, you come with me!"

Arsdale dropped next to Musselman and began to apply pressure to his chest to try to stop the bleeding. Kruse and Johnson maneuvered into the next room.

////////// **SNIPER TEAM** //////////

As soon as he heard "go," Skeeter shattered the glass out of the window. While Scott covered his left side and Guitiérrez his right, Skeeter positioned his weapon through the metal bars that had been rusted by years of exposure to the damp salt air. Sure enough, within five seconds, the door burst open and two armed guards came running in. Each man received three rounds in the chest.

As he kept the rifle aimed at the door, Skeeter called out, "Riley? Riley, you in there?"

A raspy voice answered, "Skeet? Is that you?"

"Yes, sir! We comin' to get ya! Where you at?"

"Your left."

Another man ran into the room. He made it two steps before he joined his friends.

"Can you move?"

"No—" A deep cough erupted from the corner where Riley lay. "I'm cuffed to a ring in the floor."

"Well, cover yourself up with something. We got a surprise comin'!" Then, without taking his eyes off the door, he called out, "Scott! Tell 'em to send it in!"

"You got it, Skeet! Tech, send it in! Send it in!"

"Copy!" came Khadi's voice.

There was silence for about ten seconds—the only sounds coming from Sniper Team's breathing and the gunfire on the other side of the building. Then came the growl of an accelerating vehicle, faint at first but growing louder.

With its lights out, the vehicle was hard to see. Anyone who did get a good look at it would have noticed one curious characteristic about this speeding Iveco Daily cargo van: it had no driver.

######### *TECH TEAM* #########

While Khadi lay prone with her sniper rifle aimed at the roof of Port 2, Hummel stood next to her, doing his best to keep the cargo van under control. He had estimated that the van would have enough distance to reach 60 mph—a perfect speed if his aim was true and the hastily constructed radio-control device held up. However, it would be a horrifying speed for Sniper Team if the van happened to veer right just thirty feet.

He lined it up according to his coordinates. So far, so good. Abruptly he smelled smoke. Not the comforting smell of wood-fire smoke rising through a chimney and saturating the frosty air of a cold winter's morning. This was the kind of electronic smoke that you smell in your kitchen telling you that in seconds you're going to be mixing the rest of the cake batter by hand.

Hummel's heart sank to his feet.

Hicks's team eased their way through the front rooms of the building, firing their guns at anything that moved. Kasay was limping from a wound to his right thigh, and Hicks was bleeding from where a bullet had creased his left cheek above the jawline.

Alpha Team's goal was not to move through the building, nor was it to find Riley. Their mission, along with Delta Team, was to create noise and draw as many bad guys to them as possible. The more who came their way, the fewer the rescue team would have to deal with. So they slowly moved forward, never getting too far away from the front door and their escape.

Scott heard the cargo van approaching. A movement at the far corner of the building caught his eye. Just before he fired, a voice came on his comm. "Sniper, this is Boomer. I'm rounding the corner."

Scott's feeling of relief that he hadn't taken the shot was immediately shattered by a second voice. "Sniper, this is Tech One! I've lost control of the van! Repeat, I've lost control of the van!"

"Tech One, what do you mean you've lost control?" Scott yelled.

"I lined her up true, but then my controller burned out! She should be locked in straight, but I can't guarantee it. You guys had better clear out of there!"

"I ain't movin'," Skeeter said calmly from beside Scott.

"Skeeter," came Hummel's voice again, "clear out! I can't tell you for sure where it's going to hit."

"I said, I ain't—" Skeeter's words were interrupted by a burst from his M4 as another visitor to the room checked out—"movin'."

"It's too late now anyway!" Scott shouted.

The van raced toward them, the whine of the onrushing engine growing louder. Nobody moved; all the men kept their eyes on their positions. If it was going to hit them, it was going to hit them—nothing they could do about it now.

Riley lay on the ground. He had taken cover under his chair. It was scant protection, but at least it was something. In the dim light, he could see the growing pile of bodies by the door.

How had the team found him? It had to be Scott and his computer brain. Now, as he waited for his band of brothers, he silently prayed for their protection.

A moment later the deafening sound of high-speed metal meeting stationary cinder block exploded all around him. He was thrown sideways, and he cried out in pain as the arm that was cuffed to the floor was yanked from its socket.

As the ringing in his ears from the terrible impact began to fade, it was replaced by an even more frightening sound—silence. Then the sound of automatic-weapons fire erupted in the hallway. Scott's voice sounded from the window, cutting through the din. "Hang in, Pach! They're almost there!"

Riley tried to say something in reply, but the pain in his shoulder had taken his breath away. A noise at the door caught Riley's attention, and he turned just as a huge figure came bounding into the room.

Skeeter. He was followed by a determined-looking Guitiérrez.

Riley managed a weak wave but could say nothing as a cough racked his body.

"Pach! You hold still, okay?" Skeeter said as he positioned a pair of bolt cutters around the chain on Riley's cuffs.

Riley cried out again.

"What is it?" Guitiérrez questioned.

"Arm's out!"

"Well, then, hang on, 'cause this isn't going to be pretty."

While Skeeter kept an eye on the door, Guitiérrez positioned Riley. Then with a quick jerk that caused Riley to scream and slam the cement with his good hand, Guitiérrez popped the joint back into place.

Riley launched into another fit of coughing.

"Can you walk?" Guitiérrez asked.

"Yeah, I'm fine," Riley squeaked between coughs.

"No, you ain't, Pach! Look at your feet! They been beatin' on your feet?" Skeeter asked.

"I'm fine, Skeeter!"

"Yeah, whatever," Skeeter said as he picked Riley up and threw him over his shoulder.

"Skeeter, put me down! I mean it, Skeet! That's a direct order! Put me—" A cough cut off the rest of Riley's words, but he knew they would have been wasted on the suddenly selectively deaf man anyway.

////////// **DELTA TEAM** //////////

"Rescue complete! Pull out! Pull out!" Hicks's voice came over the comm.

Kruse and Johnson each lobbed a flashbang followed by a gas canister to cover their retreat, then sprinted toward the entrance. As they ran through the front door and turned left, they saw Arsdale twenty yards ahead with Musselman on his shoulders. When they rounded the corner, their eyes were drawn to the new, large hole in the rear of the building, out of which poked the last five feet of the cargo van.

They ran on and finally reached the rendezvous site seventy-five yards down the port road. Alpha Team was twenty-five yards behind them.

Suddenly the clacking of an AK-47 broke the air. Gilly Posada dropped. Hicks, who was bringing up the rear, slid down and lay on top of him. As he did, he yelled, "Boomer! Blow it now!"

Matt Logan lifted the safety cap off the detonator, toggled the circuit on, and depressed the trigger.

Twenty-four explosive charges, eight on both the front and the back of the building and four on each of the ends, went off at once with a concussion strong enough to make the waiting team members' ears pop a football field away. Anyone in or around the building who wasn't immediately incinerated by the blasts was crushed as the warehouse's outer walls fell and its roof collapsed.

Kruse and Johnson ran back to where Hicks lay on top of Posada. They each picked a man up and carried him the rest of the way to the waiting vans. As they laid the two men in the back of the first van, they saw Guitiérrez working hard to stem the flow of blood from Musselman's chest.

Farther back in the vehicle, they saw Riley. His eyes were closed and his head was lying in Khadi's lap. Scott sat next to him trying his best to tend to some of his former lieutenant's wounds. At Riley's feet squatted Skeeter, M4 at the ready.

It would be thirty-six hours before anyone could finally convince the big man to put down his gun and leave Riley's side.

There were a lot of things in this world that CTD Midwest Division Chief Stanley Porter didn't like. He didn't like French wine. He didn't like black-tie dinners. He didn't like designated hitters. He didn't like his wife's lasagna. But what Stanley Porter truly liked least in this world were pompous, self-absorbed, shortsighted, bureaucratic dolts like Director of Homeland Security Dwayne Moss.

"All I'm saying is that we've got to take some major precautions at the PFL Cup next week," Porter said, sitting on the edge of his seat. The chair was way too soft and way too deep for him to sit back and still make his point.

"Because some PFL player turned secret agent thinks he overheard something while being tortured? I'd venture to say he was probably hearing everything from archangels to his dead grandmother," replied Secretary Moss, who was settled comfortably back in his imported Argentine leather wingback chair. His feet were kicked up on the mahogany coffee table that separated the two men, and his chin was resting on the two index fingers extended from his interlaced hands. "I mean, really, Stan, is that the best you can give me?"

"What do you want? Are you expecting an engraved invitation to the jihad party at the PFL Cup? BYOB—bring your own bomb! Mr. Secretary, you know that's not the way this business is run."

"Oh, I know all right. I've been a professional in this business for twenty-five years now."

Porter wanted to reply that he had meant the international law enforcement business, not the special-interest-kowtowing, keep-yourself-in-office-no-matter-what, governmental-leech business—but he thought better of it. "What I'm saying is that Riley Covington heard some very specific words from a man who was his best friend for two years. These words led him to believe that the PFL Cup would be the Cause's next target. He so strongly believed this to be true that it was the one message he secretly communicated in a video, after which he fully expected to be killed."

"Now, now—as you know, Stan, just because somebody believes something doesn't make it true. I could believe that the moon was made of mozzarella cheese, but it doesn't mean I'm going to go there to make a pizza." Moss failed to hold in a smile at his own witty remark.

Porter looked down at his feet, trying to control his exaspera-tion. When he composed himself enough to look up again, he said, "While that's a very valid point, Mr. Secretary, it still doesn't negate the fact that we have a potentially serious, possibly even devastating, situation on our hands."

"Don't you think that's a little overstated? From what I've been led to believe, the head and the heart of the Cause were removed in Paris and in Italy. Do we really think that they have the ability to do anything more? Especially when you think of the level of security that is already going to exist at the game. I mean, Sal Ricci would have to be Houdini to penetrate their perimeter. You don't think he's Houdini, do you, Stan?"

"No, sir, I do not think he's Houdini." *But what I wouldn't give to buckle* you *into a straitjacket and dump you in a milk can,* Porter finished to himself.

This conversation was going nowhere; Porter decided it was time to abandon intellectual integrity in favor of expediency. "When it comes down to it, you are right, sir. The evidence is shaky at best."

Secretary Moss nodded.

"I'm just concerned about what another attack on your watch might do to your future. People will forgive you for not doing anything to prevent the Platte River attack. I mean, how could you have known?"

"Impossible to anticipate," Moss agreed.

"But another attack would most likely look really bad. Think of the way your opponents could use that against you if you ever decided to seek higher office."

Secretary Moss was now leaning forward in his chair. "I see what you're saying . . . not that my personal career matters at all to me compared to national security."

"Of course not."

"I just wouldn't want anything to happen to those American citizens in L.A." He pondered this for a few moments and then shook his head. "But I'm afraid my hands are tied. The president's declared this a National Special Security Event, so the Secret Service is handling the security for this PFL Cup. And although they are technically under the Department of Homeland Security, they've always been pretty much an entity unto themselves. They don't like me intruding into their area of responsibility, nor do I like to do it."

"Yes, sir, I know. All I'm asking for is permission to take this information to the Secret Service. I'll let them know that I'm not looking to interfere at all in what they're doing for security—in fact, I can supply them with additional warm bodies from CTD if they would like. But I will ask that my two ops teams be allowed on-site and that they be given free rein."

"What? You want me to let Jim Hicks and his loose cannons into the PFL Cup? They'll probably blow the place up themselves!"

"Listen, Moss!" Porter shouted as he jumped out of his chair. Then he caught himself and slowly lowered himself back into his seat. *Remember who you're dealing with,* he told himself. *Expecting Moss to understand the ins and outs of international security issues is like asking a six-year-old to understand the intricacies of astrophysics.*

The secretary settled himself comfortably into his chair and put his feet back on the coffee table.

Porter's outburst had given the upper hand back to Moss, and the DC regretted it. "Please, sir. Hicks and company understand the Cause better than anyone I know. I'm just concerned how it might look if something happened and you had kept the most knowledgeable people out of the stadium. Besides, you're too bright a man to let that happen."

Secretary Moss smiled. He clearly knew when he was being kissed up to, and he obviously liked it. "Okay, Stan, I'll talk to Secret Service Director LeBlanc. However, I'm holding you responsible for Hicks and company's actions. Do we have an understanding?"

"Yes, sir," Porter said, rising out of his chair.

"Wait a minute. Sit . . . sit. There's one more thing. In exchange for this little arrangement, I want the Scorpion delivered here for trial. We need to show the world how America metes out justice to those who dare take her on."

Porter, recognizing another man's photo opportunity when he saw it, protested, "Sir, pardon me, but that is insane! Do you realize the risk we would be bringing to our shores by trying him here?"

"Still, I think it's important for our citizens to see the face of the man responsible for these attacks, especially when he is convicted. Besides, I want to look at this man eye to eye."

Yeah, while the flashbulbs are popping, Porter thought. "I'll see what we can do."

He rose and walked around the coffee table to the secretary. Moss extended his hand in a way that had the DC wondering if he was supposed to shake it or kiss it. He opted for the shake. He stood for a moment, staring at the secretary's extended legs, which were blocking the direct way out. Then, wisely choosing what his head told him to do over what his heart said, Porter walked back around the table and out the door.

Riley's eyes fluttered, then opened. The light in the room felt like a sledgehammer to his skull, so he quickly closed them again.

Where am I? From his brief glance, he could tell he was in a hospital room—where, he had no clue. One by one, he wiggled his fingers and toes. They all moved, though not without some serious discomfort. *So, everything is in operating order—nothing severed, nothing broken.*

Next question: how did I get here? His brain started rewinding its tape. He saw the rescue—Skeeter and Guitiérrez coming through the darkness. He saw the room where he had been cuffed to the floor; twin fires in his left wrist and shoulder protested the recollection. He saw the chair he had been tied to when they—

Lord . . . how could they have done those things to me?

He felt the knife across his chest and side, the bat against his stomach, the cane against his feet, the electrodes against—

A wave of nausea rose through his body, mercifully taking over his thoughts. He rode the wave out until his insides settled again.

He hadn't seen anyone in the moment his eyes had been open, but he knew he wasn't alone. The sound of fingers on a laptop keyboard was evidence of that. As Riley listened, he recognized a very distinct pattern—one he had heard many times before. A quick burst of keys, followed by the tap-tap-tap of the backspace.

"Hey, Scott," he rasped.

"Pach! Oh, man!" Riley heard the clap of the laptop being closed. "How're you feeling?"

"Like my head was used by Evander Holyfield as a speed bag. Any chance of dousing those lights?"

"Of course!"

When he heard the click of the overhead lights shutting off, Riley slowly cracked his eyes—this time with more long-term success. "Where am I?"

"Does something tell you we're not in Italy anymore, Dorothy?"

Scott laughed, and Riley forced a smile, though his friend's enthusiasm for Riley's consciousness was making the hammers in his head increase their pace. Seeing Riley's expression, Scott continued, "Sorry, man. You know me—mouth first, brain second. We're at Ramstein. Look familiar?"

Riley nodded faintly, thinking back to the last time he had been here. His hand traveled toward the scar on his hip but was halted by the pain that the movement caused in the rest of his body.

Scott handed him a small, clear cup of water.

Suddenly a thought thundered into Riley's mind, and he quickly turned to Scott, spilling the water as he did. "The PFL Cup! Did you get my message about the PFL Cup?"

"Yeah, we did. I passed the info on to Division Chief Porter, who was going to take it up the chain."

"I knew you'd figure it out, Scott," Riley said with a sigh of relief before a wave of nausea overtook him. He quickly signaled Scott for the small bucket that was sitting on his bed stand for just such an occasion. Riley heaved for a full minute, but nothing came out. The only nourishment he'd had over the last four days was from the IV that was still in his arm.

When he was done, he nodded to Scott, who took the empty bucket from him. As he lay back, another recollection came. This one had him glad that the overhead fluorescents were off and the only light in the room was that of the afternoon sun slipping through the blinds. Pain seared through his chest as he reached up to wipe his eyes. Quietly, he said, "Sal Ricci, Scott . . . Sal is Hakeem."

"Yeah, we know. I'm so sorry, Pach."

"I still can't . . ." Riley stopped to collect his emotions. The wound was still too raw for him to dwell there. "So, tell me how I got here," he said, changing the subject.

"Well, after the gunfight at the O.K. Corral, we booked on down to Bari, picked up al-'Aqran, then grabbed our Gulfstream at the Bari International Airport."

Riley nodded his understanding, and then a thought struck him. "Wait, wasn't our jet parked up at Aviano?"

"Yeah, but Jim called it down. He figured that us getting out of there quickly was more important than getting out of there quietly—especially with you and Gilly."

"Gilly? What happened to Gilly?" Riley asked, trying to sit up in bed but failing.

"Gilly's going to be fine. He took a bullet to the left side—cracked some ribs, but it missed the organs. Guitiérrez kept him stabilized for the two-hour flight, and then the docs here got him patched up."

"Anyone else hurt?"

"Jim got shaken up pretty good covering Gilly when we brought the building down. He's feeling all fifty-whatever of his years. And . . . well . . . I don't know if you remember Brad Musselman from the training, but he took some rounds to the shoulder and chest. He . . . he bled out before we even got on the plane."

Riley closed his eyes. The reality of a man dying while trying to rescue him rocked him. He had spent his life with the attitude that he would willingly sacrifice himself for the sake of someone else. But having the tables turned on him was not something he was prepared for.

"I know what you're thinking," Scott said, "and you would have died trying to do the same thing for him—we all would have. That's part of what we do."

Riley nodded. It certainly put his own pain in perspective. Maybe horrific things had been done to him, but at least he was still alive.

A knock on the door drew his attention. Khadi came in, and Hicks limped in behind her.

"Riley, you're awake," said Khadi, whose concern was evidenced by how quickly she walked to his bedside. She rested her hand on his arm as she struggled to compose herself.

Riley managed a small smile for her.

"Yeah, he just popped his eyes open about five minutes ago," Scott explained. "I've been telling him about Gilly and Brad."

"Jim, I'm so sorry about Brad," Riley said. "I . . . if I had . . ."

"He did it willingly," Hicks replied. "When he saw your tape, you won him over. You won all of us over. But even if he hadn't seen the tape, Brad knew what he was getting into. He died a hero."

The room was silent for a couple of minutes. Khadi pulled a chair near Riley's bed and slowly stroked his arm. The friction was shooting needles of pain through Riley's overly sensitive nerve endings, but he refused to stop her. Gentle human contact, in contrast to what he had experienced over the last days, was worth the price.

Hicks hobbled over to the windowsill. He shifted a few times, trying to find a sitting position that was comfortable. Finally he gave up and stood against the wall.

Khadi spoke up. "So, did Scott tell you what the doctors have said about you?"

"No, but let me guess. Pneumonia or something in the right lung. Infected lacerations on my chest and side. Various contusions and abrasions."

"Not bad, Dr. Covington," Scott said. "But you missed the bruised kidney and the mild concussion."

"The doctors want to keep you here for observation and recovery," Khadi informed him.

"How long?"

"They're talking about a week."

Riley shook his head and turned to Hicks. "When are we heading out of here?"

The movement of Khadi's hand on Riley's arm abruptly stopped.

"You need to listen to the doctors, Riley," Hicks answered. "Pneumonia's nothing to be—"

"Blah, blah, blah. Give me a break, Jim. What would you do in my position? Would you just lie back in a hospital bed while your team put their lives on the line?" A fit of coughing stopped Riley's words for a moment, as if audibly protesting against everything that he was saying. Eventually he continued, his voice grating in his throat. "And what would you do if you found out that your best friend was actually your worst enemy? Come on; nobody knows Sal like I do. You know that. You need me there, and I need to be there. So tell them to load me up with penicillin and get me out of here."

Hicks was silent. There was no question as to what he would do if he were in Riley's situation. But he still looked far from convinced that it was the right thing.

Khadi stared at him with fire in her eyes. "Jim, you're not actually considering this? Tell him he needs to be in a hospital where the doctors can monitor him! Tell him he needs to—"

"Okay, Riley," Hicks interrupted. "The commander here, Colonel Mark Amel, and I go way back together—all the way to Cambodia in '72. Let me talk to him."

Khadi stood up and gave Hicks a look that would have bristled the hair off a warthog, then stormed out of the room without another word to Riley or anyone else.

"I'm no great judge of the subtle signals that women give," Scott said, "but I'm thinking that Khadi might not agree with your decision."

Hicks chuckled, and Riley tried to squeeze out a smile.

"Well, I'm going to go track the colonel down," Hicks said as he walked to the door, but suddenly he stopped himself short. "I almost forgot the whole reason I came to find you, Scott. Riley, this'll interest you, too. Stan Porter got us all-access at the PFL Cup from the Secret Service. Now we just have to figure out how we're going to use it. Also, how's this for a little twist: apparently Secretary Moss wants us to bring al-'Aqran back to the States so he can put on a show trial."

"He wants what?" Scott cried. "We might as well paint a giant bull's-eye for the terrorists on whatever city hosts those proceedings. It'll be a regular old bomb-o-rama."

"Yeah, that's what Porter figured. So his recommendation was that we accidentally lose the Scorpion in one of the CIA's black-site prisons."

"Wait," Riley interjected, "are those the supposed secret Eastern European facilities? I remember hearing about them on the news. The CIA's line was that they don't really exist."

"They're right; those prisons don't exist," Hicks confirmed. "And once the Scorpion is incarcerated in one, neither will he."

SUNDAY, JANUARY 25
FEDERAL BUREAU OF INVESTIGATION,
   LOS ANGELES FIELD OFFICE
LOS ANGELES, CALIFORNIA

Jim Hicks wondered if he had made the right decision. Riley's cough hadn't been too bad the day
after they left the hospital in Germany. However,
since then, it had steadily gotten worse. He knew
it was distracting Khadi from her job. And Skeeter
was inseparable from the man.

When Hicks had gone into the men's rest-
room a few hours ago, Skeeter had been sitting
up on the sink area. Instinctively, Hicks had
looked toward the stalls, and sure enough, under
the third door were Riley's ever-present Merrell
nubuck mocs.

"Hey, Riley," Hicks had greeted him.

"Jim, make him go away," Riley pleaded.

Hicks looked at Skeeter, who defiantly looked
back. "Sorry, man, you're on your own. I don't
fight battles I can't win."

The recollection made Hicks smile. He knew
that he had made the only decision he could
make regarding Riley, who was the one man he'd
ever met whose stubbornness could come close
to matching his own. As he glanced over at him,

Hicks's eye caught Khadi's. She was sitting at the workstation across from Riley. She glared at him and turned back to her computer screen.

Hicks wondered if Khadi might need to be pulled off the team. She was excellent at what she did, but she seemed to have lost all objectivity where Riley Covington was concerned. *But she's too good an agent, and she has way too good a head on her shoulders to let her personal feelings get in the way of the overall objective,* he thought. *Still . . .*

That final *still* weighed heavily on his mind.

The crack of a can opening caught his attention. Hicks looked over in time to see Scott pouring a soda into a large plastic Dodgers cup as he walked over to Hicks's desk.

Scott snapped the cup's lid back on. As he was about to speak, a deep, throaty cough echoed through the room. He nodded toward Riley and asked Hicks, "How's he doing?"

"About the way he sounds. I figure he'll end up either better, in the hospital, or dead. Any way you look at it, I think the decision's out of my hands."

"What about next Sunday?"

"Obviously, if he's coughing like that, there's no chance of him being on the PFL Cup ops team. But even so, we'd probably be able use him as Mother, coordinating the action."

Suddenly Riley looked up from his computer and spotted the two men watching him. He gave a small smile and a nod of his head as if he knew what their discussion had been about and agreed with their conclusions. Then he went back to work.

"And I thought *you* were a hard guy to figure out," Hicks said to Scott.

"True that," Scott replied.

"Huh?"

"Oh, sorry. I just got off a conference call with my little cadre of postmodern Gen Xers back in the Room of Understanding. Sometimes it rubs off. But that does remind me of why I came here. Virgil Hernandez came across a murder in East L.A. Guy's name was Valentín Joaquín de Herrera. Now, you're probably thinking, *Mexican guy turning up dead in East L.A.? Not that unusual.* True, except this guy had a rep as a coyote. A coyote's one of the dudes who escorts folks across the border."

"I'm familiar with the term. Go on."

Scott took a long pull on his straw. Now that he was back in the States where he could add the Diet Mountain Dew Code Red to his Yoo-hoo, he was in sugary, caffeine heaven. This was his fifth 32-ounce drink today—the fifth that Hicks knew about, anyway—and it was only 3:30 p.m.

Scott stifled a cherry-chocolate belch and proceeded. "So, this guy gets taken out with one .40 cal shot to the forehead. Still not that unusual. But apparently this guy used to have a partner, Fabián Ramón Guerrero. Unfortunately for Señor Fabián, he was discovered out in the deserts of Chihuahua a few days after the Platte River attack. They pulled two slugs from his body—both .40 cal. I've got Tara trying to get those bullets from the Mexican authorities so we can run comparison ballistics on them."

Hicks put up his hand to stop Scott's monologue. "Wait, something doesn't make sense. If you're going to say Hakeem did this, then how does he get the same gun to Italy and back again?"

"Patience, Jedi master, patience. Now, Valentín spent the last four weeks or so down in Mexico City. Word is he was throwing around cash like it grew on cactuses . . . or is it cacti . . . ? cactis . . . ? cactoose . . . ?"

"Scott!"

"Okay, okay. He was throwing around money like it grew on spiky desert plants. Also, he had a gun he was showing off that he said belonged to someone else, which I guess he was holding for someone, and anyway, it was a small silver gun and it had the words *40 Tactical* printed on its side, and apparently he said the guy it belonged to had promised him another fifty grand and all he had to do was get him safely back across the border again." Scott stopped to take a deep breath. "Sorry, run-on sentence. So, Valentín's got a gun. Any guesses at what this mystery gun owner's name was?"

Hicks, who hated guessing games of any kind, just stared at Scott.

Scott made a buzzing sound. "Nice try. Valentín was telling everyone that the gun belonged to a bad man, a ruthless desperado, *un hombre malvado*—"

Hicks slammed his hand on the desk.

"—a really naughty guy code-named . . . the Cheetah."

SUNDAY, JANUARY 25
EL ESPEJO ROAD
LA MIRADA, CALIFORNIA

Her face was perfect. Round with the slightest pudge to her cheeks. Her eyes were almond shaped with heavy brows. That little nose of hers was still trying to figure out what it was going to do and in the meantime just sat softly above her small mouth. *How has she changed in the past month?* Hakeem wondered. Gently, he traced her outline on the small picture with his index finger.

My sweet Aly . . . beautiful little Alessandra. What will your life be like without me? You are my sole regret in this whole affair. The things that you'll hear about me will not be kind. If only you could understand why I'm doing what I'm doing. Hakeem lifted his finger from the picture and wiped away a single tear that had slipped down to his recently dyed blond beard. *This is not an irrational act. I am not crazy. Your grandmother and grandfather were murdered by the American government. Your great-uncle was killed by an act of terror. I'm doing this for their sake—to restore their honor. To restore* my *honor.*

Hakeem unfolded the picture so that Meg could be seen holding Alessandra on her left hip.

Your mother is a good woman. She didn't deserve the hand I dealt her. I trust her to find a good man who can raise you—a man who has not been burdened by fate the way that I have. But even though he might love you and provide a roof over your head, he will never be your father. And no matter what name he gives you, that will not be who you truly are. Because, sweet Aly, you are not a Smith or a Jones or an Anderson or even a Ricci—you are a Qasim! And what I do is not for my ancestors alone but for you! I do this to give you a better life apart from the tyranny of this evil government.

He refolded the picture, kissed the image of his daughter, and slipped the snapshot back under the insole of his shoe. He had not brought out the picture at all during the first three weeks following his escape from his former life. But now this monologue to his daughter was becoming a daily ritual. He tried to analyze where his compulsion to speak to her was coming from. All he could figure was that the reality that he would die in one week's time was affecting his mind a bit.

This status of "dead man walking" was not what he had expected it to be. He had always thought it would be a period of *one more times*. He had expected that there would be foods he would want to enjoy one more time, that he would want to experience every sunrise and sunset, that he would want to experience a woman once more this side of paradise. But the reality was that the family he was staying with had to constantly encourage him to eat, and it was hard for him to summon the motivation even to leave his room. He found himself thinking often of Meg and still felt that any physical relationship with another woman would be a betrayal.

The other person that he thought of often was Riley Covington. Why he felt guilt at leaving his former friend in the hands of his compatriots escaped him. It was Riley's fault that he was in that position, wasn't it? *He came after me! He tried to block my destiny! He should be thankful I kept him alive! And he did ultimately end up serving my purpose, didn't he?*

Hakeem had never expected al-'Aqran to be released; that wasn't the way Americans worked. What he hadn't bargained on, though, was Riley's being rescued from his cell. It had been two days since his hosts had passed that unbelievable message on to him, and he was still trying to come to grips with it. A chill spread across Hakeem's body, and he zipped his fleece jacket even though he knew that the temperature wasn't the cause of his trembling.

What was it about that man that made Hakeem so uneasy? He knew part of it was his intensity. Riley would not stop until he found Hakeem. But the chances of that were so slim. *I'm holed up in a suburb of the second most populous city in the third most populous country in the world,* he thought confidently.

The bigger part of Hakeem's uneasiness was the way Riley made him question himself. Riley was so sure of himself. His conviction of his beliefs was so strong. His strength of character was so solid. The only time Hakeem had ever questioned his own calling was with Riley in that room back in Italy. He looked down at his hand, still feeling his friend's cheek against his knuckles. *Why didn't he spit on me? That would have made things so much easier!*

A bigger question came into Hakeem's mind. *Will I be able to kill him? If he puts himself in my path again—if he tries to stop me from carrying out Allah's will for my life—will I be able to pull the trigger?* It hadn't been hard for him to kill that smuggler out in the Mexican desert. And it hadn't been hard for him to finish the job two days ago by killing the smuggler's partner after that dishonorable vermin had transported him back from Mexico to Los Angeles. *Why is Riley so different? After all, he is the epitome of the American system—rich, white, gun-toting, nationalistic, and myopic. He doesn't understand the world except through his own skewed American perspective.*

Hakeem lifted the chain off his neck and laid the brass coin that hung on it in his hand. He read the words around the edge: honor, الشرف, Ehre, τιμή, onore, honneur, честь.

Lifting the coin up, he positioned it between his eye and the sun. He looked through the small hole and saw the beams of light shining through. *Glory awaits me when this is through. True, Riley Covington is a man of honor. But so am I. So I will carry out that to which Allah has called me. And if Riley gets in my way, then no, I will not hesitate to kill him.*

TUESDAY, JANUARY 27
LOS ANGELES, CALIFORNIA

During the regular season, a PFL player's life was all about routines, habits, and ruts. Each day had its own practices, its own meetings, and its own workouts. The routine helped keep down the stress level of playing a game in front of millions of people each week. The routine was the reality in what could often become a surreal existence.

Unfortunately, when PFL Cup week rolled around, you could toss that routine out the window.

This was especially true of this year's New York Dragons vs. New York Liberty championship game. Apart from the excitement of a New York/New York rivalry, the hype surrounding the game included countless tributes and memorials for the Colorado Mustangs and Baltimore Predators. The fans were more passionate than ever, and the media took frenzy to a new level. The distractions for the players were almost unbearable.

On the Tuesday before the big game, Jesse Emrick, rookie running back for the New York Liberty, woke up to find more bags in the entryway of his hotel suite. Each night, the security guards quietly opened the players' rooms one by one to admit representatives from various companies. The reps would leave bags and bags of freebies in each suite in the hopes that maybe their shoes or their shirts would be seen protecting the feet or covering the backs of some of the players. It wasn't unusual for a player to finish the PFL Cup week with twenty or thirty pairs of shoes, countless shirts, and multiple electronic gizmos and gadgets. Many players ended up shipping their stash home via UPS or FedEx, as it would be impossible to carry their enormous haul onto the charter flight.

Emrick opened one of the bags and pulled out a beautiful black leather jacket with a Reebok logo across the back. *This'll come in handy in New York,* he thought. He hung the jacket up, then tossed the rest of the bags into the hall closet—no time to examine their contents now.

After getting dressed, Emrick checked the clock—7:25 a.m. Just enough time to get down to breakfast in the ballroom. He hurriedly left his room, nodded to the two LAPD officers stationed at the elevator, and headed downstairs.

When he exited onto the main floor, the noise wound his already tense nerves even tighter. Fans who had managed to sneak their way into the lobby shouted their greetings. The ever-present and ever-diligent press called out their requests for interviews. Emrick did what he had seen some of the veterans do—he waved and flashed a smile, then quickly made his way to breakfast.

Pancakes, waffles, oatmeal, cereals, breads, and every kind of meat commonly accepted as edible in the Western world were on the buffet table. Emrick watched as two offensive linemen stood over a warming tray, picking out fat sausages with their fingers and downing each of them in two bites. At the end of the row was an egg bar, where a third lineman was waiting for his six-egg ham-and-cheese omelet to be prepared.

The rookie back speared some fresh melon wedges, six slices of sourdough toast, and a 24-ounce glass of freshly squeezed orange juice. He was trying to eat a little bit lighter than usual. His insides had been bothering him the last couple of days, which he was sure related more to his nerves than to any virus.

When the players' stomachs were full, the team boarded buses and headed to the Rose Bowl—site of the big game.

Simply making one's way to the bus was an ordeal. Hundreds of fans crowded the driveway, forcing the uniformed members of the LAPD to create a pathway with their bodies. *If Tuesday is this bad,* Emrick wondered, *what will Sunday be like?*

When the buses arrived at the stadium, the players went to the locker room to dress in their uniforms—no pads—and then headed onto the field for the daily hour of interviews.

Emrick had played in eleven different PFL stadiums and countless college ones, but this field was different. Fifteen years ago, he had come to this stadium with his father and watched Tyrone Wheatley lead the Michigan Wolverines to a 38–31 victory over the Washington Huskies. That day he had decided he would do whatever it took to become a running back in the PFL. He breathed in the cool air, wishing his dad, who had died two years ago, could be here to see that dream fulfilled.

On most days during PFL Cup week, tents were set up at the practice facilities, and the press lined up to interview the players there. But today was special. This was the mother of all media days. Each player and coach was stationed in a different part of the stadium, and the press could talk to any or all of them at their leisure.

Because of his rookie status, Emrick's table was placed in the upper rows of section 24. He sat down and pulled out a paperback, figuring no one would want to make the trek up just to talk to a second-string rookie. When the media were let loose, he barely had time to read half a page before he had to put the book down for the day.

The sheer number of print, radio, and television reporters was staggering. They had come from all over the world. Rarely was any player without at least one reporter, while some of the star players would have fifty to seventy-five waiting at any given time. Emrick never had more than seven in his line, but the number never dropped below four.

He had just finished an interview with a lady from the *Peoria*

Journal Star when up stepped a man from Japan's TV Asahi. That interview completed, a TV crew from Eurosport moved to the front of the line. Once he even had a reporter from Al Jazeera put a microphone in his face.

At first all the media attention was a bit of a head trip for Emrick. People actually wanted to know his opinion of the coaches, the other team, the refs; they wanted to know his history and where he saw his career heading. Soon, however, the excitement wore off and tedium set in.

Despite the massive amount of media, the questions rarely varied from reporter to reporter. Emrick had heard offensive linemen constantly answer the question, "Do you feel that you guys on the line get the respect you deserve?" Kickers were asked countless times, "Is it a lot of pressure knowing that the game might ride on one kick from you?" Emrick's déjà vu question was, "Is it a dream come true to make it to the PFL Cup your rookie season?" He found it difficult to keep up the enthusiasm the fiftieth time he answered, "Yes."

And these were just the mandatory interviews. In addition to the thousands of reporters and tens of thousands of questions asked during this hour and the other daily media times, Emrick had a couple hundred requests for private interviews waiting for him back at the hotel. And he knew that his little stack of requests was nothing compared to the ones the big-name players faced.

Yesterday, one of the veteran players had seen him sorting through his pile. Emrick had been wrestling with his need to keep balance in his schedule and his feeling of obligation to fulfill at least some of these requests. The vet had snatched the stack from Emrick's hands, dropped it in the trash, and said, "See how easy it is? Keep your head in the game, boy. You ain't got no necessity for making these guys' jobs easier."

But ignoring the media requests was often easier said than done. Last night, more than a dozen Liberty players had received 1:30 a.m. phone calls from a reporter pleading, "Come on, man, do me a solid! Set me up with an interview tomorrow!" Needless to say, the tactic had been less than effective. The next day, all the Liberty players had reregistered in the hotel using pseudonyms. Emrick had been christened Bill Glover by one of the veteran running backs who said Emrick reminded him of his toddler's television hero, Little Bill. The quarterback moseyed around acting out his new name—John Wayne. The starting left guard asked to be renamed Anne Heche—everyone was sure there was a story behind that, but they were all afraid to ask.

On a typical day during the PFL Cup week, once the interview hour was mercifully concluded, the teams broke into position meetings until lunch. There was rarely anything new taught in these meetings. All the Liberty's plays and assignments had been thoroughly hashed over the previous week in their New Jersey training facility. The meetings were mainly to make sure everyone was still keeping their focus and that each player's memory of his role in every play was perfect. Then, after lunch, it would be practice until dinner.

Today was different. Rather than breaking into the meetings, the players all gathered together for a team photo. Emrick stood with the backs in the third row.

Quite a few pictures had to be taken; it seemed that every shot caught either half the team with their eyes closed or someone doing something obnoxious to one of the rookies. On the third attempt, the veterans on either side of Emrick gave him simultaneous wet willies. It took him two more pictures to get over the sensation of having those guys' damp fingers wiggling in his ears.

When the exasperated photographer finally declared that he had gotten the best photo he was going to get, the players lined up to have their network headshots filmed. These were the short video clips that would be shown when each player was first introduced and again when he did something worthy of either commendation or derision.

As Emrick stood in line, he could hear comments from the TV crews like "A little more smile . . . That's it" and "Now we're going to toss you a ball" mixing with less G-rated taunts from the waiting players. Each player's shoot took about two minutes, after which they were free to stand to the side, where they could return some of the verbal abuse that had been hurled at them.

Just before Emrick's turn, a crash echoed through the room as one of the players knocked over a Lowel ViP Pro-light from one of

the other video areas. While everyone's mocking efforts were directed at that hapless player, Emrick quickly directed his video crew to
get his shoot over with. They complied, and he slipped away verbally
unscathed.

When the headshots were completed, the players were shown
to a room where long tables were set up. Emrick found his designated
chair. Laid out in front of him were five black Sharpie Ultra Fine
Point pens. When each player had taken a seat, souvenir PFL Cup
footballs were passed down the tables. A conveyorlike efficiency was
soon achieved as each player took the ball that was passed to him,
signed it, and then passed it to the guy on his other side.

At the end of the line, each ball was checked over. Oftentimes,
instead of signing their names, some of the players would write
other messages on the balls—messages that parents wouldn't want
in the hands of their seven-year-old Liberty fans. Once the balls
were approved, they were boxed up for later distribution to owners,
coaches, staff, players, friends, and family. Emrick had already put
in a request for one that he could give to his mom. Many of the
autographed footballs ultimately ended up in the hands of dealers
and collectors.

After a half hour of autographing balls—just as Emrick's hand
really began cramping—the team packed up and headed back to
the hotel. The Liberty were staying at the Four Seasons Los Angeles
at Beverly Hills, and the Dragons at the Millennium Biltmore Hotel
Los Angeles. Emrick was pretty sure the Liberty had gotten the better end of that deal.

At the hotel, it was time for another buffet feast. For the carb
addicts, there were three different kinds of pasta, baskets of freshly
baked bread, and a cornucopia of cooked vegetables—some plain,
some loaded with butter, and some smothered with cheese. For the
protein eaters, there were deli trays, chicken, sausages of various
types, and a large warming tray filled with premium quality ten-
derloins. If anyone walked away from this lunch hungry, he just
wasn't trying.

Emrick fixed himself a peanut butter and jelly sandwich and
a plate of fettuccine Alfredo—not a combination his mom would
approve of but filling nonetheless. He sat with one of the veteran

fullbacks, who had two overflowing plates—one a sampling of many of the food choices, the other piled high with spaghetti Bolognese and meatballs.

The fullback looked at Emrick's plate, and then his eyes flashed back to his own. "Rook, you gotta eat more than that if you're gonna keep up your energy." He used his fingers to pick out two large meatballs covered with red sauce and dropped them in the middle of the rookie's plate of Alfredo. "I don't want you leaving this table until you've snarfed every last bite of that, ya hear?"

Emrick's insides churned as he wondered where those fingers had been. But experience had taught him that it was useless to argue with this man, so he quietly cleaned his plate, internally chastising himself for picking this table to sit at.

Emrick had been looking forward to Tuesday ever since the team's arrival on Sunday because today the team had the afternoon and evening off. For some, that meant hanging out in the players' massive game room, which had been fully stocked with Xboxes, GameCubes, and pinball machines in addition to the pool tables, foosball tables, poker tables, and dozens of other amusements. Any player who had relatives with him might grab a car and spend the afternoon with his wife and kids, who would be staying at a nearby hotel. Getting hooked up with a vehicle was as easy as calling the team's concierge and asking for one. Some of the big-name quarterbacks, running backs, and wide receivers might find a Lamborghini Murciélago, a Ferrari 599 GTB Fiorano, or a Rolls-Royce Phantom awaiting them. Special teams players and others would be handed the keys to a Cadillac Escalade or maybe a Mustang convertible.

Once free from the confines of the hotel, the players with kids would most likely head toward Disneyland or Universal Studios. Or maybe they'd just go to the beach for some romping in the sand. Many of the players who were accompanied only by their wives or girlfriends would cruise to Rodeo Drive for some serious shopping.

Emrick had already determined that Rodeo Drive was one place he had to avoid. Having come through the play-offs all the way from the wild card round, he, along with every other member of the team, already had $73,000 worth of postseason bonus share coming his way. If they could win the big game, that figure would double—the losers receiving a measly $38,000. But Emrick had heard that on Rodeo Drive, it wouldn't be hard for someone like him to blow his whole bonus share in one afternoon.

Emrick's real hesitation at leaving the hotel was the fans. They were everywhere. It was hard enough getting in and out of the hotel due to the throngs camped out in the parking lots and driveways. But once you were out, players who didn't hire their own personal bodyguards were taking a risk.

During the day it wasn't so bad. People were still in good moods, and the exchanges were often friendly. However, when the evening rolled around and people got a little alcohol in them, the tone changed. Often harsh words were exchanged. Shoving matches ensued. Players were sometimes called out for fights by drunken fans trying to prove they were just as tough as some "overpaid, punk PFL player who's never worked a day in his life." These incidents steadily worsened as the week went on and the tension level of the team members continued to grow. Those who could, let the taunts roll off their backs; they had their eyes on a greater prize. Those who couldn't, just didn't leave the hotel.

Emrick decided to stay at the hotel; after all, it was hard to beat luxury like this. He dreaded the possible confrontations if he went out, and he had no family with him. His mom hadn't been able to get off work to come to the game, and his two younger sisters were both freshmen at Georgetown University, thanks to his signing bonus. So for him, a day off meant relaxing by the pool if the afternoon warmed up enough and taking advantage of the full-service spa. Hopefully an outdoor California cabana massage could ease his frazzled nerves.

Dinner tonight would be no different for the players than any other night. Each team member was responsible for his own meal—although each was given $120 per diem to do it. Emrick had already arranged with a couple of other rookies to take a car (a Toyota Land Cruiser) and head to Houston's in Century City. Great food, good friends, quiet atmosphere—a perfect way to cap off the team's one down day. Player curfew was 12:30 a.m. Each man was sure to be in bed on time, knowing that the next morning the circus would begin all over again.

"Secret Service is going to have two snipers on the press box, two more up in the south scoreboard, and two more behind us in the north scoreboard," Jim Hicks was saying to Scott, Khadi, and Riley. Skeeter stood about twenty feet off to Riley's left.

"What about aircraft?" Riley asked.

"I asked Craig LeBlanc that very question. He said they're putting up their makeshift control tower just west of us on a little par-three hole at Brookside Golf Course. And they're stealing the fairways to the north of us as our helipads. The city of Pasadena is throwing a fit. Typically those fairways are reserved for parking, so our security is creating a huge mess for them. Apparently the mayor started making all kinds of threats. So LeBlanc pulls out his cell phone, dials a number, says a few words, and then hands the phone to the mayor. Turns out it's the president on the other end of the line. Shut him up pretty quick!"

"What do you know about LeBlanc?" Riley was anxious to learn more about this man upon whom so much depended.

"Well, he's been director of the Secret Service for three years now," Hicks replied. "He's really a quality guy. I'll tell you a story. Back in 1988, I was working out of Washington. Craig was there on presidential detail. Somehow I ended up in a poker game with him and a few other guys—playing Texas hold 'em before Texas hold 'em was cool. I get in a hand with Craig. I'm holding two aces, and I get a third ace in the flop. So I'm sitting pretty. I check out Craig for a tell—you know, anything that might let me know what he's thinking. Nothing. So I bet high, and he calls. The turn card is a three of hearts. No worries—I bet high, and he calls again. We come to the river card—the three of clubs. I'm thinking, *Bonus; my three aces are now a full house.* I check him again—nothing. So I go all in. Without blinking, he calls. I turn over my aces-over-threes full house; turns out he's holding a pair of threes for a four of a kind.

"I learned two things about Craig that day. First, he's got nerves of steel. I mean, come on, he didn't even get his third three until the turn. Second, Craig is a rock. He's the epitome of the stone-faced Secret Service agent. He's one of two or three guys I've ever met who has absolutely no tells when they are playing poker. That is some serious control."

"So, he can play poker," said Khadi, who apparently did not quite grasp the point of the story, "but can he run the Secret Service?"

"Listen, sweetheart, there's not that much difference between being a good director and a good poker player."

Khadi visibly bristled at Hicks's choice of words but held her tongue. She reached into her purse and pulled out her gloves. Although the temperature was in the fifties, the wind where they were standing was dropping that number by at least ten degrees. After a final glare at Hicks, Khadi asked Scott, "What are the flight restrictions?"

"Oeously, iss area—"

Riley reached over and snatched the cherry Tootsie Pop out of Scott's mouth with an audible click, causing his friend to grab his cheek and start rubbing.

"Hey! You trying to crack my teeth?" He turned back to Khadi. "As I was saying, obviously this area is under TFR—temporary flight restriction. NORAD will be monitoring a thirty-mile radius. The tower will control the three-ring circus above us of all the planes and helicopters that will have permission to fly. Hopefully we can avoid having a news chopper crashing into a blimp or something. As for our own patrols, Edwards Air Base is sending us some F-22s to make sure nobody gets any silly ideas." His answer complete, he stole the Tootsie Pop out of Riley's hand and stuck it back into his mouth.

"On the ground, there're going to be more than ten thousand security agents. That's almost one for every ten people in the area. When the president declared the NSSE, the budget flew wide open," Hicks said.

"NSSE?" Riley asked.

"National Special Security Event. That's why the Secret Service is running the security. When there's a viable threat of imminent danger, the president has the prerogative to declare an NSSE. He did it for the PFL Cup after 9/11, and he does it whenever they have something like a State of the Union address or a G8 summit or the like. After what happened at Platte River, it was a no-brainer for him. So LeBlanc has gone all out. He even has fully camouflaged SEAL snipers in the hills surrounding the teams' practice sites."

"So what's our role?" Khadi asked.

"The four of us—well, five with Riley's big shadow over there— are going to watch and wait. I'm deploying the remainder of our team with the snipers and at the various command centers. They're going to be our eyes and ears. I don't want to miss anything that's going on. I figure with my knowledge of operations, your knowledge of terrorist thinking, Scott's computer brain, Riley's insight into Sal Ricci aka Hakeem, and Skeeter's . . . uh, Skeeter's apparent grasp of ancient Roman/Carthaginian battles, we should be set."

As they walked back down the steps and to their car, Riley couldn't shake an uneasy feeling that events might not turn out to be quite as cut-and-dried as Hicks was making them out to be.

FRIDAY, JANUARY 30
EL ESPEJO ROAD
LA MIRADA, CALIFORNIA

Hakeem started from the top and worked his way
down. He was glad to see the short blond hair
falling to the ground. From the time he had dyed
it, he'd felt that the olive skin of his face looked
foolish with a blond frame. Soon the electric razor
moved from his head to his face, then down his
arms, his chest, and the rest of his body.

The only hair that wasn't shaved was that
which grew from the back of his shoulders and
funneled into a narrow strip down his spine. His
host had graciously offered to assist him with that
hard-to-reach area, but Hakeem had declined. This
process was between himself and his maker. *Allah
will forgive this one patch of impurity when he sees
the purity of my actions and my heart.*

Despite the sacredness of the process, Hakeem
found his mind wandering to the time when Meg
had removed that same stretch of body hair. They
were on their honeymoon, and Meg had mentioned her aversion to back hair. He remembered
her exact words: "Ewww, Sal, it's like mating with
a monkey." He had jokingly challenged her. "Well,
why don't you do something about it?"

Meg, never one to run away from a challenge, had disappeared into the bathroom. Hakeem expected her to come back with a razor and some sort of scented rubbing oil, but his romantic dreams were shattered when Meg returned carrying some heavy strips of paper, an applicator stick, and a big tub of goop.

For the next hour, the air surrounding their rustic, thatch-roofed cottage on the Kona shores was filled with the sounds of hair being ripped from Hakeem's body, his cries of pain, and their subsequent shrieks of laughter. In later months, they had both come to the firm conclusion that that balmy June night was when Alessandra had come into existence.

Hakeem realized his mind was drifting again and quickly grabbed the straight blade he was going to use to remove the stubble the electric razor left behind. *Allah, forgive me for my weakness,* he prayed as he brought the razor across his forearm—partially for penance and partially to regain focus. As the blood dripped into the sink, he stared at himself in the mirror. *Toughen up! Does a dead man reminisce about the past? No! He realizes that what's past is past, and he anticipates the rewards of the future.*

After stemming the flow of blood with a towel, he lathered up his head and put the razor to its proper use. He removed any traces of hair from his head and face except for his eyebrows. The whiteness of his recently shaved head would be hidden under a hat, and the paleness of his face where his beard had been would be covered with makeup. But a man with penciled-on eyebrows was still enough of an oddity to receive second and third glances. *Again, Allah, I trust you will forgive my small impurity for the sake of your greater plan.*

When he was finished shaving the rest of his body, Hakeem put on a button-down white shirt and loose white cotton pants. Then he laid out his prayer rug, knelt facing east, and pressed his forehead to the ground. He remained in that position for several minutes, trying to will himself to go through the formulaic prayer that would complete the purification process. Finally, giving up, he stretched himself out flat on the rug—his arms reaching over his head and his face pressed into the fabric.

Allah the benevolent, the merciful, forgive my lack of words. I . . .

*I just don't have the energy. You know the heart of your servant. Please
listen to my heart and not my words. Please listen to my heart and not
my words. Please listen to my heart . . .*

Hakeem repeated that phrase over and over until finally sleep
overtook him.

The break room was popular again. Small clusters of agents talked
and laughed around the twelve tables that until recently had been
empty most of the time.

The change had come two days after Mustang team had set up
at the L.A. FBI office. Riley decided he had finally had enough of
the nasty Costco bulk coffee. So, under the guise of showing deep
appreciation for the hospitality of the bureau staff, Riley had pur-
chased a Bunn Infusion Coffee Brewer Twin and seventy-five pounds
of Costa Rican Tarrazu beans. After installation, the industrial coffeemaker had begun cranking out the delicious brew into 1.5-gallon
ThermoFresh servers, two at a time, elevating Riley's status around
the office to just short of demigod.

Two of the tables were not as full as the others. At one sat
Skeeter Dawkins. People around the bureau had learned quickly that
he was a man with a mission and that he was best left to himself.
At the table next to Skeeter sat Riley and Khadi. Each had a mug of
coffee, and they were sharing an oversize blueberry muffin—tearing
off a bite at a time.

"I spoke with Meg Ricci last night—gave her my contact info,"
Riley said. "I know I probably shouldn't have, but she's having a
really hard go of it. I have no idea how she's going to handle it when
word finally leaks out of Sal's involvement in all this."

"Do you think he ever really loved her?" Khadi asked.

"In Italy, he tried to convince me that she was nothing more
than a pawn in his little game. But I remember the way they were
when they were together. They just . . . I don't know how to put

it. . . . You know how there are couples that you see and you think, *I'll give them two years*? And then there are others you can tell are going to be together their whole lives?"

Khadi nodded, using her thumb and index finger to place a portion of the muffin top in her mouth.

"These two seemed made for each other. What did I miss? How could I have been so incredibly stupid?"

"You weren't stupid, Riley. I think there are some men and women who so successfully partition their lives that they actually become two different people. At home a guy might be the loving family man—all-star husband, coach of his kids' Little League teams . . . the works. Yet when he slips into his other environment—the drug house, the hourly rate motel room, the secret rendezvous, whatever—the alter ego takes over."

"Sort of like a Jekyll and Hyde thing," Riley quipped.

Khadi smiled. "Yeah, I guess. But I think whichever world they happen to be in at any given time, the people who are around them can't imagine them in any other."

Riley took a sip of coffee, then stared at the rainbow of floating oils. Suddenly a big hand wrapped itself around his cup and pulled it away. Riley looked up and saw that the same thing had happened to Khadi's mug. "Skeeter!" he called. But the man was already halfway to the counter to refresh their coffee.

Riley gave an exasperated grunt, and Khadi touched his arm. "You know why he's doing this, don't you?" she said. "He feels guilty for what happened in Barletta."

"What? Why should he feel guilty? I ordered him away."

"Nevertheless, he still feels that he should have been with you. He thinks if he had, none of that would have ever happened to you."

"Well, I need to go straighten that out with him," Riley said as he started to rise. But Khadi's grip tightened on his arm, keeping him in his seat.

"Let him be, Riley. He's got to work it out his way. Besides, having Skeeter as a shadow is not the worst thing in the world for you."

Skeeter reappeared with the two steaming mugs. Riley mumbled his thanks, but Khadi grabbed the man's hairy wrist, looked him in the eye, and said, "Thank you, Skeeter."

Skeeter looked quickly at Riley, then back to Khadi. "Yes, ma'am," he said and returned to his table.

Riley sighed deeply—a little too deeply for his still-struggling lungs—and sent himself into a coughing fit. The coughing wasn't as bad as it had been, but it was strong enough to make the occupants of two or three tables turn around. He tried to stifle the fit with a long draw on his mug, with moderate success.

"Khadi, can I ask you a personal question?"

She responded with a noncommittal nod of her head and a shrug of her shoulders.

"Okay, and please understand where I'm coming from on this. What . . . how do you feel when you hear Muslims defending what was done at Platte River?"

Khadi remained silent.

"I'm sorry," Riley jumped in. "I should have learned my lesson last time."

"No, no, no," Khadi reassured him. "I'm trying to think of a good answer. Truthfully, I've never really analyzed it before. I think my initial response is anger. But then that turns into a profound sadness. These people are taking my religion and giving it a black eye around the world. My people and my beliefs are despised and rejected based on the actions of a minority of fools and zealots. I mean, think about how you feel when you hear of some radical Christian guy blowing up an abortion clinic or a bunch of wackos picketing the funeral of a guy who died of AIDS with signs that say 'God hates gays.' No matter what your feelings are about abortion or homosexuality, you still find yourself thinking, *I really wish they weren't playing on my team.* Does that make sense?"

"Yeah, but . . . again, don't take this the wrong way—I can point out specific places in the Bible that would blow those idiot radicals out of the water. Seriously, it would be like shooting fish in a barrel. But doesn't the Koran actually support what these terrorists are doing?"

"According to the Islamists, it does. But I would also bet that your 'idiot radicals' would claim that they could back their positions with the Bible, too."

They both picked a piece off the muffin, Riley feeling the uncomfortable squish of soft blueberry compacting itself under his fingernail. Khadi looked like she was trying to formulate a thought, so he quietly chewed.

"However," she finally said, "if we're totally being honest here . . . I will admit that there are some passages in the Koran that I don't fully understand. Don't get me wrong," she quickly added, "it doesn't make me cast doubts on my beliefs, only on my own comprehension. At least that's what I tell myself when I'm lying awake at night."

"Okay, that's an interesting qualifier."

"Yeah, I guess it is. Riley, I love my faith. I love my traditions. My family has been Muslim for generations—I love having that history. I just wish . . . I don't know. I guess I wish I knew where I stood with Allah. I often have this fear of standing at the great judgment and being one good deed out of balance. You know what I mean? One 'walking the old lady across the street' or one 'giving a homeless person a dollar' short of tipping the scales in my favor and making it to heaven."

Riley chuckled lightly. "Believe me, I know exactly what you mean. That's why I don't count on anything I do. If it was up to the way I live my life to get me into heaven, I wouldn't stand a chance. I know the junk that's in me. I live with my stupidity every day. That's why instead of depending on what I do, I depend on what Jesus Christ has done. Because He died for me, I know I don't need to worry anymore about being good enough."

"It must be nice to really believe that. I wish I could . . . but once a Muslim, always a Muslim. Islam isn't only what I believe; it's who I am. . . . You know, if it's all right with you, Riley, I'm done with this conversation for now."

"Fair enough. And thanks—for being honest and all."

Suddenly a hand reached in again to take Riley's mug. Riley seized the arm and, without looking up, said, "Skeeter, if you touch my coffee again I will see to it that you are immediately transferred to Secretary Moss's personal security detail!"

The standoff lasted about ten seconds before Skeeter finally pulled his arm away and moved back to his seat. Riley called after him, "And while we're on the subject, I've finally figured out how to go to the bathroom all by myself too—thank you very much!"

Unfortunately, Riley's outburst came during a lull in the break room's conversation. On the positive side, the ensuing round of applause was the largest he had received since the PFL.

/////////////////////

"Citizens of America, the last time I spoke to you was following the incident carried out by Allah's righteous servants in Denver, Colorado. At that time, although I introduced myself to you, I kept my face hidden. That was because my work was not yet done. Today, however, I show you who I truly am, because by the time you are watching this, I will have already gone to join my fellow martyrs.

"My name is Hakeem Qasim. Some of you may be saying, 'But isn't that Sal Ricci, the football player?' I'm sorry to tell you that you are mistaken. There never was a Sal Ricci—only Hakeem. Sal Ricci was a part I played—a part that you, in your all-encompassing desire to be entertained, were all too eager to accept as truth.

"Why did I do it, you ask through your shock and tears? Because your government is in the habit of stealing land. Your presidents steal *waqf* land—land that belongs to Allah. Don't you know that once something belongs to Allah it always belongs to Allah? You fly in with your jets, and you roll in with your tanks, and you think that you possess the land. And once you have it, you hold on to it tightly—at least until the price becomes too high. Then you hike up your skirts and run home. You are pitiful!

"Why did I do it? I did it because your presidents like to murder innocent people. They send in their missiles and leave parents without their children and children without their parents! So, you stole one family—my family—and I have stolen thousands of yours! Now, think of all the other children whose parents you have taken, and do the math! I am not alone!

"Now the truth is known—the Cheetah is out of the bag, you might say. Today I stand before you as living proof of what I said in my previous message. Nowhere are you safe. Trust no one. Remember, I was in your homes every Sunday. Even now, my image is on the walls of your children's bedrooms. My number is on the back of the jersey you are wearing. My signature is on your prize football, in your autograph book, on your favorite hat. You invited a predator into your homes—and now you've been bitten!

"So as you lay your heads down on your soft pillows tonight, remember that I am only one man . . . and there are thousands more like me. My short chapter may be done, but the book is far from being written."

Hakeem continued staring at the camera until the red light blinked off. The others in the room came forward to congratulate him on his message, but he waved them off and retreated to his bedroom.

He sat on the edge of his bed and held the brass coin that hung around his neck. Where he had expected to feel elation, he felt sorrow. Where he had expected to feel victory, he felt emptiness. And where he had expected to feel pride, he felt shame.

What will she think? What will little Aly think when she's old enough to see this? Is this truly the price of honor? Is this truly what a benevolent and merciful God would require of me in order to restore my family's name?

He continued rubbing the coin, but the smell of the metal soon became a stench in his nose. Yanking the chain from his neck, he threw the necklace against the wall.

His head dropped into his hands and he wept. He wept out of anger. He wept out of fear. He wept out of sadness. Most of all, he wept out of helplessness. He knew that no matter how he felt, he would still go through with his grand martyrdom. He had to. From the moment he had been purified, his fate had been sealed. Now he had made the video, and he was dead to the world.

SUNDAY, FEBRUARY 1
FOUR SEASONS LOS ANGELES
   AT BEVERLY HILLS
LOS ANGELES, CALIFORNIA
7:15 A.M. PST

Empty. Please let me be empty. But Jesse Emrick wasn't empty, as evidenced by another internal surge that threw him over the edge of the toilet. He had awakened at 6:15 and had been either lying or kneeling on the beautifully laid tile floor for the past hour. He got himself into a crouch, leaned over the sink, and washed his mouth out, using his hand as a cup. Then he slid back down to the floor, feeling the coolness of the marble slab vanity against his cheek.

Emrick's room wasn't the only one reverberating with this sound. All up and down the fourth and fifth floors of the hotel, one could hear players kneeling at their porcelain altars, hurling out their own personal cries of penance, and ending their prayers with a flush of the toilet.

There had been no food poisoning, nor was there a stomach parasite running rampant through the ranks. One thing, and one thing only, was leading to this discordant chorus: nerves.

The incident that had ultimately led to

Emrick's personal bowl-side meditation had occurred just prior to Friday's practice. Matt Tayse—number-two rusher in the league last season with 1,758 yards, All-Pro for the past four years, bright shining hope for a Liberty victory in the PFL Cup, Mr. Twinkle-Toes himself—had broken his ankle stepping off the bus. It was a fluke accident, a once-in-a-million mistake. It was like a great soldier preparing for the biggest battle of his life accidentally putting a bullet in his calf while cleaning his gun.

This incident didn't promote Emrick to the number-one back—that role went to third-down back, Johnson Mige, who was adding his own chorus to the medley three doors down. However, this did move Emrick into the role of lead third-down back. He was going to be the clutch go-to guy.

He dragged himself into the glass shower stall and turned the water on hot. As the dual showerheads cascaded the steaming water onto his body, he sat on the tile floor, absentmindedly picking at the grout with his fingernail.

This was one of the wonderful things about staying in these fancy hotels. Back home, once his mom and two sisters finished up, he'd get maybe two minutes of lukewarm water, tops. Here, the cleansing, hot waterfall never ended.

Emrick had forty-five minutes until the breakfast buffet downstairs, three hours until chapel, and three and a half hours until the pregame meal. *Breakfast? I'll think I'll pass. Chapel? I'll see what I can do. Pregame meal? Yes, but only because I'll get fined if I don't show.* If he wanted, allowing a half hour to get dressed, he could spend the next three hours letting the water wash his cares away.

.

SUNDAY, FEBRUARY 1
ROSE BOWL STADIUM
PASADENA, CALIFORNIA
11:30 A.M. PST

Something's not right, Riley thought. *What are we missing?* He was walking around the perimeter of the field, scanning the stands. Skeeter was next to him; Hicks was a few steps ahead.

The three men had just made a full circuit of the Rose Bowl

grounds. They'd visited the makeshift tower where Matt Logan was keeping his eye on the air traffic controllers. Also in the tower they checked in with Kim Li, who was keeping in communication with the folks from Edwards Air Force Base and NORAD. Both men had reported absolutely nothing out of the ordinary.

They had stopped by the four large trailers that were the Secret Service command and control centers. After a brief word with a very busy Director LeBlanc and his head of operations, they had spoken to Ted Hummel and Jay Kruse, who were monitoring all that was going on in the operation's "brains." The two veteran agents both felt that things were fairly well in hand.

Before going under the stands, the three men walked across the western sidelines. Looking up at the scoreboards, Hicks and Riley got a status report from the three men who were embedded there with the Secret Service snipers. Carlos Guitiérrez, over the north scoreboard, gave an all clear. Steve Kasay, atop the press box on the west side of the stadium, called out the same. Kyle Arsdale, in the south, made the report unanimous—everything was looking good.

As they walked off the field and through a tunnel, they made one last status check. "Bird One, how're things looking from there?" Hicks called into his comm system.

"Good to go," came Chris Johnson's reply from the LAPD helicopter that he had hitched a ride in.

The three men entered a small room where Scott and Khadi already sat. The two had been brainstorming possible chinks in the security's armor. Hicks took a chair next to Khadi, while Skeeter positioned himself by the door.

"You guys come up with anything yet?" Hicks asked.

Khadi shook her head. "These Secret Service guys are incredibly thorough. Everything we've come up with, they've already thought of and dealt with."

Riley walked around the table and pulled out a chair. When he sat, he put his elbows on his knees, leaned over, and locked his hands behind his neck.

"Pach, what is it? You okay?" Scott's inquiries as to his friend's quietness and distance had been growing more and more frequent.

Without raising his head, Riley answered, "There's got to be something we're missing! Sal's a smart guy. He knows what security will be like, especially after Platte River. . . ." Riley's voice caught on the last word. He took a deep breath, then looked up at the four others. "It's not going to happen again. Not on my watch! It will *not* happen again!" Riley's expression was almost pleading. The dark circles under his eyes and the paleness of his complexion attested to the fact that he was still not well. Recognizing what a pitiful character he must look like, he lowered his head and locked his hands again behind his neck.

"Don't worry, man. We're going to figure this thing out," Scott encouraged him. Turning to the rest of the group, he said, "Okay, let's start from the beginning. . . ."

SUNDAY, FEBRUARY 1
LOS ANGELES, CALIFORNIA
1:05 P.M. PST

The stack of equipment bags rose outside the bus. Emrick added his to the pile and climbed aboard. When the bus was fully loaded, the bags were transferred two at a time to the lower cargo area.

Soon the bus was humming along the freeway at seventy-five miles per hour. It was the second in a line of three motor coaches; a fourth bus, carrying the coaching staff and some overly anxious players, had left the hotel an hour before the others. Ahead of the caravan, four California Highway Patrol motorcycles and three cruisers led the way with lights flashing and sirens blaring.

Emrick stretched out on the left side of the bus, halfway back. Although his nerves were getting progressively worse, at least his stomach had calmed down. He had slowly eaten a large plate of pasta with a light butter sauce and actually managed to hold it down thus far. Like everyone else on the bus, he prayed that no one would lose it, because the resulting chain reaction would make the rest of the trip extremely unpleasant.

The bus exited the freeway and gradually maneuvered its way from San Pascual Avenue to Arroyo Boulevard. Suddenly a voice from the front said, "Yo, check it out!"

Although the stadium was not yet in view, there was no doubt as to its location. Up ahead, the sky was filled with aircraft of every sort. Emrick tried to count them all—at least four planes, six helicopters, and a blimp—stacked at different altitudes as if they were on shelves.

Along the route to the stadium from the hotel, there had been pockets of waving fans. However, once they passed under the Ventura Freeway, the celebration began in earnest. The sides of the road for that final mile were filled with thousands of frenzied people cheering and holding signs.

By the time the buses arrived at the Rose Bowl, the caravan could only inch its way forward. One of the barricades had fallen, and people had massed on the road. Finally helmeted police officers were able to push the crowd back with their Plexiglas shields, and the buses rolled down to their drop-off point.

An audible groan swept through the bus as the doors opened and the sound of Frank Sinatra singing "New York, New York" floated in. No one had anything against the great crooner, but everyone on the team had heard that song enough times in the past week to last a lifetime.

A roar went through the crowd as the first players stepped off the bus. Emrick stood up next to his seat, tightened the knot on his tie, and walked out. He didn't know what the day was going to hold for him, but he did know that he would never be the same again.

SUNDAY, FEBRUARY 1
EL ESPEJO ROAD
LA MIRADA, CALIFORNIA
1:30 P.M. PST

Hakeem drove his two fists into the floor. He had been trying to pray for the past twenty minutes—trying to focus on Allah and on the task ahead—but all his mind kept giving him were images of Alessandra and of Riley, beaten and tied to a chair.

Hakeem raised his head off the ground and, kneeling, lifted his hands toward heaven. *Allah, I am yours. Give strength to your weak servant. Accept me into your paradise.* Hakeem passed his cupped hands across his face and stood. "I am ready," he called out.

Immediately the three men who had been waiting outside the door entered. Rashid Ali Jabr was the owner of the house Hakeem had been staying in. Arshad Mahmud was the local cell leader of the Cause. The third to enter, a man Hakeem had not yet met, was a specialist hired for his particular skills. It was he who had assembled the bomb that Hakeem was now going to place on his body.

"*As-salaamu alaikum,*" this man greeted Hakeem.

"*Wa 'alaikum as-salaam.*"

"My name is Zalfikar Ali Khan. I lost my family six years ago in an American raid across the Afghanistan border into Pakistan. As you avenge your family, *inshallah*, you will be avenging mine."

Hakeem nodded silently.

Khan opened the door of the closet where an oversized vest was stored. Once it had been brought into the house, Hakeem insisted on never letting it out of his sight. The Pakistani lifted the suicide bomb with an audible grunt and placed it on the dresser.

"When I put this on you, you will feel its weight. There are twenty-seven kilos of C-4 and another seven of steel bearings. Most people couldn't walk far wearing this, but I was told that you could handle the load. . . . Just remember, it will tire you out before you expect it to."

Hakeem remained quiet.

Khan turned to the other two men. Stretching his hand out toward the vest, he said, "If you would be so kind."

As Jabr and Mahmud reached for the device, Hakeem put out a hand to stop them. He delved deeply into his pocket and pulled out the brass coin.

The medallion had been so very important to him for so long. It had been a symbol of who he truly was, a constant reminder of his purpose in life. He had been born to die. But not just to die a common death; he had been chosen—called—to die with honor.

As he looked at the three faded daggers etched into the brass, he drew strength from his roots. The words his uncle Ali had repeated to him over and over echoed in his ears: "*Never forget who you are, Hakeem. Never forget who you are.*"

Hakeem pressed the disk to his mouth and felt the warm metal on his lips. Then he slipped the coin into the mesh ball-bearing pouch that would soon be covering the left side of his chest. Turning to Jabr and Mahmud, he nodded.

"Let it down gently," Khan said to the two men, who did as they were told and then stepped away. Taking half of a metal buckle in each hand, Khan told Hakeem, "When I make this connection, there will be no turning back. Are you prepared to do this?"

The two men locked eyes, each seeing the sharpness of grief and the emptiness of revenge reflected in the other man's stare.

"Very good." And with an audible click, Khan locked the suicide vest onto Hakeem's body. Hakeem closed his eyes and breathed a deep sigh. Something cold and metallic found its way into his hand. Looking down, he saw that Khan had given him a shiny silver cylinder. "Please notice that the detonator has a metal cap on it. When you are ready, flip the cap up with your thumb and press the red button underneath."

"Is there anything else I need to know?" Hakeem asked.

"No, you are ready."

"Then please leave me."

Khan bowed slightly. "Very well. *Ma'salaama.*"

Hakeem nodded slightly without replying.

When the three men had left his room, Hakeem picked up his button-down shirt. He slid his arms through the sleeves and slowly did the buttons, staring absently at an inky scribble that had been etched in the richly finished dark wood of the dresser. A small, empty jewelry box had been strategically placed directly over the shaky red letters. But the movement of the vest on the dresser's surface had shifted the disguise, revealing the blemish. Hakeem smiled weakly as he pictured a little girl running out of paper and, the need to express herself overwhelming her common sense, scribbling her name onto her parents' prized bedroom set.

Oh, Alessandra . . .

"I have no time for this," he said out loud and pulled a canvas barn jacket over his shirt. Turning, he examined his reflection in the mirrored sliding closet door. With the vest on, he looked like a man who a couple of years ago had traded in his barbells for Budweisers. Satisfied with the effect, Hakeem removed the jacket and sat down on the edge of the bed.

The vest was definitely heavy, but he'd be able to tolerate it. Although it would be just one bomb, the explosion would be big and devastating. Besides, this was not so much about the blast itself as it was about the where and when of the attack. Today, a dagger would be thrust into the heart of the American people, and hundreds of millions worldwide would know of the weakness of this once mighty nation.

THIRTY-SIX

SUNDAY, FEBRUARY 1
ROSE BOWL STADIUM
PASADENA, CALIFORNIA
2:30 P.M. PST

"You know, today reminds me of my second PFL Cup down in Miami," said ex-coach and current analyst Buddy Minter. His contribution to the ESPN expert panel was to tell a lot of pointless stories that rarely came to a conclusion. "Except Miami was a lot warmer and we were playing the Pittsburgh Miners—wait. . . . If it was the Miners, then that would have been my third PFL Cup, and we would have been in the Galaxydome. . . . No, I'm pretty sure—"

"Well, I'll tell you what it doesn't remind me of," interrupted Willy Schaefer, former All-Pro defensive lineman for the Twin Cities Norsemen. Willy was the clown of the group, and his jokes were often as unintelligible as they were plentiful. "It doesn't remind me of New York, New York. If the Rose Bowl had to last a New York winter, it'd never bloom! Ha, ha, ha!"

"You got that right," agreed Warner Schab, a former major-league first baseman who had inexplicably made his way into the football analyst's chair. Warner rarely had an opinion of his own;

even his feature segment, "Warner's Winners," in which he predicted the results of the day's games, was scripted by a staff writer.

Dale Dewey, ESPN lead analyst and the only one on the panel who really knew what he was doing, just shook his head. Dale had never thought he would miss his stints covering curling up in Ottawa for ESPN2. But from the moment he had been placed with these buffoons, he had been pining for the good old days. "Well, it's definitely not New York. It's a beautiful sunny day in Southern California. The people of Los Angeles are really taking advantage of this rare occurrence when the PFL Cup is not being played in a PFL city. This is a huge first salvo in the city's battle for an expansion team."

"Yeah, maybe they'll call them the L.A. Can't-Keep-a-Teams! They'll play their games in U-Haul Stadium! Ha, ha, ha," Willy said.

"See you later, alligator," Warner added.

Having learned long ago to ignore most of what the rest of his team said, Dale continued, "And as you look around the sea of Liberty and Dragons jerseys, you'll see an equal number of purple number-32 James Anderson jerseys, blue number-86 Sal Ricci jerseys, and many others wearing the Predator and Mustang colors."

"Great show of support," Willy agreed in a rare serious moment.

"Awesome," Warner said.

Buddy looked like he was about to start a story, but a look from Dewey quickly shut him down. The lead analyst continued, "Security is extremely tight around the stadium, and the lines are unbelievably long. Each person entering the stadium is being individually checked."

"Yeah, I'm still having trouble walking after my examination! Ha, ha, ha," Willy interjected, pretending to shift uncomfortably in his seat.

"Ouch," Warner empathized.

"You know, that reminds me of one time when I went to the doctor to—," Buddy began.

Dale quickly jumped in. "Well, it looks like it's shaping up to be an interesting game. The Liberty could be in for it this afternoon. Everyone's going to be watching to see if they can recover from the loss of Matt Tayse due to that freak ankle injury coming off the bus."

"First step's a doozy! Ha, ha, ha!"

"No doubt."

"You know, that reminds me of when we lost Ronde Jennings in the '85 wild card game. The Dragons cleaned our clocks!"

"Interesting. Since this season's Liberty have never been known as a passing team, a lot of the yeoman's work is going to fall on the shoulders of Johnson Mige and the smallish Jesse Emrick. Mige could probably play lead back on most teams in the PFL, but Emrick's still a big question mark."

"I'm sorry to say, but I think the moment Emrick lifts his Bronx up, someone's going to knock his Battery down! Ha, ha, ha!"

"New York, New York."

"You know, he reminds me a bit of the great Wally Pearson, who, although he was slightly undersized at five-ten, still was able to lead the '85 Chicago Stockmen to a 15–1 season and, despite being kept out of the end zone, was a significant factor in their 46–10 trouncing of the Boston Colonials in PFL Cup XX."

Everyone was momentarily stunned into silence by the unexpected appropriateness of Buddy's story. "What?" Buddy asked, looking around.

Dale regained his composure and said, "So, on to 'Keys to the Game.' Willy Schaefer?"

"The Dragons know that their defense has the advantage, so it's going to be up to the offense to put some points up. The Liberty have to hope that they'll be able to find a running lane through the mighty Dragons defensive line. If they can, then they'll bring the Dragons crashing down off of their skyscraping beanstalk! Ha, ha, ha!"

"Yeah, like Jack."

Dale tried unsuccessfully to hide his eye roll. "Warner, what's your key to the game?"

Warner, caught off guard by being asked a direct question, quickly consulted his prepared sheets. "I think we're going to see a powerful defensive battle. Every point won will be a point earned. Every defensive stand will bring a team one step closer to victory. My prediction is that whoever scores first will finish last. Wait—" he looked back down at his paper—"I mean whoever scores last will finish first."

For the hundredth time, Dale wished that the network would fire Warner and put his writer on the panel instead. "What about you, Buddy? What's your key to the game?"

"You know, this game reminds me of PFL Cup XXVIII, which was held in the two-year-old, beautifully constructed, $214 million Delta Dome down in Hot-lanta. The Texas Outlaws soundly defeated the Buffalo Barrelriders by a score of 30–13. Interestingly enough, that was the only time in PFL history that the same two teams met in the PFL Cup two years in a row." Buddy turned back to Dale.

The twenty-year broadcast veteran, after vainly trying to formulate some sort of response, threw it to commercial.

/////////// 3:15 P.M. PST ///////////

"How's Hakeem going to do it?" Scott's frustration level had been steadily increasing over the past few hours. He wasn't used to being stumped. "He didn't plant explosives or anything prior to the game; the dogs have been over every inch of this stadium. He can't come in on the ground; the gates are too heavily secured for that. He can't come in from the air; besides it being impossible because of our defenses, it would be just plain silly. We've even got defenses that would intercept any rockets or missiles. And the Secret Service has checked and confirmed that no underground tunnels have been dug, as ridiculous as that possibility sounds."

"Maybe when he realized he had tipped his hand to Riley and that Riley had escaped, he called off the strike," suggested Khadi, who was sitting across the small square table from Scott. Riley and Hicks occupied the other two sides.

Riley shook his head. "That's not Sal. His knowing that I know makes it even more likely that he'll go through with it. You can chalk it up to male competitive spirit or whatever, but Sal's going to hit today. I'm sure of it."

"But how?" Scott's theme resonated through the room. Silence answered his question.

Finally Riley said, "I think he's going to walk right in."

"Sorry, Pach, there's no way. Or if somehow he does make it in, he'll be carrying nothing more than a squirt gun."

"No, Riley's right, Weatherman," Hicks chimed in. "Hakeem's coming in on the ground. I don't know how or where, but he's walking in—and he's walking in fully loaded."

Hakeem confidently walked through the gate. No one questioned him. No one searched him. No one even gave him a second look. *No one notices a dead man—a ghost floats where he wants. The Cheetah stalks silently and, before you know it, makes his kill.*

Now that he was through the gates, he slowed down. There was no rush anymore. The hard part was over; now it was a waiting game.

Hakeem's doubts had faded as he made the drive. He had always believed he *could* do what needed to be done. His biggest struggle was with whether he *should* do what needed to be done. Finally all questions had been trumped by the realization that he *must* do what needed to be done. He must do it for himself, for his family, for his people, for his posterity. America needed to be dealt with, and no matter what Riley Covington said, there was morality and justice in what he was doing.

He looked at the crowd around him. Everyone was so excited. For many, being here was a dream come true—and many others around America doubtless wished they could be here as well. That was why what he was about to do would hurt so much.

When a dream dies, it kills part of the soul.

That was Hakeem's mission: the death of a dream. *The Cheetah, dead man walking, killer of souls.*

Hakeem smiled.

Blood dripped onto his white pants and turned black as it spread to the green stripe that ran down the outside of his thigh. But Emrick didn't even notice the small chunk that had been taken out of his elbow—at least until he was sitting on the bench and a trainer ran up, cleaned the wound off, and slapped a large bandage on it.

Emrick was feeling too good to notice any pain. He looked up at the scoreboard: Liberty 7; Dragons 0.

Six of those points are mine, he exulted.

The Liberty offense had driven slowly down the field to the Dragons' 34 yard line. It was third and eight. Emrick had lined up in the backfield at the halfback position, then run a pass route that swept across the middle before he suddenly broke downfield. The ball had reached his hands when he was at the 28 yard line, and he had just kept running. One quick juke and a wicked forearm later, he was in the end zone.

It might only be the first quarter, but Emrick had the feeling that today was his day.

////////// **4:05 P.M. PST** //////////

Riley, Khadi, Scott, and Hicks sat silently around the table deep in the heart of the Rose Bowl stadium; Skeeter guarded the door. Frustration was leading to desperation. Every muffled cheer from the crowd above sent a knife into Riley's heart. He wondered how many people out there—and in here, for that matter—were going to die because of his failure. It didn't make sense. *Did I really hear Sal say what I thought I heard him say? Or was I so anxious to beat him at his own game that I read into his words?*

Riley shook the doubts from his head. He had gone over his conversation with Hakeem word for word with Hicks, Scott, and Khadi, and they all agreed with him. Sal had made it very clear that his next target was the PFL Cup. *But why? Why would he have been so forthright with his intentions? Did he actually intend to have me killed after al-'Aqran was released? And wouldn't he have known that I would try to signal something to my team? He's a smart guy. Could he have made that big of a blunder? Was it a blunder?*

The silence in the room was so intense that when Riley's cell phone rang, it caused Khadi to start, Scott to tip over in his already precariously positioned chair, and Skeeter to draw his weapon. Riley looked at the caller ID—*Meg Ricci.* He silenced the phone. "Sorry, guys."

A few moments later, the phone began ringing again. Again the caller ID showed *Meg Ricci.* Again Riley silenced the ring.

A minute passed, and then the phone began to ring once more.

"Just answer it!" Scott and Khadi said simultaneously.

Riley picked up the phone and flipped it open. "Meg, now is not—"

"Riley, I have to talk to you." Meg sounded frantic.

"Can it wait for a few—?"

"Riley, please!" There was fear in her voice, and she sounded like she was about to hyperventilate.

Riley got up from the table and walked to a corner of the small room. "Sure, Meg, of course. Take a breath, and then tell me what's going on."

Riley heard Meg take a couple of deep breaths, obviously trying to regain her composure. When she began to speak again, the frantic tone had come down a few notches, but the fear was still strong. "I . . . I was cleaning out some of Sal's stuff. I know it's probably too soon, but I just couldn't handle looking at it day in and day out. Does that make me a bad person?"

"No, of course not. Everyone handles grief differently. But what's got you all worked up?"

"Well, I was in our closet pulling out the shoes he never wore. He'd buy shoes, wear them once, and then just throw them back in the corner. Anyway, I pulled out a pair from the corner and noticed a bump in the carpet. I tried to smooth it out, because we've had trouble with this carpet ever since we put it in last year, remember?"

"Right, right. So what was it?" Riley asked, trying to move her along. He remembered Sal telling him once that Meg tended to ramble when she was upset.

"So, I try to smooth it out, but it won't smooth. I feel the bump and realize there's something under the carpet. It was a key, Riley. A key to a safe-deposit box. And along with the key were three small pieces of paper with what looks like Arabic writing on them."

Riley felt the hair rise on the back of his neck. He rushed to the table. "Meg, I'm here with some friends. I think they need to hear what you might have to say. Do you mind if I put you on speakerphone?"

Meg hesitated for a moment. "Do you have to? I mean, this is personal stuff and . . ."

"Please, Meg. This could be very, very important."

"Okay, okay. But first I need to know. Was Sal caught up in anything bad . . . you know, before he was . . . before he passed away?"

"I'll tell you what. When I get back to Denver, I'll come over and tell you everything I know. Right now, I need to hear what you've discovered. So, speakerphone?"

"Okay."

Riley pressed the button that changed the mode of the cell phone. "Meg, I'm here with Jim Hicks, Scott Ross, and Khadi Faroughi."

Scott said, "Hey, Meg."

Khadi said, "Hi, Meg. I'm so sorry about your loss."

Hicks said nothing.

"So, Meg, you were telling me about a key to a safe-deposit box that you found and some Arabic notes."

The others turned to Riley, shock on their faces. He nodded to them and gestured with his hand for them to keep it cool.

"Hi, everyone. So . . . well, I took this key to our bank yesterday. I've been up all night with this, Riley. I was trying to decide whether I should call you or not."

"You did the right thing. So you went to the bank. . . ."

"Right, I went to the bank—I figured Sal wouldn't have minded and all—and they took me back to the safe-deposit boxes. The key fit one of them, and they pulled it out and put me in a private room. I'm so glad they did, because . . . I mean, I couldn't believe what I found."

"What was it?" Riley asked.

"Money. More than $250,000 in cash. There was also some Mexican money—you know, pesos and stuff—and euros. There was also a . . . a . . ."

"Go on," Khadi encouraged.

"There was a gun—a loaded gun. Why would he have a loaded gun and thousands of dollars in a safe-deposit box, Riley?" The pace of her words was steadily increasing.

"Keep calm, Meg. Was there anything else?" Riley asked.

"A couple of papers. They look like sketches or something. One of them was of Platte River Stadium."

"Do you have the papers with you?" Scott called out. "Did they have any writing on them?"

"Riley, what's going on?" Meg asked, her fear growing even greater.

"Please, Meg, I promise I'll explain everything later. Do you have the papers with you?"

"They're right here."

"Are there any markings on the Platte River Stadium drawing?" Scott asked.

"Yeah, there are some *X*s. . . . Let me see . . . one, two, three, four, five, six, seven. Seven *X*s. Wait a second! There were seven bombers—that's what they said on the news about Platte River Stadium the night Sal was killed. I know because he was killed by the seventh bomber!" Franticness had returned and replaced the fear in Meg's voice. "Riley, was Sal somehow involved in the bombings?"

"Calm down, Meg," Riley said.

"Calm down? Don't you tell me to calm down! How can I calm down? Was Sal some sort of suicide bomber who killed himself at Platte River Stadium? Is that what you're saying?" Meg was shouting now.

"Meg! Stop!" Riley yelled. Meg stopped talking, but her shallow, rapid breathing could be heard clearly through the phone's speaker. "First of all, promise me that when you hang up this phone you will gently pick up Alessandra and the two of you will go next door to Jill's house. Do you promise me?"

Hicks was motioning for Riley to get on with it.

Riley waved him off. "Meg, promise me!"

"Okay, Riley," Meg said softly. She was crying now, and her words came between sobs.

"Now, I'm sorry, but I need to know if there were any other papers in there."

"Yes, I'm looking at one now. It's got a circle in the middle, then lines going off the circle. They look like . . . I don't know . . . like spokes or something."

"Doesn't sound like the Rose Bowl," Scott said to Riley.

"Rose Bowl? Are you at the PFL Cup, Riley? Is someone planning to—?"

"Never mind that. Is there anything else on the paper?"

Riley heard a new note of icy resolve in Meg's voice. She spoke rapidly and matter-of-factly. "There are four small *X*s on the paper. One near the end of each of the lines. Each *X* has two letters next to it—the first has *CC*, the second *AL*, the third *MT*, and the fourth *TL*. Then there's a pointy arrow—like a pyramid with no bottom. And then right in the middle is a square with some pointy-ended rectangles jutting out the top. The only other thing is a big *X* down below the square, about halfway between the square and the bottom of the last line."

"Is there anything else? Anything at all?" Riley asked.

"No, that's it. Please, Riley, please tell me what's going on." Her resolve quickly disappeared again into fear and sorrow.

"I have to go now. You're going to have to trust me that I'll give you all the answers soon. Now go get Aly, and go to your neighbors'."

"Please, Riley . . ."

"Meg, I'm sorry. Now do what I asked you!" Riley hung up the phone feeling like a total jerk for speaking to her that way. He turned to Scott.

But Scott was already zoned out.

/////////////////////

Scott's eyes were closed as he brought up a mental image of the paper Meg Ricci had just described.

A square with pointy rectangles . . . missiles? . . . He could be planning to hit a missile silo, but what good would that do? . . . Overtaking a missile silo and launching—impossible; that stuff only happens in old Frank Zagarino movies.

Xs with initials: CC, AL, MT, and TL. AL and MT could be state abbreviations, but what about the others? "Khadi, start googling combinations of those letter pairs," Scott called out of his haze, and Khadi quickly went to work on the Toughbook.

So, scratch missiles. . . . Pointy rectangles . . . Washington Monu-

ment . . . skyscrapers . . . turrets . . . turrets coming out of a square . . . or towers. . . . Yeah, towers out of a square . . . a castle. . . . Yeah, okay, good call; he's probably going to hit one of the many southern California castles.

Scott took a deep pull on his Yoo-hoo without opening his eyes. *Focus, focus! A church? Unlikely . . . and it doesn't have the layout for a broadcasting zone. . . . What if it is a castle . . . maybe a replica of some kind? . . . A castle next to a pyramid . . . Las Vegas? No, that dead border coyote points to Hakeem being in L.A., not Nevada. . . . Is it a movie studio?*

"Somebody call Tara and tell her to have her minions check for a studio lot that might have a castle and a pyramid on it," Scott said as he blindly tossed his phone toward anyone who would catch it. "Speed dial 6!"

But a studio isn't big enough. . . . Not a pyramid . . . maybe a tent. . . . A castle next to a tent? Sounds like a So-Cal used car lot. . . . Not a tent. . . . Maybe the pyramid's a mountain. . . . A castle next to a mountain?

Abruptly Scott's eyes opened. "Oh no," he said out loud. "Khadi, give me the computer!"

Scott typed a couple of words, tap-tap-tapped the backspace, corrected his typing. Everyone gathered around the screen, then gasped as they saw what he had brought up.

He pointed to an illustrated map as he read off the locations. "CC . . . to the left up here; AL . . . below it over here; MT . . . up top here; and TL . . . over on the far right. Folks, Hakeem's not coming to the PFL Cup. We were set up. He's gone to Disneyland."

SUNDAY, FEBRUARY 1
ROSE BOWL STADIUM
PASADENA, CALIFORNIA
4:15 P.M. PST

"Li, tell the folks at Edwards that we're taking two of their Black Hawks!" Hicks yelled into his comm system as he ran with Khadi, Scott, Skeeter, and Riley through the tunnel under the stands. "I want one with rotors spinning in three minutes on the north fairways! You and the rest of the team will take the other one! Logan, let the control tower know we're heading out and have them plot us a course so we don't run into some idiot news chopper! Hummel and Kruse, let Director LeBlanc know what's going on! Tell him we need SWAT at Disneyland ASAP and have him contact security at the park to let them know what's going down! The rest of you, get out of those scoreboards and to the helipad—I want you off the ground no more than four minutes after us!"

Skeeter led the group as they came out into the sunlight. His shoulder was like the prow of an icebreaker as it cut through the solid mass of people. Scott was on the phone behind him, asking Tara Walsh to send full schematics of Disneyland to his Toughbook. Hicks and Khadi were immediately behind Scott, and Riley brought up the rear. The run had brought back Riley's cough, and he seemed to be having a hard time keeping up.

Hicks could hear the assault helicopter winding up as they approached. As they broke through the row of trees lining the fairway at the golf course, he spotted the Black Hawk with its rotors up to speed. Twenty yards east, another helicopter was just starting its spin. Hicks and the others finished their run in a crouch and jumped into the cargo area.

Hicks gave the pilots a thumbs-up, and immediately the wheels left the ground. All five passengers slipped on helmets, adjusted their intercom mics, and gathered around Scott's Toughbook screen.

Scott shouted over the sound of the helicopter, "Tara just sent me this architectural map. You can see the way the park kind of spokes out from the central hub of Cinderella's castle."

"Sleeping Beauty's castle," Riley corrected, causing the three men to give him a questioning look. "What? It's written on the map!"

"Yeah, whatever, Pach," Scott said with a grin.

"Just shut up and show us again where Sal had his *X*s."

"Each one was near the end of one of the spokes. You got Critter Country, Adventureland, Mickey's Toontown, and Tomorrowland."

"What about the big *X*?" Khadi asked.

"That one was halfway between the center hub and the end of the lower line. That would put it right about here," Scott said, pointing right to the middle of Main Street, USA.

"Okay, so why all the *X*s? What's he got planned?" Hicks asked.

"Scott, pull up a Google Earth view of Disneyland," Riley said. When the image was up, Riley leaned close to the screen. "Okay, I'm thinking back to when I was there as a kid. There were shops—tons of shops lining Main Street," Riley remembered.

"Isn't it the first thing you come to after you enter?" Scott asked.

"Yeah. I remember thinking it was pretty boring as a kid; I wanted to get to the real rides."

Khadi pushed her way in front of the computer screen. "So, why all the *X*s? The most logical use for the markings are that they are bomb sites. But why bomb the extremities? There's no real impact out there."

"I hear you, Khadi," Riley said. "The only other reason I can think of for Xs is to indicate meet points. But it really seemed to me that Sal was planning on going this alone."

"Quit telling me everything the Xs aren't and start telling me what they are!" Hicks commanded.

"They're whip cracks," came a deep voice. Everyone turned to see Skeeter leaning over Khadi's shoulder, looking at the screen. "You got yourself a mule don't wanna move, you crack him a whip 'crost his back. He'll start movin'. That's what *hajji's* doing with those other four Xs. He's cracking his whip."

"Of course," Riley said. "You set off those blasts, people start running away. The only route clear of destruction is the one to the main entrance. But to get to the main entrance, they've got to squeeze through the Main Street funnel. Sal waits for the big rush down Main Street, and then he detonates the big one."

"It fits," Hicks said. "And it's better than any other guess we've got." He moved to the cockpit and asked the pilots to patch him through to Director LeBlanc.

While he waited, Hicks closed his eyes and visualized the satellite image. He saw the way all the paths converged on that one street, and the mental picture made him shudder. He prayed they weren't too late.

SUNDAY, FEBRUARY 1
DISNEYLAND
ANAHEIM, CALIFORNIA
4:20 P.M. PST

Hakeem sat on a bench in the plaza at the end of Main Street, U.S.A. He wore earbuds connected to a radio that was tuned to the football game taking place less than an hour away. It was a fast game—a fact Hakeem appreciated. Timing was crucial, and the sooner he could get this over with, the better.

Stage one was complete. As soon as Hakeem had arrived, he had hidden the four small bombs in strategic spots around the park.

The devices were concealed in shrink-wrapped cases of Disney DVD collector sets and had been given to him in a souvenir bag back at the house. If all went as planned, the small bombs would explode right as the second quarter came to an end. The big blast would come during halftime.

He turned the volume down a few notches so he could think. *I wonder if Riley's enjoying the PFL Cup,* he mused. *I wonder how he's going to feel when he realizes he was within forty miles of stopping me. Sorry, buddy, but those forty miles might as well be around the world.*

A light breeze came from the direction of a popcorn vendor. Hakeem breathed in deeply. *I wonder what heaven smells like,* he thought. The smell of the buttery popcorn became so distracting that he got up and moved to another bench out of the scent's flight path.

The park was packed. Just like the day of the Daytona 500 brought thousands of people to Disney World, Hakeem knew that the PFL Cup was contributing to the crowd today. Everywhere he looked, there were smiling and laughing families. This truly was a dream come true for many of them. He had to admit that deep down he felt bad for these people, especially the children. But in any war, innocents must die. These children were not being murdered by him. Their fate had been determined a long time ago by the actions of their own government. *Blame your president; don't blame me.*

Hakeem would have liked to have been around to watch the aftermath of this attack. But he knew that Allah had chosen and prepared him for this particular mission. The American people would be devastated by the knowledge that this icon of the nation's family values had been attacked. Their horror would only be compounded at the realization that it was one of their "heroes" who had carried out the strike.

When it came down to it, Hakeem knew he was just a pawn in this game. The Cause had existed before him, and his death would result in it becoming even stronger. This was not the Cause's swan song; it was the beginning of its symphony.

"Six minutes to go in the half with the score Liberty 14, Dragons 10," came the announcer's voice as the broadcast cut to commercial.

Six minutes left. Hakeem stood and headed down Main Street. He didn't want to be caught having to rush at the last minute.

Just six minutes. Hakeem was ready. In six minutes, while millions of eyes were glued to the television hoping to witness another wardrobe malfunction, a newsbreak would cut in—rocking their world—telling them of the carnage and devastation at what had once been the "happiest place on earth."

Hicks pointed to the computer screen. "See this central plaza area between Disneyland and California Adventure? The chopper's going to come in low and drop us right in the middle of it. We need to try to get into the park without Hakeem realizing it, or he'll set himself off wherever he is."

"I don't think he will, Jim," Riley said. "He's probably been planning this thing for a long time. He's got something he wants to say with it. I'm betting he's going to do whatever he can to carry out his plan."

"Maybe you're right; maybe you're wrong. I'm not going to take a chance. So after we drop in and get into the park, we're going to pair off and go looking for him—all except for you, Skeeter."

Skeeter started to protest, but Hicks cut him off. "Skeet, with your height, I need you in this Town Square place, right inside the entrance. I want you looking at every face that comes in or out. Got it?"

"Yes, sir." Skeeter clearly wasn't thrilled at the idea of allowing Riley out of his sight, but he was a soldier, and Hicks knew he would follow orders.

"Riley and Khadi, you take the left side of Main Street. Scott and I'll take the right. And people, we shoot to kill. Everyone got that? Riley?"

"Don't worry about me," Riley answered. "I'll be right with you."

"Fine. Any questions? Good. We're five minutes out. Lock and load."

Hakeem used the time between the two-minute warning and the end of the half to pray. All doubts were gone now. His time had almost come.

"And that'll do it for the first half, with the New York Liberty leading the New York Dragons by four," Hakeem heard through his earbuds. "Stay tuned for our halftime show, coming your way in—"

Hakeem clicked off the radio. Then he stood, dropped it in a garbage can, and walked toward the spot where his life would end.

He stopped halfway down Main Street and faced back into the park. Reaching into the pocket of his coat, he pulled out a small remote control device. On it were two buttons—one to arm and one to trigger.

The four small bombs he had planted wouldn't do much damage, but they would make a lot of noise and send up huge plumes of smoke, creating a panic that would drive the frightened people right toward him.

The first button depressed with a click and remained down.

This is for you, Father and Mother. This is for you, Uncle Ali. This is for you, sweet Alessandra.

Hakeem took his last breath of calm sanity—catching a faint smell of peppermint from the candy shop next to him—and pushed the second button.

/////////// **4:35 P.M. PST** ///////////

They were two miles out. The Black Hawk was coming in very low, just barely clearing the buildings below. Suddenly four black clouds rose up from the park ahead.

"We're late!" Hicks shouted. "Plan B! Everybody rig up! We're going to have to drop onto Town Square at the entrance to Main Street to avoid the stampede! As soon as you're down, push as hard as you can to move up that street! Hakeem will wait until the street fills up. That means we've got five minutes max before he detonates. This is it, people. Last chance."

/////////// **4:35 P.M. PST** ///////////

A stunned hush fell on the park as the mushrooms of smoke rose into the air. Everywhere around Hakeem, people froze in their tracks, eyes toward the sky.

Then came a single scream, immediately opening the flood-gates of panic as people shouted for their children and yelled for directions to the exits. Complete mayhem erupted as the guests tried to remember the way out of the park.

Satisfied, Hakeem entered the Candy Palace; he needed a place where he could wait for the few remaining minutes. All the customers inside had rushed out to see what had happened, leaving him alone with the sole remaining employee. He walked through the store and around the counter. When the girl in the old-fashioned dress began to protest, Hakeem pressed his .40 cal to her chest and pulled the trigger. The teen crumpled to the ground.

Hakeem looked back toward the entrance and noted with satisfaction that the noise and the panic outside had completely drowned out the sound of the shot. Adrenaline surged through his body as he took one last look at the girl to make sure she wasn't moving. He moved to the front display window and stood watching the passing crowd begin to grow.

So far, everything is working just as I planned.

////////// **4 : 39 P . M . PST** //////////

The Black Hawk dropped to within thirty feet of the ground over Town Square, causing the already frantic people to slip into sheer panic. Five dark shadows appeared on the sides of the helicopter, then rapidly rappelled to the ground. When the team was down, they disconnected their lines, and the helicopter lifted back up.

All around, people screamed and pointed at these five figures carrying automatic weapons. No one knew for sure whether this strange sight was the continuation of the attack or somebody coming to the rescue. No one wanted to risk finding out.

People clambered over each other, trying to escape these possible terrorists. The only ones who weren't frightened were some of the preadolescent boys who thought this show was way cooler than that cheesy one at Universal Studios. After the team separated, they were soon forgotten as the crowd continued its mad rush to the exit.

Even from inside the Candy Palace, the noise of the stampede was deafening. Parents had abandoned their strollers and were carrying their children, sometimes two and three at once. Older people were getting shoved aside as the younger ones raced past.

That right there is the root cause of what is wrong in this society!

Any ounce of pity Hakeem had ever felt for these people was gone. He slid the detonator from his sleeve and placed it in his hand. After a final quick prayer to Allah, he stepped out the door.

CHAPTER

THIRTY-EIGHT

SUNDAY, FEBRUARY 1
DISNEYLAND
ANAHEIM, CALIFORNIA
4:44 P.M. PST

Riley and Khadi fought hard against the flood of
people. The crowd was pushing all around them.
Forward progress through the sea of bodies was
made even more difficult by the people's terrified
reaction to the M4 in Riley's hands.

As they forced their way down the left side
of the street, Riley scanned the faces around him.
He could hear soft voices as they passed him—
parents whispering to their children, "It's okay,
baby," "Daddy's got you now," "Mama loves her
little angel." Several times Riley passed people
who had blood on their faces. Others were limping or being helped by family members. All kept
their eyes straight ahead, trying with everything
they had to reach their goal of the front gates.

How many of these innocent victims will be killed
if we don't get to Sal in time? Riley wondered.

His foot caught on something that almost
made him lose his balance. He looked to his left in
time to see an aluminum walker tipping over and
an elderly woman go sprawling after it. Resisting
the urge to stop and help, he pressed forward—

only once looking back to see a young man trying to help the woman back up. *Lord, please help these people!*

His height gave him a little advantage, and Riley was able to keep a fairly good view of the area around him. Khadi stuck close behind him. All the stores seemed to be abandoned—the employees either fleeing to the back lots or out the exit. Someone bumped hard into Riley's side, sending a nasty message from his mending ribs to his brain's pain sensors. He dropped one arm to protect his side.

Up ahead, under a yellow and white awning, something caught Riley's eye. In the midst of the river of flowing humanity, there was one stationary person pressed against a wall. Riley signaled to Khadi, and they pressed that direction. When they were ten yards away, the man removed his hat, dropped it onto the ground, and rubbed his bald head.

"I think I've got a visual in front of the Candy Palace!" Riley yelled into his comm unit.

"Are you sure?" Hicks's voice answered.

"Negative, not yet! Khadi, cut left and head up the storefronts. I'm going to confirm whether that's Sal."

Khadi nodded her approval. "Be careful, Riley."

Riley pushed ahead, but the mass of people made forward progress difficult. Suddenly the man looked up, and Riley locked eyes with his best friend.

Lord, don't make me do this! Not Sal! Please don't make me . . .

Surprise showed on Hakeem's face for just a moment before his body went flying backwards as a shot from Riley's M4 hit him in the left shoulder.

"It's him! It's him!" Riley cried as he struggled toward Hakeem.

"I'm on him!" came Khadi's voice in his ear. "He's down but still—"

Two shots cut through the noise, and Riley turned in time to see Khadi's head drop behind the crowd.

"NO!" he shouted just before he felt two sets of arms grab him around the neck and try to pull him to the ground. As he struggled to break their grips, he felt his rifle stripped from his hands. Another hand grabbed for his sidearm.

Riley drove his elbow into the chin of one of his assailants, sending him toppling. A low leg sweep followed by a forearm to the throat dropped the second.

Riley didn't stop to find out who these guys were, but a quick glance at the first blond-haired man lying stunned on the ground in a Mickey Mouse T-shirt told him they were Good Samaritans trying to take down the guy with the gun.

With his shoulder down, Riley drove the last few feet through to the area that had cleared around Hakeem. The terrorist was struggling to roll his body onto his mangled left side. A detonator lay just out of his reach, but he was getting close to grabbing it.

Riley dove for Hakeem, but Hakeem turned in time to fire two shots into Riley's chest.

Riley's ballistic vest stopped the bullets from penetrating his body, but the impact drove the air from his lungs. He landed on top of Hakeem, causing both men to scream in pain.

Blackness threatened to descend on Riley as Hakeem fought to push him off. Finally Riley felt his body being rolled sideways, even as he struggled to find the strength to stop Hakeem.

And then Hakeem was free. He had the detonator in his hand.

Over the sound of the screaming crowd, Riley heard Hakeem gasp, "Not this time, Riley. *Allahu akhbar!*"

A loud bang and a hot liquid spray snapped Riley out of his semiconscious state. His eyes cleared, revealing the open back of Hakeem's head. A few yards beyond, he could see Khadi lying on the ground, her gun in her hand.

Riley wanted to go to her but knew that the detonator must still be in Hakeem's hand or under his body. As he pushed himself up to look for it, a large, dark shape dove past him from behind, clipping his back and knocking him facedown again. When he looked up, he saw Skeeter lying on the ground, gingerly holding a wired metal cylinder. "'Scuse me, sir. I got the detonator. Now go get Khadi."

Riley nodded to his faithful bodyguard and stumbled toward Khadi. Sliding down next to her, he lifted her into his arms. He could feel the wetness of the blood that had pooled underneath her.

"Medic!" Riley yelled into his comm unit. "Scott, get me a medic!"

Khadi slowly shook her head. "He . . . he should have known, Riley. Never leave . . . never leave a sniper breathing."

Khadi smiled weakly, showing bloodstained teeth, rolled her head into Riley's chest, and closed her eyes.

The iguana lay on its back on a pool raft, a coconut shell drink in one scaly claw and the words *Pura Vida* in a speech balloon to the left of his mouth. The orange bucket hat upon which the lizard had been stitched was to Riley the single ugliest piece of headwear he had ever laid eyes on.

"Remind me again," he called out, "how much did you pay for that thing?"

Scott Ross, who could have been the model used to create this masterpiece, tilted the hat off of his eyes and answered from the middle of the pool, "You can't place a price on art, my friend. That's why I snagged a second one of these beauties to take back to Tara."

"She'll be thrilled."

Riley watched as a cabana girl waded over to Scott's raft with another coconut shell brimming with Yoo-hoo, three multicolored paper umbrellas, two toothpick-skewered maraschino cherries, and one bendy straw. He smiled as he laid his head back on the deck chair, enjoying the coolness of the open-sided cabana's shade.

Riley was finally getting to the point where he could close his eyes without pictures of Platte

EPILOGUE

River Stadium and Disneyland invading the darkness. But the what-ifs still plagued him—*What if I had paid more attention to Sal back in Denver? What if I had dug deeper that Christmas Eve instead of putting a tough conversation off for another day? Why was my first reaction at Disneyland to put a bullet into my friend? Was there no other way? What kind of person does that make me?*

"Skeeter," he said, knowing that this train of thought was taking him nowhere, "what time is it?"

Skeeter, one cabana over, looked up from his copy of Goldsworthy's *The Fall of Carthage*—a gift from Scott—and replied, "Five minutes since you asked last. Relax, Pach."

Riley sat up quickly and gave Skeeter an incredulous look. "Wait a second! *You're* telling *me* to relax? Excuse me, but do you see anyone else around this pool with long pants and boots on? anyone else in this sunny tropical paradise wearing all black? You look like a giant shadow of someone who's not having a good time!"

"At least it matches," Scott interjected from the pool.

"What?"

"The all black—at least it matches his piece."

"What are you talking about?"

"Well, can you imagine Skeet wearing one of those green and red tropical shirts accessorized with that black nylon shoulder holster? What a horrible fashion faux pas that would be."

"First off, I am not going to discuss clothing with you of all people—the walking fashion faux pas himself. Second . . . second, I don't even remember what this whole discussion is about."

"Score one for the faux pas," Scott said as he slipped his hat over his eyes again.

Riley stared after Scott, then leaned back into his chair again, laughing. This trip had turned out to be everything he had hoped for, especially considering that his idea for bringing the team down to Costa Rica for some much needed R and R had initially seemed like it would be a no-go. Most of the members of Mustang team had already been redeployed to their old positions. Jim Hicks had appreciated the offer but declined, saying he was concerned he would get so bored on a beach vacation that he would start trying to stir up rebels to overthrow the Costa Rican government.

But ultimately, the trip had been just what Riley needed—a lot of laughs, a little bit of adventure, and a bucketful of escape. There were no phone calls, no inquiries, no depositions, and best of all, no media. One week into the two-week trip, he was finally feeling like he was decompressing.

"Hey, Skeet, what time is it?"

"What's wrong, Mr. Covington," came a female voice from behind him, "someplace you need to be?"

Riley turned with relief to see Khadi standing there. She was dressed in hiking shorts and a wispy buttoned shirt that showed just a hint of the scarring on her shoulder. She had gone into the town of Tamarindo by herself, insisting on some "time away from the guys." Riley had wanted to send Skeeter with her, but for some reason she had felt that might defeat the away-from-the-guys aspect of her excursion.

As Khadi stretched out in the neighboring lounge chair, Riley closed his eyes again. "Actually," he answered, "I can't think of any place I'd rather be."

Dear Reader,

Lots of people have asked me how I made the jump from football to fiction. It's a fair question!

The genesis of *Monday Night Jihad* goes back about ten years to when my brother started keeping a journal of all the football stories I told. He always tried to talk me into writing a book, but for a long time it wasn't something that interested me. Then about a year and a half ago, I began to think about the possibility of incorporating a military/terrorist element with all of my own football experiences. My goal was to give readers a great story full of action, adventure, a little bit of romance, and of course, football.

After having lengthy discussions with my pastor, Rick Yohn, about the concept, I remember asking God to show me whether or not this was something He would like me to pursue. Eventually I became convinced to go forward. My desire in writing this book was—and still is—to contrast the more radical elements of Islam with what I view as *true* Christianity.

Many have attempted to distort the Jesus of the Bible, and so my hope and prayer is to honor the *real* Jesus. Second Corinthians 11:4 speaks of people who preach about a Jesus who is "different" from the true Son of God. My hope is that through this story each reader sees Jesus Christ for who He *is*—the eternal God who created all things. He is the God-man who took on human form to bring us hope. He is the one who allowed Himself to be the perfect sacrifice for us all. He is the one who suffered a brutal death on a Roman cross. He is the one who physically rose up from the grave. He is the one who now indwells all believers. He is the one who will return to take those who believe in Him to be with Him for all eternity. It is to this Jesus that I dedicate this book.

Thanks for taking the time to read *Monday Night Jihad*; I hope you enjoyed reading it as much as Steve and I have enjoyed working on it. Be looking for our next Riley Covington thriller, due in stores in early 2009!

Sincerely,

Jason Elam

JASON ELAM is a sixteen-year NFL veteran placekicker for the Atlanta Falcons.

He was born in Fort Walton Beach, Florida, and grew up in Atlanta, Georgia. In 1988, Jason received a full football scholarship to the University of Hawaii, where he played for four years, earning academic All-America and Kodak All-America honors. He graduated in 1992 with a bachelor's degree in communications and was drafted in the third round of the 1993 NFL draft by the Denver Broncos, where he played for 15 years.

In 1997 and 1998, Jason won back-to-back world championships with the Broncos and was selected to the Pro Bowl in 1995, 1998, and 2001. He is currently working on a master's degree in global apologetics at Liberty Theological Seminary and has an abiding interest in Middle East affairs, the study of Scripture, and defending the Christian faith. Jason is a licensed commercial airplane pilot, and he and his wife, Tamy, have four children.

STEVE YOHN grew up as a pastor's kid in Fresno, California, and both of those facts contributed significantly to his slightly warped perspective on life. Steve graduated from Multnomah Bible College with a BS in biblical studies while barely surviving a stint as a youth pastor.

While studying at Denver Seminary, Steve worked as a videographer for Youth for Christ International, traveling throughout the world to capture the ministry's global impact. During his more than two decades of ministry experience, both inside and outside the church, Steve has discovered his greatest satisfactions lie in writing, speaking, and one-on-one mentoring.

Surprisingly, although his hobbies are reading classic literature, translating the New Testament from Greek, and maintaining a list of the political leaders of every country worldwide over the last twenty-five years, he still occasionally gets invited to parties and has a few friends. His wife, Nancy, and their daughter are the joys of his life.

"You try it," said Scott Ross as he slid the glass across the table with his fingertips.

"You ordered it; you try it," Riley Covington countered, sliding the sweating glass back across the polished wood. The two friends were sitting at an outdoor table at Las Fresas restaurant in San Jose, Costa Rica. Skeeter Dawkins and Khadijah Faroughi rounded out the foursome.

"When I ordered guanabana juice, I thought I was going to get some sort of guava and banana mixture. This looks like they started with skim milk, added water, and then took the glass to the back so the cooks could each hawk a big, honkin' . . ." Scott stopped when he noticed Khadi looking at him. He had been trying really hard to use his verbal filter on this trip, albeit with limited success. "Let's just say that it looks like the guanabana had a bad head cold just prior to being juiced."

"Thank you, Scott. Although I'm not sure that was much of an improvement over what you were going to say," Khadi laughed. "Just try it. You might be surprised."

"My lips and this twisted tribute to post-nasal drip will never meet this side—" Scott's pledge was interrupted by a large hand grabbing the glass from in front of him.

Bringing the glass to his lips, Skeeter downed the juice in one continuous motion. He slammed the glass back onto the table, wiped the back of his hand across his mouth, then turned to the spot he had been watching down the street.

"Dude, that was my juice you just drank," Scott whined. "What's up with that?"

Riley took a sip of his fresh pineapple juice as he laughed. At the next table over, a little *tico* girl with enormous brown eyes and her hair in ponytails shyly turned around for the fourth time to watch this big, happy American man. She jumped as Riley caught her eyes and quickly spun around when Riley winked at her. The girl's mom gave Riley a smile and a nod in appreciation for acknowledging her daughter's attention.

These last two weeks in Costa Rica had been exactly what each of the four had needed to physically and emotionally recover from the events at the beginning of the year. A lot of pain had been experienced by this team, and a lot of blood had been spilled in the search for Hakeem Qasim. Only now was Riley finally feeling ready to go back to Denver to face life again.

Riley Covington knew he faced a decision when he got home. Three months ago, he was an all-pro linebacker for the Colorado Mustangs. Then, suddenly, his old life literally blew up in his face when a terrorist group bombed Platte River Stadium in Denver during a Monday night game. Nearly two thousand people were killed in that suicide attack. Because of his post-Academy years in Afghanistan as part of the Air Force Special Operations Command, he was pulled back into the Special Forces life of guns and death. *Can I really go back to professional football as if nothing ever happened? I've been franchised by the team, but do I have the passion anymore?*

"Riley . . . Riley," Khadi's voice drew him back from his thoughts. She motioned to the waitress, who was trying to put his food down.

"Oh, sorry," he said to the woman as he dropped his elbows off the table. His jaw immediately followed his elbows when he saw the plate that was put in front of him.

"Holy Mother Russia, what is that monstrosity?" Scott asked before realizing that two more were being delivered to him and Khadi.

"Pastor Jimenez told me, 'Order the *ensalada de fruta con helado*—it's just a fruit salad with ice cream.'" Riley had never seen so much fruit. His plate was overflowing with huge chunks of strawberries, pineapple, watermelon, and mango. And if that wasn't enough, three huge scoops of ice cream topped off the tropical explosion.

"I'll never be able to finish this myself," Khadi complained. "In fact, I would never forgive myself if I did finish it."

"Don't look at me. He never told me to just get one for all of us. He just said, 'Order the fruit salad.' I just assumed."

"Yeah, well we all know where that gets us, Pach," Scott said. *Pach* was Riley's nickname from his Air Force football days, when his speed and hitting power drew comparisons to the AH-64 Apache attack helicopter. "If I try to eat all this, it could make for a long, painful flight home. This stuff will shoot through me like . . . like . . . like refuse through a Canadian waterfowl," Scott finished lamely. "Dang, Khadi, this whole verbal filter thing is really a pain."

Khadi reached over and patted Scott's arm. "I know it is, and I appreciate it."

Scott called the manager of the restaurant over and had him take a picture of the three of them with their fruit salads and Skeeter with his Cuban sandwich.

"Nice smile, Skeet," Scott said as he checked out the picture in the digital viewer of his camera. "You look like someone just stole your brass knuckles."

"Mmm," replied a distracted Skeeter, who turned his attention back up the street.

"It's always great having you part of the conversation, my friend."

Riley, Khadi, and Scott attacked their fruit salads, effectively halting conversation other than the occasional "Oh, yeah" and "That's good." A passing box truck spewed black diesel exhaust into the sidewalk café, causing Riley to cough and look up for the first time in five minutes. As he waved his hand in front of his face, his eyes were drawn to Skeeter, who was so intent on something up the street that he had completely ignored his plate. "Hey, Skeet, you okay? What's up?"

Skeeter turned around, noticed his sandwich, but didn't take a bite. "I don't know, Pach. There's a couple of guys halfway down the block. Caught them looking this way a few times."

"Where're they at?"

"Your eleven."

Riley casually looked around Skeeter's big frame and saw the two men. One was sitting on a car, and the other was leaning against a building. Their close-cropped black hair and full beards seemed out of place with their surroundings. Both men were smoking. As Riley watched, a third man walked out of a *farmacia* and joined them. "Don't look now, but your two have turned into three."

"Will you two relax?" Scott said as he turned around to look at the men. "You guys have been seeing bogeymen behind . . . Whoa, hold on. They do look a little more *hajji* than *tico*."

Khadi spotted the men also. "They sure do. And I've asked you to please quit using that term."

"What? *Hajji*? That's just what we called all the Middle East folk when we were out on patrol in the 'Stans."

"First of all, this isn't the 'Stans. And second, if that's true, then I'm a *hajji*." Khadi was from a Persian family who had fled Iran just prior to the fall of the shah.

"No, that's ridiculous. *Hajjis* are guys. You'd be like a *hajjette* or something."

"Thanks, Scott. That's far less demeaning."

"They're moving," Skeeter broke in. As the four watched from the table, the men walked to the far end of the block and turned out of sight.

"There! Did you see that last guy take a quick glance back before he rounded the corner?" Riley asked.

"I'm kind of getting a bad feeling about this," Khadi said. "We need to think about making ourselves scarce."

"Good call." Riley caught the waitress's attention and made a scribbling motion on his hand indicating he was ready for the check. "Skeeter, what are you packing?" As Riley's official bodyguard, Skeeter was the only one allowed by Costa Rican immigration to bring in firearms.

"Got my HK45 and a Mark 23."

"Good. Pass your Mark to Scott under the table. Now, there's no way anyone could know we're here, so this is probably total paranoia. But it's not worth taking chances. Scott and Khadi, soon as I settle up, I want you guys to walk to the corner and hang a left. Skeeter and I will cross and head up the next street to the right. We'll meet back at the hotel soon as we can get there."

Khadi laid her hand on Riley's wrist. "I don't feel good about us all splitting up."

Riley knew that by "us all," Khadi meant the two of them. The feelings between Riley and Khadi had continued to grow over the months since they had met immediately following the Platte River Stadium attack. The only thing separating them now was the one issue big enough to keep them apart—their religious beliefs. Both Khadi's Qur'an and Riley's Bible prohibited this sort of cross-faith union. But while both could control their actions, it was much harder to control their emotions.

"I understand, Khadi. But if these really are *haj*—bad guys, I don't want you or Scott anywhere around me. Skeeter can take care—" A screech of tires made Riley jump.

"Don't matter now! Here they come," Skeeter yelled as he pushed Riley to the ground. Scott and Khadi dove for cover.

A rusting red sedan tore around the corner where the three men had gone and sped up the street. One masked man was leaning over the roof of the car, and a second was hanging out the rear driver's side window. Both were armed with AK-47s.

"Get inside!" Riley yelled to the next table. The mother grabbed her daughter and was through the front door just as the gunmen opened up.

The sound of the assault rifles combined with the shattering glass of the restaurant's windows sent screams up all around the four. Riley prayed that the mother had made it to the ground in time. Scott and Skeeter opened fire with their handguns. A shot from Scott put a hole in the knit mask of the man leaning over the roof. He flew off his side window perch and exploded the rear glass of a parked car.

All of Skeeter's shots were directed at the driver, with one finally hitting its mark. The car swerved, caught a tire, and began to roll. On the third spin, Riley could see the other gunman ejected from his window. The last Riley saw of him was when the car landed on top of him, then skidded against a delivery truck.

Riley turned toward Khadi. Blood was streaming down her cheek from a shard of glass. "You all right?"

"Yeah. How'd they know we were here?"

"I have no clue. Scott, Skeet, you guys okay?" Before they could answer, Riley heard the familiar *whoosh* of an RPG launch. "Incoming!"

All four dove to the ground just as the rocket plowed into the restaurant, showering them with pieces of the building. The explosive wave slammed hard into Riley's body and drove the air out of his lungs. Plaster dust hung like a fog, burning his eyes. He lay there gasping for breath, trying to clear his brain. He could hear screams around him, but they sounded like they were coming from down a long tunnel.

He didn't know how long he was in that state before the sound of automatic weapons fire snapped him to full consciousness. He looked to his left and saw Khadi moving slowly. Beyond her, Scott knelt behind two large fern planters and returned fire. Next to him, Skeeter was stretched out. There was blood on his forehead, and he wasn't moving.

"Scott, sit rep," Riley called out, looking for a situation report.

"Minimum three bogies with AKs hoofing it down the opposite direction from our first batch. Skeet's out but breathing. I've got two more clips for his Mark and three for his .45."

"Got it! Slide me the .45 and the clips." Scott complied.

Riley picked up the weapon and lost his fingers in the thick grooves of Skeeter's custom-made grip. However, Skeeter's gun was not unfamiliar to Riley, and he made a quick adjustment to his hold. Turning to Khadi, he said, "Scott and I are going to press these guys back. Soon as we're forward, I want you to check on Skeet."

Khadi tried to respond but started coughing instead. Tears from her grit-filled eyes were making streaks down her dusty face. She put a thumb up.

"Okay, Scott. Just like Afghanistan, except this time we're outnumbered, outgunned, and surrounded by innocent civilians."

Scott grinned, "Look out, *hajji*, here we come!"

"On *go*, you cross the street and split the fire. 3—2—1—GO!" Riley began firing up the street as Scott bolted across. His peripheral vision caught Scott suddenly veering. He turned in time to see Scott grab the first casualty's rifle off the pavement and dive behind a car. *The guy's good*.

Riley signaled Scott, who began to lay down a cover fire. Running past the corner restaurant and across the intersection, he could hear the whiz of bullets all around him. The discordant scents of freshly baked bread and gunpowder hung in the air as he flattened himself against the side of a *panadería*. Chunks of pulverized brick showered his face from the corner of the building.

Looking back at Scott, he could see him ejecting the magazines that had been taped together and shoving the fresh box into his AK-47. *That'll give him thirty more rounds*, Riley thought as he slid a new clip into his handgun. *Not much, but it'll have to do*.

Suddenly, he saw Scott's eyes get big. Scott quickly signaled to him that there was another RPG ready to fire, but he wasn't in position to get a shot at it. Riley leaned out just a touch and used the glass of the buildings up the street to give him a picture of where the gunmen were. His eye caught a dark shape stepping out into the street with a long cylinder.

Riley signaled Scott to lay fire, and then spun around the corner. His first two shots were wild as he tried to get his bearings, but the next three hit their mark. As the man fell back, his RPG fired wildly into the sky. *Lord, don't let that land in a schoolyard,* Riley prayed as he quickly advanced. Running ahead, he saw another bogey lose half his face courtesy of Scott.

A third one, Riley thought as he ran. *There's got to be a third one. There!* Up at the next intersection, a man was pulling off a mask as he rounded the corner at top speed. Riley signaled to Scott, who was now across the street and trying his best to match the linebacker stride for stride. Scott nodded, and they both went toward the corner.

Just before they reached it, the sound of a motorcycle engine kicking to life echoed down the narrow side street. Scott and Riley made a wide turn just in time to see the third gunman speeding away.

The sounds of sirens began to fill the air. The two men slumped against the building trying to catch their breath.

"How'd they know, Scott?" Riley panted. "How could they possibly have known we were down here?"

"I don't know, man. But believe me, I'm going to find out."